W9-AUH-771

MISS BEDE IS STAYING

MISS BEDE IS STAYING

Anna Gilbert

St. Martin's Press
New York

ISBN 0-312-53471-X

First published in Great Britain in 1982 by Judy Piatkus Limited.

First U.S. Edition

10 9 8 7 6 5 4 3 2 1

One

I stood at the door waving goodbye until the last pinafore had fluttered out of sight and the clatter of clogs on the steep cobbles had died away.

The schoolroom had sunk into an exhausted silence. On her high chair Miss Wheatcroft was absorbed in her last duty of the day. She was counting. A shaft of sunlight struggled through the green-tinted upper panes of the Gothic window and pointed wanly at her desk: at the box labelled 'Slate pencils'. It would not do to interrupt. I could bear to wait. In ten minutes I would be free – for ever.

'Ninety-six.' Miss Wheatcroft neatly packed away the last pencil and closed the lid. 'Just as I thought. Another one missing. And *you* know how I watch over them.' Her eyes narrowed. 'It's Jordan Finch, of course.'

'But he's scarcely ever here.'

'He was here today.'

And then without any change of manner – Miss Wheatcroft's manner rarely changed – she opened her desk and took out a parcel wrapped in white paper and tied with pink ribbon. 'I hope you will accept this with my best wishes to you both for a prosperous and happy future.'

'Oh, Miss Wheatcroft! And such lovely ribbon!' She watched severely as I undid it and opened the wrappings. 'Miss Wheatcroft!' Looking up I just caught in her eyes the softened look of love, not for me but for the gift. Then the last of the sunlight glanced on her pince-nez, concealing the brief lapse into human weakness. 'You made it yourself?'

'Naturally.'

'How kind! How very kind!'

So simple a response to the gift itself was less easy to find. It defied simplicity: a gilded frame of fretwork so complicated in design that the eye, tracing its mysterious curves, was quickly baffled. The frame enclosed a rectangle of crimson satin deeply edged with scrolls and fleur-de-lys of gold-embossed paper. Here and there an unseemly gap had been given a decent covering of white lace, for Miss Wheatcroft could not abide an unfilled space. It was to be some time before I could appreciate the workmanship in all its detail: the band of flat black beads within the frame; the edging of tiny shells within the band of beads. Miss Wheatcroft was content to watch my astonishment, her confidence complete. The creation was unique and she knew it.

'A thing of beauty,' she said. 'Yet useful – and helpful too.'

'Indeed it is. It will be.'

I had arrived at last at the dead centre, at the three words embroidered in black silk, close-packed but incisive! FEAR NO EVIL.

The conflicting demands of wood, paper, lace, beads and shells had made it difficult to fit in the message they were designed to convey. Miss Wheatcroft's solution had been to arrange the words on separate lines and in increasing size so that my attention was drawn to the last and most prominent. 'Evil,' it snarled.

'My first idea,' Miss Wheatcroft confided, 'was to work the whole text but in the event there wasn't room for it, and after all those are the words that matter. They are sufficient in themselves to give guidance both to you and your future husband, should the need arise.'

'Philip' – at the mention of his name a thrill went tingling from the crown of my head to the soles of my feet and pricked my finger-tips as if, god-like on winged sandals, he had descended from his golden cloud to stand, smiling a little, just inside the door. 'Philip will be – gratified. And I shall think of you, Miss Wheatcroft, whenever I look at it.'

'I knew you would like it. It isn't easy at first, when a young woman sets up house, to find something suitable for the centre of the mantelpiece; and in your case I dare say there will be a good many old-fashioned things to be got rid of. Your future husband's late aunt's possessions may not be to your taste.'

The possibility had not occurred to me. Philip's inheritance of Honeywick House and its contents was still so recent, Miss St Leonard's death (as the result of a fall, poor lady) had been, not to mince words, so providential, that the dazzling transformation in our lives still blinded me to anything so prosaic as a mantelpiece. Besides, our good fortune, having arrived so unexpectedly out of the blue, must surely be accepted wholesale as an act of God, or, more directly, of Miss St Leonard.

'I never knew her.' The naked joy I felt in her departure seemed to require some excuse. 'And Philip hadn't seen her since he was six. It was a tremendous surprise.'

'You have been very fortunate.'

Poor Miss Wheatcroft! My pity for her brought a rush of gratitude for my own escape from the imprisonment she was endlessly doomed to bear, here in the shabby room smelling of unwashed clothes long after their wearers had gone: marooned on her high chair in the green-tinted gloom beside the crooked map of the world we were for ever straightening, her buttoned boots perched on the second rung, well clear of the mice which crept out when the room was quiet. Poor Miss Wheatcroft!

But there had been no envy in her tone. She was studying the effect of white lace on red satin.

'I did wonder about feathers,' she said dreamily.

'It's quite perfect as it is.' I made a reverent move to replace the wrappings.

'Mr Hawthorne might like to see it,' she prompted me. 'He has his artistic side.'

'That was what I thought. I'm going to him now.' I swept the children's gifts and posies from my own desk into my bag. 'So, goodbye, Miss Wheatcroft, and thank you for all your help and patience.'

They had not always been uppermost in my mind during the two strenuous years in which we had shared this room, but in the glow brightening my departure I saw them more clearly.

'It's the end of a chapter.' She would have liked to linger for a while and talk, but the irresistible need to escape had already wafted me into my hat and jacket and out into the corridor where Mr Hawthorne sat at his desk, warmed to the point of singeing by his iron stove, cooled to the point of freezing by the draught between the two outer doors, so that he was continually putting on or taking off his long grey muffler. He put it on and stood up as I emerged from the classroom, bearing the parcel.

'Miss Wheatcroft has given you a present?' He examined it carefully. 'A marvellous affair. But surely – she seems to have made short work of the verse. "Yea, though I walk through the valley of the shadow of death, I will fear no evil".'

'There wasn't room for it all.'

'So she has turned it into an imperative. You see what happens to us, Florence. We grow used to giving commands. But could she not have found a sentiment more encouraging – for a bride? Something less bracing? But there, I'm envious. My own gift is more commonplace, I'm afraid.' He handed it to me unwrapped: a leather-bound copy of *As You Like It.* 'It seemed suitable as you're escaping into the country.'

'I shall cherish it.' I hung my head, suddenly tearful. We had studied the play together during my time as a pupil teacher before I went away to Stockwell College. Here in the murderous corridor, roasted by the stove and chilled by the draught, I had discovered the Forest of Arden, had learned the famous speeches by heart and then, lest imagination should outstrip reason, had analysed and parsed them, moving my little table as need dictated between the torrid and the frigid zone, as Mr Hawthorne put it.

'Philip will like it too.'

This was a gift I could show him without apology, with no fear that it would offend his exacting taste.

'I mustn't keep you, Florence.' Mr Hawthorne reached for his hat and we went out together. 'He will be coming to meet you, I suppose, as it's your last day.'

'Perhaps.'

If Philip had only once come to meet me, that was my fault. I had not encouraged him to come to Marshall Street, and had even been at some pains to keep him away. On that one occasion he had plainly been unfavourably impressed. The squalid alleys, the thick pall of soot from the forges down by the river and the tattered, pale-faced children had upset him. He was out of his element. Mr Hawthorne must have seen for himself that Marshall Street was simply not the sort of place Philip was used to. With relief I remembered that it didn't matter now.

'You'll come back and visit us, Florence? Gower Gill isn't far away.'

Some warm response was called for. The words rushed to my lips but in the nick of time I paused, remembering Philip's first remark when he had read the lawyer's letter.

'You can leave that dreary schoolroom, Florence, and never go back,' and he had added with almost passionate earnestness. 'You can forget Marshall Street.'

Until then I had not realised how dearly, how protectively, he cared for me. No, I would not come back.

Mr Hawthorne saw my hesitation.

'You still haven't seen the house, I believe.'

It was simply a fact. He stated it without inflection, his voice as quietly reasonable as ever. There was no need to rush into explanations as I began at once to do. Mr Hawthorne already knew the difficulties: how time and again we had been thwarted in our intention to go. The news of the legacy had come at the end of February when there was just time for me to give a month's notice of my resignation. On Saturdays Philip was at the bank. On Sundays, when we were both free, there were no suitable trains. Philip's plan to hire a gig and drive Aunt Maud and me to Gower Gill on the first Sunday in March had been foiled by a late snowstorm and that had been followed by high winds and flooding which made the roads impassable. Then had come Philip's severe attack of congestion. My heart contracted at the memory.

'Oh, but he's better now,' I finished breathlessly, 'and we've decided to wait until after we're married and go straight there from the wedding. Then we shall see our new home for the first time –'

'– as man and wife' I had meant to say, but blushingly substituted, 'together. I mean, it has seemed as though we weren't meant to go till then; and it will be such an adventure, not knowing what to expect.'

'Your aunt approves of the plan?'

'Aunt Maud says she has never known such an impulsive, scatter-brained creature as I am. But are we not lucky, Mr Hawthorne, to have a house of our own, whatever it is like? Without the legacy it would have been years before we could marry – and we've been very sensible in spite of what Aunt Maud says. Philip made a special point of writing to Miss St Leonard's lawyer about the drains and chimneys.'

'Philip must have some idea of the place. Didn't he once visit his aunt there?'

'Only once as a very little boy. He has only the most shadowy recollections.'

Of a well in the cellar, trees and a hill. Nothing more. I saw the house as a gaunt rectangle of stone exposed to the wind at the top of an incline, flanked by a ragged tree or two: and indoors, Philip and me, alone together at last.

Remembering Mr Hawthorne, I felt that he had been looking at me rather intently; but now he glanced away across the cinder-covered yard to his own house of soot-grimed brick. Above its chimneys the sky had already thickened into evening. I longed to go.

'My mother wishes to be remembered to you.'

'Please give Mrs Hawthorne my affectionate regards,' I said eagerly but the warmth could not quite outweigh the feeling of guilt. Surely I could have snatched a moment from the long day, crowded though it had been, to pop across and bid the old lady goodbye. Even now – but it was no use. I could not spare another second, especially if there was even the remotest chance that Philip might come to meet me.

'She urges you to be zealous in the matter of airing beds, particularly in a house that has stood empty for some time. It seems as good a piece of advice as any I could give you.'

'Mrs Hawthorne is always so kind. But Honeywick House hasn't been quite empty, even though Miss St Leonard didn't live there for ten years before she died. It's been let from time to time and there's a servant living in, a local woman. She will have everything ready.'

We had stopped at the gate where a sycamore had sown itself and grown with surprising persistence into a sturdy tree, now putting forth plump buds.

'That's one thing I like about Martlebury,' Mr Hawthorne observed. 'It's good for trees. Have you noticed how they grow in every nook and cranny? They say it's the soot. Hullo! Who's that?'

Beyond the bole of the tree protruded a bare foot, and then another. A boy stood up, touching the forelock of his short-cropped hair and faced us, expressionless.

'Jordan Finch? Still here?'

Mr Hawthorne knew better than to ask why he had not gone home. Whether or not Jordan had a home to go to, he was known to prefer the shelter of a bridge over the canal or the warm grating above a basement kitchen. We deduced the existence of a parent from the fact that Jordan came to school at all, however rarely, and from the regular pattern of his bruises, which Mr Hawthorne had come to know well from having treated them so often with tincture of arnica and once or twice with raw beef steak. No information could be gleaned from Jordan himself. His silent scowl, so far as I knew, was impenetrable.

Having hooked so slippery a fish, Mr Hawthorne

wasted no time on small talk.

'Three times six,' he rapped out.

'Eighteen,' Jordan replied without hesitation and was moved to add, for reasons of his own, 'pence, sir.'

'If you went north from here, which country would you come to?'

'Scotland, sir.'

'Name the first four books of the New Testament.'

'Matthew, Mark, Luke and John, sir.'

When this smart exchange was over, Mr Hawthorne laid an approving hand on Jordan's shoulder, then felt in his pocket and gave him a penny. 'Good lad. Off you go now – and see that you come to school tomorrow.'

As Jordan padded away over the cobbles, he turned to me. 'That brute of a father of his has cleared off, I'm told. No loss to Jordan but it leaves him completely on his own. I have hopes of finding a home for him with the Society for the Protection of Destitute Boys. We'll make something of him yet.' He smiled and held out his hand. 'But you and I must part, Florence. I'm sorry. We've known each other for a long time. The children will miss you and I . . .' the smile had a touch of sadness, 'We shall all miss you. You have brought colour and brightness into our lives.'

It seems to me now that I parted too lightly from so true a friend. Had I been less hopelessly lost in my own affairs, had I been able to spare a thought for anyone but Philip, I might have found more suitable words of thanks than the few I jerked out disjointedly, impatient to be gone. Perhaps he too felt less than satisfied. As I walked away, he called me back.

'Florence.' I remember how the long, narrow lines of his comforter emphasised his slimness; his thin cheeks above the soft brown beard were colourless as the segments of sky between the dusty sycamore boughs; most vividly of all I remember the unexpected gravity in his shrewd grey eyes, the inexplicable seriousness with which he said, 'If ever you need help, Florence, of any kind, you must come to me. Promise.'

'I promise.'

Was my laugh as light and empty as I now suspect? Did I actually take to my heels and run away from him as if, with all the rapturous years ahead of me, I could not exist another minute in his company? I seem to remember scurrying off without a backward glance and swooping between the terraced houses into the narrow lane that tilted steeply down to the river, until my flight was abruptly halted by an obstacle on the causeway.

'Jordan!'

He did not speak but straddled the path like Apollyon waylaying the pilgrim, and from some unimaginable recess in his bedraggled clothing produced, still scowling, a bunch of wilting watercress.

'Well, I don't really need . . .' I drew breath and groped for my purse. He shook his head, thrust the limp bundle into my hand and put his own firmly behind his back. 'You mean, it's a present? A wedding present?'

He nodded, his grubby bare feet firm on the cold cobbles. His right eye was still closed from a recent blacking. It gave him a disillusioned look; but the other eye, I fleetingly noted, was blue and steady.

Then beyond him, at the bottom of the long vista of bravely donkey-stoned doorsteps, where already a yellow mist was closing in, appeared the elegant figure of a young man in a frock-coat and tall hat. He had come after all.

A wave of happiness lifted me from the earth. There was just time for one last gesture of farewell before I floated into a loftier, brighter sphere.

'Thank you, Jordan.' In an overflow of affection I

stooped and kissed him on the cheek, the unbruised one, and skimmed away, stuffing the watercress into my pocket. Fortunately Philip had not seen my effusive and unsuitable behaviour. We met at the pieshop. He took my heavy bag. I took his arm. We walked slowly. There was so much to talk about: the wedding, for instance, and then the living happily ever after.

Two

A week later we had shaken the dust of Martlebury off our feet. We were both remarkably free of ties. Philip's father, Captain St Leonard, had served under Sir Colin Campbell and died at Lucknow. Since his mother's death Philip had lived in lodgings near the counting house of the Martlebury and District Bank, where he had worked himself up to the modest but respectable position of second accounting clerk.

My own parents had died of diphtheria when I was seven. Aunt Maud had done her duty nobly by her orphaned niece. For fifteen years we had lived together happily enough. She had waited patiently to have me off her hands before fulfilling a long cherished plan to set up house in Surrey with Helena Lincoln, her second cousin and girlhood friend. Consequently Miss St Leonard's death released Aunt Maud as well as me. The bustle of selling up, packing and setting off in our different directions left us little time for affectionate regrets.

The wedding was as quiet as could be. There was no reception. Philip had not wanted it.

'I can't wait to have you to myself,' he said, and that amply made up for the disappointment. Fortunately my dress of cream twilled florentine with spotted foulard swathing the skirt and my hat trimmed with blond lace and cream roses though, I must say, very becoming, were not too elaborate to wear for travelling. We went straight from St Matthew's Church to the railway station, broke our journey at Kirk Heron to take luncheon at the coaching inn there and caught a stopping train to Gower Gill.

The whole journey was no more than ten miles. Breathlessly consulting a county map when the news of the legacy first came, we quickly saw that Philip could travel to Martlebury every day without too much inconvenience. For a time at least there could be no question of his leaving the bank. In addition to Honeywick House with its six acres of land, he had inherited investments amounting to £5000, which would enable us to live comfortably in the country even though in marrying me Philip gained nothing but the £500 of my father's insurance, kept intact by Aunt Maud's unselfish economies.

My one anxiety at that lighthearted time was lest Honeywick House should be too grand a place for us to keep up. We scarcely knew at what level to pitch our expectations. 'Cottage', 'Lodge', 'Grange' or 'Manor' would have given a clue but 'House' told us nothing. By the time we came in sight of it on a cool clear April evening I had exhausted every combination of tree and hill that imagination could devise. Perched on the edge of my seat in the one-horse fly that took us from Gower Gill station, and shivering, in spite of my warm new dolman and the straw at my feet, I scanned the road ahead for a first sight of the village.

'You're cold.' Philip tucked the rug round my knees.

'No, not cold. Only excited. Look, Philip. Lambs!' I reached up to rub the dusty pane and refrained, remembering my new glove and, with a thrill of disbelief, the gold ring inside it. 'Do put the window down. I want to look out. I know it's undignified but there's not a soul about and I simply must see.'

I stuck out my head and shoulders and breathed the scent of grass and damp air, heard the thin bleat of sheep, caught a glimpse of moor against the pure pale sky. The driver put on his brake.

'Yon's Gower Gill. Down there.'

From the right-hand window we saw chimneys; in the hollow a church tower; then the road curved and there, framed in the window . . .

'I believe that's it.' Philip was nervous too. 'It's not actually in the village.'

At first I caught only the sidelong blink of its bow window halfway down the hill, for the house faced the road and looked across it towards fields and a hanging wood: a stone house with red tiles.

'It's small.' I abandoned the manor and the grange without a pang.

'Not so very small.' Philip spoke quickly. I had said the wrong thing. 'There's more at the back.'

'Oh, but I didn't mean . . . It's lovely, Philip.'

We got down at the wrought iron gate. Two curved steps led to a small flagged terrace. A jasmine starred with yellow flowers hung securely pinioned against the east-facing wall. Impulsively I raised my hand to the brass knocker shaped like a fox's head, then drew back, conscious of having almost blundered. But Philip gave no sign of disapproval as he knocked.

'And you're perfectly right, Philip. Look!'

Through the bow window we could see straight across a low room and out by way of a latticed window on the other side to a courtyard beyond, to other walls, other windows, to the thrilling prospect of unknown rooms ready and waiting and belonging to us – or rather to Philip. I grasped his hand, my heart brimming with love and gratitude. The gesture pleased him. He looked down, his lips shaping a kiss. We exchanged looks of longing.

The door opened. We recovered ourselves as Annie Blanche appeared, bobbing a welcome. One glance into her light blue eyes and I knew – the ferocious crispness of her cap and streamers, the glaring white of her crackling apron confirmed it – that she had dreaded our arrival.

Her expression changed as if at the sight of us whatever she had feared was dispelled.

'You've come then.' Her eyes found the blond lace and cream roses of my hat and lingered there, approving, until she remembered her prepared speech. 'Welcome, sir. Welcome, madam, I'm sure.'

She stood aside. Philip propelled me gently forward and followed me into the house. The door closed behind us, shutting out the cool twilight, shutting us in. A stuffed stoat bared its teeth at my elbow: behind glass, I discovered thankfully, catching in it the reflection of my quick recoil. There came to me as I stood in the unlit hall some notion that marriage too was a shutting out, a closing in. We were cut off together, Philip and I, in an unknown house with all its advantages and drawbacks, all its possibilities and limitations still to be explored. Behind us Annie dragged a velvet curtain over the heavy door, twitched and stretched it to cover every possible crack and secured it with a long, plump draught excluder. It was as if we would never go out again.

But then who would want to? What young woman in her senses would turn her back for an instant on a way of life enriched with so many advantages as I was blessed with? Destiny had pitched me quite simply and without reservation into a condition of ideal happiness; had pitched us both, for Philip felt as I did the rare, the improbably rare coincidence of time, place and loved one all together. On that first evening, in the newfound delight of being alone together in our own home, we didn't even bother to explore. We faced each other across the lamp-lit table and made a pretence of eating, then sat by the hearth, Philip in the wing chair which immediately became his, I on the green ottoman stool at his feet, his hand on my hair, until he brought it tumbling down.

'We can do as we like now,' he said when I protested and tried to bundle it up again. 'Are you not my wife?'

In our firelit bedroom I put back the curtains and found with surprise that there was still a world outside; but it too had been purged of earthly grossness, purified and formalised into a simple pattern of stars, bare-branched trees and silent hills. But the air was keen, a reminder, sharp as a threat, of other factors banished only for a time. I drew a quick breath of it and turned back to the rose-coloured, softly shadowed room and Philip.

In any house, in any place, my love for him would have overflowed and encompassed my surroundings, making me love them too, however unattractive in themselves. But here, I told myself in astonishment, everything was charming, every circumstance delightful.

Annie, for instance, could hardly be called a circumstance and would have been quite rightly suspicious of the word 'charm'. Nevertheless she seemed, at that peerless time, to feel personally responsible for our happiness. Meals appeared when we needed them, though in that first week we were erratic in our ways, dawdling through the days and rambling in the twilight.

'You'll be ready for a bite,' she constantly said; and constantly we were: not only ready for a bite but ravenously hungry for her homebaked bread and raised pies, roast beef and ham, scones, cakes, bramble jelly, curd tarts and honey. We had neither of us had much experience of holidays and had not thought of them as anything but a respite from hard work. Aunt Maud and I had been once or twice to the seaside. Of real country such as that surrounding Gower Gill, I knew nothing.

'You've got some colour in your cheeks, ma'am,' Annie said when a few days had passed, and she added in a burst of confidence, 'You both looked frail standing there when I opened the door that night. With living in the town, I expect. It struck me here,' – she indicated the heart within the starch and whalebone, – 'a kind of pang. Bless their hearts, they're young, I thought. They want a bit of looking after and look after them I will. It's the least I can do.'

For her too, I gathered, things had turned out well. She was a local girl, or had been: she was now turned forty, with an old mother still living in the village. Until she came to Honeywick, Annie herself had been in service with the same family in Cheshire for more than twenty years.

'But I'd been wanting to come home, ma'am. There's only Mother and me since our Sam died and she can't get about much. The woman that was seeing to things here found it quiet when the house wasn't let. It was an easy life as I could have told her but she'd had enough and went back to Martlebury where she came from. Well, when I heard there would be a place here, I thought, "This is an answer, Annie Blanche, to all your prayers." The first thing I did was to give the place a good clean out from top to bottom.'

She drew a deep, satisfied breath as she recalled the battle: a victory over superior forces. She had faced the furniture, pictures, ornaments, carpets and massed household effects of Honeywick, had been outnumbered and had triumphed.

'Then when word came that the new master and missus would be coming to live here' – her eyes met mine with a pale reflection of the panic I had seen lurking there the night we came – 'it put me in a fright. "Supposing we don't suit," I said to Mother. But the minute I clapped eyes on the two of you, "Thank God," I said. And then when I helped you off with your dolman, well, you looked a real bride.'

'Oh, Annie!' I hugged her and was glad that we had come straight from the church without changing. A travelling dress would have disappointed her.

'It put me in mind of *The Mistletoe Bough*. I've always liked that song. That's about a bride.'

Philip was coming downstairs. I drew back quickly, hoping he had not seen the hug. His behaviour was always more formal than mine. Ownership of the house had already increased his air of calm authority. After all, I told myself, this is the sort of life he was born to. I owed it to him to behave with more dignity and restraint; but with Annie it was impossible. The barriers, if they had ever existed, had gone down at the first sight of her anxious eyes; and I don't believe she ever thought of me as a mistress but always as a bride dropped from the dusk on to the doorstep, to be taken in and cared for.

Was our life too much withdrawn, our retreat too safe, suspended above the village, hemmed in by woods, undisturbed by callers? In the absence of other people the house itself made its presence felt and would have been of absorbing interest if only – here the old feeling of helplessness comes over me again – if only one could have got at it; if only one could have penetrated the vast assemblage of possessions it contained and confronted the house itself: a seventeenth century cottage enlarged in 1805 by the addition of a more elegant front portion.

Time and use had blended the two parts and made them one. But even when the first excited rush from room to room had been followed by a series of systematic tours, I found it difficult to envisage the house as a whole or to picture its rooms in relation to one another, overwhelmed as I was by the number and variety of their contents. Time and again, exhausted by the sheer impossibility of noticing them all, I retreated, bewildered, to the familiar parlour.

Alone there one morning, I gave it my full attention. It was really two rooms. An archway with a looped-up curtain led to the dining parlour with no door between; but from the fireside where I sat on my favourite stool, nothing could be seen beyond the arch but a picture of Highland cattle drinking at a brown loch enclosed by mountains of bottle green. It covered half the wall so that every meal became a loch-side picnic and put me in mind of the Queen at Balmoral.

On the sofa three identical green velvet cushions with gold tassels stood stiffly poised, each at precisely the same angle from the horizontal. And when the east window darkened suddenly, lines of April rain slanted at the same sharp angle across the fields; the brass fire irons lost their sparkle and glowed darkly. Above, on the white mantelpiece, Chelsea flower baskets and a pair of Dresden figurines flanked a clock surmounted by a bronze Neptune and two nymphs.

'How could she leave them?' I thought. 'How could she?' and tried to imagine her going away: putting on her hat upstairs and coming slowly down, her gloved hand on the banister for the last time; the fly at the door; the portmanteaux and hatboxes; the final leavetaking. Had she intended to go for good, for always, never to come back?

The rain had stopped. I got up and saw my right shoe

with its black rosette reflected in the brass fire shovel. Picked out like that with the rest of me rejected, it could be anybody's foot; another person's like all the other things in the room. Indeed it was still hard to believe that it was mine. What on earth had Philip seen in me, to choose me, Florence Lincoln? Still, in the chimney glass my face was quite becomingly flushed and I couldn't help noticing that the air at Gower Gill seemed to suit my hair.

'It was done when I came, ma'am.' Annie had appeared in the archway. Her tone was defensive. 'That china ornament. There's been a bit broken off.'

'What a shame!' One of the Dresden girls had lost a hand.

'Considering the house was let,' Annie said, 'there's been very little damage done. That's what the young man said, the lawyer's young man. He came all the way from Cheltenham not long after I came here, and made a list of everything in the house. Pages of it. It took him best part of a week to write it all down. Every blessed thing.'

I felt the crushing weight of them all as if I were sinking under a slow avalanche of metal, wood, china and stoneware, linen and plush, saucepans and kettles. In one drawer alone I had found a dozen unworn flannel bodices; in another a pile of embroidered guest towels, untouched since they had received their last stitch. With so much here already I must never buy or make another thing lest it should prove the last straw. There must come a time when one more ounce added to their load would cause the walls to crack, the floors to sag and Neptune himself, with the desperately clinging nymphs, to be submerged.

Then with a positive burst, with a crash of light, the sun came out. The window beamed. Through it and slightly above eye level where the upward slope had placed it, the garden was brimming with green light.

'Philip!' I rushed through the dining parlour to the hall. He was coming down. We met at the foot of the stairs. Ignoring the stoat, I fell into his arms. It was at least half an hour since our last embrace.

'Whatever shall we do with all these things? Having so many possessions gives me the most peculiar feeling. I feel it a kind of duty to look at them all and remember every single thing, and all the time there's something more, something I can't quite pin down and know, even now that I've seen everything.'

'But you haven't seen everything. You haven't seen the well.' He reached past me, pressed the latch of the low door set cornerwise in the wall, and pushed it open. Into the warm, thickly carpeted hall stole a breath of cold air. A half spiral of stone steps went down into darkness.

'We'll need a light,' I said half-heartedly.

'I think we can manage.' Philip bent his head under the lintel and went down. 'Leave the door open behind you and I'll open the other door into the yard.'

'There aren't any rats?' I waited halfway down, my skirts held high.

'Not many, I shouldn't think.'

'Philip!'

'This won't do.' His voice, hollow-sounding from the far end, was no longer teasing. 'This outer door wasn't locked, not even closed. I must speak to Annie. It would be the easiest thing in the world for some tramp to slip in this way and wait his chance to go up into the house.'

He pulled at the heavy door to let in more light. The ancient timber dragged on the uneven floor, which may have been the reason why Annie had left it open.

Standing a few inches ajar, it gave enough light to show the outlines of the cellar: a windowless vault with a stone sink by the outer wall, stone benches and brine tubs for cutting and salting pork, and more recent additions in the shape of buckets and brooms, a long-handled mop and garden chairs. A draught from outside ruffled the dank air. As if in protest the hall door behind me closed, cutting off my retreat.

'Suppose one should be shut in here?'

'You'd escape into the garden. Stay there while I look round. Here it is. The well.'

Having expected a canopy, a winder and handle or at the very least a pump, I was disappointed. Of the well itself there was no sign, only a great wooden lid level with the floor and clamped down by two slabs of stone. 'It must have been filled in.'

'I don't think so, though perhaps it ought to be. It would be dangerous for children.' Philip tugged at one of the slabs and eased it off the lid, a circle of oak three feet in diameter. I crept to his side as he cautiously lifted it, leaving an opening wide enough to show the dim outline of stones lining the well. 'I seem to remember a low parapet and a bit of a well head. Aunt Adelaide didn't use the water but she kept butter cool in a bucket hanging from a rope.'

I knelt down to peer over the edge and saw, like a reluctant response from the earth itself, a mysterious stirring on the water far below.

'Something moved.'

'It's the light moving, not the water. You moved your head. See.'

He took a tress of my hair and waved it over the void and the movement came again as if my presence had been noted, to be stored up and absorbed into the sinister wisdom of the house. Philip drew a deep breath.

'That's what I remember as a small boy. The smell. It frightened me somehow and yet I couldn't keep away. It's the most primitive of all the senses, the sense of smell.'

I drew back, disturbed by a purely physical reaction. Mingled with the tang of water lying in its limestone bed was something less wholesome. A whiff of ancient bones? A residue of something old and forgotten? That was it. A smell of remains.

'Do cover it up,' I said and retreated to the steps. Why had they stopped using the water? Anything, I told myself, could have happened in a house as old as this – and felt a delicious chill of horror. Anything could have got itself into the well and be lying there – or anybody. Any body! No one would know, not in such a quiet spot as this with not a house within earshot and scarcely a passer-by from morning to night. But I had sufficient sense to refrain from sharing the grisly idea with Philip. He might feel it as a slight on the property he was already so proud of.

'Listen.' He took a coin from his pocket and held it over the water. 'Strange how things come back. I remember Aunt Adelaide telling me to count the seconds as it fell.' He let it go. It seemed a long time before it met the water with a sound that was no more than a tiny infringement of the silence, yet with a sad finality. To leave the world with no more than a touch, a whisper of farewell. How simple! How unbearable a thought!

'Do put the lid back in case anyone falls in. It must be terribly deep.'

'Fifty or sixty feet, I suppose.'

I ran up to the warm hall where Aunt Adelaide's possessions waited, close-ranked, solid, dense. Rugs upon carpets, doormats upon rugs lay thick, to muffle footfalls and frustrate the least disturbing echo. The effect was to make one listen all the more intently: to stand, ears pricked, between the court cupboard and the long case clock and to be aware, for a moment, of the house in its entirety: at the bottom of the cellar steps, the earth; below the earth, the well; and above, the house rising layer on layer through ceilings and attics to roof and chimneys, so that one could never get to the bottom of it or rise above it; and I felt it, not as a shelter to keep us safe but as a separate thing, a force to be reckoned with. I turned as Philip came up out of the darkness. In the dim light from the low hall window he looked pale like Eurydice rising from below.

'You mustn't leave me,' I cried unreasonably, absurdly. 'I couldn't bear it if anything should part us.'

'How could it, you silly girl?' He laid his cheek against mine. 'Have you forgotten that we're married? Nothing can part us now.'

Sometimes, dreaming in the firelight, I can feel again the safety of that untroubled time; can see myself, snug by the fire, while Philip, candle in hand, set off on his nightly round of the house, to wind the clocks, close the shutters and bar the doors. Pride in his new possessions made him unexpectedly fussy. He worried, not without reason in such a quiet place, about tramps, burglars, intruders of any kind. We always kept the door into the cellar locked on the inside but the outer door opening into the yard had warped and had to be slammed into its frame. Except at night we didn't bother to fasten it: the sheer weight of its stout panels kept it almost closed unless the wind was from the north. Its heavy thud when Philip shut it and slid home the bolts reached me as I sat warm on the hearth rug and symbolises for me to this day a security I have never felt since then.

It could not last. The loss of Eden is to be expected. But to have known it before the serpent came has left memories of unspoilt happiness which can still outweigh the sadness of its passing.

Three

But time was bearing us steadily away from the haven of those first untroubled days. A whole week had seemed in anticipation to have no limit. We had not envisaged its end. On Monday Philip must go back to work.

We faced the unappealing fact as we walked down the hill to the stone bridge spanning the stream.

'It's silly to mind so much, I know, because we shall simply be starting on our normal life and it will be a way of life we could never have dreamed of until a few weeks ago. It's just – oh, this has been such a perfect week, Philip. If only we could go on for always like this!'

We leaned over the parapet and watched the rain-swollen stream race between budding alders.

'If only,' Philip said more prosaically, 'we could afford to live here without my wretched pittance from the bank. Going back, after all this, will be a grim business.'

We watched a slender bough travelling forlornly downstream until, to both of us at once, it became an object of pity: a victim helplessly exposed to the perils of life.

'It doesn't want to go either. Look!' I clapped my hands as it took advantage of a cross current to steer itself into a little bay. Ripple after ripple broke in white foam on its safe retreat. The bough rocked gently and remained under a sheltering bank already patterned with pale flowerheads. 'Primroses!' My spirits rose. 'It won't be so bad, dearest. I'll come to meet you every evening and you'll have all this to come home to.'

'And there'll be Sundays,' Philip said, unsmiling.

Sunday would be the one precious day in the entire week. Already when the next one came, bringing our honeymoon to an end, there lay upon it the shadow of Monday with its cruelly early rising, the quarter-mile walk to the station, the long journey, the late return.

But the morning was fine. Hawthorns bordering the lane were in full leaf, the air ringing with bird-song, as I panted uphill a few paces behind Philip.

'You must go back, Florence. I shall get on faster without you.'

I clung to him as if we were parting for all eternity, then watched him out of sight, my heart aching, my body limp, as if a limb had been torn away.

With the whole empty day before me it was difficult to settle to any one occupation, tempting to flit butterfly-like from one to another. The washerwoman, Mrs Churnside, had called for the week's linen. I seized the opportunity to speak seriously to her about Philip's shirts: he was so very particular. She promised to handle them with the care she would give to a living child and departed, wheeling the big basket on a handcart. By mid-day the need to communicate my thoughts and feelings drove me to pen and paper. I settled in a sunny corner of the courtyard, intending to write to Aunt Maud.

It was lonely with no-one to talk to, and yet the loneliness and quiet were part of the spell of the place. Here at least, out of sight of its contents, one could be aware of the house itself. The roof tiles settled and creaked as they spread themselves in the sun. Upstairs Annie was singing – 'O, the Mistletoe Bough . . .' How she loved that song!

She opened a window to shake a mop and, seeing me, refrained.

'You must have known Miss St Leonard, Annie.'

'Oh yes, ma'am. Well, not to say "knew". I never spoke to her.'

'But you saw her sometimes in the village?'

'She came to the Sunday school to teach us little ones our Catechism and the Collects.' Annie looked down into my flagged pool of sunlight enclosed in its pale golden walls. 'She was just a young lady then. A blue hat she wore with a little ostrich feather.' Annie was interested in hats.

'Then she lived here as a girl?'

Annie seemed puzzled.

'This was always her home.'

'Of course.' I had forgotten, had not really taken in the brief account Philip had given me of her history. She herself had inherited the house from the maiden aunt, another Miss St Leonard, who had adopted her. That accounted for the fact that Philip scarcely knew her – or Gower Gill. His father, Miss St Leonard's brother, had been brought up in the family home in the south of England.

'Miss Adelaide,' Annie said reminiscently.

'It's a pretty name.'

'"Honeywick House"' I wrote carefully, conscious of it, as if it were looking over my shoulder. 'How could she go away?' I cried. 'How could she leave it?'

'It was too quiet for her here.' Annie leaned out from the dark bedroom. 'A lady living alone.'

I gave up my half-hearted attempt at letter writing, corked my ink-pot and went slowly upstairs.

'It can make them odd.' Annie smoothed the counterpane into a creaseless rectangle. 'Ladies. Living alone.'

'Was Miss St Leonard odd?'

'To tell you the truth, ma'am, I don't know much about her myself. It's only what I've heard Mother say – that it might have got on her nerves. She'd see more company where she went.'

Where in fact had she gone? To one spa after another, Philip had said. His mother had had brief letters from Bath and Tunbridge Wells. The lawyer's young man who made the inventory had come from Cheltenham. Aunt Adelaide had died at Matlock. An unsettled, unsettling way of life with only a paid companion, more than one perhaps in almost ten years; whereas here she could have been at rest. Where else in the world could one hope to find this long-established harmony of stick and stone, this happy blending of house and setting? Without all these things – I picked up her silverbacked mirror, examined its angel heads in low relief and put it back between the twig-shaped china ringstand and the beaded hair-tidy – without them, how stripped bare, how naked she would feel, blown about the world like a fallen leaf!

'What was she like, Annie?'

'Fairish.' Annie pondered. 'A delicate, slight lady. Something of your own build, ma'am, but taller. And she was shortsighted. She always had an eyeglass hanging on a gold chain, I remember.'

It was from such meagre scraps of information that I began to fashion for myself a companion in the shape – as near as I could guess at it – of Aunt Adelaide. In her shadowy way she saved me from being lonely and she was much easier to get on with than a fleshly companion. She could be moulded to suit my moods. My favourite view from the window looking up the hill must have been, I persuaded myself, hers too. By the same insight it was revealed to me that she too had enjoyed a cup of chocolate in the morning and a dip into one of the blue-bound novels of Mrs Banstock. There was a whole set of them on the bookshelves under the china cup-board.

A dint here and there in the board covers, a slightly creased page, suggested that these volumes had been handled more than any of the others. She too had been under the spell of Mrs Banstock's prolific pen. In *The Lost Years* I found a bookmark with 'Forget-me-not' worked in silk with a border of stem stitch and small eyelet holes; and I imagined that she had sat here reading by the hearth until the last minute before she went away.

One small discovery interested me as I pulled out the books one by one wondering which to read first. The fly leaf of every volume was inscribed with her name and a date covering a period of twenty years. The earlier ones also bore the inscription, 'To Adelaide from Aunt Thora', in narrow script and fading ink. But from the year 1860 Aunt Adelaide had written her own name (I presumed). She had evidently gone on buying the novels after Aunt Thora died. The puzzling thing was that the date in the last volume, *The Lost Years*, was 1865. Yet we had understood that she had left Honeywick ten years ago in 1863 and had never come back. I made up my mind to ask Philip to let me see the lawyer's letters which might cast light on her movements. I had done no more than skim through them when they arrived, intent on their one item of interest at the time: the legacy.

'So Miss St Leonard did come back,' I said when Annie next came into the room. 'Was that while you were still in Cheshire?'

My question was casual. I was surprised at its effect. Annie gave what could only be described as a gasp and set down the tray with a jerk, almost spilling the chocolate.

'No, I was here, ma'am.' She hesitated and looked uncomfortable. 'I didn't know you'd heard about it. Mother thought it best not to tell you.'

'Why ever not? It wasn't at all an unusual thing for Miss St Leonard to do.' I looked again at the fly leaf. 'It was in 1865 – or later perhaps.' For of course the date proved only that she had come back some time or other after her departure in 1863.

'Oh, that?' Annie's face brightened. 'I see what you mean. Yes, Miss St Leonard did come once to see about engaging a housekeeper. She brought her companion and maid and they stayed for about a month, I believe. That was when she took on the woman from Martlebury. But I was in Cheshire at the time, like you said. Will that be all, ma'am?'

'No, indeed it isn't all. You're being mysterious, Annie. First you said you were here and then you said you were in Cheshire. And why did Mrs Blanche think you ought not to tell me that Miss St Leonard had come back?'

'I don't know what to say, ma'am.' Annie was plainly flustered. 'You took me by surprise and I thought – It was a foolish thing, not worth repeating. It's all died down now and best forgotten.' She made a tentative move towards the door.

'Annie! What was it? What happened? I absolutely insist on your telling me.'

'Well, if you must know, and I should have had more sense than to let it out – Laban Badgett claims he saw her – Miss St Leonard – here in Gower Gill – not more than a few weeks ago. It was at the end of February, so he says.' Annie emphasised the last three words as if disclaiming reponsibility for the story.

'But that was when she died, in Matlock.'

'That's what I meant about it being a piece of foolishness. Laban swore it was her but it couldn't have been. It was Nancy Badgett that told Mother. "Laban's seen the lady from Honeywick," she said, "yesterday, just before dark in that field between the churchyard and the house. She had a hood on her head." "It couldn't have been Miss St Leonard," Mother says to her, "or our Annie would have been let know she was coming. And what would she be doing all alone there in the field on a nasty day like yesterday, nearly dark at that?"'

'It does sound unlikely,' I said. 'Did Laban Badgett remember her well enough to recognise her, especially in a hood?'

'That's just what Mother said. "One woman in a hood looks much the same as another," she says. If it had been anyone else but Laban, I'd have paid no attention,' – Annie spoke doubtfully as if less convinced of the foolishness of the story than she had at first appeared – 'but Laban's not like other people. He's got gipsy blood in him from the Badgett side. His grandfather and grandmother were travelling folk. They say he has the gift of sight.'

'Are these the same Badgetts whose boy died recently?'

'Yes, ma'am.'

Annie had told me of the boy's death some months before we came to Gower Gill and of the parents' inconsolable grief.

'But you know, Annie, people sometimes persuade themselves that they have seen a ghost or a vision when they hear of a death.'

'That's right enough, ma'am. But we hadn't heard of Miss St Leonard's death then. Nobody had. And Laban never said it was a ghost he'd seen; just that he'd seen the lady from Honeywick. It wasn't until well into March that I had a letter from the lawyer at Matlock telling me she'd passed away on 26 February, a Wednesday; it gave me a queer feeling because it must have been the very day that Nancy told Mother what Laban had seen. Under the broom bushes she was standing. They grow tall there by the path. I'm sure of the day because I'd been making a woollen ball for little Linda Price's birthday . . .'

I didn't follow Annie's rambling account of all the circumstances whereby the date could be fixed, being occupied with the surprisingly vivid picture of the hooded woman in the twilight under the tall brooms.

'Was she walking towards the churchyard?' I was superstititous enough to ask.

'Laban didn't say.' Annie seemed to nerve herself to a further confession. 'I may as well tell you, ma'am, as it's come up like this, that it made me a bit nervous being here on my own and I took the liberty of fetching Mother up here to sleep. We slept in the same bed so it made no difference as far as the bedding was concerned, and there was no-one to ask.'

'It was a perfectly natural thing to do.'

'It was for the company, you see. We talked it all over. Mother hasn't a lot of faith in Laban's outlandish ways. She's never liked gipsies, they're so dirty, although Nancy's made a respectable man of him I'll give her that, and you wouldn't find a cleaner house than hers in Gower Gill. "Ten to one, Annie," Mother says, "It was a real woman, likely one of those lunatics from Gower Oaks."'

'Lunatics?' Here was another bombshell.

'"Who else but a lunatic would be there all by herself under the broom bushes on a winter night?" Mother says.'

'Do you mean to say that there is –' involuntarily I lowered my voice, lacking Mrs Blanche's robust approach to such matters, 'an asylum near here?'

'I don't know if you'd call it that exactly but Mr Drigg –'

'Mr Drigg who rents our field?'

'That's him. He's not really a doctor but he takes in a few people not quite right in their heads that need looking after.'

'A private asylum! At Gower Oaks!'

'They're harmless,' Annie said. 'In fact you never see them, and there'll be no more than two or three at a time from what I've heard. It's a goodish step from Gower Oaks to here but one of them might have wandered this way. Anyway, what with her never being seen again and me having so much to do, it all seemed to blow over. And then you came.'

Having made these interesting revelations, Annie withdrew. Such talk, I reminded myself, was exactly what one might expect in a village. Ghost or lunatic? Pondering on the rival candidates, I rejected Mr Drigg's patient, preferring on the whole to think of the hooded lady as Aunt Adelaide revisiting past scenes before departing for ever; and I settled back in my chair with a sigh of satisfaction. Dear Aunt Adelaide! She had denied us nothing, not even a ghost, her own ghost at that. What more could she do? The weird little tale aroused just the right frisson of simulated fear. A ghost three or four times removed, glimpsed over the heads, so to speak, of Annie, Mrs Blanche and the Badgetts and well away from the house, caused me no disquiet but rather increased my feeling of security, remote on my leafy hillside, in my sunny garden or by my snug fireside, indifferent to the Badgetts, Blanches and Driggs of the unsheltered world below. I sighed a little on Aunt

Adelaide's behalf, without feeling the slightest concern for her apart from an increase of sympathy which seemed to justify the morning dip into Mrs Banstock.

Too often the dip became a plunge and even a prolonged wallowing while the bronze clock ticked away an hour or more: hours of delicious leisure such as I had not yet known in my short, hardworking life. In no time at all came the scramble of preparations for Philip's return: the laying out of fresh towels and his velvet house jacket; the setting of the table; myself to array for the walk to meet him.

Sometimes I was actually there on the platform, but was more often running down the hill when he came out of the station with the slightly dazed look of a long distance swimmer wading to land. Instinctively I refrained from ever remarking on his obvious tiredness. Already I knew that no opening must be given, no cue for him to say how much he hated the long journey after a day of drudgery. It must be accepted. He must do it every day, even in winter. At the thought my heart sank.

The fresh air restored his spirits. The road took us down a deep gully of trees and out onto the open hillside above our own chimneys where the landscape lay displayed, a masterpiece softly lit from the west. But that was the trouble. The sun had set. The day was over. Week in, week out, Philip would see little more of his inheritance than this: a column of smoke from the parlour fire made to blaze for his homecoming; lamplight on the table set for late dinner; then yawning to bed; whereas I, free as a bird, could revel all and every day in the charms he would enjoy only on Saturday afternoons and Sundays. Only a saint, I reminded myself, could fail to see the unfairness of it, or having seen, feel no resentment.

'What have you been doing?' he would ask with a stiffness of the lips as if it were an effort to speak, much less smile; and he would lean his head against the chair back and listen to my catalogue of pleasant trivialities: a stray kitten; a call from Tollemy Price, the travelling dealer in paraffin and household goods. Naturally I told him about Aunt Adelaide's return in 1865.

'Suppose she had stayed, Philip.'

'Lucky for us she didn't,' he said heartlessly. 'She might still have been alive.'

As for her more dubious return in February, he was sufficiently roused to be annoyed by Laban Badgett's confounded cheek in inventing such a yarn.

'And I hope Drigg doesn't make a habit of letting his patients wander about the countryside frightening people. I gathered he was some sort of medical man with his own private hospital but I hadn't realised that his patients were of that sort.'

While he made his nightly round of the house, I raked out the fire and turned back the hearth rug. We went early to bed. I loved to lie awake and watch the stars come out over the hills; and sometimes I would wake in the night and find him lying awake too. We would talk a little with an unerring concentration on important things less easy to achieve during the day.

'I can't possibly give up the bank,' he said once, suddenly out of the dark. 'We can't afford to live here on Aunt Adelaide's money – I suppose?'

'I wonder if we could?'

Silently, yet again, we calculated.

'Apart from Annie's wages we don't spend much. Goodness knows, we haven't needed to buy anything for the house. Perhaps we could cut down on the housekeeping.' A page of my account book obligingly illuminated itself in my head, the columns neatly ruled, the careful entries: 4lbs sugar at 6d a lb.; 1lb tea at 1/– a quarter; soap – 5d. 'We live very cheaply, especially as we burn so much wood and they only charge 1/4d for butter at the farm. Do you think we should keep a few hens of our own – and a cow?' I added, suddenly ambitious.

Philip was absorbed in his own calculations.

'The lease of the pasture expires this year. I mean to put up the rent if that fellow Drigg still wants it. But what use is a miserable ten pounds or even twenty?'

'It would help. And there's my £500.' Safely invested in the 4%'s, it had become for Aunt Maud and me almost sacred, certainly untouchable. 'Only once it's gone there'll be no putting it back.'

'Better leave it,' Philip said, to my relief. 'But I think I'll go into some of Aunt Adelaide's investments. It may be possible to put the money to better use. She must have drawn on capital, living as she did, though she would have the rent of the house, of course.' He turned over. 'I say, what about setting up a pony and carriage? You could drive me to the station.'

It was much pleasanter to dream of this expensive outlay than to plan cheeseparing economies. We talked of it enthusiastically, then fell asleep. The weather for the whole of May was fine and warm. For Philip the pleasure of returning to the country after airless days in town amply made up for the tedium of the journey.

We spent blissful Saturday afternoons and Sundays in the garden, the woods and by the river; and at last one evening as we sat together, Philip in his wing chair, I on my green stool, I had something interesting to tell: a little adventure.

Four

I remember the day – the feel of it: one of those spring days, delightful not only in themselves but in the assurance they bring of a whole summer lying ahead. Walking through the wood above Honeywick, I had just heard the first cuckoo; and as the hollow notes floated across the valley, I caught sight through the trees of someone sitting on the seat by the roadside – a hat; a grey dress –a woman.

At once I was aware of having seen her before, or some such person, walking down, or up the hill; had seen and disregarded her as an unremarkable detail in a scene that offered a rich choice of more interesting things. But now in my enthusiasm for the morning, the cuckoo, the rabbits at the field's edge, I felt an impulse at least to say good day, perhaps even to chat. I put on a spurt which became an undignified trot.

All the same, when I closed the gate behind me and came out into the road, the seat was empty. Its occupant, her back to me and too far away presumably to have heard the click of the gate, was sauntering down the hill. I watched her with a sense of having lost an opportunity, and with something more: a faint feeling of rejection. What could be more foolish? And yet, I discovered, there was a reason for it: a visible reason; for the stranger was now passing the house. This took a little time if one counted from the moment she came to the cascade of stonecrop on the first corner of the wall until she passed the stable at the far end; but I particularly noticed that as she made her way past the bow window, the white door and the high garden wall with its tile coping, she never once turned her head to look, but with her gaze fixed on the village walked steadily towards it.

And so my first impression was of a mind very different from my own: a strong, unwavering personality. Her own thoughts absorbed her to the exclusion of her surroundings: of the only house on the long hill – our beautiful home. She had not deemed it worthy of a second glance. No, that wasn't true. It was not that she had weighed the house in the balance and found it wanting in interest: she had simply not looked at it at all. During the past weeks my world had shrunk to the measure of Honeywick House. The effect of that unturned head, that extraordinary indifference, was to direct my attention, fleetingly, away from the house to something else. The grey figure moving slowly downhill had changed the view.

The seat, too, was different. Its moss-covered arm rest had grown a blob of colour: the Derby china handle of a parasol leaning against it. I remember hesitating and that was unusual: I was not given to second thoughts. She would discover the loss herself and come back. She was not a person to be intruded upon: a person of taste and elegance. The grey silk parasol was discreetly edged with narrow fringe, the ferrule bright, the slim Derby handle charmingly pretty with its puce and blue flowers on white.

I picked it up and ran down the hill.

'Excuse me. I say – your parasol.'

By the churchyard wall she turned and faced me. She was the taller but I stood above her on the incline so that I could look straight into her eyes and for an instant I saw nothing beyond or below their utter darkness. Then she held out her hand for the parasol with a look of apology.

'How like me! How very like me! I'm always doing it. It was good of you.'

She said it half-smiling and I smiled too but without quite believing her. Not that any deception could be involved in so trivial a matter. It was just that her looks belied the kind of carelessness she had confessed to. In that first flash as our acquaintance sparked into life I recognised her as a person of controlled behaviour; unlikely, one would have thought, to be forgetful.

'I had walked rather a long way. The seat is very conveniently placed. I must have sat there for half an hour, dreaming.'

Were those dark eyes – opaque black pools they seemed – were they the eyes of a dreamer? She was describing her walk, the same as mine. It was her favourite too.

'You like to walk?'

There was no need to ask. Her skirt hem, clearing the dust by a few inches, revealed stout black shoes. She wore her short train tucked into a loop at her waist. Her dress was subdued, with just a black-braided flounce to simulate an overskirt. Her Rubens hat was as staid as a bonnet but for the lack of strings.

'You live here?'

Her voice was cultivated and confident, the voice of an educated woman.

I explained.

'Ah, then you're quite a newcomer.'

And she, I learned, was a visitor enjoying a quiet stay in apartments at Ivy Cottage, over the second bridge, the very last house.

Unconsciously, on my part at least, we fell into step. She pointed out the Latin inscription on the bridge. As newcomers to the district we compared notes. I lingered, not wanting to let so interesting a discovery slip from my grasp.

'Perhaps we shall meet again.'

She had already walked away as I spoke and only turned her head and bowed as if in agreement but without stopping; and I envied her poise, her cool detachment, feeling myself a trifle dusty and flushed. As usual I had been too eager.

'What sort of person?' Philip listened languidly.

'Oh, a lady. One could see that. But not rich.' And yet there had been nothing cheap, no hint of economy in her soft grey merino or in her fine lawn undersleeves with their cuff buttons of mother-of-pearl.

'She cannot be well-off or she wouldn't be staying in one of the cottages.'

'I don't know. It's picturesque down there by the stream. She sketches. And she likes the quiet, I believe.'

'What is she doing, wandering about on her own? A widow, I suppose.'

'Oh no. She's unmarried. Well, I don't know why I should say so. She seemed unmarried.'

'You silly little thing.' He ruffled my hair. I seized his hand and laid my cheek against it. 'Perhaps she sensed by the same kind of intuition that you seemed married. How old is this apparent old maid?'

'There's nothing of the old maid about her. Unless . . .' There had been a latent severity in the hat. 'Her age? Not young. I don't mean that she's old or even quite middle-aged. I'm not sure.'

It was difficult to tell. The poise I so admired had given

her an air of maturity. On the other hand one couldn't imagine that she had ever been without it, even as a child. For all I knew she might have been born with it.

Nor was it easier to tell her age the next time I saw her which, to my regret, was not until a few days later. Taking a short cut through the fields by the mill cottage I almost stumbled upon her, sitting on a cushion with a book among the cowslips under a thorn tree.

'Good morning, Mrs St Leonard.' She looked up with a humorous twinkle. 'You're surprised at my knowing your name?'

'Not really. I should have told you. The fact is – it startled me. You see, I've hardly ever been called by my married name – yet – and it made me realise – well – who I am.'

'Do you know,' she became serious, 'I think that is quite delightful. Thank you for telling me.'

Much as the remark pleased me, I was a little taken aback. It was as if we had made a sudden advance in intimacy which I did not regret, indeed I welcomed it, but which I had not intended.

'My name is Bede. Martha Bede.'

This time I had only to glance at her ungloved and ringless hand to see that I had been right.

'I must not interrupt you, Miss Bede,' I said in what I felt to be a very proper manner, but I couldn't quite bring myself to leave and stood smoothing my gloves and glancing at her book.

She got up and stamped her feet as if stiff from sitting.

'Perhaps you would like to walk?'

She nodded pleasantly, picked up her cushion and came with me to the stile and so to the bridge. I leaned over to look at the little bay under the projecting bank. The primroses had faded.

'You're looking for something?'

'It's gone. A broken bough. We watched it, Philip and I, pretending it was alive: a traveller finding a safe place to rest for a while.'

'But only for a while.' Her voice was low. Its vibrant quality gave weight to everything she said. 'It's nice to be young and still able to make believe.'

'She really is an interesting person, Philip. I wish you could meet her. She's a clergyman's daughter. I think she must be quite alone in the world.'

Philip yawned, from tiredness not boredom, though in my enthusiasm and in the absence of anything else to talk about, I was inclined to dwell on the phenomenon of Miss Bede. But he saw nothing odd in the fact that a lady of education with a knowledge of the world should choose to spend her time in Gower Gill.

'In fact,' he pointed out, 'a person must have inner resources to enjoy life in the country. Obviously she will lack company and conversation, but she may have other interests.'

'What can they be? Sheep perhaps. There are plenty of *them*.'

I giggled and we both relapsed into a senseless fit of laughter as we often did in those days; as we still did.

Miss Bede would probably have laughed too if she had been there. I learned to look for the twinkle that enlivened her normally grave expression. We met more often in the days that followed, though rarely in the village itself which she seemed to avoid. The meetings were never arranged, but I have to admit that they were not always accidental.

I knew, for instance, as I took my garden tools and basket on to the front terrace one morning, that she would be passing before long. She was at that very moment getting up from the seat and setting off down the hill. Why I should pretend to be so absorbed in the jasmine as not to notice her even when she came within speaking distance is difficult to explain. Miss Bede perhaps could have explained it better than I. She had stopped and was watching me with amused interest; and as I came to the wall and saw her face upturned, I made a discovery. At the time it did not impress me but later I re-discovered it. Miss Bede's intensely dark eyes were by far the most noticeable feature in her somewhat fleshless face; and yet it was not through them that her expression was conveyed, but by the mouth which was strong and mobile with its glimpse of large, long teeth. The eyes, so black as to allow no play of light or shadow, no change of shade either to brighten or make them darker still, gave nothing away so that one learned to disregard them, or tried to.

'A jasmine,' she remarked, 'can be a tiresome thing. You must be firm with it.'

'It's beginning to do as it likes, I'm afraid, and I'm not sure . . .'

'It must be thinned – there.' She pointed. 'No, no –'

Nothing could have been more natural than the way she pushed open the gate and joined me on the terrace. Under her instructions I snipped and tied.

'I haven't had any experience of gardening.'

'Fortunately there isn't much.'

'Oh, but there is. A long garden at the back. Would you like to go through?'

The front door stood open. I wiped my hands on my gardening apron feeling oddly hesitant: nervous even. She smiled with the merest shrug as if it hardly mattered and took a step forward: a decisive step. Inevitably then, yet still uncertainly, as if in the simple act much was involved, I ushered her into the house.

Five

My intention had been to lead Miss Bede straight through the hall and out into the garden. I had reckoned without the house; had forgotten how, on going in, one was obliged to notice it. As if she too felt that Honeywick was not a house that could simply be walked through, Miss Bede paused by the case of stuffed birds.

'Do come in and sit down.'

Had the words actually passed my lips? I'm not sure how it was that we came to be sitting in the bow window. More than once I had rehearsed such a scene. As hostess, my role would be to listen rather than talk: my manner would be dignified and cool, a manner not unlike Miss Bede's own. I had even felt my lips shaping themselves into a quizzical smile very like hers as I mentally asked her how she had passed her day.

Why then did I ardently exclaim, 'You are my very first visitor, Miss Bede,' as if my self-conscious fussing with the cushions and the strings of my apron could leave her in any doubt?

'I'm honoured,' she said simply. 'To tell you the truth I guessed it might be so. There aren't many people in Gower Gill for you to make friends with. Certainly no young people. If I cannot supply the youth, I'm happy to offer my company. Though I do think young people are best left alone in the early days of their marriage. A difficult time.'

The remark astonished me. Her low, confident voice was always impressive. I was more struck by this further proof of Miss Bede's worldly wisdom than by the fact that it wasn't really true: in our case it had not been a difficult time. But even as the thought crossed my mind, I discovered that there were problems. Somehow there and then they took shape, the shape of Philip. My anxieties were all on his behalf. They came pouring out with the hot chocolate Annie brought us. His health, his dislike of the bank. 'It's not good enough for him, Miss Bede. The St Leonards are people of breeding as you can see.' My glance round the room and its imposing contents drove the point home.

'Indeed!' Her own glance followed as briefly as politeness allowed and came back to me. 'And your own parents died when you were a child. Do you remember them at all?'

'A little.' I took the opportunity to replenish her cup with cooling chocolate. It was easier to enthuse about the gentility of Philip's family than my own. All the same it couldn't have been many minutes before Miss Bede knew most of what there was to know of my history, mediocre as it was. My father had inherited his father's stationer's business but had not had time to make good certain family debts before he died at the early age of thirty. My mother had sickened and died a few days later. My girlhood at Martlebury with Aunt Maud was quickly sketched in: my two years at Stockwell College; my first meeting with Philip at a lecture to the Martlebury Geographical Society on the subject of The Overland Route from Pekin to St Petersburg by way of Siberia. Aunt Maud was slightly acquainted with Philip's mother . . .

'Oh Miss Bede,' I ventured. 'Do you believe in love at first sight?'

She did not answer at once. For the delay there was every excuse. I blush still at having inflicted on her so banal and mawkish a question. Even then it had no sooner passed my lips than I regretted it and stared in embarrassment at the silver sugar bowl in whose convex sides Miss Bede's olive-tinted cheek appeared obscenely stretched into the cheek of a gargoyle.

But to my surprise she was apparently taking my question seriously. It was her way to give thought to the smallest thing, a habit which could only increase my already deep respect for her. A half smile softened her often severe mouth. Her eyes travelled round the room, this time less casually, taking in the blue squares of sky pressed on the small panes of the lattice and coming to rest on the fields and woods framed in the bow window opposite.

'Yes,' she said at last. 'I do believe in love at first sight. One can see – and instantly love – with so deep a passion for the – object of one's infatuation that one's entire nature is engaged.'

Her manner, her intensely dark eyes, compelled my attention, my breathless attention.

'And such love does last, doesn't it? Do you think?'

Unconsciously my tone echoed the somewhat lofty strain she had sounded.

'For ever.' She bowed her head and seemed to contemplate a rather fine brooch of emerald *en cabochon* among the ruffles of her rather costly lace. 'Nothing can displace it. One never changes.'

How thrilling that was! She had almost confided in me. I knew better than to urge her to say more. Instead I looked soulfully into the space between the occasional table and the corner cupboard. 'She has loved,' I told myself and later told Philip, 'and suffered.' It was sad but satisfactory. She had seemed to lack – what was it? – femininity. Even now that she had confessed (for what else could she have in mind but a love affair long ago, long long ago? In my romantic zeal I transported her backward in time to an altogether remoter age and even made an unsuccessful attempt to put her into white muslin and ringlets); even now that she had admitted to some tender experience, the sensitive antennae with which I explored her personality told me of something incongruous, not quite in character.

She was not entirely without good looks even at her age, poor creature. What she lacked, for all her elegance was womanly softness, I concluded, trying not to look too blatantly. She had certainly lost, if she had ever possessed it, the languishing air of a woman who loved in vain; for it must have been in vain, obviously. Were those marks of suffering that shadowed her face? She turned it obligingly to the window. It had a gauntness as if she had recently lost flesh. The eastern light through the clematis made a green hollow between her high cheekbone and the strong jutting line of her jaw.

Conscious, no doubt, of my ill-concealed interest, she smiled more widely than usual.

'The Overland Route from Pekin to St Petersburg by way of Siberia!' she observed. 'Well!' She got up.

At the change of key I gasped, then laughed in response to the sparkle of fun.

'Must you go?'

I too got up, feeling a slight awkwardness as if delicate threads had been spun which too casual a parting might break. Strange that so often in my memories of her I come upon the picture of Miss Bede in hat and gloves, poised on the brink of departure, ready to say goodbye.

'Do just look at the garden before you go.'

We walked across the courtyard to the long path leading through the flower garden to the orchard. The air felt more than usually fresh. Indoors there had been a closeness I was glad to escape. A mist of forget-me-nots clung to the path's edge. The wallflowers were in full fragrant bloom.

'They're looking their best.' My enthusiasm was superficial. I was simply at a loss for something to say.

'How do you know that?'

'Well, of course I don't. We haven't been here for a whole summer yet. I meant their best so far.'

'Who knows what lies ahead, or how much better things may be than they are now?'

'But they couldn't be.' Her words may have been playful but they struck home to my heart, bringing a sudden solemnity of mood. 'They couldn't be better than they are now.'

That being so, if any change should come, it must be for the worse. I felt a prick of fear. Upstairs Annie was singing quietly, her favourite song. It came quavering out through the open window above the lilac. All at once I felt dreadfully tired. The heavy purple blooms trembled: the steep garden and the sky above it moved out of focus and vibrated sickeningly beyond the strong central figure of Miss Bede.

'You're tired, Mrs St Leonard. Shall I call one of your servants?'

'No, no. It's nothing.'

'. . . under a strain . . . a new life in a new place . . . This strong country air will do you good but it takes a while to grow used to it . . . You must sit down and rest.'

Between her firmly curved lips I caught a glimpse of long white teeth, but it was the darkness, the extreme darkness of the eyes above them that I felt. As if moving away from the brink of a deep pool, I felt for the wall behind me and leaned against it. What *was* the matter with me?

And how keenly observant the dark eyes were. As I made a move to take her back through the house, she simultaneously reached out and placed her hand on, of all things, a wicket gate in the thick thorn hedge which I had never seen before, almost hidden as it was by the currant bush.

'This is –' she paused, then went on, 'This must be the quickest way.'

'Why, how quick of you to see it!'

'You hadn't noticed it?' Her tone was incredulous. 'Nothing could be more obvious.' She seemed to pitch her voice higher than usual and speak more emphatically than was necessary. 'I saw it at once. Perhaps you're a little shortsighted.'

'Not at all.' My head swam. I wished she would stop talking, insisting that the gate was clearly to be seen, as indeed it was now that I knew it was there: a green-painted wicket with rusted hinges and nettles growing through the slats. She had to push against them to open it.

'I think –' she seemed struck by a new idea – 'this must have been the way they went to church.'

In my lightheaded state the whine of the gate like her voice seemed loud. My ears hummed. I flinched from the inescapable facts of the gate and Miss Bede squeezing her dress through it. Sure enough a thickly overgrown path skirted the pasture on the other side.

'It will be a short cut for me.'

Her grey dress moved without haste past the tall bushes of broom. Their yellow petals clung like butterflies but their stems were dark and all seemed to point the same way, towards the churchyard. Broom, they say, is a symbol of death.

In a minute or two she had mounted the stile at the far side. Her head in its grey hat sank out of sight as she went down among the tombstones.

Almost at once the faintness left me. I felt strong again.

'It's nice for you to have a lady to talk to,' Annie said. 'You could do with a bit of company.'

Six

'Is she staying long?' Philip leaned back in his chair, eyes closed.

'She hasn't said how long.'

The reminder that Miss Bede's visit must come to an end was unwelcome. Rather surprisingly it was after a short inward debate that I arrived at this conclusion: surprising because my enjoyment of Miss Bede's company had seemed beyond doubt. Perfect as my life had been before she came, her departure would leave a gap. If she had not actually widened my horizon, she had at least made me aware of its narrowness.

'She'll get tired of Ivy Cottage. Her rooms there can scarcely provide the sort of comfort she's used to.'

'Does she complain?'

She had never mentioned their shortcomings. The thought of bare bedroom floors, damp cupboards and invading earwigs from the ivy worried me. I didn't want her to go – yet. She intrigued me. Besides, she supplied the one thing we had lacked: an audience. To be blessed with such happiness and have no-one to see it was not to be our lot.

All the same there was one further step to be taken. So far I had acted as go-between, interpreting for Miss Bede the drama she had not yet seen; preparing Philip for the spectator who had not yet taken her seat. They had still not met.

'Would it be correct for me to ask her for five o'clock tea on Saturday?'

'It's my only free day. Oh well, if you wish. I don't see that it can do any harm, though we know nothing whatever about the woman.'

'Mr Camden mentioned her to me when he called this afternoon. "I believe you know Miss Bede," he said.'

Even so very slight an indication that the vicar, who was new to the parish, also knew Miss Bede seemed to establish her as a person to be known.

'Did he say anything else about her?'

'Not really. It was the way he said it.' Pondering, I had to admit to myself that almost everything Mr Camden said struck the same cheerful note of unworldly optimism. "I believe you know the Angel Gabriel," he might say, or "I believe you have met Satan," in the same pleasantly modulated tone.

'Ask her then if you like. If you're to spend your time hobnobbing with her I ought to meet her. And it isn't as if she lived here. If you should find yourself involved in an unsuitable friendship, it will come to an end when she leaves.'

Tiny as it was in the vast scheme of things, the visit made a difference. I can review my life before and after it, as if it marked a division.

She had made the small adjustments to her toilet suitable for an occasion of this kind: that is, she wore her train loose, low shoes and kid gloves instead of thread. The white lawn of her chemisette was newly laundered. She had dressed her hair less severely and looked well. I was proud of her and guessed that Philip was not unimpressed.

Naturally the presence of a third person made a difference, and here I pause in some uncertainty as to which of us was the third. At first there could be no doubt that the outsider was Miss Bede. This was almost the first time since our marriage that Philip and I had not been alone together, if one discounted Annie and Mr Camden whose two visits had been very brief. Besides, being an outsider was the most striking aspect of Miss Bede's situation and personality, not only in relation to ourselves but to the rest of mankind. It was her detachment and independence that I had first noticed and admired.

'Florence is anxious for your opinion, Miss Bede, as always.'

'It's about my point lace.'

'The final decision rests with you, Miss Bede, as to whether it is to be Spanish, Brussels or English point.'

The familiar twinkle of amusement passed from her face to his. How good Philip was! For of course it was he who was odd man out. He had deliberately given a feminine turn to the conversation. Was not that thoughtful? I had been learning to make point lace, an accomplishment I had never had time to master and now promptly got out my bag of pink glazed calico, paper and braid.

'Which do you really like, Miss Bede?'

My own taste was for the Spanish point and it was a real pleasure when, after a careful inspection of the patterns in *Cassell's Household Guide*, Miss Bede approved my choice.

'There, Philip. It's to be the Spanish. It will be very pretty. You'll see.'

'An attractive pastime,' Miss Bede observed, 'the concocting of imitation point lace, and the results, as you say, are pretty in themselves – though never to be worn, of course.'

'Not to be . . .?' My face fell, I dare say. I had planned to make a plastron for my blue dress.

'I think not.' Miss Bede's little frown of discouragement was as kind as could be. I saw Philip look at her own lace which was genuine Brussels.

'I'm glad you told me,' I said soberly.

'It's merely a matter of taste.'

I folded the calico and put it away in my sewing bag. Aunt Maud had worn home-made lace. Why had she not *known*?

'For a parasol,' Miss Bede suggested with rather obvious tact as if she guessed that I was put out. 'Or squares of point lace sewn together would be perfectly suitable for a cushion cover.'

But I felt a sudden loss of interest in point lace. Mercifully delivered from the lapse of having worn it on my bosom, I was indeed grateful, but the peril so narrowly averted had undermined my confidence. What other social gaffes might I be guilty of, in my ignorance?

'Your bank is the Martlebury and District, I believe, Mr St Leonard?'

In no time at all Miss Bede and Philip were chatting about banking, investments, shares and so progressed to the Suez Canal of all things; thence logically enough to India, Lucknow, Philip's father's regiment and the changes in India since the days of the Company: a conversation in which each topic followed so smoothly on the one before that it was possible to lose sight of Miss Bede's skill in manipulating its course. So inevitably did it flow, so evenly did the two of them pull together that I found it difficult to get my oar in at all. After two or three attempts I had perforce to listen, and this I did for ten minutes or more.

It was gratifying to see how well they got on together: interesting too in a way, though my own taste was for talk of a more personal kind. My opportunity came when Annie put the tea things on the table in the dining parlour and quietly withdrew. Some remark of Miss Bede's as to our good fortune in having found so excellent a servant was a cue for me to enlarge on Annie's family history.

'Annie's mother is a remarkable old woman. I like her very much.'

'You speak as if she were a friend.'

'Florence is fond of scraping up acquaintance with the village people.' Philip's smile was inclined to be stiff.

'Mrs Blanche is the only person I have visited so far. She has a wonderful memory and tells me all sorts of interesting things about the village.'

'For instance?'

'For instance,' I said triumphantly, 'she told me one particularly interesting thing.' I paused tantalisingly. 'She remembers your Aunt Adelaide quite well.'

The announcement fell flat.

'I don't suppose Mrs Blanche is the only person to remember my aunt.'

'No. It was just that she told me about the time Aunt Adelaide came back in 1865. She stayed for a few weeks with her companion and maid while she looked about for a housekeeper.'

It sounded impressive. Philip relaxed.

'And then?' he asked indulgently.

'That's all.' The answer being so tame I was driven to add, 'I can't help being interested in her now that I'm living in her house and using her things.'

'It *was* her house, Florence.'

I had not realised until then how completely Philip had taken possession of it. The poise of his head, the easy assurance with which his hand rested on the chair arm, his whole manner confident and commanding, impressed me as never before.

'Miss Bede doesn't do us the honour of coming here in order to hear tales of Annie's mother.'

It was a rebuke. With a shock I realised that Philip had become master of more than the house and its inanimate contents.

For a while Miss Bede had not spoken.

'Miss St Leonard had called to see Mrs Blanche?' The question seemed to come as the result of careful thought, as if she had been studying how best to contribute to so unrewarding a conversation. 'That was kind, especially as it must have been before Annie came here.'

How quick she was! And how amiable! To take an intelligent interest in even the most trifling topic if it interested other people was – I made a mental note – a sign of good breeding.

'It was the other way round. Mrs Blanche called here two or three times to bring potatoes, eggs and honey and so on. She was more active in those days.'

'I believe we have heard enough of Mrs Blanche, Florence. Miss Bede will think we have nothing better to talk about than who saw whom in Gower Gill eight or nine years ago. You are a Londoner, Miss Bede, and cannot be expected to understand our interest in these small events. Living in a village gives one a long memory for short encounters.'

'Indeed –' Miss Bede was drawing on her gloves – 'I had not realised.'

We walked with her as far as the first bridge. When she had left us, taking the footpath by the stream to avoid the village, we stayed leaning over the parapet. An uncomfortable notion that I had not been at my best, had been indiscreet or gushing or rather naïve, made me draw close to Philip, hoping he would put his arm round me.

'You liked her?' I ventured when the hope was not

fulfilled.

'As to liking or disliking, such a thing does not arise. She is intelligent and used to good society.' He looked down at me as if viewing me from a little distance. I wondered if my hair was untidy, tried negligently to tuck a curl under my hat brim and glanced down at my front frill, aware of the horrifying possibility of a stain. 'She can guide you a little, Florence, in the way things are done.'

There were ways, then, that she and Philip knew: ways as yet unknown to me. But how gladly I would pursue them if it would please him! And what pleasanter guide could providence have supplied than Miss Bede! For the time being. After all, she would not always be here. The thought was less displeasing now.

'You're inclined to go in for rather a tattling style of conversation, Florence. It could be just a little . . .' He broke off as if reluctant to pronounce the word. Could it have been 'vulgar'?

I might have nerved myself to ask had we not been interrupted by the sound of wheels, and quickly stepped closer to the parapet as a neat brougham went by, driven by a dark-haired man in a black frock coat: Mr Drigg of Gower Oaks and tenant of our three acre field. I had not yet met him and eyed him curiously now that I knew his calling. He transferred his whip to his left hand and raised his hat with the utmost courtesy but the incident seemed to annoy Philip.

'What a cad the fellow is! Why does he dress like that?' Philip's own appearance had taken on the casual and easy air of a country gentleman at leisure. His tweed reefer and helmet hat became him every bit as well as his city clothes. The material of both was of the best. 'I'll tell you what, Florence, we must have a conveyance of some sort. I don't care to be showered with dust by such a man as Drigg.' His irritation faded with the sound of wheels and hoofs as Mr Drigg turned into his own long avenue of oaks. 'We're fortunate to have found a person of such cultivated mind and manners as Miss Bede. I haven't enjoyed such conversation for a long time.' Then after a silence I could not quite bring myself to break, 'How well it has all turned out! These past weeks have been a revelation. It was as if I had been wandering through life, dissatisfied, never feeling at home . . .'

But now? I kept still. In a moment he would say that in marrying me he had found all that he wanted. 'But now, Florence,' he would say, kissing my hand perhaps, 'now that I have you . . .' My heart swelled with pride in him; in his distinguished features, his superior speech and manners.

'But now that I have the house, it has changed my life. This is where I was meant to be. I feel it. Some men can drag out their lives on office stools but that isn't good enough for me. Thank God, I have found my element: to live under my own roof with my own bit of land to look out on. You see, if my father had lived . . .'

'Oh, I do see. Your way of life would have been so much more comfortable, more suitable.'

'Cheap lodgings! A cheap school! Mother did her best but I loathed it all. And now . . .' He turned his back on the rushing water – and on me. I too looked up the hill. From here the house dominated the hillside. It looked bigger and more imposing than I had thought it. A cloud moved. Light poured down on the walls and chimneys, bleaching them to the colour of honey, and on the roof tiles, warming them into rose and flame.

'. . . at last I have what I want. The house.'

Summer is capricious among the hills. A moment later the clouds had moved again; the radiance had gone from the sky. I shivered in my thin dress. It was difficult to know what to wear; harder still to know what to say, what to do to make him love me as I loved him.

Seven

I was soon on speaking terms with most of the folk living in the half dozen cottages on the green. One could never grow tired of Honeywick of course, but there were times when the quiet rooms with their over-abundance of things and their emptiness of people drove me to look elsewhere for the companionship I had always taken for granted. So much I would have acknowledged. I would have been less willing to admit to a feeling of discouragement, a premonition of failure at home that roused me to stretch my tether a little. In any case, as Philip said, I was too much of a nosey parker not to be interested in my neighbours. There was always some excuse to be found for scraping up acquaintance: a wedding, a confinement, a baby to dandle.

'It's like old times,' the cobbler's wife told me, 'having a lady living at Honeywick again. After Miss St Leonard left, the others all just came and went.'

'You wouldn't think of calling to see Nancy Badgett?' Annie said one morning as I was about to set off for the village.

'Do you think I should? The trouble is – Mr Badgett might be there and he might not like it.'

I was somewhat nervous of Laban Badgett and his

capacity for seeing people who were not in fact there.

'Very likely he'll be out and off on his own somewhere. He can't hardly settle in the house since they lost the boy.'

The Badgetts lived next door to Mrs Blanche. I knew something of their story. Their only child –a fine boy – had died shortly before we came to Honeywick from some wasting disease for which there was no cure or even any treatment. They had watched, helpless, as he slowly pined away. His death had left them desolate and withdrawn. Their door never stood open in the hospitable fashion of the other cottages but I had seen Nancy Badgett in the village shop: a fair-haired woman in her thirties; and had caught sight of Laban two or three times from Mrs Blanche's doorstep. He was a lean, dark-haired man, a turner by trade and some years older than his wife. It was common talk in the village that he had taken the loss of his son too hard. Grief had absorbed him so entirely that he had lost all interest in his work, his home, his wife.

'He never used to be like that,' Annie told me. 'He was a kind husband to Nancy and a rare clever workman. There's nothing he can't turn his hand to, not to mention a bit of poaching,' Annie lowered her voice though there was not a living soul within a quarter of a mile, 'but that's the gipsy in him.' Fifty years back the Badgetts had been travelling people but Laban's parents had settled and put him to a trade. 'He was late marrying and a bit wild but Nancy calmed him down and made an honest workman of him. He was doing well. But now the life's gone out of him. They'll be in a bad way if he doesn't put his hand to a bit of work. It's a real waste. And he can carve as well. He made those butter markers in the dresser drawer. You'd brighten Nancy up a bit, ma'am, and you could make the excuse of asking if Laban would fit a new leg to that chair in the back bedroom.'

We were not short of chairs. Indeed I had been gleefully on the point of making a bonfire of the one in question. To dispose of even one household item would have been a step in the right direction.

Instead I knocked on the Badgetts' door and introduced myself.

'I know you well enough, ma'am.' Nancy hesitated before asking me in, as if she had got out of the habit. But she dusted an already spotless chair and invited me to sit down. I explained about the chair leg.

'I'll ask him. It isn't that he'd want to be disobliging, ma'am, but he isn't himself. He's that gnawed at by sorrow he doesn't see what's in front of him. Every day he goes up the garden to his workshop and I listen for the sound of the lathe, praying he'll start. But nothing comes of it and when I go up he's just standing there idle. Every day he gets more like skin and bone. I watch him wasting away like I watched our Edwin. Oh, Mrs St Leonard, am I going to have to pass through the same trial again? It's more than I can bear.'

It was a comfort to her to talk, particularly to a stranger, though her distress involved me as deeply as if I had known her for years.

'He used to have Edwin up there with him from being a toddler in petticoats, and he'd make him toys: tops and hoops; and he made him a little cart. He said to me only yesterday, "I'm forgetting his face, Nancy. I used to see it as if it was printed on the air in front of me but now I can't bring it to mind. What am I going to do if I can't picture him?" he says. "It's like losing him all over again." We had neither a likeness taken nor a photograph,' Nancy explained. 'I wish we had. When I see him staring at nothing, I know he's trying to see Edwin. It's easier for me. He was the very spit of his father. I only have to look at Laban to see him again.'

'Perhaps as time passes . . .'

'There's only one thing. He's half hinted at it himself. He's best out in the open. If he could take to the road again. It's in his blood.'

'It would be a hard life.'

'That might be the saving of him. He'd have to struggle and take every chance and wear himself out to get a living. It's doing nothing that's killing him.'

'Would you go with him?'

'I'll never leave him as long as there's breath in my body. He's got his trade at his finger tips and there's a shed full of little things we could take to sell: broomheads and tool handles and spoons and bowls. I could make besoms and do bits of field work. We'd manage.'

'And then some day when he's better, you could come back.'

'God willing.' She looked round anxiously. Her kitchen was clean and comfortable. It would be an act of quiet heroism to leave it for the vagabond life she had in mind. 'Go and talk to him, ma'am, about the chair. You might get through to him.'

At first, looking in nervously, I thought the workshop was empty and in a sense it was. There was no sound or movement. He was standing quite still beside his bench, his swarthy, high-cheekboned face like a mask; and he was not just doing nothing. It was as if he had left his body standing there on the sawdust and wood shavings and gone away from it on an endless, fruitless search. I had an impression of lightness as if the form he had escaped from were an empty husk. I felt ashamed of my errand. It seemed indecent to bring him back for such a trivial reason. In fact, when I summoned up courage to speak, he gave no sign of coming back to life except to look at me and change his stance uncertainly from one foot to another as if aware that something was expected of him.

'. . . if you would call some time and look at the chair . . .'

After a while I crept away.

'There's strange blood in him,' Nancy said. 'He isn't like our folk. I don't know what to do.'

I went again several times, though it needed courage to knock and disturb the awful grief-stricken silence of the house. On this particular morning, as it happened, Nancy seemed more hopeful.

'We've talked about going away, Mrs St Leonard, ma'am,' she told me. 'It's what he needs, the sky above him and a road ahead to make him go on. He was out all day yesterday and came back calmer. I felt a difference as soon as he came in. "Shall we pack up," I said to him, "and go, just for a bit?" He didn't say anything, just nodded his head and he slept real well last night.'

'When will you go?'

'He'll want a sign,' she said simply. 'He'll do nothing without a sign.'

'What sort of sign?'

She shook her head.

'I don't know. There'll be something.'

We talked over the difficulties. They would find cheap lodging in cottages or wayside inns or make shift, if need be, to spend the night in their cart. Laban had spoken of a bobbin mill in Westmorland where he might find work. I offered her money.

'There's no need,' she said. 'We're not without but we'll not have to dally about too long. The summer's passing.'

But the warm weather remained with us, and so did Miss Bede, whom I now saw almost every day. She had taken to wearing a veil which gave an enviable touch of mystery to her already enigmatic personality. The sun, she said, was trying to the eyes and complexion. Only indoors, safe from the heat, did she put up the veil. There was an imposing deliberation in the way she did it. I used to watch with interest as her finely gloved hands folded back the delicate net over the crown of her hat until her face was revealed and the lips resumed their humorous curve as though to say: 'Now what shall we talk about?'

With our skirt hems touching confidentially, I was usually ready to begin; and yet already I had learned to restrain my tongue a little. Of Mrs Blanche I never spoke again nor of Annie who, as my chief companion, was always a source of interest. Aunt Maud, who wore point lace on her best dress, might present pitfalls as a topic of conversation, though I was beginning to think of her more fondly than when I saw her every day and I had continued stubbornly with my lacemaking. There was, to be sure, another subject on which I was well informed. That too, as things turned out, was to prove unsuitable, disastrous even.

Somehow we got into the habit of having Miss Bede to five o'clock tea on Saturdays.

'It's the only day I'm at home,' Philip reminded me when I suggested that another day might do as well. He had no need to remind me since that had been the very reason for his reluctance to invite her in the first place. Short as her visits were, they drastically reduced the time we could spend alone together, especially as it was not long before Philip fell into the habit of walking to meet Miss Bede in a leisurely sort of way; indeed more and more leisurely: sometimes tea was on the table before they strolled up the hill, deep in conversation.

One Saturday afternoon, having waited for them an hour or more, I had begun to sort out the contents of a wooden box: papers and letters hastily thrown together before I left Martlebury. I had emptied them on to the floor, only to cram them back again as the front door opened.

It was a hot day. Philip had come home wearied out after a morning in Martlebury and was still inclined to dwell on the discomforts of the city.

'You can't imagine how depressing it is. The smells, the lack of air! Sometimes I'm tempted to give it all up and never to go back.'

Miss Bede was nodding sympathetically. She was now sufficiently at home to have taken off her hat and looked cool and fresh in the chair that had become hers. It occurred to me that the olive-tinted complexion of which she took such care was not of a kind to be affected by the sun. Philip and I, being fair of skin, were both a trifle flushed.

'Any person in your position would feel the same. I have often wondered why you don't –' she paused, self-deprecating, 'I shouldn't say it.'

'Leave the bank? How gladly I would, if we could afford it!'

'Money,' Miss Bede said, 'isn't everything. This is your natural setting, this gracious way of life. It must be hard to leave it for so much of the time for the sake of mere pounds, shillings and pence.'

'And yet we're lucky to live here at all,' I felt obliged to point out. 'Most people spend all their lives struggling for pounds, shillings and pence with no hope of anything better. For that matter no life can be gracious as you call it without money, and money has to be earned.'

I must have spoken too warmly as usual. At first neither of them responded. Miss Bede seemed to be listening earnestly, her lips drawn together, with an air of conscientiously trying to understand.

'Florence is sympathetic to the lower classes. Quite rightly,' she murmured.

'I have worked for my living,' I said bluntly, 'among people worse off than myself.'

Miss Bede looked perplexed.

'But surely,' she glanced at Philip as if for confirmation, 'your pupils were young ladies of means.'

'Not at all. I taught in a Board School.'

Philip was leaning back in his chair, his eyes closed, with an expression of faint distaste; and I knew with a flash of insight that it was he who had given Miss Bede the wrong impression, deliberately. He would actually have preferred me to be a genteel governess putting Mangnall's Questions to the pampered children of rich parents for twenty pounds a year.

'Indeed. Then you worked among – street children?'

'Some of them were very poor. Life was hard in Marshall Street.' Nettled by Philip's lofty attitude, I went into detail and held forth with some eloquence, forgetting the summer scents of roses and cut grass, remembering the pall of soot, the smell of drains and of the stagnant pools where there should have been drains; and there by the grimy sycamore stood Mr Hawthorne, brown bearded, shabby and – absolutely honest. The thought startled me with its implication that others were not, and brought a swift sense of loss as if a bird had flown or some precious thing had slipped from my hands. For the first time I understood the meaning of integrity. Strange, unbelievable as it seems, a surge of homesickness for Marshall Street brought tears to my eyes; brought too a sharp revulsion from affectation and pretence. I felt in the room a pettiness of aspiration against which my soul rose in protest. To wash one's hands of honest work, to shy away from reality into a rustic dream – that was not the way to live.

'"Now am I in Arden. The more fool I. When I was at home I was in a better place."' The words came to me through the medium of Mr Hawthorne's well remembered voice.

'You have left all that behind you, Florence,' Philip was saying coldly. 'You can forget the whole wretched scene. There's certainly no need to dwell on it now.'

How anxious he had been for me to leave! With the same dreadful clarity I understood that the anxiety had not been for me because he loved me, but for himself. He had been ashamed of my connections. Was that – I tortured myself in wondering – why he had not been able to face a wedding reception lest he should be confronted with people – my friends – who would be inferior to him?

I bent over my box, pretending to busy myself with its contents. A few weeks ago, an hour ago, I would have been humbled; but now I felt the sustaining heat of anger and pride. I was proud of my training, which in those days was still rare. Why didn't Philip tell Miss Bede that I had passed my examinations with distinction? It would be her turn to be impressed. Here in this very box was my certificate, hard won, dearly prized; but I would not mention it. Deliberately I cut myself off from them both, blindly rustling the papers and blinking away tears; and by a fiendish chance a flash of crimson caught my eye. My hand closed on a hard object: Miss Wheatcroft's gift.

'Fear no Evil,' it said stoutly, starkly disregarding the worldly enticements of gilt and satin by which it was beset. It was no conscious decision but a wave of loyalty to Miss Wheatcroft, Marshall Street and all its works that lifted me from my chair and deposited me on the hearth rug.

'There!' I pushed away a Chelsea flower basket, stood the framed text next to the clock and nonchalantly resumed my seat.

'What on earth is that?'

'A wedding present from my friend Miss Wheatcroft. She intended it for our mantelpiece.'

'Did she indeed?'

'She made it herself.'

'That explains it.'

Outfaced by its garish confidence, the St Leonard possessions ceased to exist. Miss Wheatcroft's gift had become the only object in view – a souvenir of my low connections; a symbol of defiance.

'A monstrous piece of bad taste.' At Philip's tone my mood hardened. 'And now that we've seen it, pray put it away.'

'Good taste is all very well, but loyalty to one's friends is more important,' I said sententiously. 'Miss Wheatcroft must have spent hours making it.'

In her one drab room overlooking the canal, her table spread with glue pots, needle-case, beads and brushes, her face sharpened by fatigue at the end of a gruelling day, she had sat absorbed in her creation.

'Miss Wheatcroft is not my friend.'

Philip's tone excluded her not only from the favoured circle of his friends but from any kind of respectable existence. It infuriated me.

'Nor are any of these things mine, for that matter.' I glared at the Highland cattle, at Neptune and his nymphs. 'That is the only thing of my very own in this whole room.'

'Then I wish,' Philip said icily, 'it could have been a thing that a civilised person could bear to look at.'

It was to be expected that Miss Bede would feel some discomfort during these deplorable exchanges: unfortunate that she should have chosen that moment to rise.

'I really must go – if you will excuse me.'

The action, the murmured apology, the air of embarrassment, gave point to Philip's remark. She had betrayed me when there were a dozen ways in which she could have come to my rescue. But catching her eye, or rather her mouth, I saw it curve in a little grimace of regret.

'But we haven't had tea,' I wailed.

'Under the circumstances . . .'

She was gone. Who knows? If she had stayed to coax us back into good humour, or if she had never been there at all to register wry amusement declining rapidly into grieved concern, the absurd affair might not have gone beyond teasing and argument.

As it was we were both angry with a bitterness that came not from the trivial incident but from the sudden revelation of the difference in our natures. A pit of terrifying proportions yawned between us. The golden cloud was gone. I saw him, mercilessly, as he was. His cheap school, I told myself, had left him uneducated but with all the pretentiousness of shabby gentility.

'You have made a scene,' he said in angry disgust. 'What will Miss Bede think of you? You seem determined to discredit me. Come, Florence, put that dreadful thing away. I warn you that until you do, I shall not come into this room. You can sit here alone.'

He went out into the garden leaving me in a wretchedness of spirit that dragged me to the earth. Again, more distinctly than ever, I felt the inescapable seclusion of marriage like the closing of a door, and this time felt it as a threat. To have quarrelled so soon! To go on living together unloving until we were old! How was that to be endured?

'Fear no Evil,' Miss Wheatcroft admonished sternly from the mantelpiece. Drearily I contemplated the symbol of my shattered happiness but I did not take it down, and after a while I went upstairs and with long fierce stitches sewed a plastron of point lace on my blue dress.

Afterwards I walked restlessly down to the bridge. The evening was sultry. There was no-one about until Mr Drigg's brougham appeared coming slowly downhill as if from the station. This time he was not alone. The passenger inside was a young woman. As they passed, she pressed her face against the window looking so dispirited that instinctively I waved and smiled as I would have greeted a friend. She hesitated, then half raised her hand in a languid uncertain way. I felt sure that she must be one of Mr Drigg's patients.

They turned into his drive and disappeared down the avenue of wide spreading oaks. The green freshness of their young leaves was so much at variance with the girl's doleful manner that I probably exaggerated her look of fatigue, natural after a journey, into an expression of woeful appeal, hopeless even as it was made. Framed in the small window, leaning forward like Leonardo's St Anne, she had seemed the picture of despair. The dreadful thought occurred to me that she might be there against her will. She had looked almost as if she were going to prison.

I felt drawn to her by more than pity: by fellow feeling, as if in a way I was in prison too.

Eight

'My, that's pretty.' Annie stopped short on the threshold and gazed admiringly at the mantelpiece.

'Mr St Leonard dislikes it. He thinks it too ostentatious.'

The word was new to Annie. She ignored it.

'It's really showy,' she said. 'That's what I like about it. You notice it. It must have taken a lot of doing. Mother once had a pincushion something like that but not so fancy.'

I was more than ready for a chat. It was the Monday morning following a silent and gloomy Sunday. The gloom had not affected Annie. She seemed particularly happy at that time. I looked at her more closely and sensed in her a secret inward satisfaction. An hour later I saw her trot up the long garden path and disappear into the orchard. It wasn't until she came trotting down again a few minutes later that I seemed to remember that she had been carrying something. A tray? But she was empty-handed now and singing, her fair face content; and I envied her.

So that it was all the more upsetting when I went into the kitchen that evening and found her with her apron over her head, sobbing.

'Annie! Whatever is the matter?'

At first I could make nothing of the muffled explanation, except that the master had been angry and she had meant no harm. Philip and I had dined in frosty silence. He had left the table without a word and gone into the garden. Now, through the open door I saw him coming wrathfully down through the orchard. My splendid anger, my high principles, my well founded self-respect, were not proof against my curiosity.

'Whatever is wrong with Annie, Philip?'

He was, I'm sure, enormously relieved to hear me speak. His aloofness melted. I saw his eyes change and instantly loved him again. The smile I waited for didn't quite come but it already softened the corners of his mouth. In a minute he would kiss and forgive me; but at first he looked away, evading the reconciliation.

'Annie has been very foolish. You didn't know?' Seeing me dumbfounded, he went on, 'I found her out just now by accident. I've sent him off, needless to say, with a flea in his ear.'

'Who?'

'Believe it or not she's been harbouring the fellow up there in the potting shed.'

'Annie? A follower?'

'No, no. He wasn't of an age. A rough young lout. She'd been feeding him, if you please. I don't know how long. Could anything be more unwise? The two of you, alone here all day. The very thing that most worries me. We're lucky not to have been robbed, or worse.'

It had certainly been unwise, incredibly so.

'At any rate I've taken a stick to him and given him a good thrashing. I threatened to hand him over to the police if he showed his face here again.'

'Oh, Philip!'

My exclamation covered a whole range of emotions:

gratitude for his protective care; pity for the tramp; repentance; amazement at Annie's lack of judgment; but chiefly joy in being at one with him again. I flew into the parlour, snatched up Miss Wheatcroft's present and hid it under a cushion, then meekly led him in, settled him in his chair and kissed his forehead. Not until we had talked over the incident several times did I slip away to comfort Annie.

She was sitting at the kitchen table, brooding miserably over the possibility of losing her place. I reassured her. The affair, seen from her point of view, seemed much less heinous. Just a lad, he had been, half-starved and homeless but neither a tramp nor a beggar. He'd been knocked about, you could tell, and now – at the thought of yet another thrashing, Annie wept again. She had found him asleep in the potting shed three days ago among the sacks of potatoes and flower pots.

'You couldn't help wanting to mother the poor lad.' She had fed him and given him the old green waistcoat the master had thrown out. 'He'd nothing on his feet.' She picked up a half knitted sock on its needles and put it down again. 'I couldn't get his name out of him. He'd run away, you could tell. So I called him Sam, after my own brother. He was ever so willing and I let him help with chopping sticks while you were out with that Miss Bede. I didn't think there was any harm in looking after him a bit but I didn't tell because the master's so fussy about tramps and burglars.'

The boy hadn't talked much but she had felt that he was a good lad or at least not bad, given a chance. She had lost a pet, however unsuitable, and for a time was very low spirited.

For me the potting-shed affair had a happier outcome as it ended my quarrel with Philip, though as things turned out, peace would soon have been restored without its help. But I couldn't help sharing Annie's regret for the thrashing. The shed, a stone-built outhouse at the top of the orchard, would provide comfortable shelter for a homeless vagrant. I walked up there next morning and pushed open the door. It would be cosy here among the sacks and cobwebs. Idling in the sunlight by the ivy-covered window, I glanced at a row of flower pots and a pile of sand and found myself staring, Crusoe-like, at the imprint of a bare foot –a slender young foot – and I wished that Philip had been merciful.

My mood of dreamy tenderness for someone else's child arose perhaps from instinctive stirrings on behalf of my own, for it was soon after that there came a change in my life so momentous that every other circumstance in the world's history faded into oblivion. Florence St Leonard the bride followed Florence Lincoln the spinster into the past. A third individual emerged: one altogether more to be respected, in some inexplicable way more real, chosen, singled out and blessed. Philip, when I imparted the news to him, was in no doubt as to what I had been chosen for: to be mother to a long line of St Leonards.

'There will always be St Leonards here at Honeywick,' he said more than once with a largeness already patriarchal, and he happened to be saying it, or something like it, from a commanding position on the hearthrug as if referring to an establishment on the lines of Blenheim Palace, when Annie announced Miss Bede. It was not likely that she would fail to notice Philip's exalted manner even if she had not heard the speech. A whisper, a nod, an exchange of smiles made the position clear. At least I thought Miss Bede smiled. She hadn't had time to put up her veil. In fact for some reason she chose on that occasion to leave it down, so that if her face was suffused with sympathetic joy, I could not see it. Her response to our wonderful good fortune could only be deduced from a few quiet words; and she was unusually quiet. Not that I was interested in deducing Miss Bede's responses, poor woman.

Her veiled head turned this way and that as she looked from Philip to me and from me to Philip. Indeed another impression I retain of her, like the memory of her in hat and gloves continually on the point of leaving, is of Miss Bede quietly observing us, first one, then the other; and so of necessity moving her head from side to side because she was always standing or sitting between us. I recollect the feeling of having to crane my neck or raise my voice to speak to Philip across the intervening barrier of Miss Bede, as in dreams one struggles with tangled bed clothes and wakes in dread of suffocation.

Gradually, as usual, I fell silent while they talked. Since I remained in this detached condition for some time it is as well to say that my view of later events may not have been accurate or my account of them reliable. In fact the problem of distinguishing between what was and what seemed to be the truth is the gist of my story and the essence of its strangeness.

Snippets and phrases reached but did not interest me.

'You are most obliging . . . care and attention . . . constant company . . . while I'm away from home.'

'. . . set aside part of each day . . . the greater part if need be . . .'

It was one of many similar conversations. I cannot recall precisely when a new topic arose or which of them introduced it: the immense advantage it would be to set up a conveyance of some sort, immediately. If, as I think, the plan was mooted by Miss Bede, Philip seized on it at once. Expense was no longer of importance. A carriage would be useful in a hundred ways; and by a happy chance, Miss Bede was knowledgeable about horses and had been used to driving. Florence could soon be taught. Philip could be driven to the station in a trice.

'It's extraordinarily lucky,' Philip said, 'that we should have made friends with Miss Bede. I don't know what we should do without her. She's offered to advise me in choosing a horse. I'm writing to Pursley at the livery stables in Kirk Heron asking him to let me know when he has anything suitable.'

He became absorbed in the Martlebury and Kirk Heron newspapers and talked of nothing but landaus, barouches, victorias, dog carts and gigs.

'For fifty pounds,' he looked up from the advertisement column of the Kirk Heron Gazette, 'we could buy a light one-horse landau particularly suited to hilly country.'

'Oh, much less. Here are phaetons for as little as eighteen guineas.'

'Rattle-traps! I don't intend to buy a conveyance we would be ashamed to appear in. I wish Pursley would bestir himself.'

A few days later came a letter from Pursley announcing that he would be holding his monthly sale of hunters, hacks and harness horses on the last Thursday of the month. The sale would begin at eleven-thirty. The arrangements, thrashed out in all their details, did not concern me. Miss Bede would go with Philip to Kirk Heron to view the horses and would remain to bid while he went on to the bank. Miss Bede was being very, very kind. We were greatly obliged to Miss Bede.

I was still asleep when they set off at seven and was laying the table for our evening meal when the sound of wheels sent me scurrying to the door; and there they were, triumphant, mounted high behind a dapple grey, Miss Bede holding the reins, Philip at her side, having bought not only the horse but a carriage too. Only it was not the low-slung four-wheeler or small tub I had envisaged but a rakish, brassbound, yellow-painted gig.

'What do you think of it?' Philip jumped down. 'It's taken us all day.'

'You don't mean that you haven't been to the bank?'

'It just wasn't possible. Oh, I'll make it all right with old Wetherby. We heard of this gig for sale at a farm on the other side of Kirk Heron. Miss Bede pointed out that it would give you more air than a closed carriage. It's the very thing, don't you think? And this is Hector.'

From the moment I laid eyes on Hector and the gig I disliked them both. I am a little below average height and the gig seemed to me frighteningly high and lightly hung on its two great wheels. As for Hector, we were enemies from the start. I know nothing of horses and listened rather inattentively as Philip enthused over his good proportions, deep girth, broad chest, slender neck and the clean line of his legs. My instinct was to look instead at his face. It did not attract me. His eyes seemed to me to be small and to show a great deal of white. A distinct lump between them gave him an ill-tempered look. I moved away from his restless hoofs.

'Everyone feels like that at first.' Miss Bede evidently sensed my nervousness. 'You'll soon get used to him.'

'I must say Miss Bede has an eye for a horse, Florence. She picked him out, and he was actually cheaper than the cob Pursley tried to foist on to me, an animal fit for a grandfather to drive.'

'I shall never, never dare to go near him, Philip, much less harness and drive him.'

'There's no need for that at present. Miss Bede has kindly offered to take charge of him for the time being.'

I seemed to be for ever thanking Miss Bede. I thanked her again. She declined to stay for dinner and they drove down to Ivy Cottage. Having driven Hector back, Philip returned looking a little subdued. He was a long time in the stable yard. We kept his dinner hot.

'He's spirited.' He ate his dinner in silence and got up absently without waiting for his pudding. 'I think we shall have to look out for a groom. You may not be able to manage at first. There's no real difficulty . . .'

'But the expense?'

'Don't keep harping on money. Money isn't everything.'

Miss Bede had said the same thing. However unhelpful it was true. I ceased to harp on money and retreated into my private dream; but I did not retreat so far as to be unaware that between them Hector and the gig must have cost a good deal. Philip at once set about finding a groom. It was not easy. All the lads of suitable age in the village worked on the land and our groom, though his duties would be light, must always be at hand.

Meanwhile we were dependent on Miss Bede's kindness. Philip continued to walk to the station each morning but Miss Bede harnessed Hector and drove to meet him in the evenings. Our sense of obligation grew. It was Philip's idea that we must acknowledge her kindness by giving her a small present.

'A mere token,' as he put it, 'of our appreciation.'

The token proved unexpectedly difficult to find. While Philip anxiously scoured the shops in Martlebury, I suspected that he was more than once unpunctual at the bank, but I dared not interfere. It was a relief when he brought home a brooch of Florentine mosaic depicting a Roman temple, quiet enough for Miss Bede's taste and so obviously expensive as to make me refrain from asking the price.

Annie no longer bothered to ask if Miss Bede would be staying for dinner. Philip insisted that when she was with us everything must be of the best. My carefully-kept account book showed a steady rise in expenditure on meat, cream and wine. She left later and came earlier. I gathered that Philip had asked her to keep an eye on me. In fact he told me so.

'You're so impulsive sometimes. I'm glad Miss Bede can be with you while I'm in town. She'll discourage you from doing anything rash.'

I don't know how the legend arose that I was an incompetent creature likely to do foolish things; but having taken shape it persisted and would have irritated me if I had been in a less placid frame of mind.

Sometimes, emerging from my faraway state, I felt oppressed. The beautiful solitude of my first days at Honeywick had gone. During Miss Bede's brief absences I went from room to room, enjoying their quietness and thinking of my baby, lost in a tranquil dream, in which – oddly enough in the circumstances – Philip had no part; from which Miss Bede was firmly excluded.

Our bedroom had a built-out bay overlooking the garden; a pretty room, its walls papered with an old-fashioned pattern of green trellis. I liked to sit there knitting or crocheting or working on my chef d'oeuvre, a muslin baby cloak. I was not absolutely alone. One companion was often with me. Banished for a while by the arrival of Miss Bede, she now came back, making no demands, simply being there among the things that had been hers, peering through an occult eyeglass at the steadily growing layette folded away in one of her own mahogany drawers for her great-niece. It was a daughter I longed for.

'I'll call my baby Adelaide.'

I seemed to wake hearing the words and for a while lay still on the chaise-longue, my mind and limbs relaxed. But the sun had already reached the upper part of the garden where the trees were deeply green with the heavy foliage of late summer. It was time to rouse myself for our afternoon drive, a slightly longer one than usual. Miss Bede was eager to explore the upper reaches of the dale. We had often talked of going to Holleron Edge where the view was said to be spectacular, especially when the heather was at the height of its bloom as it was now. She had done so much for me. I must not disappoint her. Reluctantly I got up and bathed my face.

Annie was waiting in the hall with my outdoor things.

'You'll want this.' She put a shawl round my shoulders. 'It's warm enough down here but you'll find a difference at yon end of the dale. I don't know why you can't have a nice sit in the garden instead of trapesing about so much, especially to those god-forsaken parts.'

I tied a scarf round my hat and reminded her that Hector needed exercise.

'That animal! Who's to be put first, I'd like to know, him or you? She's there now.' Annie jerked her head in the direction of the stable. 'Now just you be careful, ma'am. Remember your condition. You're looking a bit washed out.'

She came with me into the yard where Miss Bede was waiting in the driver's seat, and she insisted on helping me up though I was as spry as ever; only the step really was high. Annie seemed far below, her upturned face anxious.

'The weather's nothing special. I wouldn't go too far, ma'am.' She tucked the heavy linen cover round my knees. 'Shall I look for you coming back in about an hour's time?'

'It will be longer, Annie.' Miss Bede pulled on the reins. 'I'd like to get to the Edge if possible.'

'A nasty, dreary place. There's nothing there but one or two tumble-down huts and some nasty bends. If it had been a nice little brougham like Mr Drigg's . . .' Her voice faded as we drove over the cobbles.

After the first few weeks, my health had been excellent but these drives were a small trial and would soon become an ordeal. The swaying of the gig brought on a slight nausea and made my back ache. I had already hinted to Miss Bede that this must be the last of our long drives. 'Then it must be the Edge,' she had decreed. The road was new to me. Fortunately it was level and well surfaced for the benefit of the waggoners who drove this way to and from the mining village at the head of the dale. I tried to forget my physical discomforts and enjoy the airing. Miss Bede and I had rather got out of the way of chatting now that we spent so much time together. I made an effort and drew her attention to the occasional cottage garden and to the purple slopes unfolding ahead but she seemed disinclined to talk. There was no-one about, until at the crossroads where a finger post pointed north to High Gower, we came upon a cart drawn up on the wide sward; a skewbald horse; a swarthy man with a red handkerchief at his throat; a fair-haired woman with a brown cloak thrown back from her shoulders.

'Gipsies,' Miss Bede said and urged Hector to a quicker pace.

But I knew better.

'It's the Badgetts. Do please stop.'

Nancy came across to speak to me.

'I'm ever so glad to see you, Mrs St Leonard. It went against the grain to leave without saying goodbye but there wasn't time.' She lowered her voice. Having looked round, Laban had gone on rearranging the cart, which was loaded with bundles of clothing, bags of tools, cooking utensils and wooden merchandise. 'We were up all night making ready.'

'Was there – a sign?' I too dropped my voice to a

whisper.

She nodded.

'He came in last night. "It'll be tomorrow, Nancy," he says. "We must go tomorrow, if we're going".'

'What was it? How did he know?'

'It was Edwin,' she whispered. 'Our own Edwin.'

'Laban saw him?'

'He saw him up on Holleron Moor, walking away. "He's gone up the dale, Nancy," Laban said, "to show us the way".'

'Oh Nancy, how strange!'

'It's something I don't understand. He came in, his face all aglow. "We must make ready," he says, "and follow the boy".'

She called to Laban. He came at once and stood bareheaded to say goodbye. It was wonderful to see the change in him. His movements were lithe, his face alert.

'Let me be your first customer,' I said. 'Please. For luck.'

He brought a tray of small household things from the cart and I bought a long beechwood spoon, smooth and graceful. We shook hands. But before we drove on, as Nancy and I exchanged our last goodbyes, Laban stood back and took a long, critical look at Hector: not the look of a clairvoyant or a seer but of a man with generations of horse-dealing ancestors behind him. He seemed unimpressed by the deep girth, broad chest and other features so pleasing to Philip and Miss Bede. His expression was not one of admiration. I saw him draw a deep breath as if about to speak, if not to explode. Nancy saw it too and nudged him. He swallowed whatever he had been about to say.

'Take care,' he said briefly instead.

Miss Bede had waited patiently without joining in the conversation. I apologised as we drove off for having whispered to Nancy. 'We didn't want Laban to hear.' I explained about the mysterious sign. 'Do you think he did actually see Edwin? Or do you suppose it could have been a vivid dream or vision?'

'It could have been a great deal of nonsense.'

Miss Bede spoke tartly. I wondered if she had seen Laban's critical look at Hector. After all, it was she who had picked him out and persuaded Philip to buy him against Pursley's advice. Pursley had recommended the unspectacular cob.

Since her mood was unsympathetic, I didn't launch into a discussion of Laban's mystic powers as I would otherwise have done, but merely said, 'Something made him feel that this was a special sort of day. I wonder if it's to be special just for them or for other people too. He has a kind of second sight, I suppose. On the whole I'd rather be without it. It's better not to know what lies ahead.'

Miss Bede was silent, looking along the white road and holding the reins lightly in her left hand. Between the top of her glove and the edge of her cuff an inch or two of wrist lay bare: a wrist unexpectedly thick for a woman of her build. I had thought of her as slender: her face certainly lacked flesh; but now, with her shoulder touching mine, I felt its squareness and the thickness of her upper arm. She was a strong woman.

The landscape was growing wilder. The hills drew nearer and took on a harder edge as the bright sweep of heather thinned into sparse patches between boulders and scree. We had left the red-tiled farms and cottages behind. On the right, half a mile ahead, rose the head-stock of a working mine and a terrace or two of slate-roofed cottages. The sun was well to the west. The east-facing hill on our left lay in deep shade. It was not easy at a first glance to distinguish the half dismantled buildings and spoil heaps of a worked-out pit from the harsh jags of outcrop stone.

'You should take the reins, Florence,' Miss Bede said as we approached a grey crag jutting out into the road fifty yards ahead. I started, and transferred my attention from the gaunt profile of rock to Miss Bede's. 'You'll never have any confidence if you don't practise. There's nothing to be afraid of while I'm here.'

She drove past the scar and drew up. We changed places, reluctantly on my part. Though docile as a lamb with Miss Bede, Hector had never taken to me. I had developed a nervous habit of watching his ears. The moment he recognised my tentative touch on the reins, they flattened ominously. I felt him shudder and my pulse leapt.

'Miss Bede won't let you do anything silly,' Philip had said more than once. How had it come to be understood between them that I was inclined, especially in connection with Hector, to be silly? 'We are all,' Miss Bede had said with the humour which failed so completely to alter the expression of her dark eyes, 'inclined to be silly in one way or another.'

She spoke a calming word to Hector, laid her hand gently on the reins and we went on, without mishap. I grew less nervous and had relapsed into my former dreamy state when the sound of running water roused me. We drove between ash and alder and came to a stone bridge over a stream: to a choice of ways. The broader road led on along the dale.

Again without speaking, Miss Bede put her hand on mine and guided Hector to the left along the narrower road. In another minute we had come to the foot of Holleron Edge. A white track – it was no more – wound up in snake-like curves between gorse-clad bluffs; wound into the very sky, now a lowering and sunless stretch of grey. Against it loomed the harsh, treeless line of the Edge. I tilted back my head to look.

'You're not thinking of going up?'

Miss Bede seemed to rouse herself.

'It isn't as steep as it looks. I'm going to lead him. No, no. You sit still. It will be a magnificent view from the top.'

'You've been here before?'

She murmured something over her shoulder about having walked this way once. I planted my feet firmly on the footboard and tried as best I could to lean my weight forward as we went slowly up between high banks. Once Hector slithered on the loose stones. Once I glanced back, saw the sickeningly steep tilt of the track behind and turned again to the narrow upward view between his nervous ears. Gradually there came over me a sensation of loneliness, of being removed from all that I knew and understood: a bewilderment as to why, from all the empty stretch of country around, we had chosen this forsaken way.

'Miss Bede.' The words came faintly and were lost in the crunch and rattle of wheels on stones. She had not heard. She had forgotten me and might have been alone. That absorbed forward thrust of her square shoulders and unturned head reminded me of my first view of her when she had walked past the house without a glance: an indifferent stranger. I had not foreseen – how could I? – that in so short a time we would become constant companions. Not exactly friends and equals: I had fallen, somehow, into her hands. What an extraordinary way of putting it when she was so kind! It was just that I so constantly adapted my ways to hers while she was so manifestly the one who led, as she was leading me now through a valley already shadowed by the onset of evening.

A heather-scented breeze from the moor top blew the

ends of my scarf over my face. I clawed them away. Another sharp bend and the view had changed. We came out of a narrow gorge to the top.

'It's glorious,' I cried and came back to life. The track levelled out between broad grass verges. Miss Bede led Hector round in a wide circle until we faced the way we had come. I could look round and down for miles: opposite, the mine workings; to the north, stone walls and sheepfolds; to the south, farms and copses; cattle like thimbles and trees like parsley stalks. From far below floated the sound of mallet strokes as a man hammered at a post.

'It's well worth it, Miss Bede. It's beautiful.'

She had the whip under her arm and was busy with the harness, altering the girth, I vaguely thought. Then she went to the horse's head and seemed to be occupied with the bridle. My scarf blew up again, blinding me. I pulled it away and holding the ends firmly, made a discovery. I saw, to my amazement, that we were not alone. Sitting quite still and quietly watching us from the bracken was a boy. His stillness, his silence, the drab colours of his clothes formed so inconspicuous a feature of the muted scene that Miss Bede had evidently not yet seen him, whereas I . . .

I jumped up, but stiffly from having sat for so long. The linen cover slid from my lap. The gig lurched. I steadied myself. As things turned out there never was time to speak. I see myself in that fatal moment poised high above the ground on the hilltop high above the valley, reaching up, taller than I had ever been.

Then – I never could tell how it happened – in what order I mean: the sudden beat of wings as a grouse rose from the heather; its dark diagonal flight; its warning cry, 'Go back, go back, go back!'; the loud crack, like a gunshot. Miss Bede stepped back quickly, her face white as paper as the horse screamed and reared.

'He means to kill me,' I thought – and then in agony – 'and my baby.'

I had just sense enough, as he plunged towards the Edge, to pull with all my strength on the reins. They seemed to come away in my hands. I fell back; saw a segment of cloud; caught a glimpse of ragged gorse overhanging the bluff. The earth fell away, then rose to meet the falling sky with such violence that I felt the impact in every tender nerve, in every muscle, every bone, with a terror so immediate, so intimate, that it seemed to single me out and strike at me alone, exposed on the cruel hillside like a sacrifice.

Nine

Then after the event that changed the world, other people came. I moved in strange company. Beyond the barrier of fever and pain, faces looked down on me. The owners of the faces spoke but would not listen, and there was so much to explain. A great weight, poised somewhere just behind my head like an overhanging rock, was not a rock at all but an obligation to explain. Sometimes it was Miss Wheatcroft who would not listen when I tried to tell her about the valley and the shadow, to convince her that I knew the whole text; and sometimes it was Aunt Adelaide who drifted with me, her limbs burning like mine, her body bruised and lacerated, sweat lying on her brow. Like me she shuddered, ice cold and fire hot, for she too had fallen. Separately but in agonising unison we had both fallen. But the downward drag, the draining of life itself, the unbearable loss could not be shared. The guilt and failure were mine. It was not I who had perished upon the sacrificial stones under the callous sky, but my baby. If only they would let me explain, the crushing burden of guilt might lift a little. My heart and spirit might be eased.

'I have to tell them, Annie, how it happened.' Recognising her with relief, I struggled to sit up.

'Lie still, love.' She bathed my face. 'And don't talk. There's no call to tell anything at all.'

And indeed, sinking back into weakness and despair, I could not tell my story; could not explain how things had happened or in what order. Confusion tormented me. The bird; the loud report; the rearing horse; and there had been some other factor. The mists of delirium shifted to disclose, against a background of tall bracken, another face.

'It was such a surprise.' I moistened my lips: it was hard to speak. 'To see him there.'

Who was it I had been so surprised to see, mysteriously striped with the green shadows of bracken leaves?

Annie's face swelled, elongated, and I lost her again for a long time, doomed as I was to go on falling and trying to explain how it had happened, to all manner of strange people.

But not to Philip. Lost though I was, I felt his absence. Even when I came to myself and found him looking down or sitting by the bed, I knew that he was not really with me.

'Well, Florence?' He tried to infuse kindness into his voice. 'You're getting better, aren't you?' And I knew that it was no good telling him how sorry I was, how guilty I felt, how I had longed for our baby and loved it from the beginning, how it had been my one thought. He had moved away.

At last there came a day when I woke and saw the trellis on the wallpaper still there, clear and steady; beyond the window a gentle movement too slow to be a bird, and then another: leaves were falling. The fever had gone; the pain came only when I moved.

'Annie.'

She was there at once. Had she ever left me?

'Thank God.' She bent and kissed my forehead.

'That's your old smile.'

She turned away and mopped her eyes. Presently she brought me a cup of broth.

'You'll get better now that the fever's left you. We thought it would never go. Every night it's been the same story. You've been wandering far way. The doctor'll want you to get up as soon as ever you can.'

'Philip?'

'He'll be over the moon,' she said gravely.

I watched the fingers of the clock and had drowsed off several times before he came home.

'This is wonderful news, Florence.' I tried to reach his hand and he took mine, but not at once, not warmly. 'Hush. Don't talk.' And I heard him say to Annie, 'Don't let her talk.'

'She's herself, thank God,' Annie said. 'In her right senses. There's been no damage there.'

It was to be a long time before I knew the details of what happened, and some of them never did come to light. Besides shock and concussion two ribs had been broken, but the worst physical damage had been the severe bruising of my whole body. In those early days of my return to life the pain of moving was so intense that I begged to be left alone but Dr Slater insisted that I was to be got up.

'You must make the effort to restore the circulation by exercise. Otherwise your body will stiffen and you may be an invalid for years. You've been lying in bed for a long time.'

Reminders that it had been a long time were not lacking. When at last Annie had got me into a chair, my head swimming from weakness, I looked round, pushing back my hair which had grown lank and unmanageable. A movement a few yards away coincided with mine. Opposite me sat an old woman swathed in a blue wrapper: a little white sickly wraith of a woman with a look of death about her. Aunt Adelaide? My heart leapt to my mouth. She too gave a nervous start and put her hand to her face, a hand on which the wedding ring hung loose. So that was the wife Philip now saw.

No wonder it had all been too much for him. As my strength returned I tried to realise the revulsion he had undergone and to forgive him, victim as he was of his own fastidious nature. The disorder, the blood, the unseemly intimacies of the sickroom must have been revolting to him. His tenderness for me had not survived them even though he saw my suffering and understood that my disappointment was greater even than his own. Whatever it was he had loved me for was gone: my lightness of heart, my flattery of his self-esteem, such good looks as I had; and also gone – the possibility must be faced – might be my ability to be mother of the long line of St Leonards he had hoped for. It would have been better to die than endure a lifetime of his disappointment, just the two of us alone together at Honeywick for the rest of our lives.

Or so I thought. In a few days I was strong enough to take a few steps without help, and with returning strength my interest in the world beyond my room revived. With it came the timid hope that the situation might after all improve. We must make a new life together. Turning things over painfully in my mind, I saw the future as a vague and colourless repetition of our first days at Honeywick. The glamour would be gone but we must try to be happy in a different way. Always at this point would come a loss of sequence in my thoughts. My mind, groping uncertainly, took hold of visible things: the yellow leaves falling; the fire; the fringe of my shawl; as if some force too strong for me to face routed my listless spirit.

'I shall soon be well enough to go downstairs,' I told Annie as she brushed my hair. 'Do you think – tomorrow perhaps?'

'It's lovely hair,' she said. 'We'll soon have it shining again.'

'Tomorrow?'

'I'll fetch out some of your dresses. When you do get about again, you'll need warmer things.'

The opposing force – I thought of it as dark and unmoving – must be faced. Some great step must be taken. Thought of the effort involved brought sweat to my brow. I held out my hands to the fire and looked at it through skeleton fingers. It was autumn. People who came into the country for summer holidays would all have gone away, gone home, those of them who had homes to go to.

'I could be all ready, dressed, in the parlour when he comes in. It will be a surprise. The brown valencia will be warm enough with my pink shawl. I won't wear stays.'

'There's something I haven't told you,' Annie said. 'Nothing to worry you. It's only for the time being, I dare say – and hope may be the case. So far as I can see there was never any need of it and Mother thinks the same, but it was not for me to speak and be snubbed. There's been plenty of that as it is. I will say for her she's kept away from you since the one and only time she came up here just after the accident.'

The new strength ebbed from my body. My hands had fallen, weightless as dry leaves, into my lap.

'Then she hasn't gone?'

Annie put down the brush and as if suddenly tired, sank on the chair at my side.

'If it upsets you,' she said slowly, 'I'll bring myself to speak to the master and tell him you're best left alone. Seeing her that one time seemed to frighten you very nigh to death, as I told the doctor, and he told her to keep away and forbade me to mention her.'

'I don't know why it is that the thought of her frightens me. It's the shock, I suppose. She was there, and so I can't bear to think of her, or him, the horse.'

'Dead and gone, so far as he's concerned, and none too soon. The evil beast. They shot him. There'll be no more trouble from him.'

Had someone been there already with a gun? That would account for the loud report. The familiar panic stirred again, the feverish worry of remembering things in the right order: the bird, the tremendous crack, the screaming horse . . .

'But I must face it, Annie. I must be strong again. As I said, I shall be waiting in the parlour when he comes home. She won't be here then . . .'

'That's just it, love, ma'am. That's what I was trying to tell you. She's here all the time.'

'You mean staying here? In the house?'

'The next day after it happened she had her things sent up. "Make Miss Bede as comfortable as you can," the master said. "She is fearfully distressed and anxious to be of help. She can have my aunt's room."'

I pictured her asleep in Aunt Adelaide's bed; or lying awake, her dark eyes exploring the innocent white ceiling.

'What has she been doing all this time?'

'It's hard to say. Here's a book for you to look at. You'll like the pictures.' She handed me an ancient copy of *The Ladies Cabinet*. I turned the pages, staring at the ladies in short dresses and gigot sleeves without seeing them. As for going downstairs, another day would do as well, not tomorrow. So long as I could stay here safe with Annie.

'Don't ever let her come up here, Annie. Not into my

room.'

'No fear of that, love. She's got all the rest of the house to roam about in.'

If Annie's intention had been to soothe me, it failed. 'All the rest of the house to roam about in.' There in a nutshell was compressed a world of disquiet. The thought of that leisurely roaming disturbed me as did the thought of her presence during all the weeks of my illness. She had been here and I had not known. For all my weakness I had just enough strength to see that my attitude to Miss Bede was irrational and unfair. The last thing I wanted was to have her in the house day and night, or anyone else for that matter; but it would not be for long now that I was getting better. When I was well, she would leave. The peculiar distress accompanying the very thought of her must stem from the accident. It was an unhealthy state of mind. She had done nothing to justify the shrinking that made me want to creep under the bedclothes and shut my eyes rather than see her again.

But I must face her. With a courage I can look back on with approval, I insisted, the very next day, on being dressed to go downstairs. Annie did my hair quite becomingly in a chignon and tied it with a pink snood. With shoes on my feet instead of slippers I felt less shrunken, more confident. Annie was folding the paisley shawl on my shoulders when there came a tap at the door.

She must have been waiting on the landing and listening for the right moment to knock. She didn't come in but waited on the threshold. Her smile, but for its hint of long teeth, would have been wistful.

'Dearest Florence.'

She held out her arms but without taking a step into the room, so that irresistibly I moved forward into them.

'So frail,' she murmured, 'and so brave.'

She, on the other hand, was in every way so strong that it seemed natural to entrust to her the solemn task of getting me downstairs. She had settled me in my chair before I remembered Annie and the quick head-shake with which Miss Bede had dismissed her offer of help. In no more than a few minutes I had grown used to Miss Bede's simple house dress and indoor shoes, her work basket and embroidery frame. Her glance at the clock, her hand on the bell pull, her quiet, 'A glass of wine and water for your mistress,' roused no more than faint surprise in a situation where even my familiar chair intrigued me by its novelty.

By the time Philip came home I was lightheaded with exhaustion. How grateful I was that Miss Bede was there to preside at dinner! When they were ready to sit down, he carried me upstairs as he had done before, in a different life. I noticed that when he put me down on the bed he was breathless, though I had lost weight and was, as Annie said, as light as a bird. It was not the time to ask him, as I longed to do, if he still loved me; if he could love me again.

I must be strong. The conviction that in some future battle all my strength would be needed made every sip of cordial, every morsel of food dutifully swallowed, into an act of preparation. I forced myelf to walk and bend and stretch, opened my window to the cold, pure air and insisted on going downstairs, first in the afternoon, then for luncheon, then in the morning.

'You are a good patient,' Dr Slater said. 'You won't need me much longer. You have had a merciful escape, and with youth on your side you should recover pretty well.' Seeing my quick look of hope he went on, 'As for children, there would be grave risk as yet. Who knows? We mustn't give up hope.'

Now that I was recovering, Miss Bede showed no sign of leaving. There was certainly no inducement to go back to Ivy Cottage at that time of the year. At Honeywick she had a fire in her bedroom every day on Philip's instructions and sometimes she withdrew there; but as a rule we were together in the parlour. She read to me from the newspaper. The world's events reached me through Miss Bede's firmly curved lips and in her low, confident voice – and failed to distract my attention from the reader. She also read to me from Mrs Banstock's novels with which she was familiar, and in some subtle way she altered them; at least I no longer enjoyed them.

'Her kindness is beyond anything,' Philip said.

'She is very kind indeed,' I responded with the mechanical promptness of a talking doll.

On the first evening that I stayed up for dinner, they dined together at the table through the arch, while I ate by the fire. When Miss Bede returned from taking my tray to the kitchen – at other times of the day she left such tasks to Annie – she went straight to the cabinet, bent to open it and only then exclaimed, 'Ah, I was forgetting.' She looked at Philip. 'Perhaps you'd rather not now that . . .'

'Florence will be going to bed directly.'

Interpreting this as consent, Miss Bede got out the chess board and set it up by Philip's chair so that he had no need to exert himself. He moved his first piece listlessly. His face in the lamplight was surely thinner than it had been when we had played together in April, but even in my concern for him I was aware of the comfortable easy nature of their companionship. The evening game had become a well established habit. I was to grow used to seeing them face to face across the board and to watching their two hands advance and retreat, Philip's white and languid, Miss Bede's strong and square. Time and again I struggled against sleep, reluctant to doze off and leave them together then wake to find them together still.

One afternoon Miss Bede and I were in the parlour, as we so often were. Reading still made my head ache but I pulled out *The Lost Years* from the shelf in the recess by the fire. It opened at the bookmark.

'Forget-me-not. It's rather touching, isn't it, especially as no one remembers her much? Stem stitch like yours – and the same kind of eyelet holes.'

I handed it to her. She examined it and glanced ruefully at her own work.

'Better than mine, I'm afraid. It's a commonplace pattern.'

'I wonder if she worked it herself.' There was something appealing in the idea of continuity: another woman stitching in the same way in the same room. My mood might have been sentimental if I had not found myself wishing passionately, almost violently, that Aunt Adelaide's successor at the fireside could have been someone other than Miss Bede. 'More likely it was a present,' I said, mastering the uncharitable wish with some difficulty. 'She must have had friends. I wonder who they were.'

Miss Bede offered no suggestion.

'Look,' she said. 'It's snowing.'

I crouched in the window-seat like a child to watch the leisurely flakes interpose their shifting pattern between the panes and sloping fields, submitting myself to the mesmeric effect of slow movement and fragmented light. Perhaps I really was mesmerised. A feeling of unreality grew on me: a doubt as to why I was there, captive between stone walls, with nothing to be seen but a steadily thickening screen between the outer world and me – and us; for of course Miss Bede was there by the fire: settled, with the same confidence as the house itself as if they belonged together. They were alike. She was its human counterpart, mysteriously established, unable to be known. Each on the surface presented an elegant composure. Had she, like the house, a darker mood safely contained, like water lying deep in limestone until the lid was lifted to release its elemental chill, pervasive, primitive, yet already corrupted by the taint of earlier influences? Had she, like the house, hidden depths?

If so she could control them. She was restrained, subtle, clever. But one thing she could not control: the sheer power of her personality. That she could not keep in check. Even at her most charming, especially then, it seeped, crept, spread itself, so that like the house she could never be ignored. I watched the deadly thrust of the delicate needle in her muscular hand. From time to time she talked with the ease of a strong intellect apparently tempered by a desire to please, to be companionable: for that was what we were – companions.

'She's biding her time,' I thought. The quaint phrase removed us still further from reality into a fairy realm of unknown motives and helpless victims. What on earth could she be biding her time for? As she mended the fire and replaced the brass tongs so that they lay exactly parallel with the poker; as she plumped the cushions and balanced each one at the same angle on the sofa, it dawned on me that she was more at home there than I was. I discovered in her not just the absence of any wish to leave – but an unawareness of the possibility of leaving. She intended to stay.

The conclusion came, not exactly as a shock; rather as the result of a long series of observations. A deep dismay made me draw closer to the cold window pane as if help might be found in the winter fields and snowcapped hedges; and almost at once I saw the absurdity of the idea: saw it too quickly perhaps. She might want to stay at Honeywick but there was no earthly way in which she could contrive it. Re-arrange cushions as she might (how dare she?) there was no doubt as to who was and who would remain mistress of the house.

She had joined me at the window. In contrast to the ethereal scene outside she seemed to have grown more substantial, more impossible to avoid. There was no sky to be seen, no summit to the hill. It was growing dark. I remembered the encircling moors, their long backs humped and silent above the village, and thought how dreadful it must be to be out there homeless in the cold dusk. From the still overcast area of my mind a cloud lifted.

'I wonder where he is?'

'Philip? He will stay in Martlebury.'

'No, not Philip.' I put my hand confusedly to my brow. The cloud was coming down again. 'Illness makes one stupid.'

'Your mind is still a little astray.' She spoke lightly. 'We mustn't worry.'

I took the vinaigrette she handed me so solicitously. The feeling of anxiety and loss refused to become a clear thought. A mental light had flickered out, leaving only an impression that it was no fit night for anyone to be out of doors.

But someone was. We both heard it, the sound of carriage wheels muffled by snow. Through the dulled panes I recognised the figure on the box.

'It's Mr Drigg. He must have been to the station.'

This time we could not see a passenger if there was one but I remembered the girl, his patient: her face pressed to the window; the appealing tilt of her head; the swiftness with which she had vanished down the long avenue of oaks. Never to be seen again?

The room was warm and safe. There was nothing to be afraid of. Miss Bede had gone into the dining parlour. I saw her through the archway. The heavy gilt frame enclosing the Highland scene enclosed her too so that the picture ceased to be a landscape and became a portrait of Miss Bede with the mountain behind her as if she had risen from the inscrutable waters of the loch.

For two days the snow kept us prisoners, Miss Bede and me at Honeywick, Philip in Martlebury. By the Friday evening it had melted sufficiently to allow trains to run. Philip trudged home later than usual, looking fagged out, and declared that he would not go to the bank the next day no matter how old Wetherby went on about it. He was too tired to eat and only drank a cup of soup. Sometime I must talk to him seriously about Miss Bede but this was not the moment.

I left them together reluctantly while I went upstairs, to the little room which Philip was still using, and spent a few minutes making sure that all was comfortable: the fire drawing well, a stone bottle between the sheets. I came out on to the landing to hear the low murmur of voices below and hesitated, wondering whether to go down again; but there had been a touch of irritation in Philip's manner when I had urged him to go to bed early and I judged it best to keep away. Much as I disliked leaving them together, I had come to dislike being with them even more. Philip had developed a habit of looking at Miss Bede before he spoke, like a child seeking approval or encouragement or even, sometimes, a reprimand.

But I made a point of rising early next morning and for the first time was installed by the coffee pot when the others came down to breakfast. Each seemed a little taken aback. Philip kissed my cheek mechanically and took his place, looking as if he had not slept.

'This is a pleasant surprise, Florence.' Miss Bede gave the effect of smiling and spoke with a heartiness that somehow conveyed a mood of gallantly facing the worst. 'You'll soon be quite yourself again, won't you, dear?'

'Yes,' I said aggressively. The note of aggression, the tremor of my hand as I poured out the coffee, did not escape her. With a little sigh she communicated her concern for me to Philip.

He ate moodily and when Annie had taken away the plates said abruptly, 'I must tell you, Florence, that I have decided to leave the bank.'

Instantly, as if at a signal, Miss Bede rose.

'I'll leave you to talk things over. No, don't get up.' She touched Philip lightly, encouragingly, on the shoulder as she went to the door.

'You told Miss Bede before you told me.'

As a first response to such momentous news, it was less petty than it sounded. Nevertheless Philip flushed with annoyance.

'We have often talked of it, while you were ill. I'm not blaming you, Florence, but naturally it hasn't been possible to confide in you and look to you for companionship for some time. Miss Bede's help has been invaluable to me in reaching this decision. It was always a foolish scheme, to live here and work in Martlebury. What's more, I'm not prepared to put up any longer with old Wetherby's infernal arrogance.'

I held my tongue. Old Wetherby must have been sorely tried by Philip's unpunctuality, occasional absences and by his condescending manner.

'You will not like being poor,' I said.

Unexpectedly I recognised a ray of hope. On £200 a year we would be too poor, too gloriously, mercifully poor to entertain a guest whose refined tastes demanded a diet of veal, cream and wine. Oh how gladly would I embrace poverty if it should prove the means of getting rid of Miss Bede!

'We can manage,' I said. 'Your health must come first. Apart from Annie's wages we don't spend much and we have enough household things to last all our lives. With just the two of us, we can live very simply. My clothes will last for ages. Do you know that Wordsworth and his sister lived for years without animal food, on bread, milk and vegetables . . .'

'Miss Bede has made a suggestion,' Philip interrupted.

I gathered my strength to hear it.

'If she were to share our expenses as a paying guest, it would help. We could go on in the same way.' He didn't look at me but leaned his head on his hand as if weary to death.

I had been prepared for conflict. This first blow almost stunned me. I hardened my heart, ignoring his haggard looks.

'No,' I said with all the firmness at my command and with an effort to behave with the restraint so much to be admired in Miss Bede. 'No, Philip. It will not do. As a matter of fact I meant to tell you. I have no wish to go on in the same way. Miss Bede has been here long enough. She must go. You must tell her – or I will.'

'I didn't expect you to be reasonable or to consider my interests before your own. You are not yourself. Miss Bede warned me what to expect. Would you rather let me ruin my health by travelling to the bank every day than accept a sensible, civilised arrangement, beneficial to us all?'

'To us all?' It was no use. Under such provocation I lost all desire to be restrained: became in fact passionate. 'Of what benefit would it be to you and me to have her here? Oh, you're thinking of the money. But it's you who are not being reasonable. We could not charge Miss Bede more than a pound a week at the most and that is only a third of your salary at the bank. For that we must live in a manner beyond our needs or wishes.'

'Miss Bede has a small annuity,' Philip said coldly and still without looking at me. 'She has offered – her generosity amazes me – to put most of it at our disposal. Added to my own income it would be enough for all three of us.'

'Then she would not be a paying guest,' I said slowly. 'Her position would be quite different. She would want an equal share in deciding how things are to be done.'

'And what would be the harm in that? Miss Bede is a lady of refinement and breeding. She knows how things should be done.'

'I could not bear it.' Trembling, I got to my feet. 'I cannot and will not bear it.'

'What will you do?'

I went and put my arms round him.

'Philip, my dearest, how can you speak so coldly? I know that since my illness you haven't felt the same towards me. I'm plain and unattractive. I've disappointed you. But I shall soon be well again. We'll be happy as we used to be when we were alone together. Give up the bank if you wish but don't, I beg of you, put us under any further obligation to Miss Bede. She has obliged us enough,' I said bitterly. In despair I sat on the chair next to his, dragged at his arms and made him look at me. 'Listen, I have found out something about Miss Bede.' His eyes were heavy, already disbelieving. My earnestness repelled and exhausted him. 'She cannot live a life of her own. She has fastened upon ours like a leech. I don't mean that she's unkind, only that she needs other people to cling to and feed on. And I believe she wants this house. Sometimes she behaves as if it was already hers.'

It was true but it sounded unconvincing. Philip's reply didn't surprise me.

'You don't know what you're saying. This house is mine. How could it ever belong to anyone else – so long as I'm here? It's because the house means so much to me that I'm prepared to take this opportunity of keeping it and caring for it. I can't do that without money.'

'If people want money they should work for it,' I said. 'She will take the house from us as she is taking you from me. If she stays, I warn you, Philip, it will drive me out of my mind. Already I feel . . .' My head ached as if it would burst.

At once I regretted the words. His expression had changed. He looked at me sharply, then looked awkwardly away.

'This is a delusion, Florence, this prejudice you have formed against Miss Bede. After a fall such as you have suffered, it is perhaps understandable. As Miss Bede says, an illness of any kind can affect the judgment, but particularly an illness such as yours.'

The drift of these remarks alarmed me. Did they think I was out of my mind? I began some confused protest then broke off. The smallest criticism of Miss Bede would only strengthen his conviction that I was prejudiced against her, irrationally so. He saw only her kindness, her unfailing courtesy. They were her strongest weapons, far more effective than my own directness. I forced myself to submit and tried to do so patiently. I too must bide my time.

As my body grew stronger, so did my powers of concentration. I read; I wrote to Aunt Maud; and recognised it as a real step towards recovery when I could speak of the accident without too much distress.

In this however I was given no encouragement.

'It would be best not to talk of it in front of Miss Bede.' Philip had come into my room for the express purpose of telling me so. 'It distresses her.'

'She's always there. How can I talk to you without talking to her?'

'She can't forgive herself for having let you take the reins.'

I stared at him in sudden enlightenment. For all my feeling of guilt – a common condition, I now know, in women who have miscarried – it had never occurred to me that I had been in any way responsible for the accident itself. Something had frightened the horse and made him bolt. I began to explain.

'Don't talk about it.' Philip cut short my confused account, not unkindly. 'Let us agree that it wouldn't have happened if Miss Bede had kept the reins. She reproaches herself. It's what one would expect of her.'

Miss Bede was competent and responsible. I, particularly where horses were concerned, was flighty and nervous. I forced myself to see the situation as Philip saw it and partly succeeded. No wonder he had lost patience with me. I had lost him his horse and gig, besides inflicting on him the other, greater disappointment followed by this long, miserable illness. He had never even mentioned the expense, much less complained of it. It was not surprising that he had turned to Miss Bede for companionship and comfort. I strove to be grateful for his forbearance, for her many acts of kindness.

All the same the accident had not been my fault. Philip must be made to understand that. It became the one thing I wanted to talk about. About the people at Blea Rigg Farm, for instance, the Buckles, who had taken me in. Mrs Buckle had put me in her best bedroom and nursed me with Annie's help until I was fit to be moved.

It was a curious feeling to know that so much had been going on without my knowledge. But it was on the disaster itself that my mind became fixed. Try as I might, I could not resist the subject for all Miss Bede's grieved looks and Philip's reproving frowns. Even when I didn't actually speak of it, I thought of it continually. Dozing over a book through the long evenings, I was there again on Holleron Edge, high in the gig above the dale. A mist, not in the scene but in my mind, obscured the details. But the conviction grew that there were forgotten factors which would somehow exonerate me if only I could remember them.

So hour after hour in the warm, low-ceilinged room we each pursued our own thoughts. Firelight reddened the curtain drawn over the archway to shut out the Highland cattle. In its genial light nothing was shabby, everything softened into concord. The uniform volumes of Mrs Banstock closed their ranks; the cushions stood at ease. Each object had its counterpart: the pairs of vases, the nymphs, the two figures at the chess board. I was the only discordant element as I struggled to clarify in my mind the last minutes before the sky seemed to fall on Holleron Edge and the earth turned against me.

And all at once one evening a missing piece slipped into place. It must have come to me half-dreaming. I woke triumphant, still spellbound by so amazing a discovery.

'Of course. There was someone who actually saw the accident. Jordan Finch.'

Ten

It was the queen, I believe, on whom Miss Bede's hand had come to rest. Flesh and ivory remained still. Taken up as I was by my discovery, I nevertheless felt the stillness and the silence: a flabbergasted silence which Philip at last broke.

'What do you mean, Florence?'

'I don't believe you saw him, Miss Bede. He was sitting in the bracken.'

'Someone you knew?' Philip said slowly, reluctantly, for some reason.

'One of the boys from Marshall Street. Wasn't it strange? Whatever was he doing there?'

I had no sooner put it like that than I felt doubtful. Nothing in the world was more improbable than that Jordan Finch and I should be on Holleron Edge together. Philip had glanced quickly at Miss Bede who remained unmoving, her hand on the ivory piece.

'What *was* he doing?'

A certain note in Philip's voice should have warned me. I believe it did.

'Nothing. Just watching.'

Again he glanced at Miss Bede. This time almost imperceptibly she shook her head: the merest hint of a signal only to be recognised by someone very close; or to someone newly alert to danger as I had become. With a concern I had not seen in him before, Philip put his hand on my brow.

'You are hot, dear.' He wheeled the painted glass screen between my face and the fire. 'Come, let me make you comfortable.'

The endearment, the kindness, brought tears to my eyes. I was still easily upset.

'Thank you, Philip. Do you suppose –' I looked up into his face. For once he stood between me and Miss Bede. 'Do you suppose we could find Jordan? He might be able to tell exactly what happened. You see, I don't really think I was careless. Something frightened the horse. There was a loud noise.'

Searching his face for understanding, I found something that alarmed me. It was compassion.

'You don't believe me, darling. You think I'm making it up.'

'Imagining it perhaps.' He held my hand in both of his. He seemed distressed. 'Is it likely that one of your pupils would be there on Holleron Edge just at that moment – and no other soul for miles around?'

'I was very surprised; and there wasn't time . . .'

'You rambled on a good deal about Marshall Street, you know, and Miss Wheatcroft in particular.' He shook my hand gently, teasingly, to show that he had long forgiven me for having such a friend as Miss Wheatcroft. 'And Aunt Adelaide. You talked about her too, my poor Florence.'

Miss Bede's silk skirt rustled as she got up. From my low chair she seemed tall as she stood over me. They both seemed tall, as if I were sinking into a concealed pit – or trap. With a flurry of panic I felt the strewn leaves give way, the camouflage of dead branches crack as I sank.

'Dr Slater warned us that there might be a recurrence of the fever.'

The word 'us' disturbed me. With an effort I sat up straight.

'I'm not feverish now,' I said. 'It may seem strange. You may not believe me. But Jordan Finch was there, watching. We must find him. Then, you see –' I think now it must have been from the look of insane cunning he found in my face that Philip recoiled – 'if he wasn't there, he'll be sure to say so and at least –' I looked from one to another, pleased with so simple a plan – 'we'll know.'

'Tell me, Florence' – Miss Bede sat down on the ottoman so that her face was close to mine. Her manner was reasonable, almost excessively so. I watched, fascinated as her red lips parted to disclose her long narrow teeth – 'how was he dressed?'

'I didn't notice.'

'Did he look just the same as when you last saw him?'

'When he gave me the watercress?' A swift glance passed between them: a glance of alarm. 'I didn't tell you, Philip.' I hastened to explain. 'It was meant to be a wedding present.'

'A bunch of watercress.' Miss Bede's tone was carefully unsurprised.

'The children gave me little things . . .'

'And he looked, when you saw him on Holleron Edge, just the same?'

'Not exactly.' What had the difference been? I considered Jordan's characteristic features. The silent scowl? He had been silent but not scowling. His expression had been steadily watchful. His face – and it was only his face that there had been time to see, striped green by bracken fronds – had been unbruised. His bare feet? 'I didn't see his feet,' I said. It sounded odd.

'He seemed better, brighter, fresher,' Miss Bede suggested before I could explain, 'than in real life?'

'It was real life,' I said soberly. Nothing could have been more real. 'It was before the accident, remember, not after.'

'The reason I asked about his appearance,' Miss Bede said quickly, 'is that there was a boy who went for help. He appeared – I don't know where he came from and although you were, or seemed to be, unconscious –' Her look of distress brought a murmur of sympathy from Philip.

'We mustn't speak of this,' he said.

'– you could have been aware of him,' Miss Bede went on bravely, 'and that might explain your feeling of having seen him before. Such things can happen in cases of concussion.'

As best I could, I described Jordan.

'The boy who fetched help from the farm knew the district.' She was obviously distressed by the memory but did not spare herself. 'He knew exactly where to go.'

'What happened to him?'

She shrugged.

'I have no idea.'

'I should like very much to see him and thank him.'

'That shouldn't be difficult,' Philip said. 'And as you say, it will settle your mind and drive the bogeys away.'

'Jordan isn't a bogey.'

'It couldn't have been Jordan, dear,' Philip began, but in response to a warning gesture from Miss Bede, continued, 'or may not have been. We must find out.'

'Yes,' Miss Bede spoke with soothing kindness. 'We'll find out, shall we? And now, I think –' she glanced deferentially at the bell rope. 'Shall I ring for Annie?'

It was sweet beyond words to feel the tenderness of

Philip's hand on mine. I clung to it, not wanting to leave him; and was overcome with a weak weariness as if my bones had dissolved.

Upstairs, I tried to tell Annie all about it.

'They don't believe me but he was there. We must find him. He saw everything.'

'Well I never.' Annie measured out a few drops from a black bottle into a glass and half filled it with water. 'Drink this. It'll help to settle you.'

'What is it?'

'Just a draught. The doctor said you were to have it if you got yourself worked up. "She must sleep", he said.'

I drank it meekly and slept well. The next morning Dr Slater called though it was not his usual time for a visit. After the customary examination he passed his hands carefully over my head. Their gentle pressure disarranged my hair but caused me no discomfort.

'You have done very well.' He took up his hat and bag and added casually, 'There's nothing you want to tell me? Nothing that worries you?'

I hesitated and was tempted to confide in so genial and impersonal an acquaintance.

'Well, it did worry me when they seemed to think . . .'

'They?'

'My husband and Miss Bede – that I'd been careless with the horse. It wasn't so, Dr Slater, and now I've found a way of proving that it wasn't my fault. You see, there was a witness to the accident.' Warmth came to my cheeks. I felt my eyes light up. He may have thought my sudden animation unnatural.

'Ah!' He put down his bag.

'A boy, a pupil in the school where I taught. He was there in the bracken, watching.'

'You spoke to him?'

'There wasn't time.'

'Had he said anything?'

I shook my head. What would Jordan of all people be likely to say? He never talked much except to Mr Hawthorne, as we all did. He was a person one could talk to with absolute trust, confident of being believed and understood.

'Tell me about him. Was he a favourite?'

I looked directly at Dr Slater and saw his eyes waver; and I resolved to say no more. Nothing would induce me to embark again on the presentation of the watercress.

'Well, we shall see,' he said unhelpfully. 'We shall see.'

I had been ready to go downstairs when he arrived. No sooner had he left me than I tidied my hair and went stiffly down, one step at a time. Fragments of conversation reached me from the hall.

'. . . confused state of mind . . . Let her talk but on no account encourage it or let this become an unhealthy interest.'

'I assure you, Dr Slater,' I called out, 'I'm not in the least confused.'

'Ah!' He started. 'And I'm delighted to hear it, my dear. Good day to you. Delighted.' He hastily opened the door and let himself out.

He must have known about Jordan even before I told him. They had talked it over and asked him to call. My anger at being treated as a foolish, irresponsible creature who could cause a horse to bolt and suffered from delusions was inflamed still further by the humiliation of having my supposed symptoms discussed with a perfect stranger. That was what she was; not a relation or even an old friend. She was nothing to me, nothing.

'You mustn't be angry, Florence.' Her low voice vibrated with concern. As always the sheer urbanity of her behaviour made it impossible to be uncivil. 'We have been so very anxious about you. "Nothing," I said to

Philip, "nothing must be left undone. No effort must be spared to make her well. Your own dear wife." Wasn't it best to consult Dr Slater when you seemed – momentarily – to have lost ground? You were thrown so violently,' she closed her eyes in pain, relieving me of their dark stare, 'there was always the possibility of an injury to the head.'

'I have had a narrow escape,' I said, 'and so had you, Miss Bede. You stepped back just in time.'

With one of the flashes of recollection that came to me with increasing frequency, I recalled the quick backward step as she took her hand from the bridle, her face as white as its olive tint could ever be; but brilliant as the flash was, it did not illuminate her movements before or after.

'You remember that?' She had gone to the window and stood with her back to me. 'Tell me, what else do you remember?'

'The grouse flying up; a loud cracking noise. A gun, I suppose.' It had come from my left as I turned my head to gaze in amazement at the figure in the bracken on the right. 'And Jordan. I remember him clearly,' I said firmly and, realising how improbable it sounded, I added, 'Very clearly.'

'His face was imprinted on your mind,' she said, 'because he was the last of your pupils you ever saw. Wasn't it a rather striking incident, when he gave you the – the present?'

'The watercress?' How ridiculous it sounded! But the incident had indeed been memorable: more striking than she knew. I had actually kissed Jordan's bruised and grubby face, then skimmed downhill clutching his present. Was it possible that two experiences had fused in my mind so that in my second, swift, fateful descent I had experienced a lightning memory of leaving Jordan behind as I had left him on the steep, cobbled street?

I went back to my room, feeling a desperate need for solitude in which to face the possibility that – in certain directions – my mind was impaired. Philip and Miss Bede believed that it was. They saw me as an object of pity, a prey to fantasies, as Philip was careful to call them.

'I know so little of your family,' he had nerved himself to say that morning. 'There was never, I suppose, any . . .' He had hestitated, hating the question. She had told him to ask, I was sure of it. 'Anyone who was . . . not . . .'

'Never,' I cried, knowing no more of my family than Aunt Maud: good sensible Aunt Maud, my father's sister. 'How can you ask?' I saw a look of sickness in his face, as if events had overtaxed his strength. Soberly, I reminded myself that Jordan Finch was not my only delusion. Daily, hourly, I had to struggle against an unreasoning resistance to Miss Bede, a tendency to imagine in her unvarying kindness a sinister quality. 'You're prejudiced,' Philip had said. I could not deny it.

But I had not been mistaken in my conviction that she intended to stay. It had seemed impossible, yet here she was, a permanent member of the household. Step by step she had invaded our lives. Since one improbability after another had hardened into reality, I was irresistibly drawn to consider the next. If I had died on Holleron Edge, what would she have done? Would she have moved on, or moved in? The thought of Philip and Miss Bede at Honeywick without me came quite naturally and lured me on to the next: was it conceivable that having manoeuvred herself into the house, she would in time manoeuvre me out?

I recognised the idea as preposterous: recognised too a desperate need to reassure myself that I couldn't possibly be – got rid of. It was sheer fantasy; and fantasy can be horribly disturbing. A chill of foreboding actually set my teeth chattering. There was no doubt that my mind was temporarily unhinged.

It took courage to tilt the looking glass and look steadily at my reflection. The face was still thin but it had filled out a little and lost its sickly pallor. The expression was melancholy and thoughtful. Wasn't it the eyes that betrayed disorders of the mind? I seemed to meet the blue gaze of an older, more sorrowful woman than I had been only a few months ago. My life was already so different from anything I had foreseen, the process of change had been so subtle, so seemingly inevitable, above all so irreversible that somehow or other, against all the laws of mathematics, two had become three. Was it possible that by the same subtle means three could become two, myself being the unwanted third – discarded? The eyes in the glass widened and showed me my own fear.

I pulled myself together. Over my dead body . . . Only death could remove me. What had I been thinking of? Philip loved me and would always put me first, would cherish me as his wife, do what was best for me. A person could not be ousted from her own home. Besides, there was nowhere one could be ousted *to*.

Turning from the glass, I opened the window and saw Miss Bede in hat and mantle make her way through the wicket gate and across the field, her skirts raised above the damp grass: and I pretended that she was going away.

'She's gone,' I would tell Philip, having rushed up the hill to meet him. 'She's gone and I'm well and happy again.'

I must make it come true. From the depths of my being rose a tide of resolution so strong that it made my body shake. I must purge the house of Miss Bede and re-establish myself: at once – as soon as she came back. I made a pretence of tidying a drawer, absorbed in my plan; and my determination had not wavered when half an hour later the front door opened and closed. As soon as she had taken off her outdoor things I would simply go downstairs and tell her how much I disliked the idea of this permanent arrangement. Had she not herself said that young people were best left alone? She was a reasonable woman; her very walk as she passed softly along the landing past my door had the measured dignity of all her actions. It was only a minute before she went down again. Now was the time to confront her. It was important to think out carefully how to put it, to equal the civility in which she generally out-did me. On no account must I lose the initiative and relapse into anger or confusion, or worst of all, tears. 'Our first year of marriage, Miss Bede . . .' At once they welled and overflowed, blurring the image in the glass, bringing a tiresome delay. As I wiped them away and tried to compose myself, I was absently aware that the front door had opened and closed again.

When at last I went downstairs it was to find Miss Bede in conversation with a visitor: Mr Drigg.

Eleven

I realised at once that she had brought him here. She had gone to Gower Oaks and asked him to come. He had lost no time. Fortunately I was on my guard and faced him, not as a neighbour and the tenant of our three-acre field but squarely as an enemy: one who offered select asylum to people not in their right minds.

Miss Bede skilfully bridged the conversational gaps while I sat icily silent. Under her influence it was impossible to be rude but he must have felt my antagonism as I raked his unpleasing countenance with critical eyes. The man had an ostentatious sheen: his shirt collar and cuffs seemed excessively white, his black hair too liberally anointed with macassar oil, his voice too rich, his lips too red. 'A cad' Philip had called him. The cast of his features was toad-like with bright, over-large eyes. And yet Philip must have consented to Miss Bede's fetching him. He would want – panic gripped me again – to do what was best for me.

'I'm happy to see you up and about again, Mrs St Leonard. The last time I called you were still very ill.'

It transpired, to my surprise, that he had called several times.

'Young people have excellent powers of recovery. I

remember . . .' He described his own experience of a bolting horse, his injuries, their treatment. 'The mishap has never troubled me since, not for an instant.'

He was trying to draw me out. I gave him no encouragement. He had an air of kindliness that I mistrusted, a smoothness which might ingratiate him with Philip who was apt to be impressed by good manners. He was persuasive and plausible. A person who was – not quite well – might be entrusted to such a man in good faith; could vanish from sight for years; for ever.

'So now you are without a conveyance,' he said, 'and very much confined to the house. It would give me great pleasure to drive you, Mrs St Leonard, with your husband's approval. An airing now and then would do you a world of good. I'm afraid –' his glance at Miss Bede seemed to me to be meaningful – 'there is room for only one passenger in comfort.'

He had come quickly to the point. I saw myself being whirled out of sight along the avenue of oaks and resolved never to set foot in his brougham under any circumstances.

'I have no taste for drives at present, thank you.'

'Miss Bede is an excellent judge of horses, I believe.' He had turned to her quickly. She seemed a little taken aback and was drawn reluctantly into a discussion of draught and saddle horses, single, double and tandem harness. I instantly saw it as a sign of his cunning that all his remarks, questions and comments were directed towards Miss Bede and seemed to exclude me. Was she familiar with this part of the country, the steep hills, the loose-surfaced roads? Had she had much recent experience of driving? He seemed unable to leave the subject of horses, accidents and our accident in particular; and when he did, it was to draw from Miss Bede a few personal details about her childhood in Sussex and drives with her father.

His interest in Miss Bede (for he kept his large, over-bright eyes directed towards her as if unable to drag them away) was so noticeable that I was diverted from my own worries and found time to wonder if she had found an admirer. I had cautiously sketched in the out-lines of a whirlwind courtship culminating in the removal of Miss Bede to Gower Oaks, when a certain expression in Mr Drigg's eyes, a coolness of observation as if he were methodically dissecting a specimen, brought me to my senses. Whatever had been Miss Bede's motives in bringing him here, his persistence was evidently distaste-ful to her. She was as near fidgeting as I had ever seen her. Mr Drigg had been describing his method of oiling harness and had gone on to ask Miss Bede's opinion of various types of bit. Why was it, I wondered, that when I had pulled on the reins, they had seemed to come away in my hands? Could I, after all, have done some stupid thing? I must never mention it.

At this moment came a diversion as a cart drew up outside, bringing the rest of Miss Bede's possessions from Ivy Cottage. With obvious relief, Miss Bede escaped, murmuring that she must speak to the carter. A fit of misery overcame me. The arrival of her luggage was the final touch. She was here to stay. There was no hope.

'You have something on your mind, Mrs St Leonard.' The man's rich voice had a deceptive warmth. One could see how skilled he was in inviting confidences, especially from people in enfeebled states of mind. I shook my head, unable to deny it, determined to resist him.

'You come from Martlebury, I believe. I know it well.'

In spite of myself I was interested.

'Do you know Marshall Street?'

'A little. This is a very different life for you.' The warm voice, the probing gaze, produced a peculiar effect. It was as though I were being soothed and at the same time scrutinised under a microscope. 'You were happy there? You loved your pupils.' He seemed to know it without my telling him. 'You must miss them.'

'I know now that I was happy but when I was there – I was all impatience to escape.'

'Not an unusual state of affairs. You have never gone back?'

'No,' I said and had thawed sufficiently to add, 'I should like more than anything to see Mr Hawthorne again.'

'You liked him?'

'More than that.' I hesitated, surprised by the strength of feeling aroused by the familiar name. It was more than liking: it was respect, reverence, love. It had even made me forget how much I detested and feared Mr Drigg. 'He would tell me – what to do,' I said incautiously.

'About what?' he asked quietly; but I was already on my guard again.

'I only meant that he gave me advice when I needed it.'

'There are times when we all need advice. Ah, Miss Bede.'

She had appeared noiselessly through the archway leading from the dining parlour. I wondered how long she had been there. Had Mr Drigg noticed my nervous recoil?

'Pray do not forget my suggestion, Mrs St Leonard. Believe me it would be an honour. A drive, I mean.'

We had risen. He looked me full in the face, nodded persuasively and smiled his too pleasant smile. I had dallied with the man long enough. Fortunately I knew my danger and inwardly gave thanks for the chance glimpse of the unfortunate girl, his patient, which had so vividly brought home to me the nature of his establishment.

'At present I am on foot. It would give me great pleasure to escort you on a short walk, if you felt inclined for it.'

He was obviously trying to draw me into another tête-à-tête. Well, he should have it. Ignoring Miss Bede, I went out with him into the hall and closed the parlour door. An hour ago I had resolved to resume a proper authority in my own home. It was time to begin.

'I believe you have some experience of mental derangement, Mr Drigg. Your patients are not in their right minds.'

'I would not describe their difficulties in quite that way.' He seemed surprised by my direct manner. Afterwards I wondered if it had been too forthright, eccentrically so.

'If you are in any doubt about my mind, if you have been brought here to discover whether or not I'm completely sane, let me tell you in the plainest terms that I am. Your help is not required, Mr Drigg. My illness confused me for a while. I see things quite clearly now.'

'I'm very glad to hear you say so.' Nothing could puncture the man's oily blandness. 'I believe you may have been mistaken as to the object of my visit but . . .'

'I understand perfectly why you came and who brought you. Good day to you, Mr Drigg.'

It was then, as I flung open the outer door, that the man outside slammed the tailboard of his cart, snarled at his horse and with a report that brought my heart to my mouth, cracked his whip. The sudden sound so unnerved me that I clung to the door, my heart pounding.

'I thought it was a gun,' I said shamefaced.

'Was it –' Mr Drigg's toadlike eyes were brilliant – 'was it at all like the report you heard on Holleron Edge?'

His tone was urgent but I was not to be lured into making any foolish comparisons.

'How could it be?'

He knew better than I that no responsible driver would crack a whip over a nervous horse on a cliff edge. I recovered myself and went indoors taking with me the odd feeling that Mr Drigg was satisfied: not pleased; but like a physician whose patient discloses the final symptom from which a diagnosis can be made. I went purposefully into the parlour, determined to speak despite the inescapable presence of Miss Bede's luggage in the hall; and only then noticed the envelope Mr Drigg had left on the table. It was addressed to Philip. The quarter's rent for the field without a doubt.

Could his visit have been perfectly innocent after all? Had he combined his duty as a tenant with a friendly call? Or was the envelope an excuse to reassure me? I couldn't be sure; nor was I any longer sure of Miss Bede's rôle in the morning's events. I nerved myself to ask her – then changed my mind.

'Well, Miss Bede,' I said instead, 'it seems we are to live together for a while. Naturally this can never be your home as it is mine, but for my part I shall try to behave as Philip wishes. I want him to be happy more than anything in the world. If things had turned out differently . . .' But for the disastrous trip to Holleron Edge, I would soon have held my baby in my arms. In spite of myself my voice failed me.

She had been listening with her head bowed and seemed dejected as if Mr Drigg's visit had oppressed her too.

'Poor Florence.' Her sympathy like everything else about her was restrained and for that reason convincing. My resentment wavered.

'Oh, Miss Bede, we must be friends.'

'What else could we be?' Her astonishment seemed so spontaneous that I was reassured.

'And make Philip happy,' I went on, conscious of my dismal collapse into childishness. 'I don't feel he loves me as he did. But I'm his wife. I want to be the one who cares for him.'

'Of course you do. Naturally. You're mistaken, I'm sure. He loves you beyond anything. I believe –' she seemed struck with remorse – 'I have interfered too much. It won't happen again. You are mistress here. You shall make all the decisions; and you won't begrudge me a place at your fireside? Remember – I have none of my own.'

She spoke with such disarming reliance on my sympathy, such resignation to her loneliness, above all with such charm, that I felt ashamed of all my wild suspicions. For the time being, there could be no question of her leaving.

Twelve

'So you want to go to Blea Rigg Farm?' Mrs Blanche put down the poker and took up her knitting needles.

'We have never thanked the Buckles for their kindness – at the time of the accident.'

'Mr St Leonard'll likely have written to them.'

'He's had so much to think of.'

'And her? Yon Miss Bede? Couldn't she go?' Mrs Blanche looked at me sharply. 'If there's to be any trapesing up the dale at this time of the year, she'd likely be better fitted for it than you.'

'It ought to be me,' I said evasively.

'You needn't feel as grateful as all that. Hattie Buckle would be in her element with all the fuss. Like a dog with two tails she'd be, would Hattie. There's not much doing up there as a rule. You gave her something to talk about for the rest of her days.' She knitted another row so rapidly that it made scarcely a pause in the conversation before she went on, 'Come a summer day, you could walk up there.'

'I want to go now.'

I nibbled a wedge of Mrs Blanche's gingerbread as I did almost every day now that I could walk out on my own again. Her cottage had become a haven into which I could escape from Miss Bede.

'Then why don't you? You've some notion in your mind, that's easy to see, so you might as well go.'

'How?'

The problem had absorbed me for weeks: how to get to Blea Rigg Farm on my own, or at least without Miss Bede, and discover the identity of the boy who had watched from the bracken. The worst had not happened. Mr Drigg had not come back and had, in fact, gone away from Gower Oaks as he frequently did. For Philip's sake I had learned to behave with such restraint that no one could suspect the effort it cost me. But I never ceased to resent Miss Bede's strange power over him.

'It might be as well for you to continue at the bank a little longer,' she had said, weighing one grave doubt against another. 'Another month or two. Since Florence wishes it.' She had looked at him carefully as if calculating his physical strength, and then at me as if placing on me the responsibility for taxing it to the utmost. She did not add, 'We must humour Florence in her present disturbed state of mind.' Not when I was there.

'Philip must do as he thinks best,' I said quickly.

'Indeed, I shouldn't dream of interfering.'

Each day he seemed to change before my eyes, to grow physically more frail, his cough more troublesome, his eyes larger and more sunken. Every day I saw his face more sullen and martyred as I kissed him goodbye and felt his kiss more perfunctory and reproachful.

All this made me wretched. But looking inward I faced a greater misery: the dread that they were right. If my mind really was disordered, then my view of everything else must be disordered too. All my capacity for worrying was directed to the stark necessity of convincing myself, if no one else, that I was perfectly – it horrified me even to use the word – sane.

I became obsessed with the thought of Jordan Finch. He was the supreme test. If it really was Jordan, improbably come to rest on Holleron Edge on that fateful day in August, then I could trust my senses; I was absolutely myself.

Feeling Mrs Blanche's keen eyes upon me, I could almost have confided in her but the anxiety was of too intimately painful a kind to share.

'How?' I repeated, wiping my fingers on my handkerchief.

'There's always a way. If you ask me, you give in a bit too easy. You're like our Annie. A little bit soft. To other folk anyway. If there's anything you want to do, you do it. I'm more sorry now for the things I never did than the daft ones I did do.' Her needles flashed. 'Tollemy Price'll be here in a few minutes. It's Thursday.'

With some effort I contrived to seem interested in Tollemy Price, travelling dealer in candles, soap, groceries and ironmongery.

'He'll be passing Blea Rigg on his way to Catblake.'

'Oh but I couldn't . . .'

'Why couldn't you if you want to? The weather's not the best for an outing but it won't snow.' She glanced out as a cat leapt on to the sill and glared balefully in, its back arched like a hairpin. 'There'll be wind however. That cat's got a gale in its tail.' She got up stiffly and banged on the pane.

'I'll get you a blanket. One of the bairns can run up and tell Annie where you've gone.' She put her hand on my shoulder. 'And I'll tell you something. When you've been and seen the place again, you'll satisfy yourself that folks are going up there all the time and coming back safe. Then you can forget about the accident. It's time you did.'

Half an hour later I was swaying between the hedgerows in Tollemy's wagon, seated in the ancient armchair he kept for an occasional passenger, wrapped in shawls and blankets and sheltered by the grey canvas awning.

'Comfortable?' Tollemy addressed me over his shoulder and through pipe-clenching teeth.

'Very. I wouldn't have believed . . .'

Gusts of wind lifted the awning and combed the winter fields where fieldfare and redwings were feeding, and brought down showers of twigs from the wayside trees.

'It'll be wild, I doubt.' Tollemy took a scarf from his pocket and tied it round his beaver hat. 'You won't have been out much since the accident. There's nowt like fresh air for putting new life into you.'

I caught the reek of his pipe and shrank to the safer side of my chair as he spat into the wind.

By this time I knew enough of country life to accept Tollemy's familiarity with my affairs without surprise. His occupation was well suited to newsgathering. He must see a good deal from his high seat.

'I'm going to thank Mr and Mrs Buckle for the help they gave. And I believe there was a boy who ran for help.'

'It'd mebbe be one of the farm hands. The two Buckle lads are grown men by now.'

I tried to picture Jordan as a farm hand: tried to recall any sign he had shown of wanting to live in the country or even of knowing that such a thing as the country existed. But Jordan had never given any sign of any emotion whatever. Still he was young, adaptable and hardened to discomfort. To one who had lived on his wits in Martlebury's squalid streets and survived the assaults of his near relations, it would be child's play to tend sheep and cattle at Blea Rigg. Was that what he was doing up there? We had come in sight of the Edge. From this distance, with steeper hills behind, it looked less spectacularly high.

The Buckles' farmhouse stood to the right of the road, half a mile short of the bridge where the track went up to Holleron Edge. Tollemy would take the level way up the dale to Catblake. At the sound of his horse bells, Mrs Buckle appeared at her door.

'Here's somebody wants to see you.'

He left me exposed to the full blast of Mrs Buckle's amazement, and of the wind which was by this time sweeping up from the south west with a force that rocked Tollemy's wagon as he drove away.

'Come in,' she gasped and closed the door behind us with some difficulty. 'I'd have recognised you anywhere,' she said when I introduced myself. 'Ee, what a going-on, love. You might have been dead.'

The kitchen at the back of the house was sheltered and warm, its big deal table given over to pastry-making. At the sight of a day-old lamb in a box on the hearth, I exclaimed in delight.

'Yes, it's coming into lambing again so I'll get on with these pasties while the oven's hot. They'll want to take them for their snap. Sit you down and get warm. That's where you was lying the last time you was here.' She nodded towards the sofa. She was a strongly-built woman with a mass of fuzzy, auburn hair and looked young to be the mother of grown-up sons. The circumstances in which we had last met had forged a bond between us. There was no standing on ceremony. 'It was a real bad do.' She scattered flour and began to roll out her pastry. 'Losing your first.'

I shed a few tears, not with the earlier bitterness of guilt and grief, but in a purely instinctive response to her sympathy.

'You'll happen have another chance,' and when I shook my head, 'Who's to say you won't? Old Dr Slater?

What does he know?'

We talked of the intricacies of childbearing in an intimate, straightforward way quite new to me.

'What's to be will be.' She snipped the edges of her tenth pasty and put the baking trays into the oven. A girl appeared from the scullery and carried off the bowls and dishes. 'Keep busy, Mrs St Leonard. That's the answer. There's always somebody to look after.' She filled a feeding bottle with warm milk. 'Here. Feed him while I mash the tea.'

I got down on my knees by the fire. The lamb's coat was unexpectedly rough. The touch of it established him not as a pet, but as a host, however frail, for life itself, imperiously demanding. He sucked feebly at first, then more vigorously. The kettle hummed. The servant girl sang as she rattled her pots and pans. After the unwholesome confinement of Honeywick, the jealous watchfulness, the uneasy threefold solitude, I felt the world brimming with purpose again.

'I came to thank you, Mrs Buckle, for rescuing me and taking me in. Without you it would all have been so much worse and I really might have died.'

'You're right there, and we were glad to do it, me and Will, seeing as your friend,' Mrs Buckle stressed the word grimly, 'was no more use than a graven image. She was sitting up there like a statue when Will came on the scene. The horse was down, heaving its sides and rolling its eyes. The gig was in splinters, the traces all twined up with the reins; and you lying there like a corpse. "She's dead," your friend says to Will.'

'Miss Bede was dreadfully shocked. I can see that now. She still can't bear to talk about it.'

'Shocked? And well she might be shocked. Our Will gave her a piece of his mind and no mistake. He's quiet, Will, till he's roused. I've never known him so wild since one of the men let the bull out and it nearly killed our Lionel. "Folly's no better than crime," he says to her. "Of all the daft ideas, taking a nesh young lady up the Edge in a spindly gig with a flighty horse!"'

Mrs Buckle's well-placed adjectives were splendidly forceful. They cast new light on the dreary affair. The folly had been Miss Bede's, not mine. I was too much relieved to bear her any grudge but simply shuffled off the burden on to her shoulders, remembering with a touch of malice how strong they were and how little there had been to tax their strength since she moved into Honeywick House.

'"If she's dead," Will says, "I know who'll be answerable for it." She just turned her eyes on him and never said a word. Like black marbles. They fair made him shiver, he told me. Then he ran up on to the moor and shouted for old Tim. He's been living in that tumble-down old shepherd's hut up there. They took the door off. It was half off anyway. And when they were laying you on it, "Thank God," Will says. "She's breathing!" And all the time she'd been sitting there as if she'd been turned to stone. She gave a big sigh and got up. "The horse must be shot," she said. I won't tell you what Will said to himself about who ought to be shot. Then when they brought you down here and we sent for the doctor, she never lifted a finger. Neither a bite nor sup passed her lips. She just sat there thinking, as if she was working out all the puzzles in creation.'

'I hadn't realised how much she must have suffered,' I said with shameful satisfaction. 'There's something else, Mrs Buckle. The boy. There was a boy, wasn't there? He was watching us from the side of the track. Miss Bede said he ran for help.'

Mrs Buckle handed me a cup of tea and sat down in the opposite chair.

'Funny about that boy. I never saw him and I can't think who he'd be. Will was mending a gate in the bottom field when it happened. He thought he heard something up on the Edge but with him hammering he couldn't be sure. Then this boy came crashing down through the gorse bushes as if he'd come right over the Edge. He'd never bothered to find the path but just came running and sliding down. It's a wonder he didn't lame himself. He gasped out that someone had been killed. That was all Will heard. "She's been killed!" Nobody's seen him since. We've asked here and there. He might have been doing odd jobs at the pit, filling tubs and that. But nobody knows who he was.'

'Old Tim,' I said. 'He might know.'

'Mebbe he does but Tim's not in a condition to tell, more's the pity.'

'You don't mean he's dead?'

'Not Tim. He won't die easy. No, he's in Kirk Heron gaol for poaching. He was caught one day in the back end, with a hare in his pocket and a brace of moor fowl under his shirt. There's no getting at Tim for a bit.'

'Oh, I do hope . . . The boy. He would fall into bad habits with a man like that.'

'He'd do that easy enough whoever he was with. Still, he's somebody's lad. My, that wind.' She went anxiously to the window. 'It'll take the tiles off. Run out, Sally, and make fast the byre door. And watch your head. You'll have a rough ride back, Mrs St Leonard.'

But matters were worse than we realised, snug as we were within the stout walls of the farmhouse. Two hours later Will Buckle came home, too weary after a day spent in the relentless wind to give me more than a nod of greeting before he went to wash in the back kitchen. But when Hattie had told him who I was and I had thanked him, he made me welcome.

'It looks as if you're meant to stay at Blea Rigg, what with one thing and another.'

I smiled, uncertain of his meaning.

'You'll not get home tonight. Tollemy'll never risk his wagon in this weather. He'll stay at the Grey Horse while morning.'

'And let's hope he'll be fit for the road then. I know Tollemy and I know the Grey Horse.' Mrs Buckle turned to me. 'You might as well settle yourself, love. Sally! Bring the clothes horse. We'll get the sheets aired.'

They brought the best linen sheets and draped them on the heavy clothes horse, where they turned pink with reflected firelight and made a snug fold for the lamb and me. The roar of the wind as it battered against the front of the house came to us subdued, and enhanced the luxury of being safe indoors. Were it not for the lambs out there in the cold . . .

'The cold doesn't bother them,' Mrs Buckle told me, 'so long as it keeps dry. It's the wet that does the mischief.'

When we had finished supper of broth, boiled bacon and pease pudding and the men had gone back to the fields, I listened drowsily to Mrs Buckle's unending stream of talk, chiefly about her sons' wives: one feckless and thriftless, the other 'mean as sin, like all Catblake folk'. But I was pleased to find that she had known Aunt Adelaide. 'A pretty looking lady, shortsighted and not too strong. She used to go to church regular with the old lady and they would drive about in the landau. I'll tell you what she used to make me think of,' Mrs Buckle confided with an unexpected burst of poetry. 'A crushed flower, stuck away up there on the hill. The old Miss St Leonard was a bit on the stiff side but everybody liked Miss Adelaide. She was shy with having been kept down from being a girl, but you could talk to her. Not like some. It was a shame she went away and died elsewhere among strangers.'

It was comforting to submit to the timeless flow of fireside talk: the unfolding of other people's lives in simple words like old tales. Far away beyond the barrier of wind lay Honeywick, shrunk to the size of a doll's house. From this safe distance I could accept the two figures at the chess board as one accepts a picture in a story book. To be the odd-man-out was unbearable only when one was there. For a few hours I felt light-hearted and carefree. They didn't need me. In coming to Blea Rigg I had not found what I was looking for. Whether or not the boy was Jordan I might never know: but my gratitude to him was stronger than ever. Not only had he run for help, heedless of gorse needles and treacherous stones: he had also given me the excuse for this delightful holiday.

And if it was Jordan, where was he now? I stood on the front step the next morning and looked up at Holleron Edge. The wind had died. The sky was blue as a thrush's egg, the air bright as crystal, the smallest sound clear as a bell. From the pit half a mile away came the clatter of tubs, the whirr of winding gear. They were a rough lot up there according to Mrs Buckle. A wicked lot.

'Don't let him slip through your fingers, Florence.' I knew what Mr Hawthorne would say. 'Save him if you can.'

It would do no harm to enquire. I could walk up there with no risk of missing Tollemy. I would meet him on the way or find him before he left the Grey Horse. All at once I was anxious to find Jordan but no longer for my own sake: I was cured of any doubts about my sanity and already felt the first stirring of anger that anyone else should doubt it; but for Jordan's own sake I should try to rescue him. He had never had a fair chance.

I was about to go indoors to tell Mrs Buckle where I was going, when Will appeared, climbing the stile from the next field. I went to meet him. He had been out all night. His eyes were red-rimmed and heavy.

'The wind's dropped.'

'Mr Buckle, I want to ask you about that boy. What was he like?'

He stopped and eased his hat from his brow. His dog flopped down at his side, panting; and for a moment it was so quiet that the dog's quick breaths infected the morning with a mood of anxiety. I looked up sharply. High on Holleron Edge something had moved. I stared until the Edge itself seemed to shimmer and sway against the aquamarine sky; but I saw nothing, only jackdaws rising and falling from the pale rock.

'That's a puzzle. He wasn't a boy I'd ever seen before. If he was to walk up this track, I'd know him straight away but as for telling what he was like . . . I couldn't hardly make out his way of speaking either, just that there was someone lying dead up there, and I was off like a shot.'

'A thin boy, with blue eyes?' Will shook his head though in doubt rather than denial. 'Ragged perhaps? I'm just wondering if it could be a boy I know.'

'Ah! Now then! He had a long green striped waistcoat on, half a mile too long for him. It came very nigh to his knees.'

Then it wasn't Jordan. The boy in the bracken was the boy Annie had sheltered. I remembered her tearful confession. 'I gave him the green waistcoat. You put it in the ragbag although there was years of wear in it'! A fine twill with covered buttons. 'But not the kind of thing I care to wear now,' Philip had said when I remonstrated. It had not suited his new rôle as country gentleman.

My first reaction was one of bitter disappointment, but

presently the complicated tangle of regret was replaced by a much simpler emotion. Why had Philip seen fit to thrash the boy and send him away? It would have cost us nothing to give him shelter. As it was we had driven him into the company of poachers and worse. Yet he had played the Good Samaritan. He had repaid our unkindness with an act of service, hurling himself down the rock face without regard for life or limb.

The morning air no longer seemed brilliant: only cold. There was still no sign of Tollemy but in the other direction I caught sight of a horse and carriage coming up the road at a trot. They vanished behind the overhanging scar and soon reappeared. With some misgiving I recognised the brougham and its driver, and walked to the gate.

'I've come to fetch you home, Mrs St Leonard.' Mr Drigg seemed to have lost his blandness. 'Your husband is very ill.'

Thirteen

It never occurred to me to doubt him. The clear, sharp air of Blea Rigg had restored my sense of reality and the brisk urgency of Mr Drigg's manner banished any lingering suspicion that I was destined to become a prisoner at Gower Oaks. Such a possibility never entered my head. My one thought was to be with Philip. There was not a minute to lose – barely time to take leave of the Buckles. Mr Drigg explained the situation briefly as he handed me into the brougham where I had sworn never to set foot, then mounted the box and drove off. I had nothing to do but brood in growing anxiety on the stark facts.

'Your husband must have been a sick man for some time,' Mr Drigg had said tersely. 'He came home very late last night in a state of complete collapse. He was coughing blood. A haemorrhage of the lungs, I'm afraid, brought on by exposure and exhaustion.'

'But why was he so late?'

There had been a mishap on the railway. A tree had blown down and blocked the branch line. Passengers for Gower Gill had been put down at Kirk Heron, where no cabman would turn out in such a gale. Philip had decided to walk the five miles home to Honeywick, much of the way in open country where there was no shelter from the wind. It had been after eleven when he stumbled home.

Into the arms of Miss Bede, not mine. In this crisis I had not only failed him but given her an opportunity she would not waste. Sure enough when I rushed into the house, anxious, remorseful, apologetic, she was standing there in the hall, gravely in charge.

'Wait!' She restrained me as I was about to brush past her and run upstairs. 'He's resting. You must not disturb him, not until you have taken off your things and calmed yourself.'

'What does the doctor say? Is he still here?'

Miss Bede shook her head.

'I'm afraid, Florence, you must have forgotten the promise –' she hesitated before adding sorrowfully – 'that you insisted on my giving you.'

'Promise?'

'Never to interfere. You reminded me that caring for Philip was your responsibility, naturally: you are his wife. I respect you for feeling as you do. It was hard to know what course to take; and so, as you weren't here . . .'

'Do you mean that the doctor has not been sent for?'

'Now that you are here, I think you had better send for him at once.'

Her tightly-compressed lips conveyed more than reproach; rather a grieved awareness that retribution was at work: more simply, that I was to blame: we must all suffer for my childish insistence on my rights, my irresponsible disregard of my duties.

'I wish you had sent for him.'

It was all my fault; but I could not understand why she should have taken so great a risk.

I had certainly appealed to her not to interfere but I was not aware of having demanded a promise. She spoke of it as a sacred vow to be kept at all costs, even when

Philip's life was at stake. The lack of proportion between the two issues worried me and added to my nervousness as I untied my bonnet with trembling fingers. There was something abnormal in her ability to sit motionless in a crisis like a graven image.

I ran upstairs, dropping my dolman on the landing and taking a deep breath, opened the door.

'Philip. Darling.' They had propped him up with pillows. I had the feeling that without them he could not have raised his head. He seemed, in the short interval since I had seen him, to have moved far from me into another and more dangerous element where all his remaining strength was needed simply to breathe, and with every breath his chest heaved painfully. I sank to my knees at his side.

'Where have you been?' His lips moved feebly. There was no smile or warmth of recognition in his eyes.

I explained, ashamed.

'But I wish – Oh, Philip, how I wish I had been here! You've been so ill. I'll never leave you again, never.'

I laid my head on his hand, trying to reach him; my whole life if need be would be spent in nursing him; and when I looked up, he was looking past me at the door, expectantly, as if waiting for someone else to come in.

'Dr Slater must be fetched. I'll send Annie. But I'll come back, dearest, at once.'

He closed his eyes and did not speak.

'Annie.' I went quickly into the kitchen. 'Put on your things at once and go for Dr Slater.'

'Thank God you're here, ma'am.' She crammed on her bonnet and thrust her feet into her boots.

'Oh Annie! Couldn't you have insisted?'

'I tried.' Tears ran down her cheeks. She didn't stop to wipe them away. 'She let him sit there on the hall chair. He'd evidently fallen. His clothes were all wet. "Your mistress will soon be here," she says. "She must decide." "Well, at least let's get him to bed," I says. "She'll not be back tonight now." She sat by his bed, just watching him. It was me that thought of Mr Drigg.'

Dr Slater's wrath was hard to bear. I accepted it as part of my punishment.

'I cannot understand why Miss Bede thought it more important to humour you than to protect your husband's life. I don't understand it at all.' He glared at me. 'Tantrums and moods are to be expected in an invalid but you're not ill now, Mrs St Leonard. You must put your own whims to one side and tend to your husband. It's a pity Miss Bede wasn't able to handle the situation with her usual good sense. As it happens, I'm afraid . . . Well, rest is the most important thing now. The only thing. His mother, I understand, went off in a consumption.'

He applied a blister to Philip's side and to the soles of his feet, prescribed a low diet and forbade red meat and wine.

'If only,' Miss Bede stood at the window and watched him go, 'If only Philip had left the bank in December as I first suggested!'

'It was my fault,' I said brusquely. 'I didn't want him to. I was wrong.'

It had been because of her. Philip's proposal to leave the bank had been bound up with her willingness to share the household expenses. 'You had better go on a little longer,' she had said, 'since Florence wishes it.' Yet she had come, bag and baggage, fulfilling her part of the bargain before his resignation made it necessary. A confused feeling that nothing had worked out as I had intended did nothing to appease my conscience. My objections now seemed contemptible: another example of the tantrums Dr Salter had reproved me for.

Having been wrong in so many ways, I must now,

more than ever, be right; only in these altered circumstances it was harder than ever to know the right course to take: whether to follow my instinct, which was to nurse Philip entirely by myself, or to defer to Miss Bede, who was far more experienced than I, though I had less faith in her unerring good sense than had Dr Slater.

As usual the decision was made for me.

'I have not forgotten my promise, Florence. No, I won't be tempted to interfere. You shall do it all yourself. It is your privilege and duty.'

I accepted gladly. I would be the perfect nurse. Here was an opportunity to put everything right again by my own efforts, not only to restore Philip to health but to make good all my mistakes. In so far as the barrier between us had arisen through any fault of mine, it must be spirited away by the devotion I would lavish on him. He would never be disappointed in me again. Brimming with zeal, I gave my whole mind to the preparation of the meals he picked at listlessly; the temperature of the milk; the age of the chicken; the consistency of the arrowroot; and changed bed linen several times a week until Mrs Churnside passed from rejoicing to consternation.

'You'll kill yourself,' Annie said, 'running up and down stairs when you're still far from strong. Let me do it – or *her*.'

'I must do it myself. Don't you see?'

'What I see is' – to my dismay gentle Annie beat her hand furiously on the table – 'that the two of you are fading away before my very eyes while she sits like a duchess, preening herself with her hands folded in her lap.'

This wildly confused description of Miss Bede made me smile. Her quiet composure may have been all the more striking at that time because I myself was so entirely without it. Scurrying from kitchen to bedroom with bowls and jugs and trays and lamps, I occasionally caught sight of myself in a looking-glass: hair uncurled, anxious-eyed, strained. Only gradually did it dawn on me how skilfully Miss Bede had arranged things. By nobly resisting the temptation to interfere, she had left herself free to sit for hours by Philip's bed or chair. Even when he slept, she seemed always to be there, so that when he woke, she was the first object on which his eyes rested – and remained.

'You're looking tired,' Miss Bede murmured as I set down the heavy tray. My vision blurred by sleeplessness and fatigue, I saw her brows and eyes as one dark area above her smiling mouth with its long white teeth. 'You should let me help. But I know you like to do it all yourself.'

Having established myself as mistress of the house, I took on the duties of master too. Every night I wearily made a tour of the outbuildings; then, taking the bronze candlestick from the hall, went round the house to wind the clocks, close and bar the shutters, chain and bolt the doors. More than once I had to put from my mind the fancy that it was too late: the house had already been invaded.

'You don't like it, do you? You always leave it till last.' Miss Bede watched sympathetically as, candle in hand, I pushed open the cellar door and drew my shawl closer in the current of cold air. 'You should let me go down. I don't mind.'

But she never did; and gradually I forgot my dislike of the dank, echoing place, its lurking rats and smell of decay. It took no more than a minute to run down the steps, dart across to the back door, dodging to avoid the stone slabs on the cover of the well, and slide home the heavy bolts. Since the draught between the two doors often put out the candle, I got into the habit of leaving it in the recess halfway down the steps and could have carried out the whole operation quite easily in the dark.

As February slipped by and the days grew longer, I grew more tranquil. Hard work, so wearisome at first, must actually have helped to restore my health. There was deep satisfaction in nursing my husband. His helplessness made him dearer to me than when he had hovered above the schoolroom in Marshall Street, godlike and glamorous. If the passing days brought no improvement in his condition, neither did it appear to grow worse. Had we been alone together, I could almost have been happy.

It was my turn now to sit with Miss Bede in the evenings during the short spells when neither of us was upstairs with Philip. I cannot remember how we passed the time but her conversation was never dull. She probably exerted herself to restore our old friendly companionship. I had always responded to her charm and was less prickly now that I felt less inferior. After all, she too could do silly things though I would never add to her remorse by telling her how foolish it had been to take a spindly gig and a flighty horse, not to mention a nesh young lady, up Holleron Edge. The trip to Blea Rigg had restored my natural buoyancy. There was nothing now – my confident glance embraced the whole room and became fixed for a while on the frail fabric which Miss Bede's needle was piercing with minute and merciless precision – nothing that I could not deal with.

It was just that her relationship with Philip was – curious. It was not love. I knew that, partly because there was no rapture in it. If, looking past me at each other, they had exchanged looks of love (despite the absurd discrepancy in their ages) I would have sensed the longing and the pain; but they would not have been able to hide the glow of happiness that warms the hearts of even the most hopeless lovers. Nor, for that matter, would I have been able to endure the anguish of it, much less observe their strange attachment with even this degree of calm, much as I hated it. If I had thought of it as love, I would simply have died of misery, I told myself. But neither of them – I thought – was of a nature to be possessed by love. By this time I had learned that it was not my shortcomings that had estranged Philip from me but his own lack of warmth; and she – if she loved him – how could she let him lie desperately ill without medical care all night while she waited, absorbed in her own impenetrable thoughts? That was not an act of love, and as an error of judgment it was more than usually silly.

Yet she believed in love at first sight: that the object of one's infatuation could engage one's whole nature, as she had put it, gazing raptly at the blue squares of sky beyond the lattice. An odd sort of way to describe the person one loved. Some sad affair long ago must have dried up her affections. She was living on without them, letting the passionless days go by in this quiet place. Poverty, I supposed, had brought her here. How else could she live on a small annuity except as a paying guest in someone else's home? No, it wasn't love. And Philip? The weakness in his nature responded to the strength in hers. Her refinement flattered his snobbery. I thought of it tenderly as an inherent weakness like the weakness in his lungs.

Upstairs a door opened.

'Mr Drigg is coming down.' Miss Bede put down her work and went quickly into the hall. I glanced at the clock. He had stayed later than usual. I had stopped resenting his visits now that he came two or three times a week to sit with Philip and read to him from the *Gazette* or the *Cornhill*. In our feminine household Philip needed a man's company, even if the man himself I could not yet like or altogether trust. He must have been discouraged by the stiffness of my manner and rarely came into the parlour, but this time he appeared at the door which Miss Bede had left open when she went upstairs, promptly seizing the opportunity of finding Philip alone.

'Mrs St Leonard.'

'Pray sit down, Mr Drigg.'

He declined my offer of refreshment and sat glumly holding his shining hat by the brim.

'Your husband . . .'

'Philip is no worse?' I jumped up in a flurry but he motioned me to sit down again.

'I believe Miss Bede has gone up to him?' It was not quite a question but I was aware of some appeal as if he sought my confirmation or approval. 'There was no outward change. You know as well as I do, ma'am, that his complaint may lie dormant for some time – or – as sometimes happens, suddenly progress.'

'I must go to him.'

'Believe me, there is no need for alarm. I found him no worse, more animated in fact. After I had read to him we talked a little about old times. Your husband wanted to talk about his aunt.'

I must have looked astonished: Philip had never shown much interest in poor Aunt Adelaide.

'You knew her?'

'Indeed I did. I was one of her few visitors here. When your husband mentioned her, I needed no encouragement to talk about the old days of our friendship.' He looked round with an expression which on a more appealing face would have seemed affectionate. 'You haven't changed the room, I see.'

'Scarcely at all. It has always seemed to me to be hers.

It would be ungrateful to alter it too much.'

He gave me a quick look of approval and was all at once more at ease.

'Did you see her when she came back?'

'Alas, no, to my everlasting regret. I happened to be in Leipzig on a visit to my friend Dr Wilhelm Wundt. We were both interested in Fechner's book on the relation of mind to matter and I went out there to discuss it with him. Wundt was more impressed than I. My own approach to problems of the mind would be less scientific, more intuitive, arising from the careful observation of an individual's whole life and circumstances, wherever possible. But I mustn't bore you. The sad fact is that when I came home it was to find that my old friend had been to Honeywick and gone away again. I never saw her again. But I had only myself to blame. It was I who advised her to go away in the first place.'

'Why did you do that?'

'I thought a holiday would be good for her. Miss Adelaide confessed to me that she had melancholy moods. A single woman without family ties, alone in the world – a woman of leisure, I mean – is in some danger.' The word was unexpected. I thought it exaggerated and Mr Drigg apparently felt the need to qualify it. 'Either she will retreat into herself and lose contact with other people or . . . but I didn't intend to inflict on you theories that cannot possibly interest you as they do me.'

'What is the other – danger?'

'The affections must either wither from lack of nourishment or else find some outlet. She may lavish them on some unsuitable object or form a strong attachment of a kind that could be harmful.'

'Harmful?'

'It could lead to eccentric or unsuitable behaviour.'

He was looking even more uneasy than before. With

some idea of giving a pleasanter turn to the conversation I said, 'If my baby had been a girl, I meant to call her Adelaide.'

'Nothing would have pleased her more. She was a warm-hearted, loving soul.'

Mr Drigg was certainly not a handsome man but it had been cruel to think of his peculiarly large eyes as toad-like. When he spoke of Aunt Adelaide his eyes were not peculiar at all but thoughtful and gentle.

'She must have valued your friendship,' I said slowly. 'We have not heard of any other friends she had.'

'She was good enough to give me her confidence and consult me on matters connected with her property. I helped her to draft her will when the elder Miss St Leonard died. That was a good many years ago.'

'You advised her to go away,' I said, 'and afterwards you were sorry?'

'I never intended it to be for so long, nor was that her intention when she went away. The advice was good, or at least well meant. She was not suited to loneliness, though, if I may confide in you, Mrs St Leonard, she need not have been alone.' A faint colour stained his sallow cheeks. 'But apart from material things, and she had enough of those, what had I to offer a lady like her?'

'You never asked her?'

'I could never quite presume.'

'She would have liked to be asked.'

'You think so?' His face had softened so that its very outlines seemed changed. 'Then I regret more than ever that I lacked courage, even though it was hopeless.'

If he had asked her and she had accepted, the whole story would have been different. We might never have come here but would have gone on working and saving and longing and loving, and since he had confided in me, I went so far as to say:

'If only she had come back, she might have . . .' It was difficult to say that she might have married him, and so add to his regret. Instead I said, '. . . she might have lived longer and we would have stayed in Martlebury.'

'You would have been happier?'

'I believe we might,' I said reluctantly.

'You have not the same feeling for the property that your husband has.' Mr Drigg's face had grown sombre again.

'Not the same, perhaps.' My feelings for Honeywick were too complicated to convey to Mr Drigg or even to comprehend myself.

'It is natural in his present condition that your husband's thoughts should take a certain direction. That was what I wanted to talk about when I came in, but it was tempting to talk of old times with such a sympathetic listener. Your husband confided to me that he was doubtful of your attachment to the house. He is troubled, I believe, about its future.' Mr Drigg spoke abruptly as if bent on getting out the words as best he could.

'Do you mean' – I stared at him aghast – 'that Philip thinks he might die?'

Mr Drigg must have thought the question naïve. It certainly showed my failure to grasp the gravity of Philip's condition. The thought had not entered my head that he would, that he could die. It could not be that all my care, all my burning devotion, would not save him. I felt the colour drain from my face.

He looked wretchedly uncomfortable. Beads of perspiration stood out on his brow. He took out a snow-white handkerchief and dabbed at them.

'Forgive me. The last thing I intended was to distress you. But surely when a man is gravely ill, he is obliged to set his affairs in order. Your husband asked my advice about a lawyer. I was glad to give him the name of my own, Salt, Annot and Salt of Kirk Heron. A most respectable firm. They were also his aunt's lawyers. They drew up her will and arranged the letting of the house.'

'But Philip has no need to make a will. He made one in Martlebury as soon as we were married, leaving everything to me.'

'So he told me. A very proper thing. And this evening when he asked my advice, I urged him not to make any change.'

'Why should he think of any change?'

It distressed me even to mention, much less seriously contemplate the disposal of Philip's property; but Mr Drigg was now determined to finish a task for which he clearly had little taste, and he floundered on with a good deal of awkwardness and hesitation.

'I told him that in his present state he should on no account be prevailed upon to alter the arrangements he has already made. He has some fixed idea . . . I'm not sure. . . . May I ask – forgive me, but the situation is unusual and my feeling for his aunt gives me the privilege of an old friend – is Miss Bede a relative of yours, or of his on his mother's side? A family connection through marriage perhaps? No? Only a close friend?'

It was so exceedingly difficult to explain our precise connection with Miss Bede so as to justify an arrangement which now seemed more than ever unwise; so difficult to think clearly, in my mounting panic and despair, of anything but Philip, that I sat silent; and into the silence came faint sounds from upstairs. She was coming. I gripped the arms of my chair and saw Mr Drigg glance at my whitened knuckles. His large eyes were brilliant with the mingling of observation and understanding I had noticed, with some discomfort, before;

but this time I trusted it and trusted him.

'If I may advise you,' he spoke quickly, 'encourage your husband to leave things as they are. On no account should he consider any form of trust or joint life interest. Believe me, an outsider and an older man can often see a situation more clearly. As it happened I could not refuse your husband's request to give him the name of my lawyer but I'm sure that Salt and Annot would give him exactly the same advice as I have done.'

He stopped abruptly and wiped his brow. Miss Bede was standing in the archway, having come quietly through the dining parlour. Her distinction of manner was in sharp contrast to his awkwardness as she released the curtain from its loop and let it fall, to enclose us in the front part of the room.

'Philip is asleep.'

She made it sound like a benediction, as if she had soothed him to rest after the intrusion of the day; as if from all the troubles of his waking hours she had dismissed him; and now, with a courteous nod she seemed to dismiss Mr Drigg, who took his shining forehead and worried eyes out of the room and out of the house.

'He's gone. Now we can be comfortable together. And you can tell me what he had to say.'

But I didn't tell her. Instead I went to the kitchen and prepared Philip's tray for the next morning, trying to face the bitter knowledge that there might actually be a limit to the number of times I would measure out oatmeal for his gruel. It could not be true. He could not fail to get well if I gave all my thoughts and energy and will to caring for him. When Annie had gone to bed I hung over the last of the fire, my tears falling on the hot bars with small desperate hisses until the iron grew cold and the chill of night spread all around me.

Fourteen

During the next week Mr Drigg came more often and his visits reduced the amount of time Miss Bede spent with Philip. There were days when he sat at the bedside for hours on end. Some half-formed notion that he hoped to direct Philip's mind into other channels than the disposal of his property, that is to say, into other channels than those chosen by Miss Bede, made me think of him as an ally when I thought of him at all, which was not often. Much of what he had said went over my head unheeded, but whatever his intentions, he had impressed on me the terrifying possibility that Philip would die.

At once the whole structure and meaning of life were changed. It was as though my actual vision changed so that I saw nothing but Philip, enlarged, clearer, nearer and dearer than ever before. Miraculously, the utter concentration of all my heart and soul upon him restored his confidence in me. It fed his need to be supported, cherished, put first. Now that it was almost too late, the old tenderness revived, not only mine but his. We passed into a mood so tranquil that it would have been perfect happiness had it not been flawed by the very circumstance that created it: the knowledge that it must end – and soon.

There were times when he was confident of getting well and I was deceived, not recognising the hectic optimism so often a symptom of his disease. On one of his better days I helped him into a chair in his small bedroom looking down the hill to the church. Annie had brought in a bowl of snowdrops picked from the garden, where the mild sunshine held a hint of spring; but I stayed all day with Philip and took my meals with him, eating with as little appetite as he did. We sat hand in hand by the fire as we had done when we first came to Honeywick less than a year ago.

'You're quiet, Florence.'

'I was thinking of the evening we came.' There had been lambs and wild daffodils; the air was pure and strong with its mingled promise and threat; my body so brimful with life that I might have had wings like the thrush calling from the pear tree, its throat throbbing with joy. 'I've never worn my wedding dress again, not once. Aunt Maud was so sure that it would be just the thing for small evening entertainments, as she called them.'

'I like that blue dress you're wearing. Is that lace on the front? What are you laughing at?' He touched my hair. 'It's growing pretty again.' Presently he added, 'We haven't . . . It hasn't been quite as we hoped but you haven't – been unhappy, Florence?'

It was as if some inkling came to him of the mental turmoil I had endured. His look of sudden misgiving was more than I could bear.

'I didn't know what happiness was until we came here.'

He smiled, satisfied with the half-truth.

'And now you're tiring yourself, looking after me.'

'There's nothing else in the world I want to do.'

'When you were ill, I didn't . . .'

'That was different,' I said quickly. 'Besides, you were working. I wish . . . It was all my fault that you went on so long at the bank.'

'And yet you were right. I couldn't have faced being poor again.'

'It would have been hard.'

At least we had been spared the pinch of poverty. The cost of our illnesses had made inroads on our savings but we had been able to leave Aunt Adelaide's capital untouched. We talked about the early days in Martlebury, the thrill of the legacy, our arrival at Honeywick; and all the while the thrush went on singing under the window: the same thrush perhaps. It was always the same in spring, no matter who lived or died or failed to be born.

Only on one subject were we divided, or could have been, had not my whole soul been devoted to preserving the precious harmony we shared. Pervading every nook and cranny of the house as she did, it was not surprising that she crept into our conversation. Her influence had been far more profound than I had supposed. During those long evenings he had spent with her, already weakened by the disease which must have long been active, his lack of vitality had made him an easy victim to her excess of it. His mind had lain open to receive her counsels, her suggestions, her attitudes and beliefs; and had absorbed them with passive acceptance as a light fabric takes a darker stain. Some of the attitudes and beliefs surprised me.

'You'll get well now that you have no need to worry about the bank,' I said all the more confidently because I no longer believed it. 'Isn't it lucky that you can lead a quiet country life. We have so much to be thankful for.'

'You feel that too? You can't think how often I've lain there thinking of the blessing Miss Bede has been to us.

It was a happy chance, if it was chance, that brought her here.'

'What else could it be but chance?'

The plain question rose from a much more complex range of possibilities, not to be explored at such a time as this when nothing mattered except to be alone with Philip, for the morsel of time that remained.

'I believe it was the Divine Will.' Philip's answer startled me. 'There was a time when I would have mocked at anything of the kind but my illness has made me think more deeply and clearly.' I held my tongue. His thinking had never been deep or clear. I knew him now, and only loved him more for his wrongheadedness. 'She thinks so too. We have often talked of it. Her mind is so much more profound than most. "There is a great deal," she said to me once, "that we can never know, only feel and respond to without understanding." Yes, I see her coming as an act of God. What would I have done without her when you were ill, Florence? She has helped me in a practical way though she is far from well off and I have felt ashamed to let her pay for such simple accommodation. But her companionship, her influence, are beyond price, as I have told her. Something must be done . . .'

His voice died away as if stifled by some confusion of the mind. A moment of hysteria shocked me with the wild fancy that he could not die because she had not yet told him how to leave the world. But she had evidently laid down certain guiding lines, had hinted at possibilities he would not otherwise have thought of. Mr Drigg's warning took on a clearer meaning.

'Her goodness must not go unrewarded.'

I thought his face had altered yet again even since yesterday. The dark hollows at his temples were tinged with blue; his features had grown sharp. They gave an anxious cast to his face. There was inward anxiety too.

'Don't think of such things, not now. It tires you.' I held him close.

'I've sometimes wondered – in fact we've talked of it – whether some legal provision could be made for her.'

'You've spoken about it, to Miss Bede?'

'Yes. The subject arose somehow – as to the future. As she pointed out, you are young. If I were to die, you might – in time – marry again.'

He looked pitifully downcast.

'How could she dream of such a thing?' I burst out furiously.

'Well, you might. Someone is sure to love you. In that case I wouldn't like to think of the house being sold to strangers. It has taken hold of me somehow. Miss Bede understands how I feel; and as her situation is uncertain and she has no other home . . .'

His cough troubled him. As always, it racked me too. It was almost more than I could bear to feel his thin body convulsed and see the weakness bring sweat to his brow.

'But Drigg has advised me that there would be difficulties.' He took the handkerchief from his lips. To my relief it was unstained. 'Legal difficulties. He insisted so strongly that I felt too confused to make up my mind. I hadn't realised, in fact I still don't see the complications he hints at and there hasn't been time – I haven't felt like going into them. It seems to make my head swim.' He pressed his hand to his side. I helped him back to bed and he leaned gratefully against the pillows. His eyes were troubled, large and deep in their sockets.

I waited, hoping he would fall asleep but presently he revived.

'Florence.' He seized my hand and held it with feverish anxiety. 'She was homeless and we took her in . . .'

The solemn Biblical echoes frightened me. I could not deal with this new, religious aspect of Miss Bede's presence. How could I explain to him that her coming had been quite different: that she bore no resemblance to the naked and hungry, the homeless and oppressed? Whether he saw her as the future guardian of Honeywick, heaven-sent to keep it from the hands of strangers, or as a roofless outcast whom he must succour and protect, neither of these figments appealed to me. I prided myself – in my arrogance and folly – on seeing Miss Bede for what she really was: a charming, intelligent but rather overpowering visitor who had outstayed her welcome; and I wished with all my heart that she would take her charm and intelligence elsewhere. But it was useless to hope for so happy a release at present; and beyond the present lay a future so painful that nothing, not even Miss Bede, could make it worse. The next moment this conviction was unexpectedly put to the test.

Philip had been watching me anxiously.

'Promise me,' he said suddenly, 'if I'm not able to make provision for her, promise me, dearest, that you won't send her away.'

If I had been struck dumb I could hardly have found it more difficult to reply. The idea that in any circumstances I could be responsible for Miss Bede, who could be sent away like a telegram or an unwanted servant, staggered me, as did the immediate discovery that to refrain from sending her away was to keep her with me – always. The future could, after all, be even darker than I had foreseen. My silence distressed Philip. He struggled to sit up.

'Lie still. You'll bring on the cough.'

He murmured something about Salt and Annot and not letting her go back to Ivy Cottage.

'I must speak to Drigg again. It must be thought about. You won't turn her away, Florence? Promise.'

Still I hesitated. For all my love for him, for all my

obstinate hope that he would, against all seeming probability, live, still a small reasonable voice within me urged that he would die whether I promised or not. If I did promise, he would go, leaving me the thoroughly unwanted legacy of Miss Bede. There would be no freedom ever again from her darkly observant stare. I saw her as my companion figure facing me across the parlour; but we were not a pair: two pieces brought together by chance, ill-matched. Then I saw Philip's eyes fixed unhappily upon me and in their shadowed depths an appeal too pitiful to resist. I couldn't disappoint him or worry him. Not now. It was to soothe him that I recklessly put my whole future at risk.

'I won't turn her away. But don't leave me, Philip. Stay with me. Please. Try not to leave me.'

He smiled and seemed at peace. In a few minutes he fell into an exhausted sleep. There was no more, really, that I could do for him. And when he was gone, I thought, struggling to find in the surrounding wilderness some grain of comfort, she wouldn't want to stay. Like me she would find the house impossible without him: empty for all its crowded rooms, haunted, a beautiful shell enclosing only memories like echoes of the living sea. Crouched by the bed, my head against the white valance, I too fell asleep and dreamed of our wedding, a dream filled with the rapturous sense of beginning all over again: and woke to face the end.

And after all I was grateful to her for being there, or if not grateful, resigned. If she had schemed to take from me what was mine, she failed. At the very end it was my hand that Philip blindly reached for, not hers. My name was the last word he spoke. We were alone together and united as we had never been in the closest embrace. All that was best in him stayed with me. The vital, loving part of me died with him, leaving only my body alive. 'My youth is over,' I thought, in the first agony of loss. 'From now on I shall always be old.'

So that in one respect Miss Bede and I grew closer. The gap of years between us closed a little. Now that he was dead Philip became a bond holding us together whereas, alive, he had made us rivals. Without her there would have been no one to talk to about him, no one who had known him. She had become part of the house. If in the stony blankness of my grief there were times when she was no more to me than one of the Dresden figures or a picture on the wall; if she seemed, sitting quietly by the fire, just one more object, a late addition to the medley of things that hung on Honeywick's walls or filled its cupboards and drawers to overflowing, at least she was an object that could speak and move and save me from the immense silence: not just the absence of sound but an element palpable as water that sometimes threatened me as if rising from the earth to flood the hall and stairs and fill the whole house with the odour of decay.

The impression was not entirely fanciful. At that season of the year, early spring, and in the early autumn, there actually were movements of water in the limestone below the foundations of the house. Moisture oozed up between the flagstones in the back kitchen and lay inches deep for a few days, then disappeared in response to the same mysterious natural law.

When I made my nightly rounds, the cellar floor was wet enough to soak the thin soles of my house shoes. A chilly moisture clung to the surface of the stone benches. A hateful place. Having made fast the outer door, I always ran back up the steps with relief. And yet to make the candle-lit descent was like keeping tryst with Philip. The sliding of bolts and turning of keys had been important to him. The small duty became a binding obligation sacred to his memory. Sometimes, turning at the top of the steps to latch the door, with a catch of the breath I seemed to see him rising again, his pale lips smiling; and stepping into the warm hall, I would remember with a swift agony of grief how he had said, 'Nothing can part us now,' as he put his arms round me, just there, at the bottom of the stairs.

But now as often as not it would be Miss Bede who stood there or at the parlour door, ready to talk. But not too much. Her manner was subdued, but by something other than sorrow. I was not so blinded by grief as to be unaware of her lack of it. If she cried for Philip, she cried alone. I never saw a tear in her eyes. Not until long afterwards did I remember her curious behaviour at the end after Dr Slater, whispering on the landing, warned us that it could not last long: Philip had sunk into half consciousness. The doctor and I went back into the bedroom. Miss Bede followed, stood at the bed looking at Philip, then without a word went out and shut the door behind her. She never went back, never looked at him again. It was as if, in closing the door, she closed an episode: as if she collaborated in our instinctive need to forget her: or – for my view of her has changed since then – as if she saw that whatever might have been was not to be, not then, not yet. One could have imagined her pouring water from her ewer into the basin and carefully, thoroughly, washing her hands. More than ever, after the funeral, she gave the impression of being absorbed in her own thoughts – or plans? – leaving me absorbed in mine. Her restraint and quietness suited me. I had dreaded and been prepared to resent any attempt on her part to share my loss.

I had grown used to her. I was not glad to have her there: gladness was not possible; but I was grateful and could sometimes even believe that her coming had been, as Philip said, providential.

Fifteen

Standing at the parlour window one morning a few weeks after the funeral, I saw Mr Drigg drive up to the front door and get down, leaving a passenger in the brougham.

'If it is not inconvenient to you, Mrs St Leonard,' he began in his serious, fussy way as Annie showed him in, 'to receive a visitor for no more than a few minutes . . . We are on our way to the station.'

I went out and waited on the steps to greet her as he helped her down.

'Miss Fairfold wanted very much to meet you.'

Mystified, I held out my hand to a well-dressed, dark-haired young woman of about my own age.

'You don't remember me?' She smiled. 'I saw you one day last summer down by the bridge. You waved to me. I'm not surprised that you don't recognise me. That was the day I arrived and I was so ill then . . .'

'And you're better. I'm delighted.' Seeing her smiling and composed and with a look of health as if she had benefited from rest and country air, I felt a thrill of genuine pleasure.

'I've always hoped to see you again and thank you. Yes,' as I remonstrated, 'it was a small thing but at the time it was exactly the right thing, the only kind of message that could reach me when I had no strength to talk or act or even any wish to live. You seemed to be smiling and waving from another world, one that I had left, or lost, and you looked so full of life. You reminded me what it was like to be really alive.'

'You must have suffered a great deal.'

'If ever we meet again, I'll tell you about it. It was too much for me. I gave way and had to be helped. That's why when Mr Drigg told me that your husband had died, I wanted to see you and tell you how sorry I am. But not only that.' She laid her hand on mine. 'It's my turn to remind you that one can be – not happy again in the same way – but one can recover and be peaceful and content.'

She went on to speak of the healing atmosphere at Gower Oaks, of Mr Drigg's wisdom and the homely kindness of his housekeeper and servants.

'I'm going home now. If only there had been an opportunity of knowing you! But you have been ill yourself, and then your husband. I believe you have a friend living with you, a close friend? That must be a great comfort.' She gave me her card and begged me if ever I was in Martlebury to visit her in her parents' home. 'If ever you need advice, you can confide in Mr Drigg. He has a deep understanding of people and especially of depressed and unusual states of mind.'

He had seized the opportunity of engaging Miss Bede in conversation while we talked. His interest in her had apparently not diminished. Now he came to remind Miss Fairfold that it was time to leave. This time it was she who smiled and waved as they drove off.

'To think that I used to dislike poor Mr Drigg!' I observed to Miss Bede. 'And so did Philip. One never knows how people are going to turn out. It's simply a question of getting to know them better.'

'I believe you may be right.' She seemed struck by so sage and original a suggestion. 'But in Mr Drigg's case,' her tone was dry, 'I hope we shan't be getting to know him very much better. You're inclined to be too whole-hearted in your judgments, Florence. An impulsive little thing!'

I didn't respond to her teasing smile but escaped to the garden where I walked up and down the path, spreading my skirts the whole width of the flagged way so that there was no room for anyone else. From the wicket gate I could look across to the churchyard where Philip lay. Behind me the garden was bright with daffodils but their scent was stifled by the musty, dry smell of my voluminous black crape. How could Miss Fairfold speak of being content and at peace again? The ancient gate creaked under my listless weight. I pushed it open and, stepping into the field, looked up at the unchanging hills behind the church tower; but I could think only of the change in me, of what a different person I had been on the sunny morning when Miss Bede had discovered the gate and gone this way. I had watched her walking in the shade of the tall broom bushes to the stile, to disappear among the tombstones as if she were going away, actually going away . . .

Mr Drigg came again one morning when I was turning out the contents of Philip's desk in the little room over the porch which he had used as his study. I called to Annie to show him up. We could be alone. There was no room in the tiny apartment for a third person. It was then that he raised the subject of a change of scene.

'Oh, I don't know. You advised Aunt Adelaide to go away,' I reminded him, 'and afterwards you were sorry.'

'The advice was good, whatever the outcome.' There was always an earnestness in Mr Drigg's manner and now he looked so very serious that I regretted having mentioned Aunt Adelaide. 'It never occurred to me that she would stay away. She needed a change and stimulating company – and so do you.'

'These are the letters from her lawyer.' They had just been returned to me with a whole parcel of other documents from Philip's solicitor in Martlebury, and a letter to the effect that some small point remained to be settled with Miss St Leonard's lawyer before Philip's estate could be wound up. I undid the red tape with which Philip had methodically tied the letters relating to Aunt Adelaide's property, written a year past February and March. The whole of that business had been conducted by post. Since the bank would not release Philip for more than one day, he had been unable either to see his aunt's lawyer or to attend her funeral. 'I wanted to ask you about something that puzzles me, Mr Drigg. Is it usual to have more than one lawyer?'

'Not to employ more than one at a time. Or do you mean – is it usual to change from one to another? That can happen of course. Personally I have never felt any need to change.'

'But Aunt Adelaide must have changed. So far as I can make out, she employed several lawyers. Well, three.'

'Three!'

'You said she was once a client of Salt and Annot at Kirk Heron, didn't you? Well, Annie told me that the man who came to make an inventory was from Cheltenham. That was just after Annie came here. And these letters are from' – I glanced at the notepaper – 'Bretherby and Butterwick of Matlock, where she died.'

'You surprise me.' Mr Drigg seemed disturbed if not alarmed by such inconsistency on Aunt Adelaide's part. 'What can have possessed her? I cannot think what reason she could have for consulting a lawyer in every spa and watering place in the land.'

'Not every one.'

In having even three lawyers poor Aunt Adelaide had evidently offended against some canon of legal etiquette. Conscious of my ignorance in such matters, I gave my attention to Philip's correspondence with Bretherby and Butterwick and read their first letter carefully. It had been written on the 27th February, 1873 to inform Philip of his aunt's death and the fact that he was her sole beneficiary. The second letter had evidently enclosed a copy of the will and, in answer presumably to Philip's enquiry, informed him that Miss St Leonard had died after a short illness, the result of a fall. Messrs Bretherby and Butterwick looked forward to an early visit from Mr St Leonard, when they would be pleased to supply any further information he desired.

'How self-centred we were!' I handed the letter remorsefully to Mr Drigg. 'We scarcely gave a thought to Aunt Adelaide herself.'

'It was a great grief to me that I didn't hear of her death in time to attend the funeral.' Mr Drigg sounded even more remorseful. 'Such a very dear friend! But by the time the news reached me it was too late.'

I opened the thick parchment folds of the will and was surprised to see the date: 26th February, 1873, the very day before her death. For a woman of property, Aunt Adelaide had been slow to make a will; almost too slow as far as we were concerned. She had acted in the nick of time. And yet, on reflection, I realised that if she had died intestate, the property would still have come to Philip, since she had no other relative.

'She must have known that she was dying,' I said, 'and that there wasn't time to send to Kirk Heron or Cheltenham for a lawyer. I should have thought somehow that she would have made a will long before.'

'But she did. May I?' I handed him the document and he looked quickly through the half dozen paragraphs. 'This is precisely the will she instructed Salt and Annot to draw up for her when the elder Miss St Leonard died, fifteen years ago – or more. We talked it over together.'

'Then why should she go to the trouble of doing it all over again? Perhaps she had forgotten.' I remembered my own doubts and uncertainties. 'When she was ill, her mind may not have been clear.'

'Bretherby and Butterwick must have been satisfied that she was capable of making a will.' He hesitated, looking troubled. 'She may have felt an urgent wish to rectify some decision she regretted.'

'Do you mean that she had made another will in between, one that she repented of. I know – at Cheltenham! Then we were even more fortunate than we knew.'

A very short delay on Aunt Adelaide's part would have deprived Philip of his legacy. It would probably have gone instead to some deserving charity, which Aunt Adelaide had suddenly and unaccountably ceased to approve of on the very point of death; or more likely a revival of long dimmed family feeling had irradiated her last moments like a sunset glow. She had deserted the cause of Decayed Gentlewomen or the Heathen Overseas and pinned to the mast the colours of her clan, the St Leonards, before she went down, or on, or up.

So I mused, uninterrupted by Mr Drigg. He had folded the various documents and laid them in an orderly row on the table. I retrieved the second letter and glanced again at the last sentence.

'The remaining small items of business can wait, as you suggest, until you do us the favour of visiting us . . .'

Philip had never gone to Matlock. Within a year he too had been obliged to hand on Honeywick House with all its effects – to me, of all people. I felt oppressed at being advanced so swiftly from a supporting to a leading role in the house's history. From sheer inability to grasp all its implications, I could think only of postponing them.

'Perhaps I will go away, Mr Drigg.' I gathered up the papers and put them back in the desk. 'Aunt Maud has asked me to go to her in Surrey for a long visit. She lives with a relative, Cousin Helena . . .'

Mr Drigg literally sighed with relief, as if he really cared what became of me.

'That would be excellent. I'm convinced of it. In fact, no other solution occurs to me at present.'

'Solution?' I had not been aware of a problem apart from the purely private one, a surfeit of Miss Bede.

'That is the wrong word,' he said hastily. 'But you do need a period of change – in which to find a new direction.' Rather abstractedly, I thought, he told me of his own plans. He would shortly be making another visit to the continent. His old friend Dr Wilhelm Wundt was about to publish his *Physiological Psychology*, which would be a landmark in the new science of the mind. 'Not that I am in sympathy with any theory which attempts to systematise the human mind,' he told me anxiously. 'However, tell me, would it be possible for you to leave for Surrey quite soon? Before I set off on my travels, I mean. There seems no reason for delay and if you have made up your mind, it would be good for you to busy yourself with packing. Miss Bede, I take it,' he said casually, 'will be making her own arrangements.'

'I haven't spoken to her about it.'

'You are thinking of a long visit? Two or three months perhaps? Then I shall certainly be back before you. And there's Annie Blanche, of course. A very good sort of woman, sensible and reliable.' The thought of Annie seemed to cheer him.

He wished me goodbye but I remember that he came every day until I left, as if anxious to keep a neighbourly eye on me. And in the event I didn't go to Surrey. Having left my letter unfinished for a day or two, I felt a growing reluctance to commit myself. I was too restless to fit into a different household and eventually Aunt Maud and I agreed to take a holiday together instead. Annie would take the opportunity of going to Cheshire to visit old friends. For a few days she existed in such a state of mysterious excitement that my suspicions might have been roused if I had been less fully occupied with my own arrangements. Since Annie would not be there, it seemed at first that I would have to close the house. On the whole it was a relief when Miss Bede offered to stay, even though it meant her looking after herself.

Aunt Maud left the choice of holiday resort to me. With the whole country to choose from, I was at first too listless to fix on any place for more than a few minutes at a time, until the fancy came to me to let Aunt Adelaide choose; to follow her in the flesh, relentless visitor of spas and watering places as she was, as I had followed her in spirit through Mrs Banstock's novels. Of all the places she had visited, Matlock had been the last. There, if anywhere, some trace of her remained. The whimsical thought pleased me at a time when little else did.

'It's to be Matlock,' I told Miss Bede at breakfast one morning.

'Matlock!' she said at last. I had thought she was never going to speak and wondered if she harboured some slight resentment at being left.

'Have you ever been there?'

'As a matter of fact I have.' The note of enforced candour in her voice suggested that she was not impressed by my choice. 'But it was some time ago. It may have changed.' She seemed to hope so as her long teeth sank into a morsel of toast and demolished it. 'Rather bleak, I thought.'

'I may even meet people who knew Aunt Adelaide. It isn't so long, just over a year since she died.'

It was a bright morning. The sun shone full on the window and found unsuspected greens and blues in the Highland loch. The single pearl set in black enamel in Miss Bede's lace jabot shone coldly. She had left off wearing the emerald as unsuitable in a house of mourning.

'I can't think why you want to go.' She handed me her cup. I filled it and she sipped slowly, thoughtfully.

'I've quite made up my mind.'

'If you must –' her shrug made the best of Matlock's limited resources – 'then you had better stay at the Hydro. A little world on its own. You'll have plenty of company there. There'll be no need to go beyond its gardens and you can take the waters.'

'She's staying here on her own, is she?' Annie looked doubtful. 'Well, if any soot falls or the taps drip, she can see to them, I suppose, and she can surely see her way to keeping mice off the pantry shelves. Mrs Churnside'll come in daily if she gets the chance. But there'll be a rare cleaning round when we get back.'

'How fortunate,' Aunt Maud wrote in similar though not identical vein, 'that you have a friend to look after your house while you're away! There will be no need to worry about intruders. One hears such strange stories. There are so many undesirable people at large. We shall have a great deal to talk about and I have always wanted to go to Matlock.'

'You'll have the house to yourself,' I said as Miss Bede handed the last of my bags into the cab.

She stood on the sunny terrace with the fox's head

looking over her shoulder. As we started up the hill I leaned out to wave, but she had already gone in and shut the door.

Sixteen

The music of the Trio Berenice was of a kind to be listened to without strain, comfortable as the well-upholstered chairs but less robust, even at times swooning into faintness as if overwhelmed by the thick carpets and mahogany-panelled walls. Recovering, it reached the long, open windows and dissolved into the warm twilight. Through a small forest of shrubs in oriental pots, between the spreading leaves of tall palms, craning my neck, I could see the distant profile of the pianist and the wrists of the violinist as his bow lingered upon the final note. He bowed and beamed.

'I must say,' Aunt Maud took the opportunity afforded by a faint spatter of applause to whisper, 'it is expensive but it's worth every penny, once in a while.'

'I'm glad you're enjoying it.'

'I mean,' she glanced round, anxious not to be overheard, 'we could have found a cheaper place but after all it will be something to talk about, to have stayed at the Hydro. Do you know, it just suits me.'

Her green silk with guipure trimming and her black lace cap suited her too, as did her life in Surrey, apparently, for she seemed in blooming health.

'There'll be tea presently,' she said in pleased anticipation.

With this treat in store we walked out into the garden and explored once more its grottoes and pools, flower-beds and shrubberies. Already Aunt Maud had made the acquaintance of other guests, some of whom had come, like ourselves, for a holiday; others, invalid or elderly, had come to take the thermal cure. I thought it a little hard on the management that Aunt Maud, newly arrived, appeared so much healthier than those who had spent the winter and spring there. Having made a careful study of *Smedley's Practical Hydropathy*, she was inclined to be sceptical.

'"Vital heat is life: deficiency of it weakness and disease: absence of it death." That's what it says here. At first I thought it rather striking but now I've read it again, I'm not sure that it is so very helpful. But I do agree with what Mr Smedley says about drugs, leeches and cupping. They ruin the constitution. Water, he says, will cure anything. Of course that is going too far. No wonder the doctors resent it. Still, a good dose of rue tea every morning for a fortnight in spring was all I ever gave you.'

It was, I discovered, the one bitter memory of our life together. I had forgotten how easy and natural a relationship it had been; how little had been needed to make her happy. Here, in her unaffected enjoyment of wearing her best dress in the morning and taking her meals in the plush and mahogany dining-room, she was always ready to chat and to give her new acquaintances the benefit of a little straightforward sensible advice.

'You're paying all that money,' she was fond of saying. 'Let us hope you'll feel some improvement.'

If the attendant glared as he swiftly wheeled the bath-chair away and if the patient in it looked all at once anxious, Aunt Maud didn't notice, having other advice to give.

'Ah, Mrs Weller, you're looking better. I wondered if the veal had been too rich for you. At our age we must be careful.'

This robust directness would once have embarrassed me. Aunt Maud was neither vulgar nor coarse but neither was she intimidated by other people nor even aware of the social nuances to which, until recently, I had given such careful thought. But by this time I had seen the hollowness of much that was genteel; had had enough of subtlety and the careful avoidance of plain speaking. Aunt Maud might do as she liked, be as she liked, so long as she was not Miss Bede, whose merciful absence I found more salutary than an ocean of spa water. At Aunt Maud's side I strolled through the days; admired the scenery; listened to the Trio Berenice; and all the time my heart ached for Philip; but my mind and spirit revived and grew strong again from sheer relief at no longer being with Miss Bede.

However, she had been right in one respect. The Hydro provided a complete way of life for those who preferred its enclosed world to the steep lanes and back-breaking hills of Matlock. One gruelling ascent of Dob Lane on our first morning proved more than enough for Aunt Maud.

'If you want to explore, Florence, you must do it without me,' she gasped. 'I shall be perfectly happy to stay in the garden. But I do wish you had someone to walk with. It isn't good for you to roam about on your own, moping.'

One morning I had made my way past the old church and climbed the steep path to a point where, from a convenient seat, I could command a view of the whole dale. It was evidently a popular walk. I enjoyed watching other holiday makers in couples or family parties as they scrambled up the incline or came triumphantly down. Then for a few minutes I was alone, until the sound of footsteps tramping down the hill roused me to look up the path for a first glimpse of their owner: a slender, brown-bearded man in a tweed jacket and knickerbockers with field glasses slung over one shoulder and a botanist's vasculum over the other.

I looked; could not believe my eyes; got up and stood in the middle of the path directly in his way. He approached, walking quickly; saw me; recognised me. We spoke at the same moment.

'Florence!'

'Mr Hawthorne!'

In my joy I held out both hands. He took them in his. His expression changed from delighted surprise to concern – to consternation.

'Something has happened to you – and you're in mourning.'

He recognised them as two distinct facts: that I was changed, and not only by bereavement.

'Philip,' I said.

'My poor Florence. I had not heard . . . And you've been ill, I can see. Come,' he drew me to the seat, 'you must tell me all about it.'

'Oh, Mr Hawthorne, I'm so very glad to see you. So very glad. You see, it's been . . . There has been so much . . . And no-one to tell.'

He unslung his field glasses and placed them with his hat and specimen tin in the middle of the seat, taking a little time over the operation. I knew that he was giving me time to compose myself. Then he sat down at the opposite end.

'Tell me,' he said briefly.

I wiped my eyes and obeyed.

'At first it was – perfect happiness – and in a way – at the end too.'

'Then you have been luckier than most, Florence, no matter what happened in between. Go on.'

I went on, taking a long time over so painfully short a history and I found that it was easier to speak of events than of my feelings; and that the events, uncoloured by my feelings about them, did not convey a true impression of life at Honeywick House. But I must have conveyed it well enough to hold Mr Hawthorne's interest, though that had been in no more doubt than his sympathy and understanding.

'There's nothing really wrong with Miss Bede,' I explained and paused to examine the statement. My plain tale had stripped her of all those subtle attributes that had seemed to single her out as being – not wrong exactly but not altogether – right. 'Now that I'm away from her I can see her good qualities and Philip acted for the best in letting her come to live with us. It was just . . .'

'If she had been the most delightful person in the world – if she had been a saint from heaven (not necessarily the same thing) you would have resented her, under the circumstances. As for Philip, it wasn't surprising that she had a strong influence over him. It's not long since his mother died. He had been used to the devoted attention of an older woman.'

'And he never complained about all the fuss and expense of the accident, but my illness changed me. You saw yourself, Mr Hawthorne, that I am changed. It worried me to see how plain I have grown but now of course it doesn't matter.'

'Plain?' He examined my face, critically, his head tilted as if looking at a portrait – and smiled. 'That was not the change I saw. As for the accident and the boy in the bracken – it was Jordan Finch without a doubt. And so was the boy in the potting shed.'

'You really think so? Of course. I should have known. Poor Jordan!'

'He has never been seen in Marshall Street since you left, Florence. It was you who kept him there. He obviously felt that without you whatever we had to offer was of no use to him, and he may well have been right. Jordan will learn all he needs to know without any more schooling. Oh yes, he would be astute enough to find out where you had gone and to follow you. The name Gower Gill would be enough. He wouldn't be the first to set off on a romantic errand of that kind – and where else would he want to go? You weren't surprised when Orlando turned up in the Forest of Arden, were you? But I must confess it grieves me to think that he has gone off somewhere believing his beloved Miss Lincoln to be dead. How would that affect him – to lose the brightness and inspiration from a life as drab as Jordan's? I wish you could have found him. We've let him slip through our fingers.'

He told me about the work of the Society for the Protection of Destitute Boys of which he was a trustee.

'Of all the hundreds in Martlebury alone we can take no more than twenty-two, and even their future is far from settled. The Home itself is so dilapidated that it isn't much better than the slums some of them were born in. When it rains in the night, I lie awake and wonder if the dormitory ceiling will hold out. The roof leaks in five places. Apart from the income from the original endowment in 1832, we haven't a penny to bless ourselves with.' We sighed over the Destitute Boys. 'I miss you, Florence. You were always . . .' He didn't tell me what I always was, but together we grew more cheerful. I asked if my successor had settled happily in Marshall Street.

'Ah, Miss Partridge.' Mr Hawthorne clutched at his hair. 'A serious-minded young woman, well qualified to teach music. The most refined young woman it has been my misfortune to come across. She tells me almost daily how much she would prefer a private position with a good family where her music would be appreciated. When I'm not praying for the roof of the Home, I pray that Miss Partridge may take flight and settle in fresh fields.'

We laughed so much over Miss Partridge that I forgave her for having dared to take my place. Then we talked about Matlock and the fine specimens of ferns he had found in the narrow fissure in the rocks near the top of High Tor, by which time I felt more normal and cheerful than I had felt for a long time.

'I'll take you there – and have you seen Masson Cavern? You don't mean to say that you spend all your time drinking tea and spa water?'

He and his mother were staying at Matlock Bath.

'Much prettier than Matlock, don't you think – and less pretentious. I bring mother here every year for two weeks. We have rooms at Cliff Foot, rather more modest than the Hydro, but clean and comfortable.'

Until now I had never seen him except in Marshall Street. Whether from the effect of fresh air and exercise or the rare holiday mood, he seemed to have grown younger and more carefree, whereas I in one short year had grown older. But perhaps in some respects I had improved a little. I lost no time in calling on Mrs Hawthorne, remembering remorsefully how I had left Marshall Street without bidding her goodbye. Aunt Maud went with me on that first call and we were made so welcome that for the rest of their visit I spent almost as much time in Mrs Hawthorne's front parlour at Cliff Foot as in the more opulent Hydro.

'You must let Giles show you the sights,' the old lady said. 'Your company is just what he needs. He's never happy unless he's teaching somebody something and he's always thought a lot of you.'

I was not aware of being taught as we explored the caverns and cliff walks and climbed the Heights of Abraham, though Mr Hawthorne was informative on the subject of flowers and fossils, fluorspar and cinnebar and Roman lead mines; but he discouraged me from brooding and made me look out upon a physical world grown interesting again.

And what could have been more interesting, daunting though it might sound, than the effect of carbonic acid upon water passing through limestone rock, especially as it was demonstrated by the petrifying well in the pleasure ground by the river: a great grey saucer in the rock where water fell in an unending spray upon a strange medley of objects, encrusting them with lime and turning them grey too: an abandoned doll, a shoe, a bird's nest . . . They fascinated and repelled me.

'An unseemly collection,' Mr Hawthorne called it. It was distasteful, he thought, to see things preserved which by their very nature were meant to decay.

'Like us?' I asked.

'Exactly. I've never cared for the idea of being embalmed – though the human counterpart of this would be a death mask. They're not really being turned to stone, you see, only encrusted, but so heavily that it amounts to the same thing.'

But I liked the quaint eeriness of the place. It was fun to identify the stony relics and wonder who had left them there – and why.

'I believe you're foolish enough to want to cast an

offering into the pool yourself,' Mr Hawthorne said sternly.

'Oh no! Not really. Well, yes, I should,' I said defiantly. 'As a matter of fact I should love to.'

'Then let me buy you a suitable souvenir. One that can be sacrificed without regret.'

We searched the shop windows, discussing the merits of the assorted merchandise and trying to decide which of many rival claimants was the most useless. Since it must also be the cheapest, the choice was postponed day after day, as we laughed and argued over a teapot in the shape of a windmill, a cigar box covered in feathers, a papier mâché model of Riber Castle (Mr Hawthorne's pet abomination). Just in time, on his very last day, we found it: a pottery celery dish in the shape of a recumbent frog, in lurid shades of yellow and green.

'It's a shame,' said the girl who took our twopences at the gate when I handed her the dish. 'Are you *sure*?'

'Quite sure,' Mr Hawthorne said. 'Here is one thing that can only be changed for the better.'

'You'll have to come again next year. By that time you'll hardly recognise it.'

'That will be a blessing we shall look forward to.'

'I'll find a good place for it.' She was a friendly creature and seemed to have taken to us. 'If you're wanting a sit-down, they make a nice cup of tea over there.' She nodded towards the wooden pavilion by the river.

'The Petrifying Tea-Room, no doubt,' Mr Hawthorne said. 'How can we resist it?'

We sat down at one of the white-clothed tables on the verandah and presently the same girl brought us a steaming pot. Her advice had not been entirely disinterested.

'You work here too?'

'That's right." She lingered with the empty tray. We were her only customers. 'Mr Tanner took me on as an assistant to help in all the departments. He has the boats on the river as well.'

'You must have an interesting life,' I said.

'It's not what I really care for. We're very quiet a lot of the time. I've always been in good private service, until a year and a half ago. Still, you can't have everything you want in this world.' Her voice was quiet, lacking breath, so that each sentence died away in a sigh. Her face was rather long and oval with a little too much prominence to the grey eyes: a sensitive, melancholy face.

'I'm afraid she's right.' Mr Hawthorne almost sighed too. Certainly his smile was tinged with regret. 'She has learned a hard lesson: not to want anything too much. A sensible course if one can follow it.'

'It does sound rather dull though. I wonder if she really has learned to accept what she can have, without wanting more.'

The girl had gone to the verandah rail and was gazing somewhat dejectedly, I thought, at the river.

'So long as she avoids the error of wanting the wrong thing – like Faust.'

'I don't believe she is the very least bit like Faust.'

'You see,' Mr Hawthorne could not resist giving me a homily, 'the danger of wanting a thing too much is that you may get it in the end, with disastrous results, if it happens to be the wrong thing.'

'But how can one know – what not to want?'

'The thing in itself may be neither good nor bad but the desire for it may be wrong. To crave for a thing unsuitably, excessively, until every other impulse is suppressed . . .'

'So that one's whole nature is engaged.'

'An excellent way of putting it.' Mr Hawthorne repeated the phrase approvingly.

'It isn't my own. It came into my mind . . . I must have

read it somewhere.'

'That's interesting. What have you been reading lately.'

Shamefaced, I confessed.

'It didn't sound like Mrs Banstock. Her novels are my mother's favourites. You must talk to her about them. Only I'm afraid there isn't much time now. I must thank you, Florence, for spending so much of your holiday with her, and with me.'

'It has been' – I felt so downcast that it was difficult to find words – 'the most wonderful comfort to me. Do you remember the day I left school? You said that if ever I needed help of any kind I must come to you.'

'I remember. But you didn't come.'

'Not actually, but I thought of you often and remembered your ideas and ways of thinking. You looked very serious when you said it, as if you really thought I might need help.'

He had grown serious again, his eyes shrewd and kind as they had been then.

'You're quite right. I had a premonition, if you like to call it that. There was something too exalted in the way you rushed into the future. Even allowing for the raptures perfectly proper to a bride, it seemed to me too sudden, rash and ill-advised; and then, I knew just enough of Philip to see that his physique was delicate. He hadn't the look of long life, Florence. I've seen so much of his disease in Martlebury.'

I nodded, unable to speak.

'I felt that no man could have equalled the expectations you had of him. Remember that, if ever you felt him to be a lesser man than you had hoped. Remember too that he was already in the grip of a terrible malady. You must take care of your own health, Florence.'

We had left the pleasure grounds and were walking

back to his lodgings but now he stopped on the pavement, regardless of passers-by.

'And perhaps there was another reason why I urged you to come to me if ever you were in need. One of the sad things in a schoolmaster's life is that one is always being left behind. Perhaps I didn't want you to slip through my fingers any more than Jordan.'

'Oh I won't. And I've had a splendid idea. Why do not you and Mrs Hawthorne come to spend a day at Honeywick? Do you think she would like it?'

'I'm sure of it.'

Our last quarter of an hour together was spent in planning their visit. We parted in happy expectation of meeting again soon.

The happiness faded as I walked slowly back to Aunt Maud, resigning myself to her company for the rest of our holiday. The weather was breaking. I was still some distance from the Hydro when it began to rain. Unprovided with an umbrella, anxious for my bonnet, I looked round for shelter. On my left a door stood open to reveal a tempting porch and a glass-fronted door within. I cautiously mounted the steps and was reassured by a brass plate: it was not a private house.

I waited for the rain to stop and waited in vain. Five long minutes passed. Yawning, I glanced at the brass plate. *Bretherby and Butterwick*, it declared reproachfully, reminding me why it was that with the whole country to choose from I had chosen Matlock.

I rang the bell.

Seventeen

The sight of a young woman in deep mourning (though by this time I had left off my peak and veil) aroused in Mr Butterwick a chivalrous response. He rose and ushered me to a chair, his expression sympathetic and at the same time suitably attentive to the wishes of a prospective client. But his manner stiffened when I told him my name.

'Ah yes. We have heard from your late husband's solicitor.' He rang for a clerk and bade him bring the St Leonard papers. 'We were formerly in correspondence with your husband in connection with his aunt's estate. More than a year ago, if my memory is correct. Our last letter, as I recall, was not answered. We had expected a visit from Mr St Leonard . . .'

I explained. 'It was negligent, Mr Butterwick, but we had so very many things to think of and there was nothing . . .' I stopped, feeling some awkwardness. It was unseemly to tell him the truth, that once possessed of all that Aunt Adelaide had left, we had felt no further need to write to him, even to acknowledge his last letter. Our behaviour had been shamefully casual. I now learned that it had not even been based on a correct assumption. The house and its innumerable contents were not quite all that Aunt Adelaide had left.

'A trunk,' Mr Butterwick informed me coldly, 'containing the lady's personal effects, was deposited, sealed and padlocked, in the strong room of the County Bank here in Matlock, awaiting Mr St Leonard's instructions. We understood from his last letter that he intended to call upon us – and wrote to inform him that the remaining small items of business could be discussed when he did us that favour.'

'It was foolish of us not to think of the things she had with her. You would like me to arrange to have the trunk collected?'

Whether or not Mr Butterwick interpreted this as yet one more sign of our heartless self-interest, he raised his hand before I had finished.

'One moment, Mrs St Leonard. According to your husband's solicitors, his estate is not yet wound up.'

'There is some small point, I believe.'

'A point,' Mr Butterwick conceded majestically, 'concerning which we are in communication with them.' It dawned on me what the point must be. 'You must understand that until your husband's affairs are settled, the trunk is not your property, ma'am. And,' he continued – vindictively, I thought – 'it has been impossible for us to conclude our business with your husband while some of Miss St Leonard's property remains unclaimed in our hands, albeit lodged for safekeeping with the bank.'

Our carelessness had evidently involved us in one of those legal dilemmas which can lead to endless delay. I could not claim the box until Philip's affairs were wound up and this could not be until the box was claimed.

'What do you suggest?' It was surprising after such a short acquaintance how deeply I disliked Mr Butterwick.

'If you wish, it can be arranged for the trunk to be

placed in the hands of your husband's solicitors. You may, however, see the contents in my presence.'

'Thank you. I am in no hurry to see them. But I shall be pleased to settle my account with you as soon as you are in a position to let my solicitor have it,' I said with awful dignity and rose to leave. It was not from Mr Butterwick that I could learn the interesting details of Aunt Adelaide I had longed to hear. As a source of information on any human situation other than a legal one, Mr Butterwick must not be looked to. His niggling pomposity almost made me abandon Aunt Adelaide once again. Yet having got so far, it would be a pity to lose the opportunity of finding out at least the circumstances of her illness.

'You saw Miss St Leonard,' I began, 'before she died . . .'

'Only on the occasion when I drew up the will.' A last minute affair, it had been in the middle of the night. His hand on the door handle, Mr Butterwick recalled the occasion with distaste. Miss St Leonard had been a fairly recent arrival in Matlock, a visitor, quite a stranger to him. The doctor had assured him that though physically weak she was perfectly clear in her mind. Indeed he was himself satisfied as to her mental clarity. Beyond that, he had clearly no interest in a client who had inconsiderately robbed him of a night's sleep.

'As to the contents of the trunk – they comprise all that we found in her rooms when her landlady summoned us after our client's decease. A situation thoroughly unsatisfactory to us as executors. We were dependent on the honesty of those around her and since there was no relative . . .' He opened the door and bowed, with a glance at his desk as if anxious to return to the affairs of more satisfactory clients.

His indifference revived all my affectionate concern

for Aunt Adelaide, together with the hope that some gentler influence than Mr Butterwick's had softened her last hours. I determined to find out.

Masson View, he was able to tell me, was the name of the house where she had rented the first floor. I left him, resolving to take the first opportunity of calling there, and hurried off through the rain to the Hydro, feeling heartily sick of lawyers, as Aunt Adelaide must have been. Only the most urgent of all reasons, the knowledge that she was dying, could have driven her to summon Mr Butterwick at dead of night. A sudden wave of pity for her in that midnight dilemma destroyed my appetite for lunch. And yet there would have been no dilemma if she had been content with the first will made fifteen years ago; or if she had not felt that sudden last minute revulsion from the second will, made presumably at Cheltenham.

'People change their minds,' Aunt Maud said when she had heard a recital of my morning's activities. 'As a matter of fact I may as well tell you now that my bits and pieces are to be divided between you and Helena. There'll be a little money if I haven't spent it all by then. It's all settled. I won't change *my* mind. You'll have your mother's rosebud teaset.' She helped herself to green peas. 'And the hexagonal walnut table. Remember, all the drawers are false but *one*: and I thought you'd like the Bohemian glass. You used to like looking through it when you were a little girl. "It's all pink, the sky and everything," you used to say!'

I thanked her, feeling that it would take more than Bohemian glass to colour the world rose again, and wondering where on earth I would put the teaset and the hexagonal table, burdened as I already was with more glass, china and furniture than even the most careless housewife could break or shed in an entire lifetime. It was more than ever a matter for rejoicing that Aunt Maud looked so well and likely to survive for some time.

'It makes one think.' Aunt Maud finished her cutlet thoughtfully. 'Suppose you were suddenly to drop down dead.' She considered the proposition with a detachment I could not quite share. 'It isn't likely, but anything can happen. What would happen to all your things at Honeywick House – and for that matter, the house itself? If things had turned out differently . . . But as it is, with no family . . . If you ask me, the sooner you make a will the better.'

I nodded to the waiter to take away my unfinished cutlet.

'You can't think how tired I am of wills, Aunt Maud.'

She looked me over with the concentration she had given to my appearance before sending me off to school as a child, her expression critical, absorbed, entirely devoted to my interests, as it had been when she straightened my bonnet and swooped upon an undone boot button: a look that now warmed my heart. I had missed it.

'I'm just beginning to realise what you've been through. Would you like me to come back with you to Gower Gill and keep an eye on you? I promised Helena that I would be back in three weeks. Since that seizure she depends on me a good deal and one general servant can't do everything, as you know. But she would understand, I'm sure.'

'There's no need, Aunt Maud. But I'd love you to come. You haven't even seen Honeywick yet. When Cousin Helena is better you could both come for a long visit.' I paused, wondering what Aunt Maud would make of Miss Bede and said with less confidence, 'I shall manage. You mustn't worry about me.'

'Well, we shall have to see what the future holds.

You're certainly looking better than you did when we first came. It gave me a shock to see you so run down and frail-looking. It's a good thing you have this Miss Bede with you. At first I thought it rather odd and unwise to take a paying guest, but as things have turned out you need an older woman as a companion, especially in such a quiet place.'

'And there's Annie,' I reminded her. 'She's so dependable. I don't know what we should do without her.'

As it happened, I was soon to find out. We had not long left the dining-room when I was handed a letter from Annie herself, unexpectedly returned home from Cheshire. It fairly took the wind out of my sails.

'It will come as a surprise' – Annie's letter was a model of careful penmanship but a little stilted considering its shattering contents – '. . . Mr Hunter . . . thought it over . . . decided to accept . . .'

'Annie is going to be married, quite soon, to the coachman at the house in Cheshire where she was in service.'

Aghast, I read the letter again. Mr Hunter and his wife were her old friends. He was now a widower. Annie was losing no time in letting me know so that I could look round for someone else. It was unreasonable to feel not only let down but panic-stricken. I re-read the letter several times, trying to rejoice in Annie's well-deserved good fortune: a nice little house facing the park, a room for Mrs Blanche, a respectable position in life. Already I detected a new confidence in Annie's somewhat formal style. The letter conveyed in fact a month's warning, a blow indeed. Without Annie, life at Honeywick was unimaginable. She had already 'taken the liberty' of collecting her things from her little room over the kitchen and was arranging to remove her mother, lock, stock and barrel, to Cheshire.

If regret at leaving me did not feature so strongly in the letter as might have been expected, I should have been the first to understand. Annie's departure from Honeywick was no more headlong and heedless than my own flight from Marshall Street.

I wrote to her at once, telling her how sorry and how delighted her news had made me and tried not to let the sorrow outweigh the delight. I also wrote to Miss Bede who would already have heard the news from Annie herself when she went to Honeywick to pack her things. It became a long letter in which I told her of my meeting with the Hawthornes and my interview with Mr Butterwick and my intention of calling at Masson View.

Aunt Maud declined to come with me.

'It's too much of an effort to toil up Dob Lane afterwards. You can tell me all about it.'

She took her crochet bag into the tea garden where I left her to make her own contribution to the subdued murmur of conversation that ebbed and flowed in the warm, moist air under the hanging baskets and palm leaves and clambering passion flower.

Masson View stood back from the road, one of a short white-stuccoed terrace of Regency houses in a tree-lined street. Its velvet-swathed windows, broad, shallow steps, stone pilasters and portico gave it an air of quiet distinction. There seemed nothing squalid or seedy about the place where Aunt Adelaide had passed her last days. The nobly-panelled door stood open to the warm afternoon, revealing within a black-and-white tiled hall with a leopard-skin rug, brass gong and tall blue vases of pampas grass.

The maid invited me to wait there while she took my card to her mistress – and presently returned.

'Mrs Catchbent is at home, ma'am. Will you come

up?'

I followed her up an unusually steep and long staircase to a back parlour overlooking the garden.

'Mrs St Leonard, ma'am.'

I was about to enter the room when something moved at the far end of the landing; a head peering round a door: a woman's head. It disappeared immediately and the door was quietly closed.

Mrs Catchbent was elderly, white-haired and black-capped. She impressed me at once as a lady of the utmost correctness of manner, speech and dress. Circumstances had evidently compelled her to add to an insufficient income by letting part of her house but the dignity of her severely corseted figure, the rustling, if slightly rusty folds of her good silk and the rings dimly shining through her lace mittens, made it clear that in happier days Mrs Catchbent might have held her own in the most exalted company.

She was too well-bred to ask me to sit down but contrived a sort of displacement of her person without actually rising and a stately inclination towards the chair she desired me to take. Drawing upon the deepest resources of politeness at my disposal, I apologised for having imposed upon her a visit from a perfect stranger.

'Perhaps, having seen my name, you will guess why I am here.'

This cautious venture proved altogether too widely open to conjecture to be acceptable to Mrs Catchbent.

'You are Mrs Philip St Leonard of Honeywick House, Gower Gill,' she reminded me.

I bowed, unable to contradict. 'I believe you knew my husband's aunt, Miss Adelaide St Leonard.'

'That is so.'

I know now that Mrs Catchbent's immense restraint arose from other factors besides the hours she had spent in girlhood strapped to a backboard while enunciating prunes and prisms. Even then, without any direct experience of a court of law, I detected in her the careful phrasing of a reluctant witness.

'She lived here?'

'Miss St Leonard occupied the first floor front rooms for a period of two months.'

'And I believe,' I laboured on, 'she – in fact – died here.'

The ramrod supporting Mrs Catchbent seemed to stiffen. Her eyes took on a colder blue. She became, if possible, more remote but she did nevertheless incline her head faintly in acknowledgment of so undeniable a circumstance as death.

'I will not allude to the extreme inconvenience and extra work,' she said. 'Miss St Leonard's possessions were put together under my personal supervision and that of Mr Butterwick's assistant. In the absence of any relative I saw to it that no responsibility was left to servants. I myself hired a cab, at my own expense, and drove to Messrs Bretherby and Butterwick where I delivered a trunk to them for safekeeping.'

I thanked her.

'You must have had a great deal of worry and upset.' If my manner was too warmly plebeian it was from a desperate conviction that it was no use trying to rise to Mrs Catchbent's level. 'It was not Miss St Leonard's possessions I came to enquire after. I only wanted to hear about her. Herself. What sort of person she was . . .'

A look of distaste penetrated Mrs Catchbent's reserve: not, I quickly saw, distaste for Aunt Adelaide, but for the question. No personal and therefore illbred remark of any kind would ever be drawn from those discriminating lips.

I tried again. 'And how she died.' Even I heard something faintly offensive in the question. Mrs Catchbent's delicate nostrils quivered with resentment.

'It was Dr Archibald who attended Miss St Leonard,' she brought herself to say. 'Questions relating to her illness would be more properly put to him.'

'It was a short illness, I believe.'

'Miss St Leonard was ill for less than two days. Naturally I did all that could be expected but you must realise that this is not a boarding house.' Mrs Catchbent pronounced the term faintly. 'Miss St Leonard had taken a suite of rooms on lease. Our relationship was not that of landlady and boarder but of landlord and tenant.'

It was at this moment, when I was almost overcome by the wearisome sensation of aiming my puny arrows at a well-fortified stronghold, that we were interrupted by the entrance of the maid.

'Beg pardon, ma'am. The gentleman from Staindrops.'

Mrs Catchbent's nod of acquiescence, her politely frigid glance at my chair as if I were no longer in it but had already made way for the next visitor, effected between them so masterly a dismissal that I found myself at the door without knowing how it had been contrived.

'One thing, Mrs St Leonard,' Mrs Catchbent actually raised her hand to detain me. 'The stair-carpet then, a year past February, was precisely the same stair-carpet as you walked upon to reach this room. Best quality Wilton and then almost new. I beg you will be so good as to examine it carefully as you go down. You will find neither wear nor tear in it nor loose rail or rod. As it is now, so was it then. More than that I have no need to say. Good day to you, ma'am.'

Mystified by this information, so significantly and sonorously expressed, I came out onto the landing as the gentleman from Staindrops mounted the stairs and was shown into the room, where the maid was detained for a minute by her mistress. I wondered whether to let myself out and was still hesitating, lost in astonishment, before beginning my examination of the stair-carpet, when the door opened at the far end of the landing, a head appeared and a voice hissed my name.

'You are, aren't you? Mrs St Leonard, I mean.' A small middle-aged lady emerged and came quickly and a little furtively towards me. She was fashionably dressed and wore a good deal of jewellery. 'I heard Minnie announce you. It must be a relation, I said to myself. Of Miss St Leonard. Such a distinguished name. Mine is Petch. Mrs Petch. Do come in. I'm longing to talk.' She took me by the hand and positively dragged me into her own apartment. 'You see, these were her rooms, and that,' she pointed enthusiastically to the bedroom door, 'is where she died.'

Eighteen

So sudden a change in the situation was disconcerting. Instead of the beggarly drops of information wrung with so much effort from Mr Butterwick and Mrs Catchbent I was confronted in the person of Mrs Petch by a stream in spate which soon threatened to become a torrent.

'If only I had known! You will take tea? My maid is out but it won't take a minute.' I took refuge by the window while she cleared writing materials from the table and took teacups from a cupboard. 'The kettle won't be long. Fortunately I always have a fire. This is not a mild climate but I like it and so did Miss St Leonard. I expect you're staying at the Hydro. Don't you find it uncomfortably overheated? Miss St Leonard disliked it too, the very idea of it. "Never the Hydro," she often said – and laughed. An infectious laugh. "One might as well go to prison as be shut in there," she would say.'

'You were friends?'

'There, it's beginning to sing already.' She had moved the kettle from the hob to the coals. 'Friends? She was a very pleasant person. I miss her. But of course it's an immense advantage to have these rooms. I was downstairs, you see, and I always coveted this suite. For one thing, the view . . .'

It was magnificent, the huge mass of tree-clad rock, its foliage pierced here and there by naked limestone scars. I summoned up a suitable murmur of admiration but without feeling any pleasure in the scene. The truth is that no sooner had I crossed Mrs Petch's threshold than I felt uneasy. The room seemed full of small, restless movements against a background of barely audible sounds. I shared the window with a green parrot in a cage, its perch exactly my height. Our eyes met, mine guarded and embarrassed, the parrot's blatantly staring. It gave the impression, as parrots do when not speaking, of being about to speak if not to scream hideously. The white lace curtains were too stiffly starched to blow freely in the breeze from the open sash and yet they were not still, but seemed to breathe faintly, in and out, as if only just alive. On the mantelpiece a pair of green glass vases with dangling lustres were more responsive: their continual thin tinkling, together with the rustle of Mrs Petch's silk dress, the purr of the kettle, the ticking of an ormolu clock, the creak of the bedroom door as she trotted in and out, created an atmosphere of unrest.

'Just putting things straight,' she explained, disappearing for the third time, and I conceived the horrible fancy that she was busily reconstructing the scene of Aunt Adelaide's death, busily and happily, for I could see that she was still unreservedly happy at having seized the unexpected opportunity of taking over the rooms.

'You like Bath biscuits?' She returned and taking four from a velvet-covered tin, laid them on a plate. 'Tell me' – her eyes sparkled – 'did you come in for some of her jewellery? You're a relation-in-law, I suppose. She had some lovely things. Her brooches and her lace! My dear! And I'm quite a connoisseur.' She cast an expert eye over my toilette. 'Of course you can't wear them when you're in mourning. Your husband? I'm so sorry. But what a pity not to be able to wear them.'

'Such things must still be in the trunk at the Bank.'

'I only hope everything *is* there. There was no-one belonging to her and I'm bound to say, Mrs St Leonard, that I was never altogether sure of that maid, Bella. She was clean, and fond of Miss St Leonard but – well – how shall I put it? With rather too much imagination for her station.'

'Do you mean – she told lies?'

'I simply don't know. Her mistress trusted her but one can never rule out the possibility of a dishonest servant, especially at such a time.' Mrs Petch poured water into the teapot to warm it, and rinsed it round, speculatively. The green glass lustres swung and sparkled and tinkled.

'But Mrs Catchbent herself packed up Aunt Adelaide's things.'

'All that she found in these rooms.' Mrs Petch nodded significantly. 'It will be interesting to see when the trunk is opened just what is there – and what is *not*. But of course you won't know, will you? And it's no business of mine.' She showed her first sign of regret.

'Where is Bella now?'

'I believe she stayed on in Matlock, but I've never seen her since. Oh, I've no wish to blacken the girl's character but there would certainly be temptations and it would be very difficult to prove anything, wouldn't it? Especially by this time. There was one particularly fine brooch . . .'

If only, in trying to reach Aunt Adelaide, one could overcome the immovable obstacle of her possessions! Never was a woman so hedged in by tangible objects. I tried to introduce the subject of her illness but had to wait until the lace and brooches had been exhausted and be grateful when the swelling tide of Mrs Petch's conversation deposited a fact or two about their wearer within reach.

'It was all over in no time,' she told me when at last I could thrust in a question. 'Pneumonia set in. It often does after a shock to the system. She hadn't a chance, as I suppose Mrs Catchbent told you.'

'Mrs Catchbent told me nothing really. She seemed – offended.'

'They do dislike a death. Landladies, I mean. They simply hate it. Naturally. Though I was there, perfectly willing to take over the lease. I can well afford it. Mr Petch left me well off and these rooms are exactly to my taste. Of course I didn't enthuse about them to her but she had no cause for complaint. She lost nothing by Miss St Leonard's death. And in this case there was nothing for her to do. Your husband's aunt was well looked after. But there was the extra coming and going, the doctor, the lawyer, at dead of night too, and then the undertaker's men. It was Bretherby and Butterwick who saw to the funeral. All properly done but I gather that there is no headstone yet. Perhaps that was why you came to Matlock?'

The uneasiness remained. There was nothing in her prattling gossip, her evident enjoyment of the whole episode, to comfort me. I turned away from her and looked out, or rather, looked into the menacing face of rock which seemed at the same moment to step forward and glare at me; and with a gasp I discovered why it was that the soaring cliff with its jutting white crags frightened me. A memory of Holleron Edge made my head swim, my knees tremble. With it came another memory, a circumstance I had never consciously thought of though it had haunted me in the delirium following my own fall: the fact that Aunt Adelaide too had fallen. And no wonder. The very houses here seemed about to fall, perched precariously among the trees above the gorge, where pathways tumbled steeply and ancient steps covered with moss and slime led down into caverns harbouring pools of fathomless depths. Where else in the world would a woman be more likely to fall to her death, to turn and twist like a rag doll fluttering helplessly from the top of Masson Hill – or High Tor – or the Heights of Abraham?

'She fell, the lawyer said.'

'There!' Mrs Petch set the silver teapot triumphantly on its stand and drew a second chair to the table. 'Now, do you take sugar? Yes, it was the fall, poor dear, that brought on the pneumonia, besides the broken hip. Oh, and other injuries. She was very shortsighted and it seems she had mislaid her lorgnette. She would never wear spectacles. It was vanity of course but who could blame her? She always looked charming. One doesn't have to be young. That was something I learned from Miss St Leonard. The best of materials and good jewellery can certainly flatter, and she wasn't really old, was she? A little on the wrong side of fifty, would you say? But then you never met her. Still your husband would know. And so much to live for. She had a fine house, I understand, when she chose to settle down.'

I left the view to the parrot and sat down at the table.

'Tell me, Mrs Petch, where did the accident happen?'

'Why here of course, in this very house. Bless you, she fell down the stairs. The ones you came up. She must have caught her foot . . .'

'In the stair-carpet?'

Mrs Petch waved the sugar tongs in mock reproof.

'One mustn't even suggest such a thing. One simply dare not mention the possibility. She could just as easily have stumbled over her skirt, though why she was going down at that time of night I can't think. It has often puzzled me.' She offered Bath biscuits. 'The noise woke me. Unbelievable! How she survived, I mean. They're so steep and she came crashing down from the very top to the bottom. I was downstairs then, you see. "That can't be a person," I said and sat up in bed. It was more like a sack of potatoes. I was there in a minute, first on the scene. Well, almost. There are certain things one cannot rush out without doing. By that time they were coming.'

'They?'

'Well, Bella. She ran down in her nightdress. A servant can, you know. She knelt beside her. "Oh, ma'am," she said, so tenderly. "What've you done? Oh, my poor little madam." It was affecting.' Mrs Petch was affected all over again and positively closed her lips. The small agitations of the room could be heard again – the movement of claws and feathers and beak as the speechless parrot prepared to speak. At any minute it would screech a word, a name . . .

'Then – it was a relief I can tell you –' Mrs Petch stooped to retrieve a fallen teaspoon and I missed a word, '. . . came. She had evidently been sound asleep. She was still tying the girdle of her dressing-gown and seemed dazed.'

'Whom did you say? Mrs Catchbent?'

'No, no.' Mrs Petch stared. 'Miss Goodlock.'

I suppose it was the eldritch shriek of the parrot that chiefly startled me though I should have been prepared for it; but the totally unexpected arrival on the scene of Miss Goodlock startled me too. I had simply forgotten that there would be a third member of Aunt Adelaide's household.

'Aunt Adelaide's companion?'

'Poor Miss Goodlock. Now she,' Mrs Petch had peered into the teapot and now emphasised the pronoun by closing the lid with a snap, 'she was the one I felt sorry for. I've always thought, and used to say to Mr Petch many a time, there can be nothing more depressing than the life of a paid companion; to be at the beck and call of another, day in, day out; to be paid for being pleasant and companionable. "That will never be your fate, my love," Mr Petch said. Not that Miss St Leonard was ever inconsiderate. She was more of a friend to poor Miss Goodlock and consulted her far more than was necessary. What I mean is – when Miss St Leonard went crashing down those stairs, Miss Goodlock's life was shattered too.'

'You mean in that she lost her position?'

'Her livelihood, her bed and board, and always in such luxury. The shock! She must have known that she would never find such a position again. If one had to be a companion, no one could have been more fortunate in a mistress. I've often thought of her.'

'Did she find another situation?'

'I don't know. That was almost the last I saw of her, at the top of the stairs, looking down, her face as white as this cloth. She left without saying goodbye when Miss St Leonard died, two days later. She didn't even wait for the funeral. I suppose she just couldn't bear up any longer.'

It seemed typical of her subordinate rôle, that silent fading away with scarcely a murmur of farewell. But I couldn't help wishing that she had stayed just a little longer, to see the very last of the woman she had spent so much time with. Still, Mrs Petch, Mrs Catchbent, Mr Butterwick and Bella – it was not a list in which to find much comfort – must have filled the place of relatives. It remained for me to arrange a suitable memorial for her grave. That was the very least I could do for her after all she had done for me. I reached for my gloves.

'Must you go?'

'I have intruded on you too long already.' Now that I had come a little closer to Aunt Adelaide and could picture her here, I wondered if her presence would still be felt at Honeywick when I returned. A persistent feeling that it was her home, not mine, made me exclaim, 'I wish she had not led so wandering a life. Why should she choose to live in rooms instead of in her own beautiful home? Did she ever say? Would she have gone back in the end, if she had lived?'

'Strange that you should ask. I used to wonder the same thing myself. In fact we talked of it sometimes. "Goodie is for ever urging me," she would say. That was her name for Miss Goodlock. "Goodie is for ever urging me to go back to Honeywick and settle there." "And why don't you?" I asked, more than once. She would laugh. It was rather a charming laugh. "It's so dreadfully full of things, Mrs Petch," she said. "Possessions have been the bane of my life. They weigh me down. Some day I must take up the burden again but for a while it is delightful to carry just a few things about with me from place to place. We're like two snails, I tell Goodie, putting out our horns and creeping from spa to spa!" Yes, she would have gone home in the end, only as it happened, the end was rather different.' As if aware that tragedy loomed somewhere in the phrase, Mrs Petch paused then drew back safely into trivialities. 'Do come again.' Reluctantly she opened the door, admitting a draught which drew a tinkling crescendo from the glass lustres and an indignant movement from the parrot. 'You haven't seen the bedroom.'

'Another time . . . You've been very kind.'

'Well, there's nothing of hers there. Nothing left of her here at all. Oh, just one thing. Now let me see. I put it in one of these.' She trotted to a cabinet and pulled out half-a-dozen tiny drawers. 'Here. It isn't much of a memento, but you might like to have something that was hers.'

I took it: an affair of twisted gold wire at the end of an ivory handle. A lorgnette.

'We took out the bits of glass, crushed to pieces. My maid found it right underneath the wardrobe when she went under with a brush, at the very back. She is most thorough, I will say that for her. "It looks like a pair of eye-glasses," she said. It must have been dropped – and been trodden on.'

I needed no memento of Aunt Adelaide, having more than enough already, but this one had a peculiarly personal quality, the one thing she had always had with her, the one thing she had been unable to do without.

'It's a puzzle how it got there,' Mrs Petch said, 'right at the very back. She would be lost without it. Quite helpless. She was so very shortsighted. No wonder she fell.'

Nineteen

I knew her now. A lady in her early fifties: elegantly dressed, amiable, kind to her servants, possessed of a charmingly infectious laugh: a lady who preferred the independence of private rooms to the overheated, enclosed atmosphere of the Hydro: one who enjoyed a way of life too extravagant to last long, and enjoyed it all the more because of her restricted girlhood when she had sat in the landau like a crushed flower at Aunt Thora's side. Her only diversions then (so far as I knew) had been to teach in the Sunday school and crouch myopically over the novels of Mrs Banstock. Death had robbed her of an unknown number of harmless happy years and prevented her from ever going back to end her days, mellowed and resigned, among all the worldly goods Aunt Thora had handed on to her. We were alike, Aunt Adelaide and I, in feeling the burden of our inheritance.

But the impression I took away with me as I went cautiously down the stairs, my skirt held high, was a more disturbing one; of a helpless woman groping, half blind, in search of her lorgnette, then falling in the dark, tumbling down the whole flight like a sack of potatoes. But even without her eye-glasses she must have known her bearings. One would have to be very shortsighted indeed not to know where the stairs were. It seemed likely that she had been intending to come down and had been betrayed, for all her fastidiousness in dress, by an unstitched hem: had caught her heel in it . . . or her toe? It was certainly odd that she had been coming down at that late hour when all her rooms were on the first floor.

Having made my own way down successfully, absently noting the impeccable state of Mrs Çatchbent's stair-carpet, I turned and looked up. It was an unusually long and steep flight. To Miss Goodlock, standing whitefaced and dazed at the top, it would seem a long way to look down at Aunt Adelaide lying in a crumpled mass of silk and lawn at the bottom, maimed, unconscious perhaps; and at Bella who was already there first on the scene, while Mrs Petch made those essential adjustments to her appearance which a servant was free to neglect. There had been no mention of a broken lamp or any threat of fire – or damage to the stair-carpet from spilt oil. Aunt Adelaide must have been making her foolhardy journey downstairs not only without her eye-glasses but without a lamp. But of course it was possible – emerging into the warm afternoon I felt more cheerful – it was quite possible that she had been carrying her eye-glasses when she came downstairs and that they had been crushed and twisted in the fall. It would be afterwards that they had been accidentally kicked under the wardrobe – in the commotion: kicked so vigorously that they had gone right to the very back.

And at least she had never been alone: never lonely. No-one who paid for companionship need ever be alone; nor for that matter could the paid companion, a creature whose success in her calling depended on an ability to fade into the background, to interpose herself like a patternless screen between her employer and solitude.

My interest veered towards Miss Goodlock. It was a tribute to her powers of self-effacement that Mrs Catchbent had not even mentioned her, though to be sure mentioning things was not Mrs Catchbent's forte. Still, she and Aunt Adelaide had lived together for years; their relationship had been close; Miss Goodlock had most to lose by Aunt Adelaide's death.

These reflections weighed a little on my spirits and spoilt the last days of my holiday. There was no reason why I should not stay on after Aunt Maud left as she pointed out several times and was still pointing out when I saw her off at the railway station.

'I don't feel altogether happy about you.' She leaned out of the carriage window looking, in her magenta hat with an ostrich plume and her dark grey cape, like a reliable and sensible mother hen. 'You've got a far-away, lost look about you. I wish I could have persuaded you to come back with me. You won't change your mind and come in a day or two? Well, then why not stay on at the Hydro for another week, simply for the rest? Without your Annie, you're going to be run off your feet.'

I shook my head and did not confide to her either my growing reluctance to go home or my equal disinclination to stay.

'We'll meet again soon.'

Having settled herself for the journey, she got down again and gave me a warm hug.

'I don't know when I enjoyed myself so much, thanks to you, though it wasn't to enjoy myself that I came. Don't think I haven't felt how you've been grieving for Philip but you haven't inflicted your grief on other people. You were always a dear good girl. I only hope . . . I often wondered if he knew what a treasure he had got. Now promise you'll come and see us soon – and you'll write?'

'Often. And thank you, Aunt Maud. I shall miss you dreadfully.'

She left me lonely and restless. The Hydro, when I went dolefully back, seemed to have grown in size. Alone at my table in the dining-room I felt alternately mouse-like and monstrously conspicuous. Aunt Maud's friends, a surprising number, pressed me to join them but they must have found me dull company. When my trunk was packed and sent on ahead, most of my time was spent in retracing the walks I had enjoyed with Mr Hawthorne. I missed him too.

Already into the mornings and evenings had crept the first scents of autumn. The windless days held the hushed stillness of things coming to an end, as if at a breath the dense ranks of green on the wooded slopes would change to yellow and brown, shrivel and fall. I was almost glad when my last day came, though it brought nearer the prospect of winter at Honeywick without Philip, with only Miss Bede. I must write to her about my return.

From these sad thoughts I took refuge in action, though of a limited and unadventurous kind. Before leaving Matlock I was determined to see the contents of Aunt Adelaide's box even if I could not take possession of them. As Mr Butterwick found himself too busy to take me to the bank, his assistant, young Mr Bretherby, came with me instead. The box, a deep, tin-lined trunk, was brought out and unlocked, and under his friendly eye I went through the contents.

Aunt Adelaide had travelled light, if they were anything to go by. Even allowing for her resistance to possessions, the provision she appeared to have made for ten years of residence away from home was surprisingly sparse: astonishingly so for a lady with a reputation for dressing well and with a fondness for lace and jewellery of a quality to impress that interested connoisseuse, Mrs Petch. There were piles of underwear folded by Mrs Catchbent's own hand – or Bella's – and dresses, all modish and little worn. She had apparently stayed slim: they would have fitted me except for the length. Which had she been wearing when she tripped and fell? I ran my fingers round the hems and found no break in the stitching; but there were too many petticoats to put them all to the test. A white paper packet contained lace jabots and cuffs but they were yellowing and obviously discarded. A worn leather jewel box held a signet ring, a plain locket and chain and a garnet parure. The only other things were a few books, a set of shell-handled manicure and sewing aids, a writing-case and a bundle of letters tied with ribbon. Nothing of value. The best had gone. It could have been the perfume still scenting the petticoats and dresses that gave poignancy to this intrusion into her last days: a light, sweet, stale scent of lily of the valley.

I hesitated before untying the letters. They were not mine. It was hard to say whose they legally were.

'May I?'

'Certainly, Mrs St Leonard,' Mr Bretherby hastened to say. He was an agreeable young man.

I did no more than glance at the letters; but one signature caught my eye on a letter dated 1861, the ink faded to a pale brown. Abel Drigg. I must tell him that she had kept it. It would comfort him like a greeting across the years from an old friend. With Mr Bretherby's help I put everything back.

'I'm sure,' he began, 'you will not have much longer to wait.'

'Oh, I don't want these things, Mr Bretherby, none of them. I already have so much. It was only to find out . . .'

But it seemed wiser not to explain. There was little doubt that Aunt Adelaide had been robbed. As Mrs Petch had pointed out, there had been temptation. She had suspected Bella – but what did it matter now?

Besides, in all Mrs Petch's nerve-racking prattle, one item had been more pleasing than the rest: 'Oh, my poor little madam,' Bella had said tenderly, having run downstairs in her nightdress in the headlong fashion Mrs Petch and Miss Goodlock were too genteel to indulge in. My heart warmed to Bella; but reason told me that no amount of tenderness to a living mistress need prevent her from robbing a dead one.

'If there is anything at all I can do, Mrs St Leonard.' When he had locked the trunk, Mr Bretherby showed a disposition to linger. It flashed through my mind that if Bella should still be at large in Matlock, he would be the very person to help me to find her. But I was determined to leave the next day; and though it would be interesting to talk to Bella, it might also prove embarrassing to penetrate the cloud under which Mrs Petch had placed her. Any enquiries about Aunt Adelaide's affairs, if they were needed, should have been made a year past February. The sudden recollection of our carefree indifference at that time brought so painful a sadness that I parted from Mr Bretherby with only a brief word of thanks and walked off, scarcely noticing my direction, until I found myself in the one main street which ran alongside the river, and presently came to the pleasure gardens.

There were few visitors about, even at the petrifying well. On impulse I paid my twopence and went to look again at the strange assortment of lime-encrusted objects among which our celery dish flaunted its hideous yellow and green with the confidence of a newcomer. Had it paled a little?

'It's too soon. You can't expect to see any difference

yet.'

The melancholy young woman had followed me and stood staring down at her exhibits with the air of disillusioned resignation that was peculiarly hers.

'I'm just filling in time,' I explained.

'You're on your own today. The gentleman's gone, I expect. A nice gentleman,' she conceded gloomily. 'They come and go. There's not many about.' She glanced round, so that it wasn't clear whether she referred to the scarcity of nice gentlemen or the lack of visitors. 'Will you be having a cup of tea?'

'No, I don't think so.'

'You'd be surprised, I dare say,' she said presently, 'but all those things have a story behind them.'

'I can imagine that.' Indeed it was as if the grey toy engine and trumpet, the bowler hat and coal shovel, the kettle and branched candlestick, bore silent witness to a civilisation turned to stone.

'People mostly put in things they don't want. But me –' the ghost of an inward flame enlivened her pale face and somewhat prominent eyes, 'I'm different. What I put there was something precious. I put it there so that it would last, for ever.'

It was not surprising if the place itself had a lowering effect upon her spirits, especially in its present quiet mood. For a time we neither of us spoke. The ceaseless spray of bright water, undeterred by the greyness of its future, suggested an optimism we neither of us shared.

'I'm looking at it now.' She directed her mournful gaze towards the pool but I could not be sure, among so many articles, which one she meant or whether it would spoil the drama with which she had invested the occasion if I bluntly asked.

'Is it precious because it reminds you of someone?' I suggested instead. 'You cared for it because you cared for the person who gave it to you?'

'Cared for? I should just think I did. It wasn't exactly given to me but it belonged to the one I cared for, the dearest in the whole world.'

She left me and edged her way round the projecting rim of the six-foot pool.

'That's it.' She pointed, not at the trumpet, bowler hat or candelabra, but at another object approximately oval in shape like the wider end of a small fire extinguisher sadly crushed. 'It's been there over a year now but it doesn't seem more than a day or two since I saw it on her head. It's the one she wore for church. "I'll take that one," I thought. "Not too fancy and with a sort of religious feeling about it." Cared for, you said. I cared for her for ten years and now she's gone, I can't seem to find myself. That's the only thing of hers I had. It was no good to anyone. "Take it," she would have said. She was always giving things away. Then when I came here it seemed just the right thing to put in the pool, seeing there was no one to put a stone over her grave. It's better than a statue or an urn; more unusual. Every time I see it I think of her, my little mistress, dead and gone.'

A faint suspicion deepened into certainty as she spoke.

'You must be Bella?' There was no need to ask. I was sure of it even before she nodded, her deer-like eyes startled.

As for the precious object lying in the pool like a grey crustacean come crawling to its eternal rest – with a shudder I identified it as Aunt Adelaide's Sunday bonnet.

The thing was grotesque, both pitiful and repulsive as it lay abjectly submitting to the endless, maddening drip of water. But the influence of natural forces, of water and stone, had not turned it into a thing of nature. The outline of crown and brim were still there and had still a hideous touch of coquetry. One could even imagine a head inside – cheeks – a chin – a mouth smiling – an infectious laugh – though what one saw was a hard, cold, colourless monstrosity, a hybrid neither natural nor man-made. It was, as Bella rightly said, an unusual memorial. The situation was in every way bizarre; and yet it served a purpose, demonstrating in a single dramatic stroke that Aunt Adelaide had, after all, been sincerely mourned. Bella's eccentric act of remembrance had surely been prompted by a grief so genuine that it roused sorrow in me too: a deeper sorrow than it had yet been possible to feel for an unknown woman. Of those I had met, Bella was the first, the only person who had been with her at the end and had really *cared*.

As to her honesty – was it likely that she would steal the best of her mistress's jewellery and then sentimentalise over her church-going bonnet? It was possible, but at that moment I thought less about her moral standards than about her tenderness to Aunt Adelaide. Whether she had always been the strange, fey creature she now was, who can tell? She must always have had, as Mrs Petch put it, too much imagination for her station or indeed for any station. Perhaps we were two of a kind. The fact is that as we stood together in that grey limbo of water and stone, one part of me at least was disposed to believe every word she spoke. A less rational attitude to life than hers could scarcely be imagined, and yet her interpretation of the facts I was soon to hear was of a kind I could accept, just as she accepted me as a connection of her late employer without much surprise, indeed with something like fatalism.

Or was it more than that? Some deep-rooted sense of a purpose working itself out on her behalf may have accounted for her vaguely worded hints and exclamations when she discovered who I was.

'I always knew – there was a kind of feeling here –' in her breast, 'that it wasn't finished with.'

There was no one about, not even Mr Tanner. I sat down at one of the garden tables and begged her to take the seat opposite so that we could talk. She did not come at once to the heart of the matter. It may have been her manner, a smouldering violence of feeling long suppressed, that convinced me from the outset that the matter had a heart: or rather a festering source of suffering and pain. She fidgeted with a bunch of keys she wore on a chain at her waist, swallowed nervously as if playing for time, then suddenly found an opening, one which surprised me.

'You're madam's nephew's wife – widow, I should say.' The girl's nature was emotional. Her eyes suffused in sympathy and indeed I had the impression that tears were never far from the surface. 'Then you must live at Honeywick House. I wonder if it's still the same.'

'You know Honeywick? Of course, you must have been with Miss St Leonard in the old days.'

Not when she lived at Gower Gill, Bella told me. She had entered Aunt Adelaide's service at Bath, some ten years ago, personally recommended by the lady she worked for, who was reducing her establishment. But a year later she had gone with her new mistress to Honeywick, a short visit before they went on to Cheltenham.

'It was a change to be in the country. It was springtime when we went there and there was blossom everywhere. You could stand at the back door in that little courtyard and hear the cuckoo in the woods.'

'It's beautiful there in spring. It's always beautiful.'

'That's what I thought. But it was quiet. We hardly saw a soul except an old woman that brought potatoes and eggs and honey.'

'Mrs Blanche.'

'Yes, that was her name. I couldn't have brought it to mind until you mentioned it. I used to chat to her at the back door but she never came in. When we'd been there for a bit, it began to . . . but I don't know. You could hardly blame the house.'

'Blame it?'

'When I think about it now, it gives me a funny feeling.' She looked away across the river at the steep incline beyond, but with an air of inward vision as if she saw instead the road curving down to Gower Gill and the house halfway down. I saw it too, with the sidelong glint of sun on its bow window, and felt again the familiar impression its rooms could sometimes give of containing more than could be seen, concealing more than could be known.

'I've tried to puzzle it out sometimes, whether a place can be bad or whether it's people that turn it that way: a wicked person. It could be the two coming together, the person and the place.'

'Are you trying to tell me that something happened at Honeywick, something wicked?'

'It started there.'

Afterwards perhaps I would recover my senses. Even then the feeling of unreality was strong enough to put me on my guard, to remind me that I was listening to one of Bella's stories in a situation well suited to the suspension of disbelief: solitude, a forest of leaves breathlessly waiting to fall, a river haze to shroud boats and walls and chimneys, a diffused light to suggest rather than clarify details.

'Did Miss St Leonard enjoy being at home again?' I achieved a blend of briskness and remote interest which seemed to me admirably normal. But Bella was much better at sustaining an atmosphere of abnormality likely at any moment to decline into horror than I was at dispelling it.

'If she'd enjoyed it, she would have stayed, wouldn't she? For the life of me I can't make up my mind whether it would have been better if she had.' Her quick look at me was appealing as if she longed to unburden herself.

'And Miss Goodlock? Did she like being at Honeywick?'

My vision of her, quietly absorbed in her small commonplace duties, did not prepare me for Bella's reply.

'She was in heaven, as if she was walking on air.' She brought forth the unexpected image with a flash but with a curious moroseness, as if occupied with thoughts by no means heavenly.

It had been, I gathered, a sudden flowering for Miss Goodlock, an upward surge of the spirit, a state of being I could understand. Had I not experienced it myself? Had not I too been intoxicated by the cold spring twilights and mild afternoons, the moonlight and stars above the velvet trees, the birds, the lambs, the cowslips; by sunlight on porcelain and silver, above all by the permanence of stone on stone, of floors worn smooth by generations of women moving on the same errands year after year? If, like Miss Goodlock, I had been doomed to lose it after one short month, would it not have haunted me like a glimpse of Eden? Indeed that was exactly how the first month at Honeywick now seemed to me: a lost Paradise.

And not only to me.

'She was always on at the mistress to go back. A hint here, a hint there. She would harp on about everything that went wrong when we were in rooms; the laundry, the draughts. "It doesn't suit you here," she would say.'

I thought of her as a meek beast of burden stopping to

roll a patient eye backward in protest. In spite of her hopelessly subordinate position, as a dependant without rights or expectations, Goodie had no doubt found ways of managing a mistress so amiable and considerate. But not, apparently, on the one point that mattered to her.

'"Then let's move on," the mistress would say, teasing her. "We'll go to Tunbridge Wells. I know what you would like, Goodie, but now that I've spread my wings, I won't go back to the nest, not yet. Not until I'm old," she said. The very day before she died, I heard her say it.' Bella's expression darkened. She looked down at the keys in her lap and laid them out like fingers of a hand. 'It was Miss Goodlock's birthday. They were out paying calls before dinner and afterwards they talked. "It's no use, Goodie," the mistress said. "You'll never persuade me." I took them a pot of chocolate before I went to bed. They sat up late.'

I had been right about Aunt Adelaide's taste for chocolate, but about Miss Goodlock I was now less sure. Except for her extraordinary enthusiasm for Honeywick, she had seemed the sort of person to be thought of in negative terms, the most striking thing about her being her inactivity – and, for that matter, her absence. It was odd that so very little had been heard of her: nothing, in fact, so far as Philip and I were concerned. She had left before the funeral, I recollected. For ten years glued to Aunt Adelaide's side, then – hey presto! – she was gone like a puff of smoke. One would have expected her to pay her last respects by following so kind a mistress to the grave. She just couldn't bear up any longer, Mrs Petch had supposed; but viewed impartially, it was more as if she had washed her hands of Aunt Adelaide. The notion teased me by its resemblance to some more recent circumstance which I could not bring to mind.

'Miss Goodlock left rather abruptly, I understand, and didn't stay for the funeral. I believe she was very upset. Are you still in touch with her?'

'Upset?' Bella repeated sharply. 'In touch?'

Her sudden glare, her air of recoiling swiftly from a rattlesnake, made me jump. They also brought the dim Miss Goodlock into much sharper relief.

'Do you mean,' I asked, now treading carefully on new ground, 'that you disliked her?'

Bella drew a deep breath and seemed to look through and beyond me to a prospect so repellent that it paled even her lips.

'No,' she said bitterly, 'she didn't stay for the funeral. I'd sat up with my dear little mistress all night. She died at first light. No more than an hour later Miss Goodlock had gone, bag and baggage. Nobody knows how she got her boxes downstairs. She'd get a man at the street end to wheel her things to the station – and not only her own things either. There'd be those she'd helped herself to,' she concluded with slow and venomous emphasis.

'You're accusing her of theft?'

Only a very brief calculation was needed to discover that if Bella was honest, Miss Goodlock was not. It had not occurred to me that the weight of probability was equally balanced between them.

'Why didn't you tell the lawyer?'

'I tried to tell the lady downstairs. It wasn't any good trying to tell Mrs Catchbent. She's too high and mighty to open her eyes or ears to the likes of me. But Mrs Petch had been a bit friendly with my mistress, though far beneath her. "None of your stories, Bella," she says. "Is it likely that a lady such as poor Miss Goodlock would stoop to such conduct?" she says and tossed me a nasty look. "Thieves," she says, and gives her ear-rings a shake, "are always quick to accuse someone else." So I shut my mouth and kept it shut. It made no difference to the only one that mattered. And it brought home to me . . .'

There was obviously something more to come, something unusually difficult to put into words. I found myself sitting forward on the edge of my chair and watching Bella's lips anxiously in the certain knowledge that a host of worries on Aunt Adelaide's behalf, at first so dimly imagined, so intuitive as to be no more than inklings, were steadily taking shape – an unwelcome shape.

'It brought home to me that it was no good trying to tell the other thing I knew.' Bella's eyes were suddenly appealing. 'Though it's lain like a weight on my heart. There'll come a day, I thought, when the Lord will send somebody that will listen and believe me.'

'Tell me.'

Again she swallowed nervously, fearing perhaps that I would listen and not believe whatever monstrous thing it was that she laboured to bring forth.

'You didn't know her. It's hard to explain what she was like.'

'She? You mean Miss Goodlock?'

'The wickedness. You couldn't put your finger on anything, she was so clever. It was always there but I felt it for the first time when we were in the country like I told you. If we'd gone back . . .' My face must have reflected her look of strain. Who knew better than I how readily the seeds of discord could germinate in Honeywick's hothouse atmosphere, how vigorously they could grow? But wickedness?

'It was certainly wicked to rob her mistress when she had been treated so kindly, almost as a friend. Miss St Leonard must have been quite fond of her.'

'The mistress loved her,' Bella said deliberately, as if under compulsion to tell a bitter truth. 'Like a sister. She thought the sun shone out of her.'

'I believe you exaggerate a little, Bella,' I said after a pause for further mental adjustment. 'From all I can make out Miss St Leonard was a sweet and affectionate person. All the same . . .'

Like all good story-tellers Bella was quick to sense the weakening of her spell. She became direct. Leaning forward, she thrust her face close to mine. I saw a nerve twitch under her right eye. Her lips quivered.

'She loved her well enough to leave her everything she had, every stick and stone, every penny, every cup and every saucer, every stitch she wore. She'd have had them all, Mrs St Leonard, if she could have waited.'

'You mean she stole . . .?'

'What's stealing?' Bella demanded contemptuously. 'There's worse things than stealing. The mistress made a will – at Cheltenham it was – after we left Gower Gill. The house was to be Miss Goodlock's. I heard them talking. "You love it more than I do, Goodie," she said. "It shall be your reward, only be patient. Some day it will be your own." But she couldn't wait. I'm telling you God's truth. She couldn't wait.'

Bella had got to her feet, her keys jangling. I reached out and gripped her by the arm.

'Come here,' I commanded, grasping her sleeve so firmly that the stitches came away – and I too got up. 'Tell me what you mean. What was the other thing, the thing you never told?'

My sternness brought a look of eerie triumph to her pale face.

'I mean that Miss Goodlock,' she pronounced the name with loathing, 'couldn't wait for the mistress to die. She murdered her. That's what I mean. It was murder. Murder.'

'How can you say such a terrible thing? How can you

know?'

'Because my mistress told me. That's how I know.' Bella spoke with terrible simplicity. 'I held her in my arms and she told me. "She meant to kill me, Bella," she said. "I don't want to live. She has broken my heart."'

Twenty

It was the broken heart I grieved for, more even than the bruised and broken body. The savage blow from behind that sent Aunt Adelaide hurtling down the steep stairs was no more unexpected, no more ruthless than the betrayal it expressed. The physical violence and the contemptuous cruelty were equally vile. 'After all these years, Bella,' she had murmured in the feebleness and confusion of her fallen world. 'I have loved her, all these years . . .'

Having unburdened herself of the long-stored memory, Bella broke down and sobbed. I waited – shocked, shaken, horrified, almost convinced, entirely convinced, so long as sympathy and imagination dominated my other faculties – and I seemed to give way, like Aunt Adelaide, under a blow that was more than physical. Even when I began to think clearly again, I could not disbelieve. The tragedy, reaching me indirectly through the medium of Bella, was all the more poignant because it came stripped of irrelevant detail: I saw only the three women and the stairs. As a medium Bella might be faulty, warped by jealousy, ill-balanced, ignorant. All the same it was impossible to see her heaving shoulders and streaming eyes and not to believe her.

Besides, such facts as could be known supported her version of the grim affair, most convincing of all the fact that she was here. Whether or not Aunt Adelaide had been murdered, she had certainly been robbed. If Bella had helped herself to her mistress's most valuable pieces of jewellery, it was unlikely that she would have stayed here within reach of discovery, nor would she have needed to toil for Mr Tanner as waitress and collector of twopences. On the other hand Miss Goodlock stood condemned of theft, if not worse, by her otherwise unaccountable disappearance. The drab, dutiful Miss Goodlock had vanished in every sense, had never existed, except in my imagination; but how could I have imagined her as she really was – clever, crafty, covetous, above all violent. And far from having the most to lose by Aunt Adelaide's death, as chief beneficiary she had the most to gain.

'It was the house she wanted,' Bella said, 'and couldn't wait for any longer. They sat up late talking. They usually played piquet but they couldn't play that night because madam had lost her eye-glasses. It's as plain to me as daylight,' she raised her blotched and tear-stained face, 'that devil had taken them. I'd looked everywhere and couldn't find them and afterwards I looked again. It frightens me when I think of the mistress sitting there talking, and not being able to read the expression on that wicked face. What she did must have been intended, and no-one would ever believe that it hadn't been an accident.'

Certainly no-one would have believed Bella. Her tendency to an unrestrained flow of feeling must always have exceeded the conventional primness expected of a servant. She had always been too lavishly herself to win the approval of Mrs Catchbent or Mrs Petch, too emotional by far for Mr Butterwick. The thought that Aunt

Adelaide had liked and trusted her made me like Aunt Adelaide more, a sign, I suppose, that I too trusted Bella. At any rate I was glad to hear that her faithful service had not gone unrewarded.

'There's money sewn into my stays,' Aunt Adelaide had said. 'Seventy pounds in notes. Take it. It's yours. She shall have nothing, nothing.' And then she had sent for the lawyer.

'I've still got it, ma'am,' Bella said miserably. 'I've never felt sure, but she did say I was to have it, I swear, as God is my judge.'

'There's no doubt that the money is yours, Bella.'

It was a source of deep, vindictive satisfaction that Miss Goodlock had made such a hash of things. As a murderess she was not only loathsome but incompetent. Aunt Adelaide had lived long enough to thwart her evil purpose. More clearly than ever I realised by what a fine hair's breadth Honeywick had become Philip's and now mine. An insufficiency of force in that fiendish blow, an unexpected toughness in Aunt Adelaide's physique, more likely an abnormal flare up of spirit which had sustained her long enough to re-arrange her affairs: these things had not only robbed Miss Goodlock of her inheritance but had put her to flight, with only the things she could cram into her boxes. The thing she had most wanted was lost to her for ever: Honeywick.

As for me, I had no choice but to go back. It was extraordinarily difficult to get up and leave Bella, to give my mind to the trivial matters of packing and travelling, until suddenly I was inspired by a remarkable idea. Two problems could be solved in one happy stroke. I needed a servant; Bella had suffered, been cast upon the world, had undergone severe mental strain: it was almost a duty not to leave her here.

'Bella! Would you like to come to Honeywick as my

cook-housemaid?' I explained, warming to the idea. 'It would be like old times for you. You would feel near to Miss St Leonard there among her things in her old home. I believe, if she could know, it would be the very thing she would like.'

Her face brightened.

'I can just picture it.' Her eyes were dreamy. She wiped the tears from her cheeks. 'The parlour in particular. All those pretty things. My, the dusting.' She remembered it with a certain relish. 'It'd be like the old life in some ways. And yet it would be a new beginning. There's nothing to keep me here.'

'I must go home tomorrow and of course you'll have to work your notice, but I'll write to you and tell you exactly how to come . . .'

We discussed her position; she had no relatives or ties of any kind apart from some cousins in Bath where she came from. I felt more and more pleased with my plan. A well-trained, faithful servant had fallen into my lap and Bella herself deserved a stroke of good luck such as this. It occurred to me that if she continued in low spirits – a sign, I thought, of habitual melancholia – Mr Drigg might be consulted. Oh, it was an excellent idea, one which brightened to some extent the gloom of our conversation; but not much: Bella's figure, when I looked back from the road had already lost its clarity of outline in the hazy light above the water and taken on an unearthly, prophetic quality as if she had played her part and would melt into the grey air. The place, the mood, have remained dreamlike in their strangeness and horror.

'This letter should reach you tomorrow morning,' I wrote to Miss Bede, 'but I shall be home in the evening. There will be a wait at Kirk Heron. I shall arrive at Gower Gill at ten minutes to eight. There is no need to order a cab. I dare say my trunk has already arrived and I shall only have one bag with me.

'The past few days have been distressing. I have found out a good deal about Aunt Adelaide which has upset me deeply and which I cannot put down in a letter. Strangest of all, I have found her maid and have engaged her in Annie's place. Is it not lucky? We met entirely by chance. I might easily have left without seeing her. How it would have pleased Aunt Adelaide! It seemed the least I could do, to take her under my wing, and almost as if it were meant to be, since we have lost Annie . . .'

I was just in time to hand my letter to the clerk at the desk in the hall at the Hydro as he closed the mail bag.

'There's one for you, madam. It came on the last post.'

It was from Mr Drigg, a short note written from Gower Oaks. He reminded me of my promise to let him know the day of my return and actually offered to come to Matlock and fetch me home. What could have been kinder? I asked the clerk for pen and paper with the intention of writing a brief reply.

'I'm afraid it's too late for this evening's despatch, madam.'

Even as he spoke, the outer door swung to after the man who was taking the sealed bag to the Post Office.

'It doesn't matter.'

Except to show my gratitude for his thoughtfulness there was no need to write when I should shortly be seeing him; and so, as it happened, no one at Gower Gill knew of my return home – except Miss Bede.

Twenty-one

She was waiting on the platform when my train drew in at Gower Gill station: an unobtrusive figure in a cloak and an old, deep-brimmed bonnet which shadowed her face. She looked less elegant than serviceable and reliable. I was almost pleased to see her. At least I would not be returning to an empty house.

'Welcome home, Florence.'

Her voice was quiet and low as ever: she was never effusive; but she had been thoughtful in a practical way.

'You said there was no need to order the cab, but it felt like rain and I brought this.'

I got down and she helped me into it: a hooded mantle of dove-coloured worsted.

'How kind!' It was a handsome garment, lined and faced with twilled blue silk. 'And how nice it smells! Like flowers. I've never seen you wearing this.'

'It's too tight for me – now,' she added in afterthought, unnecessarily, for it must presumably have fitted her at some time.

'It's almost right for me except the length.'

It more than covered my black dress and jacket. Holding it up would be a nuisance. And how hot it was as she pulled the hood over my bonnet! But I could not protest when she had carried it all the way from Honeywick. Having tucked me into it, she picked up my bag.

'Oh please, let me . . .'

'Nonsense. It's as light as a feather. Give me your ticket.'

It was pleasant to be taken care of. We followed the half dozen other passengers to the barrier. They were all strangers to me, guests on their way to a local shooting lodge, no doubt, for grooms were carrying their luggage to a waiting brake. The railway clerk taking the tickets was too preoccupied to greet me and pass the time of day though he knew me well enough; or he may have mistaken us for members of the house party. Dressed as we were, we must have looked like a lady travelling with her lady's maid, both well protected from the weather.

Too well protected, for there was no sign of rain. It was a gusty wind that faced us as we climbed the hill: a dry, dust-laden wind rustling the overhanging trees and bringing down the first sear leaves. Low cloud threatened an early nightfall.

'You had my letter then? There is so much to tell.'

'Indeed there must be. You found your aunt well?'

With her usual skill she turned the conversation to Aunt Maud as a restful alternative, especially in these circumstances, to Aunt Adelaide. This was certainly not the time or place, as I panted uphill a step or two behind and already perspiring in my mantle and hood, to embark on the terrible story I had hinted at in my letter.

'You were right about the Hydro. It exactly suited Aunt Maud.'

But not Aunt Adelaide, I recalled. One might as well go to prison, she and Mrs Petch had agreed, as stay in the Hydro and know nothing of what went on outside. If I had stayed safely in the Hydro, I might never have met Bella.

'I'm glad you were comfortable. You must tell me all about it.'

But when the lane brought us to the top of our own hill and we came out of the deep cleft between tree-clad banks into the open again, I had no wish to talk. The sad scent of dying heather, a glimpse of distant headstones in the churchyard, moved me to an agony of longing for Philip. Honeywick lay below, unlit from within. A fitful grey sheen caught the bow window and left it dark again as clouds moved above the colourless hills beyond.

I started as a hunting owl swerved from a pale-barked birch on our left and sailed above our heads: deliberate, elusive, scarcely seen before it was gone.

'Do let me take the bag.' Contrite, I remembered Miss Bede. 'I shouldn't let you.'

'But I insist. I'm much stronger than you.' In spite of the bag she had been walking quickly as if borne up by a strong tide of energy. It was hard to keep up with her. 'And we're almost there.'

In the shade of the east-facing terrace, the fox's head grinned and gleamed as bright as – no, brighter than – ever. The flag-stones, the white paint, the door step, the flower pots, were all immaculate as if recently brushed, wiped, swept, watered and divested of withered petals and leaves.

'Mrs Churnside has come regularly,' I observed.

Miss Bede set down the bag, brought out the key from her pocket, opened the door and ushered me in like a guest.

'I told her I could manage without her.'

The hall smelt of beeswax and flowers. There were old-fashioned moss roses, freshly cut, in a bowl.

'You've done everything yourself?'

It was not what I would have expected. It was even, as I recalled Miss Bede's capacity for sitting with her hands folded in her lap – astonishing. A flicker of uneasiness troubled me: a warning that things had changed, though not physically. The hall, lit only by one low window, was almost dark. The feel of the house, forgotten and now recollected as I stood at the foot of the stairs, was in no way different, only more intensely familiar, as I breathed again its dense atmosphere of rugs on carpets, and door mats on rugs; of heavy curtains, massed ranks of pictures, mirrors. Miss Bede struck a match and lit the lamp; and there was the stoat, crouching, teeth bared, as if caught in a moment of ferocity and doomed to go on snarling for ever.

'But Mrs Churnside would be disappointed,' I said. 'She needs the money.'

'I gave her some to keep her happy – and to keep her away.'

'Then you've been quite alone all this time.'

Lamplight crept up the long-case clock as far as its bland face. Miss Bede untied her deep-brimmed bonnet and I saw her clearly for the first time that evening. She was thinner, and different in some other way. Not exactly younger-looking. Her most striking characteristics, I now realise, were of an ageless kind, typical of no particular decade in life, but mature.

'I've been kept busy.'

She turned, having adjusted the wick, and seeing me in the lamplight, caught her breath sharply as if startled at finding me there.

'You must have been. Still, it's wonderful, isn't it, that we shall have Bella? Meeting her was an amazing stroke of luck.'

'Ah yes. Bella,' she said. 'I'll take your bag upstairs.'

I had expected her to say more; to find the discovery of Bella more remarkable. She went up lightly. Watching her from the bottom of the stairs until she vanished into the darkness of the landing, I groped mentally for the key to the change in her. She had not only grown thinner but less substantial in some way other than physical; more inwardly directed; less outwardly responsive. It was as if by a tiny margin she had become less a creature of flesh and blood than the embodiment of an idea, or a mood: a mood of – elation. A long spell of having the house to herself had suited her. She had always liked it; liked being here.

I turned, and in the long glass behind me saw what she had seen, and with a similar catch of the breath: a faceless woman in a hood. It could have been – anybody. One woman in a hood, as Mrs Blanche had pointed out, is like any other woman in a hood. Like a flash there came to me a memory of the woman Laban Badgett had seen one evening a year past February on the field path between the house and the churchyard. I knew now who it might have been. Not Aunt Adelaide, who at that time had been already dead; not a bodiless phantom at all, nor one of Mr Drigg's patients, but Miss Goodlock in travelling dress, come for a last look at the inheritance she had longed for, risked damnation for, and lost.

The idea, once conceived, rapidly gained strength and threatened to possess my mind. The hateful Miss Goodlock here, in Gower Gill! I was almost sure of it. Something in her appearance on the path which went nowhere but to Honeywick's side gate had roused in Laban a feeling of familiarity and misled him into thinking it must be the lady of the house. It would be like Miss Goodlock, I thought bitterly, to have actually been wearing Aunt Adelaide's clothes: something she had stolen, common thief that she was – and worse.

The whole suffocating weight of that infinitely worse thing she had done thickened the very air and threatened to stifle me. I went into the parlour, slowly undoing the loops and buttons of the mantle. Miss Bede ran downstairs and went briskly into the kitchen.

'I haven't told you yet,' I said over my shoulder, 'what I found out. It was – oh, so terrible.'

My voice faded into a yawning sigh. She had not heard; or at least she did not answer.

'It didn't rain,' I called, taking refuge in banality as I folded the mantle and draped it on the sofa. My skin felt hot and dry after the journey. The fire burned low. As always in old houses in summer it did not so much warm as ventilate the room. I was glad of it as a focal point, somewhere to settle, and sank down on my green stool only to be overcome with misery at the sight of Philip's empty chair. The absence of his hand caressing my hair was a positive sensation, cruel as a blow. I got up and roamed restlessly about the room. After the spacious Hydro, the parlour felt small and would have been claustrophobically so had it not been for the open archway to the dining parlour offering escape: but framing – for she had quietly appeared there – Miss Bede.

'It was amazing, wasn't it, that I should meet Bella? She was working in the pleasure gardens.'

'I don't understand how you recognised her.' Miss Bede put down the lamp on the writing table. 'It couldn't have been that she recognised you.'

'It was something she said. Everything suddenly fitted together. I had already been to Aunt Adelaide's rooms in Masson View, you see, and talked to the people there.' Having begun with some animation, I stopped, daunted by the memory of Mrs Petch and Mrs Catchbent. It was all too much, simply too much to tell just yet. 'She's supposed to give a month's warning, Bella, I mean. But she thought her employer, Mr Tanner, might release her sooner as the season is nearly over. He may be quite glad to let her go almost at once and I promised to make up the money she would lose in wages . . .'

'Will she write to you?' The question was casual. 'Or suddenly arrive?'

'I've already given her the fare. She will write, at least she said so; but it wouldn't at all surprise me if she simply turned up without warning. She's a strange girl. But I'm sure she was a faithful servant to Aunt Adelaide and loved her dearly. I wonder what you'll think of her. I haven't told you yet, what she told me about Aunt Adelaide's death.'

I shivered and felt less inclined that ever to embark on the story.

'What do you say to having supper here by the fire, as you used to do when you were ill? I have the tray almost ready.'

'It would be very pleasant. Let me help.'

'No, you sit still. I'll do it.'

Her kindness touched me. How thoughtful she was! With the same lightness as if she were treading on air, she went into the dining parlour and came back with a cloth and cutlery. I watched idly as she pulled out the little gate-legged table.

'How beautifully you've kept everything!' Cloth and napkins were freshly laundered, knives scoured, forks polished.

Her smile, as she looked round, was tender. Again I found, or fancied I found in it, a trace of suppressed exaltation, a euphoria she could not quite subdue. Could she actually be excited at having me home again? What nonsense! Kind as she was, attentive to my needs (unusually so), in a curious way it was as if she didn't notice me; as if she had not yet taken me in as a living person: Florence – her landlady, I thought, with an hysterical recollection of Mrs Catchbent and her superior status as a landlord. I was still, in this first hour of my return, an intruder into the life Miss Bede had made for herself while she had been alone. A woman living alone, Mr Drigg said, was liable to strange aberrations from the normal. I suppressed another yawn, conscious of her physical energy as she glided in and out.

She had been lavishing it on the house. The room had never looked better. In its way, in its blending of the natural and artificial, it was perfect: a haphazard assembly of porcelain, glass, fabric and wood brought into harmony with the space it enclosed, and moulded into a small work of art through generations of cherishing, the shapes and colours interspersed with enchanting glimpses of hills and trees and sky beyond the two windows. In this detached mood, I discovered it all again like a newcomer and understood how a person could fall in love with it, especially a person with nothing else to love or live for, with no home of her own: a dependant paid to be pleasant in other people's homes. Only, to want a thing too much could be disastrous; and to have it in the end – that could bring catastrophe, if it happened to be the wrong thing to want: someone else's property.

The thought was ominous. It threatened to lead me into ways I could not face just yet. Instead I pulled out the nearest volume of Mrs Banstock. The embroidered bookmark fluttered to the floor. Forget-me-not, it pleaded.

And at once as if in instant obedience, I remembered her. I felt the room peopled again with those who had left it. What more likely than that the bookmark had been a gift to Aunt Adelaide from her faithful companion? I dropped it like a hot coal. With sudden nausea I recollected that not only Aunt Adelaide and Bella but also Miss Goodlock had known this room. She had sat here. Where? Involuntarily I moved over to Philip's chair. This, I thought, leaning back my head where his had rested, was where I would always sit. Here I felt safer and could not see it empty of his beloved form. Being the most comfortable, it had probably been Aunt Adelaide's chair. *She* – the other – must have sat opposite. Blankness confronted me. No single detail of her appearance floated up from the void into which she had vanished. A plainly-dressed woman, quietly spoken, head bent over her embroidery; but a strong woman, who could carry her own boxes down Mrs Catchbent's steep stairs; a woman of thick wrists and strong shoulders.

Save for the clock's ticking and the occasional light fall of wood ash there was no sound. But tired though I was, I could not relapse into drowsiness and I sat stiffly, struggling against a growing disgust at the thought of that evil presence – here. No picture came, no image of her face or form; but the knowledge that she had wormed her way into the house sickened me as if a loathsome, low-bellied creature had crawled out from below the skirting board or oozed its way up out of the cellar. To think that she had actually been here: Aunt Adelaide's murderess, as she was to become. She had stood on the hearth-rug to warm her hands at the fire, or in the archway, her hand on the curtain – and at least once since then had lurked outside, to be seen by Laban Badgett and mistaken for Aunt Adelaide. And after that . . .? She must have gone away.

But not to stay away. Would she not hover like a baneful insect, vanishing for a time but inescapably drawn back to the irresistible light and warmth of the place she had fallen in love with. Simply to be here was for her to be in heaven; to walk with a lighter step; to float in a rarer air. One can see and instantly love; one could fall in love not with a person but with a place, a house. One could lust after it, scheme, deceive and murder to possess the object of one's infatuation; and having failed, one could try again. A place would not lose its beauty as a person might. Age could only add to its charm; so that the longer one waited, the more irresistible it would become.

'Such love lasts, do you think?' It was I who had put the question, thinking of another kind of love as I stared soulfully into the space between the occasional table and the corner cupboard.

'For ever,' she had replied, turning her eyes unwillingly from the vignette of leaves and green sloping fields framed in the window. 'One never changes.'

Not Miss Goodlock: Miss Bede.

A soft, shirring sound roused me: a gentle sliding movement on my left as the mantle slipped from the sofa to the floor, helpless to resist the smoothness of its silk lining and the weight of its heavy worsted. It subsided as if it had swooned – or died – leaving a faint, flower-like perfume, suitable for a funeral. Lily of the valley?

One moment I breathed naturally in a familiar world whose ways I knew, though they were darker and more dreadful ways than I could have dreamed of until a short time ago. A moment later and the morass opened at my very feet. My lungs were filled with the stench of evil here with me in the house.

She had indeed come back to Honeywick, bringing into my home the taint of murder. A feeling of shame, as if she had drawn me into her cruel usage of Aunt Adelaide made me physically ill. For more than a year I had lived with her like an accomplice, admiring the brooches, the rings, the lace, the parasol she had stolen from a dying woman, a kind and innocent friend.

'There! Now we can be more comfortable.'

My companion had brought in food and chocolate in the silver pot. On the last night, Bella said, they had sat up late, drinking chocolate and talking. I almost lost my head; dared not look at her; dared not looked away; dared not stay silent; but rushed into speech and said the first thing that came into my head.

'There was a trunk of Aunt Adelaide's things. They let me look at them.' I draped the mantle over the back of the sofa with insane care, my hands stiff and numb. 'There was scarcely anything really. She disliked having too many possessions. Mrs Petch told me. The woman who took her rooms. She only wanted the few things she could take with her.'

Miss Bede's manner was only half attentive as she arranged the table to her liking, and when she spoke her remark had the accommodating ease of one who had spent her life in affable small talk.

'Like a snail,' she suggested, 'creeping from place to place, taking everything with it.'

The phrase, light as gossamer, floated across from Matlock to Gower Gill, spanning the gulf between past and present, the living and the dead. 'Creeping from spa to spa,' Aunt Adelaide had said. I had not thought the comparison with the snail particularly apt when Mrs Petch repeated it. It is not the snail's way to leave its house behind. It was no more apt now. The words had been slipped mechanically, unthinkingly, into a familiar groove.

'Do come and sit down.'

I forced myself to watch her as she poured chocolate into the two cups. From the half smile, the satisfied sigh, the cool, slightly distant way in which she acknowledged my presence without feeling it, I sensed in her a subtle alteration she had for once been unable to control.

'You asked me if anything had happened while you were away.' She fingered the silver-clawed sugar tongs for the sheer pleasure of touching them. 'Nothing. Absolutely nothing.' She laughed gently from joy in the unchanging state of her precious Honeywick. 'Except that the back kitchen floor has been flooded again. You know, we might be able to put a stop to it by having the well drained or sealed off in some way.'

She talked of springs and pumps and pipes. I didn't listen. Something else had happened besides the flooding of the kitchen floor. Alone here in the house she loved, at one with all its moods, wiping and polishing and folding its countless contents, moving from room to room, she had crossed the threshold from wanting to having. The scheming and longing were over. She believed herself actually to be mistress, felt herself to be. Her preparation of the meal, her entire welcoming behaviour were not directed towards my comfort: they were simply appropriate to her rôle. All this was clear to me as I sat sick and ill, hating her with such intensity that it must surely be visible. She must see and feel it even through the haze of unreality in which she seemed to float.

'You aren't eating anything.'

The wry smile and the quizzical lift of the eyebrows were familiar but she spoke from a formal distance, isolated by make-believe as she had been by the inscrutable veil I so much admired. It was not the sun she had retreated from but the sharp eyes of Mrs Blanche. There was just a chance that the old lady might have caught a glimpse of her when she brought honey and eggs to the back door. How easy, after all, the deception had been! What unsuspecting babes she must have thought us, Philip and me! What innocent lambs inviting in the wolf and making it welcome! But now security had made her a little deaf, a little blind. She suspected nothing of my inward turmoil. She had grown so well used to deceiving us that my stupidity could be taken for granted. So that for once, in a way, the advantage was mine. For once I knew what lay behind her enigmatic dark stare; what thoughts occupied her darker mind; whereas she could not know mine.

'I'm not hungry,' I said and caught a glimpse of myself, green-faced, in the chimney glass as I went to the window and pushed it open.

'You're too warm?' The tone was that of a hostess, conventionally anxious for the comfort of a guest.

The air revived me. Across the road the thorns creaked in the warm wind. To the east the sky was heaped with dark blue clouds pricked by a few stars. I felt the remoteness of their beauty, of all that was beautiful and good. If I were to challenge her: 'You are Miss Goodlock. You killed Aunt Adelaide,' what would she say?

'You are not yourself, Florence, not yet, not quite.' I knew the tone exactly. It would be soothing and urbane, but naturally wounded: it was not the sort of remark to be accepted without protest.

More likely she would kill me, or try to, and not for the first time. I discovered that the white face of Miss Goodlock at the top of Mrs Catchbent's stairs was indistinguishable from the white face of Miss Bede on Holleron Edge. It was perfectly obvious to me now that the accident had been contrived. Philip had boasted that there would always be St Leonards at Honeywick. A new generation would be the last thing she would want. Behind her veil she had calculated and decided. It was my lot to be removed first. There must be no heir. Philip would have his turn later.

'I took so much trouble.' She sounded aggrieved, but playfully so. 'And you haven't eaten a crumb.'

Turning, I saw her looking with concern at my plate and cup.

I could fly at her, tear out her hair, batter her with the fire irons; and she, being so much the stronger, would kill me, by strangling perhaps. It wouldn't matter in the least; but to precipitate the crisis, to fill the quiet room with fierce movement and noise, was unthinkable; or rather, my ability to think of it robbed me of the reckless savagery which was the only state in which I could bear to lay hands on her – to touch her.

'Early to bed? You're very tired, and so quiet.'

'It has all been so unpleasant and distressing – about Aunt Adelaide.'

It was she who had taught me to prevaricate in this smooth fashion. My lips formed the words stiffly. It seemed impossible that she could not feel the hatred and contempt that swelled my throat. 'And then the journey.'

'Your holiday hasn't done you any good. Not a bit.'

She drained her cup, then deftly, lovingly, replaced the china on the tray, believing, in the glamour of her delusion, that they were hers. Presently she took them away, passing under her archway through her dining parlour to her kitchen.

Yes, for once I had the advantage. She could have no idea that I knew. She had also taught me the art of biding one's time, though by temperament I was ill-suited to it. With dismay I discovered that the situation had no foreseeable end. To survive in this horrible state, alone here with a murderess, to live with her and share my meals with her, might just be tolerable provided some term could be set to it, some date to look forward to, some climax.

Such words are ludicrously inadequate to describe my utter helplessness. I simply didn't know how to deal with her. She should be denounced, locked up, brought to justice. But how could this be done without a shadow of evidence of guilt. There had been nothing visibly amiss in Miss Bede's conduct. There was nothing to connect her with Miss Goodlock. What, for that matter, could be proved against Miss Goodlock? In any case Miss Goodlock could never be found. She had presumably ceased to exist when she became Miss Bede; or was it Miss Bede who had never really existed? There was a peculiar horror in trying to accept the two as one, like a double-headed monster twice as destructive as any single enemy could be. Between them, called by whichever name, they were responsible for all the wretchedness of my life.

And never in my life had I felt so completely alone. No one knew that I had come home. Even the railway clerk had not recognised me, swathed as I was in the hood which Miss Bede had so thoughtfully provided to conceal my identity. Mrs Churnside had been paid to keep away. The Badgetts were gone. Since the accident, on the very day they went away, I had been housebound for months and had lost touch with the village folk, all except Mrs Blanche. She too had left, and Annie. Mr Drigg didn't know where I was. Philip was dead, dead. I was marooned here on the hillside a quarter of a mile from the nearest dwelling.

I went back to the fire and stared at the mantelpiece so thickly thronged with ornaments that there was scarcely room for my icy fingertips. All those pretty things! With a gasp of relief I remembered Bella.

Twenty-two

My ordeal would, after all, come to an end. Simply to have another person there, of any kind, would ease the intolerable tension. But in this dilemma Bella was the one person who could bridge the gap between Matlock and Gower Gill. She would arrive on the doorstep and recognise Miss Goodlock.

I saw it all clearly: her pale melancholy face; her large eyes nervous as a deer's under her plain bonnet, for she would still be wearing her outdoor things; her sudden recoil as from a rattlesnake; her revulsion; her fury. I even saw the look of angry accusation she would turn on me as she felt herself betrayed.

It was at this point that imagination failed me: failed entirely to tell me what would happen next. The clear picture of Bella's arrival disintegrated into meaningless fragments. She would never believe that I had brought her here innocently, not knowing that the other lady in our household of two was Miss Goodlock. That was the least of my problems. After Bella, struggling between astonishment and rage, had denounced her enemy, what then? It was difficult to think of the one she accused as remaining merely passive, standing head bowed in shame before the accusing finger; impossible to imagine her out-witted and defeated. The prospect of some dreadful skirmish, an actual physical onslaught by Bella on Miss Bede, could not be ruled out – nor could the reverse. Of the two it was Miss Bede – or Goodlock – who had shown herself capable of physical violence. I cringed at the thought; and in my shrinking cowardice was unreasonable enough to clutch at the one straw to present itself, and an unpromising straw it was: that I would not be the only one to have foreseen the implications of Bella's arrival. 'Will she just arrive?' she had asked casually. She must have seen Bella instantly as a threat. She would deal with it. There was nothing she could not deal with.

In my anxiety I couldn't remember precisely what arrangement I had made with Bella. I must write to her now, at once, and post the letter in the morning. At the earliest it would reach her the day after tomorrow. The irony of taking my letter sedately to the Post Office and then returning to have lunch with the woman who had killed Aunt Adelaide did not strike me as I worried over the actual message. Bella must be warned. My heart contracted as I thought of what I might be leading her into; yet I wanted her to come. Indeed she must come and do what no one else could do: identify Miss Goodlock. But the plans I had made for her future and my own and Miss Bede's had gone hopelessly awry. There was nothing whatever to replace them. Except for the obvious fact that Miss Bede – or Miss Goodlock – must be got rid of, I had no plan in mind, nor even any notion of what to do now, this minute.

Neptune chimed the half hour: half past nine. The mellow notes came to me from a lost age, a sedate and gracious way of life. Mechanically I compared the dial with that of my watch as I had done every night since Philip took to his bed. It had been his habit and became mine. It brought a merciful quietening of spirit and taught me what I must do. So long as she did not suspect that I knew, everything must go on in exactly the old way, down to the smallest detail. Moreover the old routine would save me from having to talk to her or look at her. In half an hour I could go to my room, sit down alone and think clearly before writing to Bella.

I went into the hall. The candlesticks, polished and wax free, stood as usual on the table. They had been fitted with new candles. I lit the one in the big bronze candlestick.

'Florence! You're not going to . . .' She came out of the kitchen, untying the strings of her apron. 'Not tonight. You're much too tired.'

'It doesn't tire me.' I felt her watching me as I went upstairs.

Of all the memories of Honeywick that haunt me – sublimely happy, painful, terrifying – it is the memory of the nightly ritual that remains most constantly. Philip had made it more than a practical household task to secure the shutters and doors, rake out and guard the fires. For him it was an excuse to take a last loving look at the house at the end of the day. For me it became a last loving tribute to Philip; so that there was always love in it; and I am glad that on this particular evening I was blessed with a brief return to the tender mood of earlier days and, in spite of everything, with some feeling for the house itself, though I came no nearer than ever to understanding what my feeling for it was.

I went from room to room and as I made fast casements agitated by the gusty wind and shut out the darkening garden, hills and sky, I could have fancied that each room quietly awaited its turn to be looked at; offered its pale walls and dark furniture to the wan candle-light; suffered the invasion of its shadows, knowing there was nothing to conceal. They were faultless. She had tended them with unflagging devotion. Something like admiration made me pause at the door of her room. I could imagine how while I was away she had come each night to stand here – or there – to be ravished by fresh vistas and new angles, by sudden patches of sky and stars, the glitter of trinkets on the dressing tables, the curves of chairs and tables. I almost understood her passion.

She was in the hall when I went down.

'Let me do the rest. I've finished in the kitchen.' She reached out to take the candlestick. 'Come. I insist.'

This time the proprietary manner irked me as she must have known it would. My sympathy melted. The sheer cheek of it! The presumption affected me more just then than her infinitely worse offences.

'Now that I'm home again,' I said firmly, 'I must do things as usual in my own way.'

She gave in at once with a half-humorous gesture of agreement.

'Yes, yes. Of course. I'm interfering again. I only thought . . . for once.'

'It won't take me long.'

She opened the cellar door for me. Her dark eyes with a candle burning in each of them were the last things I saw as I went down.

Behind me the door swung to and closed with a quiet click of the latch. Immediately a gust of wind from the yard door put out the light. But I was impatient now to be finished with the least pleasant part of this self-imposed duty. It would not be the first time I had crossed in the dark to the far door. It stood a few inches ajar and gave a measure of light so that I could make out the shapes of the stone benches. Over there by the far wall were the brine tubs and to their left in the corner behind the yard door stood a huddle of mops and brooms.

The air was cold and damp like the air of a cavern. I went down step by step, anxious not to stub my toes on the heavy stones securing the thick oaken lid of the well. The routine was coming back to me. I had learned to walk four or five paces forward, then round the lid, leaving it on my left as I turned towards the outer door. Then I would heave it into its frame, shoot the bolts and come back with the well on my right to the foot of the steps.

A sudden revulsion from the dreary place made me resolve that this would be the last time. In future the yard door would be kept locked all the time. There was no need to use the cellar for buckets and garden furniture as Annie had done. For one thing it was too damp here for wicker chairs. There were plenty of outhouses. It was simply a question of going a few yards further up the garden with buckets, potato sacks and brooms. I would tell Bella.

The thought of Bella temporarily distracted me from my whereabouts. I had forgotten the abnormality of the situation. Bella would come and there would be some fearful crisis. I must give my mind to that. Yet here I was, planning her household duties as if there was nothing else to think of.

I stopped dead. It was the smell that warned me: the cold smell of water stealing up from the depths of the earth: a dank odour tainted with the residue of decaying matter and so pungent that it cleft the surrounding air, chilly as it was, and made it harmlessly tepid, except in one place, to my left. The well was uncovered.

I felt about with my left foot and touched the wooden cover only two paces from the bottom step. The stones had been moved, the cover pulled aside. Actually I could make it out now, the great hole, black against the grey flags. To skirt the cover on my left while it was in this unusual position would have been to step straight into the well. If I had run down the steps and skimmed across the cellar with one of my swallow-like darts . . . Even now, another step was more than I could risk.

I listened and guessed that on the other side of the hall door she was listening too. This was the moment she had prepared for as she dragged the stones from the position they had lain in for years, straining her strong muscles and powerful shoulders; then heaved aside the cover to leave the well gaping wide; a drop of fifty feet into darkness: oblivion. Then when I had fallen, she would open the door and come down, set down her candle, look into the well, see perhaps some trace, and satisfied, replace the cover and stones. No-one would know where I was or what I had discovered about her. If, having escaped, I went back now to the hall, she would drag me down again and push me in. It would be easier, less unpleasant if I went tumbling and splashing to my death alone; but that curious elation of hers would not long be quenched by the distasteful business of having to force me in. And afterwards if there were questions, she would have answers. 'Mrs St Leonard has not come back . . . Florence is still away . . . She has written . . . She has not written . . . I shall look after things until she comes back . . .'

All this I understood with the clear insight that comes to those in extreme danger. A moment more and I had passed from the paralysis of terror to white-hot rage. Standing there under the low vault, on the brink of death, I became a fiend possessed. The evil I had always thought of as an external danger attacked me from within, seized my heart and soul and filled me with an inward burning. Nothing in the house at the moment could outdo me in wickedness and rage, nothing in the world, not even she who had murdered Aunt Adelaide, killed my baby, bewitched Philip, ruined our marriage. Sinful as she was, she could not equal me in the power of hating. I felt in my throat and lungs the reek of water once life-giving but somehow grown foul, its natural sweetness polluted; and felt that I too had been corrupted.

The house above was still. She was waiting. I must not disappoint her. She must be satisfied. In the same moment that I grasped her intention I knew what my revenge would be. My purpose, as ruthless and cunning as any she could devise, came to me complete in all its details and set me tingling with a resolution as callous in its way as hers, and more macabre. The danger of wanting a thing too much was that one might get it, with disastrous results. She should have exactly what she wanted; the house she had coveted and risked her soul for with all its contents complete and with the addition of a permanent companion: a murdered girl.

I softly put down the heavy candlestick, stepped back to a safe distance from the well, untied and unhooked my skirt and stepped out of it, then my white silk petticoat, moving with quick precision as if I had become the instrument of whatever it was that possessed me. Two or three minutes had passed. I must be quick; and yet she would not, could not come – not yet. She would be waiting, white-faced, baffled by the silence . . .

I tore off my shoes and wrapped them with the candlestick in my skirt and petticoat. Then, not without a sick trembling as if it was to be a real death, I contrived a little commotion by beating on the oak cover as if I had stumbled against it in the dark, knelt down, groping for the edge of the well with one hand, holding the bundle in the other. Last and most terrible of all – an act which I cannot think of without losing all sense of my own identity – I leaned over. My head and shoulders drooped over the cavity. I screamed. I cannot tell what sort of sound it was that reverberated between the stone walls of the well, whether muffled, hollow or shrill. There is reason to think it sounded authentic, a crazy shattering of the silence like the cry of a terrified creature leaving the world. Waking in the night, I have heard it inside my skull, desolate as the howl of hyenas. The cold air caught my throat. Almost as an afterthought I dropped in the bundle and heard it ricochet from the upright walls, and in a little while meet the water. I dared to look down and saw nothing but an orb of darkness. But perhaps she would catch a glimpse of white petticoat as she leaned over, shuddering, before she replaced the cover.

It was then that I heard her call. 'Florence. Florence.' With the sound still in my ears, I crept to the yard door, slipped round it and into the blessed air, into the garden smelling of mint, into the wind. I stole behind the currant bush to the wicket gate. There I waited. Afterwards my feet and ankles were swollen and red with nettle stings but I did not feel their prick.

The hall window was still uncurtained and yellow with homely candle-light. From the back window of the parlour came the steadier glow from the lamp. I shrank closer to the hedge. In a little while the hall window dimmed. She must have nerved herself to pick up the candle. She must be opening the cellar door and going slowly down the steps. A few minutes passed. Then the yard door was slammed from within; the top bolt slid into its socket; then the lower one. It was after a much longer interval that a dull scraping sound reached me faintly. The cover was being replaced. There came a heavy thud, followed by another as the two stones were heaved back into position. All was safe. A body could slowly moulder there and no one need ever know. Nor would she ever know that there was none. She need never leave; would never want to. She could do me no more harm. I need never see her again. Never.

The rattle of the hall shutters roused me to my situation. A rectangle of light edged their panels, then vanished. She had drawn the curtains.

The fiendish anger left me. Shivering, I dragged myself away along the field path in my stocking feet and cotton petticoat, passed the tall clumps of broom and climbed the stile into the churchyard. Bats were fluttering about the black yew trees. I picked my way in and out of the tombstones and across the cold mounds to Philip's grave and lay face down on the grass.

Close to him like this, I felt the distance between us as never before. Another inch or two, an incautious step in the dark, and I would have followed him to wherever he had gone. Instead I had drawn back from the abyss and knew it now to be immeasurably wide, impossible to cross. In saving myself, I had lost him again. Worse still, I was glad of it. In my slowly growing gratitude for being alive, I felt more keenly than ever before the reality of his death. Lying with my face in the grass, with no other sound than the wind's dry rustling in the leaves, I took my real farewell of him. It was the final separation to know that he was dead and yet to want to live.

Turning, I watched the stars come and go in a dark blue windy sky. The thin bleat of a sheep came to me from a universe empty of people. Night airs crept across the sleeping fields and touched my cheeks and brow bringing a message: a new sensation. I felt light like them and for the first time in my life strangely free; as free as a woman ever can be.

Twenty-three

'I blame myself,' Mr Drigg said. 'There must have been some way in which I could have saved you from the ordeal. Not that any reasonable person could have foreseen such villainy.'

Once again I reassured him. The wine had done me good; but even without it I believe the feeling of lightness would have remained: the unutterable relief of having shed a burden too heavy for me to bear alone.

'All the same,' he persisted, 'it was wrong of me simply to observe the situation, though in fact there was remarkably little one could do. And yet, the case is so extraordinarily interesting.'

His eyes grew bright. As if in compunction he got up and found another cushion though I was already as comfortable as he and his housekeeper could make me. Wearing one of her skirts and wrapped in a rug, I simmered gently by a blazing fire to which Mr Drigg now added another log, his face rapt. He dusted his fingers absently on his coat tails: a sure sign of excitement in so fastidious a man.

'Except,' he went on, 'that it is not in any sense a case, as I have had to remind myself. The woman is not to be thought of as a patient. Hers is a moral disorder . . .'

I declined his offer of more wine. I did not need it, being sufficiently borne up by a new inner strength. It is not every day that one escapes being murdered, not that the most recent escape had been my first. To my gratitude for having been twice blessedly preserved was added the welcome sensation of hearing her discussed as Mr Darwin might have enlarged upon a specimen of wingless beetle or hairless dog. It removed her to a safer distance, a state of affairs Mr Drigg may have intended as he resumed both his chair and the absorbing topic, viewing the woman – there was really no other way of referring to her – from a standpoint refreshingly different from my own.

'Every individual is unique. We are each of us the sole heir of our particular circumstances; and think, I beg of you, Mrs St Leonard, think of the peculiar circumstances affecting this case. This woman, I should say.'

To tell the truth, I was tired of thinking of them: sated in fact by their unusual richness as food for thought. Nevertheless one circumstance had escaped my attention: a factor of special interest to Mr Drigg.

'The assumed name.' He brought his palms together in a restrained gesture of applause. 'That accounts for a good deal. Time and again I was baffled by a quality in her which I could not define. In exploring personality it is generally possible to reach at last to the sensitive point: the quick, as it were. In her case I failed to reach it. She could never be natural, you see. There was always a glancing off, an impenetrable shell. But the moment you told me of the change of name – Ah! I thought, that's it. It is not sufficiently understood how inseparable from our sense of reality is our acceptance of the fact that we are what we are called.'

It evidently cheered him to find some excuse for his failure to penetrate to the heart of the woman, as he continued to call her, though it seemed likely that she was Miss Goodlock rather than Miss Bede.

'You must not reproach yourself, Mr Drigg,' I said when he continued to do so. 'We suffered from our own mistakes and ignorance. How could you know or suspect the sort of person we had become involved with?'

'How? It shouldn't have been so very difficult. You see, there is something I haven't told you. A confession, if you like,' and as I stared in wonder he added sorrowfully, 'I was warned.'

'About her?'

'About her. As clear a warning as a man might hear – and neglect. I've been wanting to tell you the story for a long time, and more than ever since you came here tonight.' He shook his head at the memory of my arrival on his door step, wild-eyed and shoeless, in my black bodice and white cotton petticoat. 'Are you too tired to hear it now? In the morning perhaps.'

'Now if you please,' I said, quite at a loss as to who could have warned him.

'Then here it is.' He placed his hands on his knees and leaned towards me, his unusually large eyes growing mild as he forsook his professional manner and became his warm-hearted other self. 'For years I've been in the habit of spending a month or six weeks in early autumn with my sister and her husband. They live in Hammerdale, about ten miles north of Catblake. My sister looks forward to my visit. She says it helps her to face the winter. They have long winters up there. For that matter it will soon be time for me to leave again.

'However – it was when I was on my way there last August that the incident happened. It seemed then to be quite unconnected with Gower Gill or anyone in it. I didn't take the road that goes up the dale. Instead I took the upper road. I have property up there, two or three cottages, and I took the opportunity to see about some repairs. One good woman begged me to take a meal and I was much later in leaving than I had planned. I struck across Holleron Moor by a bit of a track and came on to the bridle path leading down the hill to Catblake – a shorter, and I always think a safer way than the road through the gully, which I don't need to remind you is not suitable for horses.' Mr Drigg's expressive face was becoming gloomy, even lugubrious. 'Certainly Daisy was happier on the green way, and her hooves hardly made a sound on the turf; so that I heard quite clearly, coming from the gorse bushes to the left of the path, something completely unexpected. The sound of sobbing. I stopped and saw a boy lying on the ground face down in – what shall I say? – I can only call it an abandonment of grief.'

'A boy in a green waistcoat?'

'Yes. Then you know who it was?'

'There was a boy who ran for help after the accident,' I said cautiously, feeling almost as startled as Mr Drigg himself. If the boy in the green waistcoat was the boy I took him for, the sobbing seemed strangely out of character.

Mr Drigg nodded and went on: '"Come, my boy," I said. "What's wrong?" He didn't seem to hear me. I got down and went to him. I could see that he was in a very poor state, half-starved and neglected; and I thought at first his distress was due to exhaustion and despair. But it was more than that. I gave him brandy from my pocket flask – and that was probably a mistake. It fuddled his wits, or so I thought. However, I got him to his feet. He was deeply shocked and it was hard to get a word out of him until all at once he burst out. "She's been killed." "Who's been killed, my boy?" I said. "Tell me," thinking of his mother or sister perhaps. He could have been a lad from one of the miners' cottages. In fact it didn't occur to me for a while that he was not. He spoke some name. "Slink?" I said and he had to repeat it several times before I made it into Miss Link or some such name.'

'Lincoln,' I said. 'My maiden name.'

'Of course! The name meant nothing to me then. He blurted out a garbled story of a bolting horse, a lady killed – and another woman. The bad 'un, he called her. He had been roaming about on the moor, I gathered, when he saw a gig coming up the hill. He had hidden in the bracken and watched, thinking there might be a penny to be got for holding the horse's head. He saw what happened and had evidently recognised the ladies. According to him the bad one had unfastened the curb chain and loosened the bridle, cracked the whip to frighten the horse and watched it bolt towards the Edge, completely out of control. By the way, I have gradually given shape in my mind to a story that was nothing more than a few broken sentences then. There seemed no sense in what he said. "She stands outside at night and watches," he said. "Outside where?" I asked and he pointed vaguely down the dale. I took it that the brandy had loosened his tongue and gone to his head – and didn't believe him.'

'Poor Jordan,' I said. He must have seen her standing outside the house and watching at the time when he himself was hiding in the potting shed. That was before she had come to stay at Honeywick. Like an unaccepted lover she had hung about the house at night: by day she had walked past it, giving no sign, as if she could not bear to see it and not have it.

'Needless to say the boy's story strikes me very differently now. He kept on pointing to the Edge, half a mile away, but I had neither time nor inclination to go out of my way. Besides it was too late. He said something about a farmer and I assumed that help had been fetched. I took him up behindme and rode on to Catblake. There's an inn of sorts there, the Grey Horse. I gave the landlord a shilling and told him to feed the boy and give him a mattress somewhere. Some gentleman further down the dale had thrashed him, he told me, for loitering on his property. I knew no-one of the name of Link or Slink and when I came home at the end of September and heard that young Mrs St Leonard was ill, there was no reason whatever to connect her with the incident. By that time I had forgotten the boy.

'Imagine my feelings when Miss Bede called on me to tell me that her young friend was suffering from delusions after being thrown from a gig, and might be the better for a period of rest and seclusion at Gower Oaks. Even so' – he gave a despairing shrug – 'there was only the tale of a young vagabond stupefied with hunger and half-drunk with brandy to shake my confidence in a lady of such impeccable manners and refinement. All the same it was shaken. I was on my guard against her from the start and my mistrust increased when I met the young lady in question and found in her nothing but the most robust sanity and courage. Physical delicacy there was, to be sure, and some nervous strain. Without having the least right to intrude, I was interested as to what could be causing it. And as for the boy, there was something about him, for all his wretched appearance, that appealed to me. He was not entirely as I have described him. There was a kind of fortitude, I suppose, that only the very strongest feeling would undermine, such as his concern for poor Miss Lincoln.' Mr Drigg sighed. 'A very deep concern.'

I was as deeply touched. Jordan Finch, the brave, impassive, stony-hearted Jordan, had cried, not for his own miseries but for me. For all my anxiety on his behalf, I felt a touch of selfish joy. There had been a chink in Jordan's armour which I, all undeserving, had found. A warm sense of having been loved and missed comforted me more than the fire or the wine. As Mrs St Leonard I had sometimes failed. As Miss Lincoln I had perhaps been more successful – and not only in my relentless pursuit of the capes and bays of Britain and the multiplication tables. There was a place in the world which I had occupied usefully. Confidence came flooding back; and it was Jordan who restored it. We had each of us met some need in the other. I marvelled at his faculty for turning up at critical moments in my life and grieved that he had slipped away again, believing me to be dead.

'I told him where I lived,' Mr Drigg said, when we had talked over the whole episode, 'and made him repeat the name. We could have found him something to do here.'

'He never came?'

'I'm afraid not. I left him leaning against the wall of the Grey Horse with his cap pulled over his eyes and his hands in his pockets . . .'

There was no hope of finding him now, a whole year later. It was unlikely that I would see him again. He had gone out of my life but not without changing it. He had altered its direction. Like a signpost appearing through mist to a lost traveller, he had pointed the way I must take. I had no doubt that it was the right one.

'We shall have to decide what is best for you to do,' Mr Drigg said when at last I got to my feet. The household had long since gone to bed. It was past one o'clock. I apologised for having kept him up so late. 'Tomorrow, not now. You must do nothing in haste. As for her –' he shook his head, 'we must talk it over. You may count on my help.'

'I should be grateful for your advice, Mr Drigg. But I

have already decided how it must be for her – and for me.'

I told him and saw perplexity, concern and disapproval in his mobile face.

'To leave her there in possession, alone with the consequences of her own misdeeds! That would be justice, I suppose, of a kind, provided . . . Are you not taking something for granted? Her remorse, I mean. Is it wise, or safe, to assume that she will feel – as she ought to feel?'

He waited a little anxiously for my response. But I was weary of thinking and talking. He must have sensed my mood.

'You are overwrought, my dear. As to what you suggest, it is an unusual course. Not at all one that I would have advised or expected. An unworldly decision. But for the time being it may be the right one, for you at any rate, though on the surface it is quixotic. Yes, that is the word.' He repeated it. 'And as for her –' his eyes brightened as if confronted with a web-toed pigeon or a fossilized horse – 'it will be interesting, extraordinarily interesting.'

We had reached agreement if from different motives. His warning had meant nothing to me. My mind was fixed upon Miss Bede's remorse. Anguished soul-searching was to be her punishment. In the torture chamber, they say, victim and torturer can become strangely involved in an unnatural closeness. I can see now that Miss Bede's personality had possessed me so entirely as to be inseparable from my own. A sinister twist in our mutual entanglement had reversed our roles, leaving me the torturer, her the victim. But I was far too much wrought upon by anger, fear and despair to judge her wisely or to see how unlikely it was that she would feel as I would have felt if her guilt had been mine.

'Everyone,' I told Mr Drigg gravely, 'however wicked, must have a conscience,' and left him looking thoughtful as I went to my room.

But not to bed. Sleep was out of the question. I was still sitting fully dressed in Mrs Townley's ample skirt and shawl when the sky grew light. Leaning on the windowsill, I looked south towards Honeywick. It stood on the hill above Mr Drigg's trees; invisible, then indistinct until, as the light grew, it took fitful shape; a wall, a gable end, a chimney of native stone; as if the house had grown out of the sloping fields or the fields had drawn aside to expose it. It seemed destined to last as long almost as the hills, the earth, and the water lying in its depths; but in the early grey-blue light it could be seen like a thing of air, indifferent in the heartless perfection of its own beauty to those who lived in it, whether they left or stayed.

I could be heartless too. Daylight found me as implacable as stone. She would stay where she had chosen to be. She would live with an axe poised above her head. I would see to it that none of the enquiries she expected would be made. Waiting daily, hourly, to be called to account, she would be left alone. The lies, deceit and subterfuges she would be involved in would meet with no resistance. The axe would never fall. She had, as she thought, committed the perfect crime and must suffer the perfect punishment: to live a murderess in solitary confinement with her victim always there. All I need do to consign her to endless suffering was to make sure that she never saw the living Florence again.

Having reached this monstrous conclusion, I watched the gentle blue of early autumn fill the sky. A column of white smoke rose from Honeywick's kitchen chimney, from the first of a lifetime of lonely fires. I watched it without pity, then lay down and slept.

Twenty-four

It was mid-morning but we had lit the gas. The yellow light shone dimly back from the misted Gothic windows and glistened on the damp walls. We had hung the wettest shawls and mufflers on the fireguard. The most dilapidated boots stood in a limp, uneven row below. The smallest of their owners sat in a privileged half circle round the stove, their bare feet dangling in the warmth; isolated from the rest of us by a faint steam like shabby cherubs on a cloud. It was still raining.

We were always slightly keyed up when Miss Wheatcroft was in charge as she now was. Mr Hawthorne had been obliged to go out. He had gone off a quarter of an hour ago in galoshes and waterproof, looking depressed, to an emergency meeting of the Society for the Protection of Destitute Boys.

'I'm afraid it will be bad news,' he said. 'The weather is against us. When I heard the rain in the night, I knew that we were coming to the end. There's no hope for the dormitory ceiling, no hope at all, and the repairs will be beyond us.'

'I'm sorry,' Miss Wheatcroft said. 'The Society has meant so much to you. Considering the vast sums of money wasted in profligate living, it does seem a shame.'

'And think of those boys. Twenty-two of them to be housed somehow. We can't turn them out on to the streets again. Ah well.' He unfurled his umbrella. 'We must salvage what we can from the wreck. I can rely on you to take charge, Miss Wheatcroft.'

Miss Wheatcroft bowed and became in some mysterious way more essentially herself. We all braced ourselves as if in response to a tightening of inner springs.

'He feels it,' she observed as the outer door closed on Mr Hawthorne. 'There's always something to worry him. But he's been looking happier lately. We were both relieved when Miss Partridge left. She had no idea . . . simply no idea.'

She straightened the map of the world and took up her cane.

'By a transitive verb,' she informed Standard VI, 'we mean a verb whereby an action is carried across from the subject to the object. The dog bit the boy.' She pointed at the blackboard and described a sweeping curve with the cane from the word 'dog' to the word 'boy'.

An imaginary line divided the schoolroom. Miss Wheatcroft and I, six feet apart, heard and ignored each other like rival hucksters in a market.

'Put down your pencils,' I said to my own flock, having come to the end of the dictation, 'and sit up.'

When every slate lay squarely on its desk and every pair of arms was folded across its owner's chest, I gave the signal and my class burst into that well-tried safeguard against lawless diversions, the five times table. Moving in spite of myself to its compulsive rhythm, I set off to mark the dictations. There were sixty of them this morning.

'James Caudle is eating toffee,' Miss Wheatcroft said out of the corner of her mouth as I passed by. 'Act cautiously or he may choke and there would be endless trouble. He's from a respectable home but the boy has gaol-bird written all over him. I sometimes wonder whether all this talk about heredity . . .' and without any change of manner – Miss Wheatcroft's manner never changed – she wrote rapidly in her unfailingly regular script, 'The farmer sowed the seed. The cook baked a pie. The squirrel hid a nut.'

I glared at James Caudle whose jaws became still.

'Boys who eat toffee when they are saying their tables could choke.' I passed on the message in ringing, prophetic tones and later to my annoyance had to remove a moist sticky substance from the heel of my shoe.

It was dinner time before Miss Wheatcroft found time to develop the subject of heredity and James Caudle.

'One never knows what breeding will throw up.' She unwrapped a cheese sandwich from a white napkin. 'Or why. Some dark destiny may be working itself out in him of which his parents may be guiltless.'

Unconsciously she raised her buttoned boots to the second rung of her high chair though there was little danger from mice, the room being half full of children who had come provided with pasties and apples rather than risk another wetting by going home to dinner.

'It's on days such as this,' Miss Wheatcroft indicated the steady slide of rain on the windows, 'that you must be especially glad to be back in town.'

A smell of burning boot prevented me from answering at once but when I had rescued the dried footwear and distributed it to the appropriate feet, she returned to the topic.

'I was always a little dubious as to whether you would take to rural life. Even if all had gone well, I mean. Like me you were brought up in town. There's no denying it, town life is so much more – what shall I say?' She munched correctly, considering.

'Safer,' she might have said. I sneezed carefully into my handkerchief, having picked up another cold. Oh, so much safer!

'More restful. Especially now that we have the horse trams in Peel Road. By the by, you are comfortable in your rooms? The reason I ask is that there is one to let on my landing. It's a little larger than mine and the rent is two shillings a week more. But I dare say you have no need to consider the odd shilling now. To be truthful it isn't as good a room as mine. Being at the back it has no view of the canal but there is a very good deep cupboard. I don't mind confessing that the cupboard has sometimes tempted me – or would have done had it not been for the higher rent. Since I have taken up rug-making I'm hard pressed sometimes to – well, to move at all.'

'It must be difficult to find room for the frames and canvasses in addition to your painting and sewing things.'

'It is indeed. But then there is the convenience of having everything immediately to hand. I told my landlady that I would mention the room. You are rather far from Marshall Street at present.'

'Oh, but the Fairfolds have made me so very comfortable,' I said, 'and I can tell you in confidence that the rent is lower than it should be for such a large room and in such a pleasant district as Barton Square.'

'You've been lucky again,' she said without envy. There was no denying the good fortune but the word 'again' made me ponder. 'And since your own house is let, you need have no financial worries. You can afford to take up some interesting and worthwhile pastime.'

She pointed out the advantages of rug-making. Yes, I felt safe with Miss Wheatcroft. She had witnessed my launching and seen me sail away into strange seas; and with the same calm interest had been here on the quay to welcome me back; for I think she was pleased if only at the excellence of my judgment in preferring Marshall Street to Gower Gill. In this she was unlike Mr Hawthorne who had been troubled by a decision which seemed to him a backward step.

'You're young, Florence, and should go forward, especially as you have the means. Of course I'm delighted to have you here again. It was extraordinarily convenient that Miss Partridge should take flight just at the right moment. Between ourselves any moment would have been the right one.' He could smile now over the memory of Miss Partridge. 'And it's gratifying to know that her musical talent will be appreciated in a more refined atmosphere. But as to whether you are doing the right thing . . .'

I had not confided in him. Only Mr Drigg knew how my life at Honeywick had ended; or, more accurately, how my life had almost ended at Honeywick. I had written to Bella explaining that my circumstances had changed. She replied on a torn piece of notepaper that it was just as well: Mr Tanner had been 'furious' at the very mention of her leaving; and no wonder, since he had apparently cherished tender feelings towards Bella for some time. His declaration had been followed, astonishingly, by a proposal of marriage. Bella wrote in resignation rather than rapture:

'He's decided to go to America, business is that bad here. He has a brother there in the hotel business in a big way.' She was not sure exactly where. 'There's a big waterfall there. Very big. I'm sick of water what with the river and them boats here and it turns my stomach to think of all that ocean.'

That was the last I ever heard of Bella but I have often

thought of her, anxious-eyed, unworldly, and always in a watery element as if half-dissolved in mist and spray.

On Mr Drigg's advice I had taken Mary Fairfold at her word and sought her out at her parents' home in Barton Square. They had all been as kind and welcoming as if we had been lifelong friends. It was assumed that Honeywick was let once again, this time to the friend who had shared it with us.

'You've caught another cold,' Miss Wheatcroft said as I sneezed again. 'Living in the country has undermined your health. I saw that at once. It will take you a little time to recover your tone. Have you tried wrapping a stocking round your throat when you go to bed? And a boiled onion does help.'

I bit into my own bread and cheese and took a furtive peep at the dates of the Plantagenet kings in *Highways of History Book II*. It would never do to let Miss Wheatcroft know that my memory of the Henrys was becoming blurred. In fact Henry III had almost slipped away. Sniffing, between bites, I pinned him down to 1216 with a sigh of relief; and there came to me through the restless room, penetrating the smell of worn clothes and damp hair, of chalk and mice and cheese and children, a whiff of the old familiar happiness, together with a touch of eager anticipation which was quite new. I glanced at the door.

'He should be back by this time,' Miss Wheatcroft observed. 'Of course if the Society is actually to be wound up, it will be a long meeting. If by any chance he shouldn't be back in time for Hereward the Wake, I think the best thing would be for you to take the girls for needlework all the afternoon while I . . .'

Whatever fate she had intended for the boys they were delivered from by the arrival of Mr Hawthorne. We heard him in the porch. Someone ran to open the inner door. Someone else ran to take his umbrella. From the corridor came the sound of his voice raised to an unusually high pitch; not in anger; I was sure of that and sat up scarcely able to wait.

'You're smiling,' Miss Wheatcroft pointed out.

'Was I smiling? It was just that Mr Hawthorne sounded – excited.'

He was there, had burst into the room, his coat darkly patched with wet.

'Miss Wheatcroft! Miss Lincoln! I mean, Mrs St Leonard! Florence! What do you think? You cannot guess. The most astonishing thing . . .'

Rain dripped from his sleeves and boots. His face was alight. He advanced radiant, leaving wet footprints on the floor. We waited. Miss Wheatcroft remained calm but she held a sandwich motionless halfway to her lips. The warm tide of anticipation swelled. My cheeks grew hot.

'The roof?' I prompted cunningly. 'The dormitory ceiling?'

'Oh, the ceiling came down. Nobody was hurt. Buckets everywhere.' He spoke recklessly, almost gaily.

'Take off your wet things, Mr Hawthorne,' suggested Miss Wheatcroft, 'and tell us what has happened.'

'The fact is' – he looked triumphantly from her to me – 'we have been reprieved. We have found a benefactor. The Society for the Protection of Destitute Boys is solvent. Not only solvent but wealthy. A gift. We have received a splendid gift – at the eleventh hour. Do you know how much?' His voice broke. He mopped his face.

'How can we possibly know, Mr Hawthorne?' Miss Wheatcroft said.

'Four thousand and nine hundred pounds. There! I knew you'd be astonished.' He struggled out of his coat. Someone ran to hang it up. 'I must tell you about it. All five trustees were there. We arrived in funereal mood. The Master and Matron were deeply worried. They had been moving beds out of the puddles and trying to get the blankets dried when they heard that there was to be an extraordinary meeting. Naturally they feared the worst. Well, there we sat, facing the end. "I have news for you, gentlemen," said Bolding, the Secretary, and produced a letter from the Martlebury and District Bank. He read it aloud. I won't deny there was a commotion. Somebody cheered. We all applauded, clapped one another on the back, congratulated the Master, had in the Matron. She burst into tears . . .'

'Some wealthy manufacturer,' Miss Wheatcroft surmised. 'One who has risen from the gutter and has not forgotten his origins as so many of them have.'

'Perhaps. You may well be right, Miss Wheatcroft. You generally are.'

'You don't know?'

'The gift is anonymous. In my opinion that makes it all the more worthy. It must have been given in a spirit of pure charity with no wish to impress the public. But the giver will be blessed, whoever he is. Just think – far from having to find homes for those twenty-two lads, we'll be able to take in more. Find better premises. The prospects are dazzling.'

'You have no idea who it might be?'

'No notion, Miss Wheatcroft.' He turned to me so abruptly that I jumped. 'Do you know, Florence, I feel as I did when you and Philip came into your legacy. It was as if good fortune fell from the skies. You remember the feeling?'

'I do remember.'

'You said four thousand and nine hundred pounds,' said Miss Wheatcroft.

'Exactly. And you, Miss Wheatcroft,' said Mr Hawthorne jovially, 'will have no difficulty in working out the income it will bring. Come now, Florence,' when Miss Wheatcroft did not instantly reply, 'at four per cent?'

I had every reason to know; but before I could impress him with the speed of my arithmetic, Miss Wheatcroft remarked, 'It seems to me an odd sum.'

'In what way? Odd in the sense of unusual? There I do agree.'

'I meant odd in the sense of its not being a round sum. A wealthy benefactor, I should have thought, would have given five thousand. It's as though a hundred pounds had been deducted for some reason.'

'We must not cavil, Miss Wheatcroft. A quarter of the sum would have been generous beyond our dreams. Now, if you'll excuse me, I must slip over to the house.'

'Mrs Hawthorne doesn't know yet?' I roused myself to ask, my voice trembling in spite of my assumed calm.

'It will be a great joy to her. She has grown thoroughly tired of hearing me moan about the Boys' Home. What a wonderful day this has been!'

'You mustn't go out without a coat, Mr Hawthorne.'

Someone ran with the waterproof. Someone else brought the umbrella. But he waved them aside and was gone looking, as Miss Wheatcroft said, ten years younger.

'He is always so taken up with one problem or another that one thinks of him as an older man. Older, I mean, than he actually is. No, I don't know exactly but still on the right side of forty. Mrs Hawthorne once told me that his birthday is the same as the Princess Royal's. They were born on the same day, 21st November' – Miss Wheatcroft rarely forgot a date – 'but not in the same year. Mr Hawthorne is four years older than Her Royal Highness. Judging by her portrait in Bateson's print shop in Market Street, she looks a good deal younger than Mr Hawthorne but then she was obviously very much got up for the occasion in her state robes and tiara. It's difficult to make comparisons. Their situations are very different.'

'They are indeed.'

'All the same I do feel that four thousand nine hundred pounds is an odd sum . . .'

Again I was obliged to agree. My respect for Miss Wheatcroft's acumen deepened. After careful thought I had kept one hundred pounds of Aunt Adelaide's capital and had arranged with Bretherby and Butterwick for a headstone to be erected over her grave. A small sum was spent on clothes to equip me respectably for the life of a school ma'am. The rest would serve as a nest egg.

I could not have explained why it was necessary to give it all up: the house, its contents and the money too. They had never really been mine. They had caused nothing but trouble. My instinct was to break free of them. And now at last some good had come out of the miserable affair. Twenty-two boys – and more – would be housed, clothed and fed, and saved from the hardship which had driven Jordan like an outcast into the wilderness. Mr Hawthorne was happy. Now I could begin to be happy too.

Miss Wheatcroft had come to the end of her one daily indulgence: a peppermint. She looked at her watch, smoothed her well-disciplined hair, dabbed the corners of her mouth with a handkerchief; then got down from the chair, straightened the map of the world and rang the bell for afternoon school.

Twenty-five

After that one dramatic day we resumed our monotonous routine. It was as easy to fit into Marshall Street's narrow mould as if I had never left it. I had no time to think of anything except how to deal with the demands of each harassing minute. For hours on end, then for days and weeks, it was possible to forget the past, at least during the day.

It was Mary Fairfold who helped me through the evenings. We had instantly been drawn together when Mr Drigg brought her to call at Honeywick and now we became friends. When her parents generously offered me a room in their house, they may have had her welfare in mind as well as my own. We were company for each other. She was well again and busied herself with a number of charitable works, but her cheerfulness was always of a quiet kind as if still shadowed by the experiences which had led to her breakdown. By this time I knew them. She had been attached since her schoolroom days to a cousin, a naval officer, to whom she had become engaged. There were long separations but the date of their wedding was fixed when he was reported killed in an incident in the China seas. Months passed. Mary had schooled herself to resignation and was struggling back to normal life when news came that he was safe. Scarcely had there been time for her emotions to soar from misery to joy when she heard that he had died of a fever on the voyage home. The tragic ordeal she had undergone would have undermined a constitution much more robust than hers. Mr Drigg had rescued her from a state of mental and physical distress which had left her – as she said herself – old for her years.

We talked endlessly in her room or mine. Our tastes were similar and we were almost of an age. We were continually marvelling over the fact that we had grown up in Martlebury without ever having met; but it was not really surprising. As the only daughter of a wealthy steel manufacturer, Mary moved in a sphere very different from mine; but she had been brought up to live simply and was familiar with the poverty and sickness in Martlebury's slums; so that we were closer in sympathy than would normally have been the case. I believe she even envied me a little.

'I'm only playing at being useful,' she once said.

'You've been truly useful to a good many people,' I assured her. 'And especially to me.'

The Fairfolds had a wide circle of acquaintance and were hospitably inclined. Their musical evenings in particular brought pleasant company to the roomy house in Barton Square. I remember being surprised, at the first of these I attended, to meet Mr Hawthorne there. He had apparently known the Fairfolds for years and shared a number of their interests.

'Father thinks highly of him,' Mary told me. 'He has tried to persuade him to look for a better appointment in a pleasanter district. With his gifts and qualifications he would have no difficulty in finding one but nothing will induce him to leave Marshall Street. I never knew a man so indifferent to his own advantage – and he's so charming and amusing. You're fortunate, Florence, not only to work with him but to have been taught by him.'

The admiration was mutual.

'Mary Fairfold is an unusual person,' Mr Hawthorne said when I once had occasion to mention her. 'She has suffered a great deal without losing her natural warmth and interest in other people. In fact her powers of sympathy have increased. Her ordeal has left her without bitterness – and that is not always the case.'

Was there a slight emphasis on the word 'her'? For some reason, though I agreed with every word of Mr Hawthorne's speech – delivered with a certain thoughtful deliberation – it left me feeling slightly uncomfortable. At any rate, I thought a little stiffly, he seemed to find nothing to disapprove of in *Mary*. He had spoken of her as warmly as she had of him: more warmly perhaps? Nothing seemed more likely than that their mutual admiration would eventually turn to love if it had not done so already. She was beautiful and good, I told myself, making a brave effort to rise to her high level of selflessness and not quite succeeding. He would comfort and protect her. I had never thought of Mr Hawthorne in such a light, but now it occurred to me that any woman would be lucky to have him for a husband.

Sometimes when there was a penny reading or a magic lantern show in the schoolroom, Mary came and we went home together in a cab. Often she and I and Mr Hawthorne walked back to Barton Square together after a lecture or a concert. I watched them closely and found no reason to alter my conclusion that they were suited to each other. They must marry. 'What could be more delightful?' I asked myself soberly and saw it as my plain duty to push the business on. If the situation had been different, if Mary had discovered, let us say, that Mr Hawthorne had fallen in love with me, would she not have done all she could to promote my happiness? I must take her as my model – and so I did, but with a small, secret feeling of injustice. Was it not hard to have fallen into the hands of the wickedest of women and then, without a pause for recovery, to be subjected to the undoubted strain of living with the noblest and best? Still, I must rise to the occasion. Tentatively and rather skilfully, it seemed to me, I put out one or two feelers. So far as I could make out, though Mary had known Mr Hawthorne for years, it was only recently that they had become friends.

'Since you came home from Gower Gill?' I suggested, having seen to it that the topic cropped up quite naturally while we were enjoying a confidential chat over my fire one evening.

'Even more recently than that,' Mary said after a moment's thought. She looked a trifle embarrassed. 'We have seen more of him – quite lately.'

Her hesitation deepened my suspicions.

'He has never married. Don't you think that strange?'

Again I was aware of a slight awkwardness as if a choice of answers was being considered, though the one she made was trite enough.

'Oh, I don't know.'

'He can afford to marry. Not that he is well off, of course. But neither was Philip when we were engaged.' A fresh idea came to me. 'But if he should happen to fall in love with a woman who was better off, he might not feel it right to make her an offer.'

'You may be right.' To my surprise Mary now spoke firmly. It was as if she was relieved to hear me broach a subject she had already given thought to. 'It could be as you say. He would not think that dreary schoolhouse a suitable home for a woman who had been used to something better; to – beautiful and comfortable surroundings.'

She looked at me thoughtfully as if she wanted to be reassured. I was a little surprised that she should use the word 'beautiful' of the house in Barton Square, though it was certainly comfortable; but my immediate attention was fixed on something else she had said.

'I wouldn't call it dreary.' For some reason I felt impelled to defend the schoolhouse. 'It's no worse than other small houses of its kind – and not so small either. A woman must adopt her husband's style of living. It can't be much more difficult to lower one's standard of comfort than it is to get used to a higher style of living. That can be very difficult. At least if Mr Hawthorne's wife was well off, she wouldn't have the worry of always having to be grateful.'

Mary nodded and looked enlightened, as well she might, by such a piece of self-revelation.

'Mrs Hawthorne has a good-sized parlour,' I went on, 'and it's very comfortable on winter evenings. If the schoolhouse is good enough for Mrs Hawthorne and good enough for me – though goodness knows I don't count for much,' I added modestly, 'it's good enough for anyone.'

My warmth seemed to have a cheering effect on Mary.

'I know you enjoy your visits to Mrs Hawthorne. You're fond of the old lady, aren't you?'

'Very. We got to know each other well when we were staying in Matlock. She would be easy to get on with, as a mother-in-law, I mean, if Mr Hawthorne should marry. But I'm afraid she is getting old. As a matter of fact she said to me only the other evening how it worried her to think that she must leave him. "He never thinks of his own comfort," she said, "and with no wife to look after him . . ."'

'He would be lonely,' Mary said with feeling.

Having so diplomatically overcome two possible obstacles to her alliance with Mr Hawthorne, I tackled a third.

'In my opinion it can be an advantage for a man to be older than his wife, by more than the usual number of years. Philip was three years older than I but we were both foolish and inexperienced. I should think,' I said after a brief calculation, 'even as much as fourteen years could still be an advantage.'

Again Mary seemed happy to agree.

'Especially,' I said tactfully, 'when there has been suffering and sadness, for the woman, I mean. They have the effect of making her more mature. In such a case as that, the difference in age would matter even less.'

'I'm sure it would not matter at all,' Mary said heartily. 'Not to two people who were perfectly suited to each other in every other way.'

The barriers were falling without resistance. It was almost too easy to demolish them. Gratifying as it was to be able to help Mary in this way after all she had done for me, I felt obscurely depressed and had to force myself to face the last obstacle of all. It was the most difficult to overcome but once it was surmounted, Mary must see that there was nothing to keep her from marrying Mr Hawthorne. I would welcome their happiness as I would have welcomed my own. Yet somehow, as my conviction grew, my enthusiasm waned.

'Marriage is such a very serious matter, far more serious and full of difficulties than one can know beforehand,' I began.

'Indeed, I have often been surprised that people should embark on it lightly. But when a man has so many good qualities . . .'

She had evidently thought it over carefully. I must not seem to be discouraging her. With an effort I went on:

'I was thinking that if a woman has loved someone else in the past, she might feel it disloyal to love another person.' It was excruciatingly difficult to put it in such a way as not to offend her and I almost gave up. After all, it was none of my business. For all that, I felt involved: quite deeply involved.

'I don't think it would be disloyal to love again in a different way and in different circumstances,' Mary said earnestly. She seemed to have no difficulty in finding words. 'If I had died and John had lived, there would have been no disloyalty to me in his loving someone else some day. Nothing could ever change his love for me or mine for him; and I'm sure you feel the same about Philip.'

I was surprised by her directness. She had obviously given careful consideration to a situation into which I had blundered with my usual impulsive haste. She certainly needed no help from me.

'You're tired, Florence, and I've been keeping you up.' She went to the door. 'Any woman would be fortunate,' she said, 'to win the affection of such a man as Mr Hawthorne.'

It was exactly what I had thought and had meant to say. I had obviously been right about her feeling for him; and I congratulated myself, as I sat up late watching the fire die, on having put things in such a way as to ease her mind. She had responded eagerly when I praised the schoolhouse, she had agreed that age made no difference and had herself pointed out that a person could love for a second time without disloyalty to the dead. I was glad to have been of even the smallest use in helping her to these conclusions; glad to have been of help to the two people whom I now cared for more than anyone else in the world. Some such feeling was necessary to counteract the curious depression that seemed to have come upon me: a sensation such as a barrister would have if he found himself pleading for the wrong client.

Talk of Matlock had made me think of the absurd celery dish in the shape of a frog and of our light-hearted search for it as we had wandered from one shop window to another, pouring scorn on the cigar box covered with feathers and the papier mâché model of Riber Castle. With all her virtues – because of them, no doubt – Mary would not have found it such fun as Mr Hawthorne and I had done. But then she didn't know him as well as I did. She did not see him every day of her life. Every morning when I arrived he was already at his desk in the corridor; and he was there to bid me goodbye every evening when I left. I could summon up his features in a second: the rather thin face, the brown beard, the grey eyes that missed nothing. Dreaming by the cold hearth, I saw their shrewdness softened by a tender light and felt my own lips relax into a smile. He wasn't handsome like Philip: there was simply no comparison; but he imparted a feeling of strength and energy. No one could be better company – to a person who knew him well. Mary scarcely knew him at all.

If they had reached an understanding, they were in no hurry to let it be known. As the evenings grew lighter, we strolled together in the Botanical gardens or round the bandstand in the park and Mr Hawthorne often came back to Barton Square for supper. The talk that followed was stimulating and not confined to the gentlemen. Mary and I were encouraged to air our views on books, ideas and even politics, in which I had never until then taken the slightest interest though Mary was better informed. Occasionally I found her in close conversation with Mr Hawthorne; and withdrew hastily, embarrassed at having butted in. When we parted for the summer holidays, I said goodbye with the secret conviction that by the time we met again they would have announced their engagement.

I spent a month with Aunt Maud and Cousin Helena in Surrey without ever reaching the point of confessing what had become of Philip's legacy. Time and again I felt the falseness of my position and was ashamed of it but instead of unburdening myself to Aunt Maud, I let the days slip by in harmless gossip and a round of sedate visits.

'You seem to have lost your tongue, Florence,' Aunt Maud said more than once. 'We must have a good long talk.'

Some finesse was needed to see that we never did. It was inevitable that I should be drawn into evasions and even lies.

'I hope you aren't losing your interest in dress. You seem to have brought very little with you. Helena was looking forward to having someone young and prettily dressed to stay. Oh, you look very nice. You always did. And you're one of the lucky people who improve as they get older. It's the cheek bones, I think. But you mustn't turn into one of those dreary-looking martinets, especially as you have plenty of money behind you.' A new idea occurred to her. 'I suppose Miss Bede does pay her rent regularly.'

'Oh, the rent – yes.'

'How much does she pay?'

Cornered, I wildly sought about for a sum, recalled that she had paid thirty shillings a week as her share of the housekeeping and hastily doubled the amount.

'Philip's aunt lived very well on her rents and the interest from her capital, didn't she? I can't quite understand why you feel obliged to work so hard. Oh, I'm entirely in favour of your doing something to occupy your mind but there are so many things you could do without standing on your feet from morning to night. And you were always picking up colds in that damp part of Martlebury. You'll have to go back to Honeywick some time. Still, it's early days yet. And the house won't go away.'

Nor would its occupant, I silently reminded myself. She would never leave, and I could never face her, never. My mind slid away from the problem as if incapable of looking at it steadily.

'You'll be coming out of mourning in a few months,' Aunt Maud reminded me. She talked of clothes: of which of my dresses could be adapted for half mourning. 'There was your grey taffeta. It did suit you. Your wedding dress will be of no use but I would love to see you in it again. You looked a picture, Florence. Did you ever wear it for little social evenings?'

'There was never an opportunity.'

It was the wedding dress that did the mischief. At the memory of its softly shining skirt swathed with spotted foulard – of Annie's delight in the blond lace and cream roses of my hat – I lapsed unexpectedly into sentimental tears.

'There now, I'm sorry,' Aunt Maud said. 'I've upset you by stirring up the past.'

It was hard, I told myself, sobbing, when she considerately left me to myself, to having nothing of my own; not even Philip's photograph; or my wedding presents; not even the wooden spoon I had bought from the Badgetts for luck. Somewhere in a drawer in the room overlooking the garden, carefully wrapped in a linen cloth like a shroud, lay the unfinished muslin baby cloak. It was very hard. But there had been no help for it.

Thinking of the dear simple things that had been my very own among all those that I had never wanted, I progressed, shuddering, to the thought of my skirt and silk petticoat and shoes. How could I ever explain to Aunt Maud (she was weighing out sugar for strawberry jam) the stern logic of that moment on the brink of the well? How could I convey to her in simple words the sequence of events which led to it and to the peculiar, irresistible outcome? Safely removed from the nightmare, I came near to seeing my flight as a dispassionate onlooker might see it, and discovered it to have been an act of lunacy. But a sleepless night brought no solution to the problem of what I should have done instead. Moreover the one certainty, that the affair was finished, was no certainty at all. The affair was not finished. Far from being rid of Miss Bede, I had her still on my hands. Her punishment might be endless; but endless too was my predicament.

'You must simply turn her out,' Aunt Maud would say briskly having grown a little red-faced and breathless in her astonishment. 'I'll come with you. We'll stand over her until she has packed her things. She can't have many of her own, from what you've told me. You can keep your eyes open in case she helps herself to anything else. She'd be very lucky to get off so lightly when she ought to be in prison – or worse. As for letting her stay there – I really wonder, Florence, if you were in your right mind . . .'

The dread of having my sanity questioned once again made me shiver.

'But it would be impossible to take any legal action against her, Aunt Maud,' I would explain. 'Nothing can be proved. As it is she *is* in prison and suffering the torture of remorse, knowing she has murdered one person and believing she has murdered two.'

It was a mistake to put the thing into words at all, even mentally. Expressed in such terms, the punishment sounded as cold-blooded as the crime, making my behaviour seem as bad as her own. Torture can never be justified. Yet I could face such home truths more readily than I could face Miss Bede. To arrive at Honeywick with Aunt Maud while the station fly waited at the door, to knock – or would Aunt Maud insist on walking straight in? – and confront my tenant, was a prospect far more appalling than the more distant prospect of confronting my Maker and rendering a true account of all my follies, weaknesses and sins.

Aunt Maud carefully refrained from stirring up the past again but when we parted, she gave me one of her keen, critical, affectionate looks.

'It doesn't do to bottle things up,' she said.

Lest they might explode, I supposed, imagining the sudden shock of flying cork and shattered glass. After a climax such as that, one could start again, putting new wine into a new bottle. But the very essence of my situation was its unending sameness. No climax could come unless I myself caused it to happen. On the long journey back to Martlebury there was plenty of time to brood on the painful prospect of re-visiting Honeywick and to decide again and again that I could never go. There was time too to penetrate to the very heart of my dilemma. In leaving the woman alone, I had thought only of punishing her to the last sting of remorse. The fact was that once again I had submitted my will to hers.

Even without Aunt Maud's stirring, memories would naturally have awakened, but hers had been the first direct reference to the house and tenant since my conversation with Mr Drigg more than a year ago. No sooner had Aunt Maud mentioned her name than Miss Bede took shape again and showed no sign of having lost her power to violate my privacy. The sight of a perfect stranger in a Rubens hat as we passed through a station brought me to the edge of my seat. When I arrived at Barton Square and went straight to my room, I gasped to find a woman in a plain house dress and low shoes sitting in the chair opposite my own by the hearth.

'Whatever's the matter, Florence?' Mary got up and hugged me. 'You look as if you'd seen a ghost. I shouldn't have come in but I wanted to be the first to welcome you.'

'I never was so glad to see you in all my life.'

Outwardly my life in Martlebury continued to be all that could be wished. If anything, in my second year at Marshall Street, it had improved. My circle of friends widened and the dearest of them grew closer. Mr Hawthorne came often to the house, not only when there were other guests but alone. But the untroubled peace I had hoped for and almost found had gone again and would not come back. I felt on edge. For one thing I was always expecting to hear of an engagement between Mary and Mr Hawthorne – expecting and dreading. It would bring a change for me as well as for them and I was careful to persuade myself that for that reason alone I would prefer not to hear of it. But matters did not progress. Once I nerved myself to hint to Mary of Mr Hawthorne's intentions.

'You are a little goose, Florence,' she said.

It would be like them to postpone their marriage out of consideration for Mrs Hawthorne. The old lady was failing and grew much feebler that winter. I spent as much time with her as I could and often spent my whole evening in the schoolhouse. In spite of Mary's rather contemptuous description of it, I liked the shabby old house, its cosiness when the curtains were drawn and the feeling of security that came from the sounds of passers-by and carts, subdued by the thick walls. At eight o'clock Mr Hawthorne would bring my hat and mantle and we walked back to Barton Square through gas-lit streets, past the hot potato and coffee stalls and the chestnut seller's brazier, then through the more genteel avenues where carriages waited and one caught glimpses through the bare trees of richly-furnished rooms and leaping firelight.

I fell into the habit of staying on in the schoolroom after the children and even Miss Wheatcroft had gone home. There was always plenty to do and Mr Hawthorne was always there at his desk in the corridor. I would hear the scrape of his chair as he moved it out of the draught and nearer to the stove; or away from the stove and into the draught; until the caretaker's wife came with her long broom and swept us out. If he came in to chat while I ruled margins or filled inkwells, I sometimes saw to it that from time to time we talked about Mary; and I sang her praises, half hoping but not altogether wanting to rouse him to some ardent response. 'I've been meaning to tell you, Florence,' he might confide; or, 'Tell me honestly, do you think she would . . .?' But all he ever said was: 'I'm glad you have found such a steadfast friend,' or something of the kind. And once he said, 'You've been fortunate in your choice of a friend,' and startled me by adding, 'this time.'

He could not have intended it as such, but the phrase was a reminder of a former friend whom I was much happier to forget. If she came at the slightest summons, it was because under the surface of consciousness she was always there. To my alarm she now penetrated the schoolroom where so far I had been free of her; and threatened to spoil one of the occupations which had been giving me a good deal of pleasure.

I had taken it upon myself to renew the wall calendar intended for the younger children: a series of long, banner-like devices, one for each month, with appropriate scenes and an accompanying rhyme: 'January brings the snow, makes our feet and fingers glow. February brings the rain, fills the frozen dykes again,' and so on. I enjoyed the work and spent far more time on it than was necessary. Consequently, one evening towards the end of May I had still not finished my illustration for the month of June.

Miss Wheatcroft had left at her usual time, twenty-four minutes to the second after four, her invariable rule based on some mysterious calculation. In preparation for a prompt and resolute start on the next day, she had filled the upper part of her blackboard with the simple, perfect and continuous tenses, past, present and future, of the verb 'to know', passive voice, third person singular, neuter gender. 'It is known, it has been known, it will be known . . .' They supplied a background to my thoughts like the intoning of some oriental prayer as I spread out my paper and paints on the big sewing table.

At first the work had been, as Miss Wheatcroft would have agreed, an interesting and worthwhile pastime, but I was aware of a growing listlessness and sometimes sat for minutes on end wondering what it was in the little scenes I had concocted that failed to satisfy me – apart, that is, from my lack of skill in drawing. It was while I was considering how best to depict the month of June for children who had never spent so much as a day in the country, that Mr Hawthorne came in. He looked gravely at Miss Wheatcroft's blackboard, its upper half filled with variations on the theme of the verb 'to know'.

'Dear me!' he said with a sigh. 'I hadn't realised how very much there was and has been and still is to be known. We must press on, Florence, before time runs out.'

He straightened the map of the world and made a slow

tour of the room, examining the illustrations I had finished – for the first five months of the year – with as much care as he might have given to five masterpieces in a gallery. I felt embarrassed and could not help following his progress, looking as he looked: at the brown hens in grass stippled with cowslips: the arch of a bridge: a wooden seat shaded by trees: bushes of yellow and green broom: a stile in a stone wall: all harmless and innocent as could be. Subjects had come thick and fast. But seeing them as a whole, I discovered why the work, so pleasant at first, had become a burden. The choice of scenes had been almost unconscious but together they suggested a time and a place I had no wish to recreate. Together they formed a background lacking only the central figure. She had been there all the time, on the seat, the stile, the bridge, determined to push her way in – even here.

I sat down quietly, forcing myself to control the morbid fear, a kind of hysteria, that set my whole body trembling. It was as if all the discipline and hard work, all the wholesome influences of the past two years had never been. The angry bitterness had left me but I remembered it and felt ashamed; and I came near to feeling again the bewilderment and panic that had driven me away.

'And this, I suppose' – Mr Hawthorne was pointing – 'is your house – and this – and this?'

A gable end; a chimney stack with clouds above; a gate in a thorn hedge; all hinted at the existence of a house just out of sight, not to be faced squarely and seen sensibly for what it was: simply an affair of mortar and stone, tile and timber; no more.

'You're no artist, Florence, but you've caught the spirit of the country. Is it because of Philip that you can't bear to go back?'

'No.' I was startled into a direct answer. 'It isn't that.'

My voice shook. 'It isn't that.'

He came and stood beside me.

'But there is a reason? There must be. I thought perhaps you might feel that by staying away you could keep the memory unchanged.'

I could only shake my head.

'Otherwise you would naturally want to see your property, and especially when it's in such a beautiful place.' He waited. I tried to speak, feeling as if the whole weight of Honeywick with all it contained had stirred and moved nearer, and threatened once more to crush me. His next words were quietly spoken. 'I have never seen a lovelier spot.'

I looked up, more than astonished, aghast.

'You know it?'

'A little. You once invited me. Do you remember?' His tone was lightly reproachful but he looked serious with a frown between his brows. 'When nothing came of the invitation, I took it upon myself to spend a day there on my own, soon after you came here, when I found that all was not well with you.'

'I didn't think . . .'

'You didn't think I'd notice. How could I help it? Knowing you as I do, how could I not see that you were suffering from some wound more harmful than grief. You were different from the girl I had met in the summer at Matlock.'

'You never told me.'

'That shouldn't surprise you, considering how very little you have told me.'

Tears blurred the rabbits and cowslips, then spotted the clean white paper as I looked down, longing to tell him everything: to lay my head on his shoulder – the amazing thought took me unawares – and beg him to help; and at the same time, just in time, I thought of

Mary and how much better it would be if dear Mary did not exist; how easy it would be to be very careless indeed of Mary's interests.

'In a village like Gower Gill,' he said, 'one can generally find someone to chat to – and I happened to find one person who was kind enough to invite me in as soon as I mentioned your name.' He may have sensed my sudden alarm for he added quickly, 'Yes, I've talked to Drigg.'

'Oh – Mr Drigg.' For a moment I had imagined another meeting and had disliked the idea with almost feverish intensity.

'Come, Florence. Look at me.'

He put his hand gently under my chin as he would have done to one of the children. I looked into the sensitive face of a man who, in all the years I had known him, had never a thought to spare for himself. It was not of himself that he was thinking now. It was no trouble of his own that brought the frown to his brow: or the tenderness to his eyes.

'Drigg gave me his version but it's yours I want to hear. I've waited too long. Isn't it time you told me all that's been troubling you – and let me share it? It isn't like you to be bitter. You should have nothing to do with revenge and hatred, you of all people, my dearest Florence.' He glanced at Miss Wheatcroft's blackboard and smiled. 'You who have been and are being and will always be so dearly loved, so very deeply loved.'

I wonder now that it ever needed to be said. Even then, if there was astonishment, I have forgotten it. I remember only the delighted recognition that it had always been so: he had always loved me. As for me, another kind of love, precious as only the first can be, had taught me how deep, how settled and untroubled a love I felt for him.

Happiness simplified everything. It was all nonsense

about Mary. She would never have made a suitable wife for Giles, I told myself with a confidence both ruthless and serene. Mary was equally sure of this and laughed immoderately – for her – when she tricked me into confessing my plans for them. 'We wondered when you would come to your senses,' she said.

I told Giles everything. To have so tender and sympathetic a listener was an indescribable comfort.

'I had no idea, my darling,' he said,' how much you had suffered. But it's all over now and done with.'

It was tempting to believe him. In addition to the whole story of Miss Bede, I had a confession to make.

'It's about money, Giles. You must not think me rich.'

I had no sooner mentioned the Boys' Home than with one startled look he guessed my secret.

'So it was you? You take my breath away. Why, Florence, it was a wonderful idea. You never did a better thing in all your life.' His amusement, delight and approval warmed my heart.

'So there is only the £500 from my father. It isn't much.'

'Then we're well matched. My own savings don't amount to much more and I must confess to feeling happier without the St Leonard money. I have all I want in the world now, Florence; more than I ever hoped for. No man could be more blessed.'

'And of course there is the house,' I reminded him.

'Ah yes, the house. It worries you, I know.'

Simply to talk about it restored my common sense. With Giles to advise me I saw that the situation at Gower Gill was quite straightforward. Miss Bede must be told to leave. The house could then be put into the hands of an agent and let in a more satisfactory way. A letter was all that was required; or Giles would go himself.

But we both knew that I must go. Only by confronting

her could I release her – and myself. She must be shown the error of her ways and forgiven. What could be simpler?

But not yet. Autumn slipped away, and winter. Spring brought Marshall Street's grubby sycamore into leaf, violets to the flower-sellers' baskets and a bowl of tadpoles to the schoolroom; and still I felt no impulse to go. The obligation haunted me. I vowed that the ordeal must be got through somehow before our wedding in July; and let the early days of June pass without going.

One morning I woke from a strange dream in which a stifling darkness held me prisoner. I could not move. Someone was singing – *The Mistletoe Bough*. 'It's a song about a bride,' a voice said. Then a heavy curtain was drawn back. I heard the rattle of its rings. Doors and shutters opened, letting in the light. The air became suffused with the soft brightness of a summer morning at Honeywick.

I woke to a new kind of serenity compounded of tender memory and fresh hope. In so blessed a mood anything was possible: especially an errand of peace and forgiveness.

Twenty-six

A cuckoo called as we came out from the trees on to the green hillside where ewes were grazing. We paused by the seat. The whole scene was empty of human life except for one person: a man – or boy – leaning over the parapet of the bridge far below and looking, in his slouch hat and red scarf, like the conventional figure in a landscape, put there to show the proportions of its natural features or to epitomise their rural character.

'A place can be too beautiful,' Giles said. 'It leaves no good thing to be wished for.' He put his arm round me. 'You're nervous.'

'Not really. Yes, dreadfully.'

'You wait here and let me go.'

'She may not be there. She may have gone away.'

'There's only one way to find out.'

A wisp of smoke crept up from the kitchen chimney. We watched it disperse and vanish in the sunlight. I straightened my sash and smoothed my gloves.

'I'll follow slowly,' Giles said. 'And in ten minutes I shall knock.'

We had arranged exactly how it must be.

On either side of the lane sweet cicely grew tall, its blossoms as high as my head, so that the way to the house was creamy white and fragrant. The country silence, breathlessly deep, pressed on my ears as I went down through the aromatic sweetness. Roses and honeysuckle were in bloom round the bow window.

A few yards from the gate I stopped to compose myself. I had rehearsed my part. When she had recovered from the shock of seeing me alive, I would speak to her gravely with a courage and openness denied me in the past. I would tell her that I knew all her evil designs, all her wickedness not only towards me but towards Aunt Adelaide; it had been no more than she deserved to leave her under the false impression that she had murdered me; there had been ample time for her to examine her conscience; and now, under the circumstances, it was only reasonable to ask her to leave as soon as she could make other arrangements. Then – with what a wealth of forbearance in my tone would I pass from frankness to forgiveness! Our unhappy relationship would end in gentleness, purged of all evil. The thought brought tears to my eyes.

But still I hesitated. What would be the effect on her of this sudden apparition, this resurrection of one long dead; even though I brought healing and peace to appease the torment of her guilt? With some notion of softening the blow, I pulled down my veil as she used to do, but awkwardly, my hands unsteady. She must not recognise me until I had spoken and prepared her for the shock. Through the soft silk net I saw the chimneys waver. The roof tiles shimmered in the warm air. The old walls, already half lost in flowers, became a shade less real.

I listened as from an open window came a small sustained sound: a contented crooning like the murmur of bees in the honeysuckle or the cooing of wood pigeons in the ash tree: a woman's voice, but so intimately attuned to the summer mood of the place that it might have been the house itself breaking into husky song.

For a moment I fancied it was Annie singing but the tune – and voice – were different. Presently came the sound of water running from a tap. The door opened. A woman in a sacking apron came out with a bucket and knelt at the door step. I had not thought of a servant. She was not young: round-shouldered and a bit of a slattern. Her hair was coming down. But she was quick and deft. It was not long before her brisk, accustomed movements brought the task to an end. She wrung out the floor-cloth, ran a duster over the shining door panels and went inside.

I mounted the three shallow steps, glancing through the bow window as I passed along the terrace. The parlour was empty. I lifted the fox's head and was dismayed by the loudness of my knock. At first there was no response, only a cessation of small sounds within. Then a bucket handle clanked; there came a rustling in the hall; a hesitation; the handle turned. A woman stood there bundling up her hair; a woman with a stoop; a sallow face seamed with fine lines; black eyes underlined with shadows almost as black. Looking into the light, she could not see me, safe behind my veil: the one person she had counted on never seeing again. I must speak, must prepare her.

But a quiver had passed over her face like a shadow. Her lips parted.

'Florence.' The low voice was unchanged. 'My dear Florence. I thought you would never come.'

The simple words were quietly spoken. They reached me with the urgency of an alarm bell. My whole being awoke with a bound to the warning they conveyed. Something had gone wrong with my plans. Those were not the words of a murderess suddenly confronted by her victim newly risen from the grave.

Like an actor who has been given the wrong cue, I stood dumbfounded. She leaned forward with a look of – could it be tenderness? – kissed me on the cheek and drew me, dazed, out of the warm daylight into the cool hall. The clock, the stuffed birds, the stoat, were all there unchanged. Only one thing was unfamiliar. I saw it at once for it was where I could not help looking: a padlock on the cellar door. She saw my glance.

'Yes.' She drew a deep breath and released it in a shuddering sigh. 'I vowed that it must never happen again. I have never forgiven myself. You might have been – oh, my dear, you might have died a terrible death and it would have been my fault. My fault, Florence.'

It was not just a matter of one false clue. She had taken over my part. It was I who was to have accused her. The penitence, the self-reproach, these I had counted on but not yet. I had first to tell her that I had outwitted her and was now come to forgive her. This time, at last, the initiative was to have been mine. Yet it had passed at once to her. I felt it slip inevitably away.

She glanced over my head into the looking glass and with a final twist subdued her hair. There were streaks of white in it. Her black skirt was blotched with soda stains. She had been caught unawares but her recovery had been splendid. All the confusion so far had been mine.

'It's been so long, Florence, to wait for you to come back. Do you realise that if I hadn't seen you there by the wicket gate that night, I would have thought – and gone on thinking all this time – *that you were dead?*'

I might have known that she was impossible to deceive, being so long practised in deceit. One shrewd glance from the back window as I stood shivering among the nettles had undone my brilliant, infamous scheme for revenge. I had meant to cheat her into thinking me dead. Instead it was I who had been deluded all this time, she who had known the truth. She had known that I was alive, known that I would come back. But even now I had not grasped the full extent of my blunder.

'You behaved so strangely in going away without a word. You gave me no chance to explain.'

'Explain?' I believe it was the first word I had spoken.

'Why the well was uncovered. You must have known – oh, how I have longed to tell you! – that it was a sheer oversight. I simply forgot to put the cover back.' She clutched her brow. Its furrows deepened remorsefully. 'There was no excuse. But I had had so much to do on my own while you were away on holiday. Remember? You had just come home. You seemed so absent-minded. Your thoughts were far away. I couldn't reach you. I felt that you weren't listening when I told you my theory about the water.'

I was certainly listening now, fascinated.

'It had occurred to me that the flooding in the kitchen might be due to changes in the level of water in the well. I had made a few simple experiments with a weighted line. Interfering as usual.' She smiled sadly. One of her long teeth was spotted with decay. 'I told you while we were having supper that night.'

She took my unwilling hand and led me, bemused, into the parlour.

'She would never think, I told myself, Florence would never believe that I had left the well uncovered *on purpose*.' Her mouth, her whole person seemed to droop, overcome as she was by the tragedy of being misunderstood. 'Why should I want to harm you when you had been so kind, so loving to me?'

Loving? With my senses keyed to their highest pitch, I heard the false note. My treatment of her had never been loving. Admiring, respectful, friendly – all these, but never loving. More strongly than ever I was conscious of something theatrical in the situation. Impossible not to feel the skilful arrangement of words and movements one expects in a play; impossible not to wonder if she was slightly overplaying her part.

All the same, if a mighty wave had overturned the house I could not have felt a more devastating conviction that everything had gone wrong; or – and in that dreadful moment the alternative seemed even worse – that everything would have been right but for my own folly, my own infinite capacity for leaping to false conclusions.

In an embarrassment so acute that it seemed to melt the marrow of my bones I sat down and tremulously put up my veil in the forlorn hope of seeing things more clearly. She too had sunk into a chair. Our skirt hems touched confidentially as of old. The toes of her shoes were scuffed and worn. I looked out at the gate.

'You saw me there?'

She nodded. She was sitting desolate, head bowed, hands limp in the lap of her shabby skirt. Their nails were torn and not absolutely clean, their joints calloused and red.

'How many times have I pictured you as you turned away and left me, to suffer as I did!'

Was it possible that I had misjudged her; that she had never meant to harm me? In my agitation I tried to recall the events of that last evening. I had been certain then. My conviction had never wavered – until now.

She was describing the misery of rejection. To be left so heartlessly! She offered the word regretfully with a sad shake of her head. In bothering about the flooded kitchen she had only been doing her best for the house. That was her sole reason for uncovering the well. When I was longer than usual in the cellar – 'If only you had let me do it for once!' – she had suddenly remembered and had called to me. Then later when she saw me at the gate, it had been a tremendous relief. But she had never imagined that I would go without a word, obviously thinking – the worst.

Had she thought me mad, in my white petticoat? She hadn't mentioned it. For a number of reasons I didn't mention it either. At the thought of my extraordinary behaviour in the cellar, I grew hot. At the same time, though the details of that dreadful time were still confused in my mind, there came back to me something at least of the horror they had aroused. I remembered the candle flame reflected in her watchful eyes as I went down the cellar steps. How could she have forgotten that the well was uncovered, she who calculated every move she made, every word she uttered? A tiny incident rose from the past and isolated itself from a host of long-buried impressions; and I saw her in her Rubens hat by the churchyard wall as she turned apologetically to take her parasol: 'I'm always doing it, always forgetting things,' she had said.

I didn't believe her. In that first moment I had felt intuitively that she was not a careless person; and later I had been sufficiently suspicious to wonder if she had left the parasol as an excuse to make my acquaintance. For all my prickling consciousness of error piled on error, the same intuition warned me not to believe her now. Three years is a long time; long enough for me to forget the precise course of events as difficult to pin down as straws blown in the wind; but also long enough for her to prepare her story; to rehearse to the last syllable her own defence.

She raised her head with a snake-like movement of her yellow, wrinkled neck. I too sat up and strove to recover myself. Even if I had wronged her at the end, that didn't mean that she was blameless. I recollected that there had been other things, a great many other things, but one terrible thing above all. Remnants of my tattered past came back to me. It was absurd to let her upset me again or to shake my firm intention. Whatever mistakes I had made (*if* I had made them) the fact remained, when all was said and done, that this was my house. Everything in it was mine. She had no right to be there. I had come to tell her.

But before I could begin, she said almost shyly, 'There are some things, possessions of your own which I'm sure you must have wanted. I have them all ready packed lest anything should happen to them.' Her eagerness to oblige was embarrassing, even pitiful. 'The box is in the cupboard under the stairs. And there is something else. My position here has been irregular. I have paid no rent. It has been a constant worry to me. Perhaps that was what you came to see about – one of the things, that is.'

She spoke with such delicacy of feeling as made it more difficult than ever to plunge boldly into the much more distasteful lapses I had come to charge her with. 'I have done everything in my power to keep the house as you would want it.'

That was true at any rate. The house at least had kept its graciousness and elegance, whereas she . . .

She had forgotten me. She was looking round the room, reviewing each object, and there were many objects. Her lips, heavily grooved now at their corners, relaxed into an expression of pride. The darkness of her deeply shadowed eyes was lit by a dawning elation, a hint of excitement.

'As to the tenancy, we have talked it over, my future husband and I.' In the relief of remembering Giles I went on with a rush, gracelessly, 'He's waiting outside.'

I felt a sudden stillness. She had not been prepared for this. The fanatical light had gone from her eyes. They were wary now as she listened to my disjointed explanation.

'So you are to be married again.' She was careful to sound unsurprised as if to spare my feelings, and at once I felt guilty of disloyalty to Philip.

'Next month.'

'So soon.' She swallowed nervously. 'Then all this –' Her gesture, sad and loving, embraced the contents of the room: the silent cattle on the wall, the geometrically poised cushions, the books, and implied the existence of the rooms above – 'all this will be his. Everything will belong to your husband.'

Again I felt a thrill of relief. Such a loophole had not occurred to me. So far Giles had only advised and sympathised. When we were married, the entire responsibility for the house and its contents, including Miss Bede, would pass legally to him. The temptation to shuffle off the burden and lay it upon him, to use him as a means of escaping from this intolerable interview, involved me in a brief inward struggle before I rejected it sternly.

'To us both,' I said.

She seemed to be suffering. I must be careful not to misjudge her again: not to mistake for artifice what might be a genuine response to some painful emotion. Her eyes seemed misted, whether with rising tears or doubt or calculation, it would have been impossible to say. They were looking across the room at the bureau, at Philip's photograph in its silver frame.

'Poor Philip!' Her lips trembled.

The mention of his name, the sight of his face, revived a host of anxieties. With the sensation of crossing a quicksand rather than a carpet I went and picked up the photograph. He was sitting with a studied negligence but the pose of his head was assured and his expression confident. The fair face held no hint of any kind of doubt.

'Her kindness is beyond anything,' he might at any moment have said.

Had he been right, after all, to trust her? Had all her guilt existed only in my imagination, warped and distorted as it had become in the lonely hours when as odd-man-out, the unwanted third, I had watched them together, content in each other's company? At the thought jealousy came flooding back, more powerful than any of the wounding sensations I had yet suffered, and with it a revival of the old bitter anger and hatred, a determination to spare her no longer, to beat her at last into submission to my will.

'I found out that you are Miss Goodlock,' I said bluntly. 'You can't deny that, can you?' And I turned on her abruptly to surprise her start of guilt.

But I was not quick enough, if it was ever there. She was leaning forward, puzzled and anxious. A frown knit her brows as she waited for me to explain.

'I didn't quite catch . . .' she said at last.

'Miss Goodlock.' My voice was loud and crude. I was suddenly apprehensive.

'Who is Miss Goodlock?'

Who indeed? The question was put in so reasonable a tone as to force me into a rational response. Who was she? A woman I had never seen. A terrible misgiving seized me. Why had I been so sure? What had been as clear as daylight three years ago was now vague and confused. It was all hearsay, all conjecture. My attention riveted on Miss Bede's puzzled frown, my faculties paralysed by doubt, I felt all confidence ebb away. If she was innocent in the matter of the well, she could be equally innocent of all imposture, all deception. The flimsy structure of evidence against her collapsed. There are a dozen ways in which a woman may form a fine collection of brooches, rings and lace. More than one woman without a home of her own might long for a charming house.

I summoned all my courage.

'I thought you were Miss Goodlock, Aunt Adelaide's companion who . . .' It was an impossible thing to say but I had come determined to say it and would despise myself for ever if it remained unsaid, '. . . who murdered and robbed her. Bella told me,' I added with an attempt at defiance, and as I spoke it was as if from an immense distance I saw Bella fade into the haze above the river, a bodiless phantom, a voice uttering a message no-one but me would believe. And even supposing it were true and Miss Goodlock was indeed as black as Bella had painted her, what proof could there ever be that she was also Miss Bede? The links binding the two into one were light as gossamer: a word, a perfume, a few silken embroidery stitches. All the same I made a final effort. 'And I thought you were trying to rob and murder me too.'

Silence fell. My cheeks burned. The roses at the window, a misguided butterfly on the curtain, the guileless figures on the mantelpiece, the smooth-faced clock – all witnessed and quietly ignored the preposterous words I had inflicted on the room.

She stood rigid, her shoulders raised in an attitude of agony as from a sword thrust. Then she sighed, relaxed and made a little gesture of acceptance and understanding. In its quiet resignation it was rather beautiful.

'My poor Florence.' Her voice was warm with sympathy and forgiveness. 'I'm afraid at that time you were not quite yourself. Not quite. There was your illness, you see.'

It was possible. My mind and senses could have deceived me, enfeebled as they were by fever, delirium, physical weakness and grief. Now, with a new detachment, I saw the whole drama enacted again, from the spring day when she first came into my life to the grey evening when I left her. To a sane and unprejudiced audience her every action, every word, taken at face value would seem sincere, civilised, even kind. Her performance had been faultless. No shred of tangible evidence existed to cast doubt on anything she had done or said. She was always plausible, then – and now.

'It was all a dreadful mistake, wasn't it?' she said. 'A delusion. But you're better now, aren't you?' The least shade of doubt in her tone was perhaps a warning: a reminder that my recovery was very recent; might indeed still be in question. 'You'll be happy again.'

Her restraint was exquisite. She had not uttered a word of reproach – or denial; but she came and looked over my shoulder at the photograph.

'Dear Philip. If he could know. Thank God he never did. So generous, so good. He gave me the most precious of all gifts, a home.' She seemed overcome but presently she said, 'You have so much – and I . . .'

Her voice was unsteady. She turned from me and wistfully touched the Chelsea flower baskets, the Dresden figurines. She passed a calloused, broken-nailed finger over Neptune's beard and caressed the nymphs. She had no-one, no living soul to love, and wanted none. She had wanted only the house. It had enslaved her. Her passion to possess and cherish it was heartfelt, her love of it entire, her fidelity to it absolute.

I started. She had stooped swiftly. Where I had sat, the imprint of my shoes remained, faintly edged with wayside dust. I watched as she reached anxiously for the long-handled hearth shovel and brush to sweep it up. Even at such a time as this the house claimed her. In her devotion to it she was as single-minded and pure of heart as any priestess. I understood with a kind of awe that in this one thing she was honest. The discovery seemed by contrast to emphasise the falseness of every other aspect of her life; but I could no longer trust my judgment, nor were there any longer other aspects to her life, only this, her obsession with Honeywick. It had isolated her in a cruelly unequal companionship. No employer could have exploited her more ruthlessly. Alone with the house, she toiled to meet its relentless demands and could not rest from the compulsion to invent more.

She had carefully replaced the shovel and brush and was leaning wearily on the table by Philip's chair until suddenly mindful of its polished surface, she snatched away her hand and rubbed at the fingerprints with her sleeve. I found myself feeling sorry for her with the pity one feels in the presence of an incurable illness.

Yet the time had come to tell her, if I was ever going to tell her, that she must go. Still, I could not quite bring myself to deliver the final blow, nor for the moment could I remember just why her departure was so essential.

'Giles will be coming . . .'

'He won't . . . You wouldn't . . .' For the first time I saw her agitated. The dark eyes, once so unfathomable, looked out at me from a private world of pain. She was breathing quickly, in suspense. 'You won't turn me away?'

The pathos was new but not the words. They were almost the words that Philip had used. Hearing them, I heard again the pitifully feeble insistence in his voice and felt again the heavy drag at my heart: 'You won't turn her away, Florence?' It had been an entreaty, not a command, though the house was his, not mine. I had never really felt it to be mine, never really wanted it. 'Her goodness must not go unrewarded,' he had said.

Her goodness? Perhaps her love for the house was goodness of a kind, the only kind she was capable of. Turned adrift with no direction for her voyage, what would become of her? What harm might come of it to others as well as to herself?

She was looking down at the table top. Days, years, decades of polishing had given it the soft gleam of a limpid pool, darkened now by her brooding shadow.

'This is my world,' she said. 'You cannot send me away, Florence. Not now.'

Even then I hesitated, staring at Philip's confident face. His dream of a long line of St Leonard's at Honeywick had not been fulfilled. There were no St Leonards left. In another month I too would have changed my name. It was hard that all his hopes and plans had gone awry. He had died too soon to bring them to fruition. He would have remembered Miss Bede in his will if Mr Drigg had not intervened. She and I might have – I shuddered at the thought – shared the inheritance, living here together, mutually dependent, as inseparably related as the sun and moon, and as distant from each other.

'No,' I said at last. 'I won't turn you away.'

But instead of putting the photograph in my bag as I had intended I put it back on the bureau, telling myself that there must always be one St Leonard at Honeywick. Besides, the place had taken hold of him. It was too late to rescue him. He would want to stay – with her.

Suddenly I was in a flurry to leave, moved by the superstitious conviction that it would be better for Giles to stay outside; much better for him not to come within the circle of her influence. If I had my way, they should never never meet. One never knew . . . Even Giles . . . I went quickly to the door; said something about my solicitor: he would write to her about the rent; my address would be the School House, Marshall Street, Martlebury; the box with my things could be sent there.

She had bowed her head in her hands. The long agony

of suspense was over. She was weeping. At least I thought she was weeping. Afterwards I couldn't be sure. I couldn't be sure of anything except that I pitied her; and pity is the most irresistible of emotions, far harder to withstand than hatred, suspicion or the spirit of revenge, as no doubt she knew. Yes, she must certainly have taken that into account. She must certainly have given careful thought to her last move.

There was no sign of Giles. Then as I stood looking up the lane, I heard him behind me, hurrying up from the village. We stood in the thick, warm fragrance of creamy blossom. I gabbled out an explanation.

'I must have been mistaken, Giles. I was wrong – about everything, I think. She was pathetic and sad – and much older. I said she could stay.'

The bees murmured ecstatically as they rolled and tumbled in the sweet cicely. Only then, my senses reeling like theirs, did I remember the soft crooning from within the house: a wordless song of ineffable contentment. But she had been unhappy, hurt, remorseful. She had just told me so.

'Only – could one possibly forget to cover a well? And there were other things.'

A great many other things. They came back to me now to cling and buzz as persistently as the bees. Why, having seen me at the wicket gate, had she not rushed out there and then to explain that it had been an oversight to leave the well uncovered? Instead she had bolted the door and drawn the curtains, thankful to be rid of me on any terms, indifferent to any story I might tell so long as she could have the house to herself, already weaving the complex web of her defence for when it should be needed. And why, on Holleron Edge, had she deliberately undone Hector's curb chain and lashed him with the whip if not to send me to my death, or at least to make sure that no infant St Leonard complicated her schemes to possess the house, some day, somehow? As for Miss Goodlock – she had not actually denied being Miss Goodlock, and over that lady there still hung an ominous cloud.

'There must have been some truth in Bella's story,' I said wildly. 'Aunt Adelaide certainly changed her will at the last minute. She must have had some reason for turning against Miss Goodlock. And that mantle. I was sure it was Aunt Adelaide's.'

Doubts beset me thick and fast. As usual I had let myself be manipulated; she had outwitted me; she was lonely and lost, shabby and, in one direction at least, out of her mind.

'Yes, yes.' Giles tucked my arm in his. Incredulously I realised that he hadn't really been listening: Giles, who always listened. He had simply been waiting for me to stop so that he could burst forth with some astonishing piece of news. Most inappropriately he was smiling.

'You must tell me all about it. We must deal with Miss Bede. But do you think, just for a while, we could forget her?' He was leading me gently but firmly towards the bridge. 'I have something to show you. A discovery.' Then seeing that I was put out, he stopped. 'You have sometimes regretted ever having come to Gower Gill, haven't you? But good has come of it, my darling. A most wonderful thing. Look.'

The country fellow in the slouch hat was still there: a tall lad, younger than I had thought, with a lithe, muscular body and bronzed complexion, and a scarlet handkerchief knotted round his throat. He was no longer leaning on the parapet but standing eagerly upright. I saw Giles's delighted smile on his lips too. He swept off his hat.

'You won't remember me, Miss Lincoln.'

But I did, though his voice had broken since last we met and I had to look up to him now.

'Jordan!'

I held out my hand. He took it without awkwardness. We beamed at each other. It was a moment of utter happiness.

'This is a great day for me, sir.' He turned to Giles. 'Seeing you and Miss Lincoln both here all of a sudden. Mrs St Leonard, I mean. Many a time I've wondered if I'd ever clap eyes on you again.'

It was the longest speech I had ever heard from him. The change in him was miraculous.

'Where have you been all this time, Jordan? And whatever in the world are you doing here?'

'This is where I live. That's my home.' He spoke casually to conceal his pride in it and pointed to the green where in front of one of the cottages a skewbald horse was tethered. There was washing on a line, the smell of baking bread.

'They're back!' I cried. 'The Badgetts have come back.'

'And Jordan has come back with them,' Giles told me. 'He's been with them all the time.'

'That's right,' Jordan said. 'We've been well nigh all over England, even to London. Laban and I went there for a day – and a day was just about enough. A bit too much like Martlebury.'

I ran on. The door stood open. Nancy turned from the oven, her face flushed. We hugged each other. I demanded the whole story.

After we had parted that day, they made their way slowly up the dale to Catblake, arriving there in the evening. They had found Jordan leaning against the wall of the inn, hands in pockets, cap hiding his eyes, as Mr

Drigg had left him.

'That's the boy I saw on Holleron Moor,' Laban said. 'It wasn't Edwin. It wasn't a sign.'

'Never mind, love,' Nancy said. 'Whoever he is or isn't, he needs a friend.'

She had won his confidence and coaxed his history from him. Fortunately on one point at least she had been able to comfort him at once. Near Blea Rigg the Badgetts had met Tollemy Price and heard that Mrs St Leonard had been involved in an accident, had narrowly escaped death (and no wonder with that horse, Laban said), but there was hope that she would recover from her injuries.

'You were the one that really brought us together,' Nancy told me. 'It was finding that we all knew you that made us friends from the start. "Let's take him, Laban," I said. "Just think if it was Edwin with neither kith nor kin and nowhere to go."'

They had taken to one another. The hazards of their wandering life had bound them together in close affection. They told us all about it as we sat down to an impromptu meal: how Jordan had been handyman, groom and pedlar and had actually taught Laban to read. They had come home so that in return Laban could teach Jordan his own trade. Nothing could be more just, more reassuring, more delightful. They had all three suffered and been given a miraculous second chance of happiness. It was an occasion of indescribable satisfaction to us all.

I had not been in touch with Mr Drigg since I left and Giles and I had intended to call at Gower Oaks, but it was no surprise to learn that he was once more away from home. On the whole I was content to postpone another meeting, having now to face the uncomfortable possibility that I had unintentionally misled him on the subject of Miss Bede. We sat talking under Laban's apple tree until it was time to leave if we were to catch our train. Nancy and Jordan came with us up the hill to set us on our way – past Honeywick with an amber sky behind it, its garden walls gilded with stonecrop, its fox's head shining like gold.

But the lane was cool in the long shadow of the house. The effect was sobering. Our light-hearted chatter died away.

'A quiet spot for anyone living alone,' Nancy remarked. 'They say Mr Drigg visits there but I don't know of another soul that does. Still she sounds happy.'

Through an open window there had drifted into the scented evening that most contented of sounds, the voice of someone singing to herself.

'That's the right place for such as her,' Jordan was moved to say. 'Out of harm's way.'

'She's a clever woman,' Giles said, remembering her existence. He bent his head closer to mine. 'Much cleverer than you, my dear Florence. You were no match for her.'

'She's a bad 'un,' Jordan said. 'She's best kept away from.'

Our eyes met. His were blue and steady, disillusioned and kind. Jordan was not likely to have made a mistake. He knew the wickedness of the world and was resigned to it.

With a sudden expansion of the spirit like the unfolding of wings, I accepted it too – the dark side of life. There was no escaping it. It was there, as impossible to overlook as the breathtaking beauty of the place. In my memory of Honeywick, seen for the last time in that hour of luminous sky and long shadows, the elements of light and darkness are for ever counterpoised. The two strands, sinister and lovely, are indivisible. I have long since given up the attempt to disentangle them.

For some reason, at the sound of our voices perhaps, the singing had ceased. I saw – or thought I saw – deeply framed in roses and honeysuckle, a face at the window, watching us out of sight.

Twenty-seven

I have not seen her since. Years have passed but time and distance have so far failed to clarify her ambiguous image. In fact my attitude to Miss Bede has become even less rational, if that is possible. It is hard to explain how completely in this one respect such reasoning faculties as I possess have been thrown into disorder, as if routed by a superior magic. It is not a word to use lightly but there are moments when I am still half-convinced that in those days at Honeywick there was witchcraft at work.

This mood persists even though quite recently we have come nearer to discovering the truth. Indeed it is now almost certain . . . But in the early days of our marriage it was different. From time to time, snug by the schoolhouse fire, we used to talk the whole thing over, naturally; but inconclusively, as if peering at the strange affair through the fog that never leaves Marshall Street for long. Was she Miss Goodlock? By careful enquiry we might have established her identity. That no such steps have been taken is my own fault. I have never been able to overcome my *extreme reluctance* to involve Giles in the affair, as would inevitably have happened if enquiries had been made. It has needed some ingenuity to prevent him from ever meeting Miss Bede but so far I have kept them apart. To this day we have never gone back to Gower Gill; not yet.

Jordan visits us two or three times a year bringing news of the village, but it is a long time since he so much as mentioned the house half-way up the hill, an unchanging feature of the scene which he takes for granted like the true countryman he has become.

Nor have we ever gone back to Matlock. In the winter after we were married, Mrs Hawthorne died. It was she who had loved to spend her holidays at Matlock Bath. We could neither of us have been happy there without her. Yet there, if anywhere, I might have ferreted out more information about Miss Goodlock.

But it has so happened that of the three people who could have identified her, only one remains there. Bella has vanished into the New World, leaving no trace. Mrs Petch has left Matlock, as I discovered a year or two after our marriage when Giles and I, having spent two weeks with Aunt Maud, went on to Brighton to visit an old school friend of Giles.

On one of our morning strolls along the crowded sea front I stayed too long watching a Punch and Judy show and found that the others had walked on without me. It was a hot day. Judging it best to wait until they came back, I took advantage of the shade under an awning outside one of the more expensive-looking hotels. A cab piled high with luggage awaited a departing guest. Presently she appeared, a small, middle-aged lady, fashionably dressed, whom I had seen somewhere before. She was already seated when I remembered.

'Mrs Petch!'

She didn't recognise me. I had to remind her that I had once called on her in Matlock.

'Dear me, Matlock!' She spoke vaguely, her mind on her journey. 'That must have been a good while ago.'

'My name was St Leonard then.'

'Oh yes. Mrs St Leonard.' Memory revived. With rather more interest she scanned my unassuming grey dress and hat, noted, I feel sure, my deplorable lack of jewellery and prepared to forget me again.

'Then you no longer live at Matlock? I remember how pleased you were with your rooms at Masson View.'

'The rooms were well enough but – I'm very sensitive as I dare say you noticed – and there was something, an atmosphere.' For an instant her ear-rings ceased to bob. 'I was beginning to have uncomfortable feelings. Morbid, if you know what I mean. My maid noticed it too. Where is she by the way? Yes, I do remember you now.'

'I must not detain you, Mrs Petch, but I have often wished . . .'

'I'm sorry. You must excuse me. I have rather a long journey ahead of me. To Lyme Regis. I shall stay there – for a while. The company is said to be quite superior; to the company here in Brighton, I mean.'

She eyed such of the bags as were within sight with a distracted air and seemed to be counting them. It was not an opportune moment; nor was it one to be missed.

'I have always regretted not asking you for a little more information about Miss Goodlock.'

'Miss Goodlock?' Mrs Petch's gaze, briefly withdrawn from her Gladstone bag, was blank.

'Miss St Leonard's companion. We spoke of her, you know.'

'Did we? I had forgotten all about her. Now has that girl given me the keys?' She groped in her reticule. 'Miss Goodlock! Well! Did you say that she was dead?'

'No. I don't know what became of her. I only wanted to ask you . . . What was she like? Her appearance, I mean.'

'Goodness gracious!' Mrs Petch was nonplussed, even

a little offended. 'Her appearance? In her position? She was always so much in the background, naturally. She knew how to efface herself, I will say that for her. I scarcely noticed her except to feel sorry for the poor creature, as one does. If anything I am too sympathetic. Rather drab in her dress of course.'

'Was she tall, short, dark, fair?'

'Fair? Oh no. Miss St Leonard was fair-complexioned. But the companion . . . Ah, there you are,' as her maid hurried out. 'Have you the keys? Then we can go.' Seeing that I did not budge, she made a conscientious effort. 'So far as I can recollect, she was dark. Dark-eyed. I do remember once thinking that with better clothes she might have looked quite distinguished, even interesting, if one can use such a word.'

I think one could. One could certainly use it of Miss Bede.

There remains Mrs Catchbent, who, for all I know, is still living at Masson View. As a source of information she can be eliminated. One does not put personal questions to an ice-clad mountain peak. Only the most urgent necessity would induce me ever to set foot on her stair-carpet again.

Still, if it had not been for my determination to protect Giles from any involvement with Miss Bede, I might have felt it my duty to pursue the matter to the furthest possible limit. But I was soon rescued from any such well-intentioned folly; rescued as from all other trials and difficulties by Giles himself.

It was not long after we were married that two trunks arrived separately by rail. One had been despatched at my request from Matlock by Messrs Bretherby and Butterwick who had at long last succeeded in winding up Aunt Adelaide's estate; the other came from Gower

Gill. We had them taken up to the attic where for a long time they remained unopened. In nursing Mrs Hawthorne and learning the ways of my new household, I had plenty to do. It was only gradually that I found the time and inclination to sort out their contents and to reflect on the curious way in which the lives of their owners had become entwined: Aunt Adelaide's with mine. The two trunks standing side by side with their lids open to reveal the few garments and worthless trinkets in hers, the girlish dresses, inexpensive wedding presents and handful of books in mine, seemed to symbolise our joint retreat from the rich inheritance which had fallen to each of us in turn.

Such thoughts teased me as I rummaged in the attic. It was after an hour spent in this way that I sat one evening at the parlour table with a duster and brush in a painstaking attempt to clean, bead by bead and shell by shell, Miss Wheatcroft's long-neglected wedding gift. There was nothing for it but to blow into the intricate fretwork curves where neither duster nor brush would reach, an action which brought me face to face at close quarters with the three words embroidered in black silk.

'It was strange, Giles, wasn't it, that Miss Wheatcroft should have warned me? But I'm still not sure about the evil. It was there, I know, and I certainly feared it in spite of Miss Wheatcroft; but it became part of me; I felt it in my heart. Perhaps it was there all the time and not an external thing at all. And I still don't know whether at any time I did the right thing, especially in leaving her there. But I really don't see what else I could have done,' I added more loudly, thinking he hadn't heard.

But I was mistaken. He had been both listening and watching and as usual he knew how to deal with my tiresome uncertainty.

'Florence,' he said with a great show of sternness, 'I'll

have no more of this. It is no longer a question of what you should or should not have done. Honeywick House is mine and any decisions about it will be mine too. I absolutely and positively forbid you' – his severity was awful to witness – 'to interfere. I forbid it. Do you hear?'

'Oh Giles.' I went and knelt beside him. 'How good you are! It's such a comfort to be positively forbidden to do what I would absolutely hate to do. You'll see what an obedient wife I shall be.'

I drew the curtains across the dark window and turned back to the fire. And so, again and again, for one reason or another, we shelved the matter and there were long periods when I was able to forget it.

But truth, however long obscured, will find its own way of stealing into the light. We still have one link with Honeywick and with Miss Bede. In disposing of the contents of Aunt Adelaide's trunk I came upon the letter from Mr Drigg and sent it to him. He wrote at once and the correspondence has continued, though until recently he wrote no more than twice a year. Nancy Badgett was right: he had gone on calling at Honeywick as he had done in Aunt Adelaide's time and in mine. I guessed that his sentimental affection for the house as Aunt Adelaide's old home had been overtaken by an interest of a different kind; and this suspicion was confirmed when Giles discovered, in one of the new scientific journals lent him by Mary's father, an article entitled: *Some observations on the psychology of females living alone: a study in obsessive states of mind*, over the initials A.D.

In his most recent letter Mr Drigg related an odd but deeply significant incident. Indeed, to tell it was his chief purpose in writing. In passing the house one afternoon, on impulse, he called. No-one answered his knock. Having waited a while, he ventured in and found Miss Bede asleep in the parlour . . .

'She had fallen asleep in the wing chair,' he wrote. 'It was a sleep of exhaustion. Some coarse work had fallen from her hand. The room, I thought, looked neglected. She did not wake. I was able to study her face in repose . . .'

(I felt a slight creeping of the flesh. He would make good use of such an opportunity: the specimen pinned out, unconscious: her enigmatic eyes closed: his eagerly penetrating.)

'. . . It was a shock to see how she has aged,' he went on. 'She is quite emaciated and her person is sadly neglected. I sat down and waited. At length she woke. I doubt if she had fully returned to reality or indeed if she has been aware of it for a long time. But she sat up with an expression I had not seen in her before: a manner both submissive and apologetic. "I must have fallen asleep," she said, and looked uneasily about her as though disturbed to find herself in that particular chair. "*Miss St Leonard* is in her room. I will tell her that you are here."

'My opportunity had come. I acted promptly. "Thank you, Miss Goodlock," I said and held my breath, relying on the sheer power of the name. She stood up as if bewildered. (Hearing one's name can act as a summons to the whole personality, as I may have pointed out to you before. The theory is of particular interest to me.) Then having made so decisive a thrust, I did not hesitate but went on: "I trust Miss Adelaide is well. Her health, I know, is not robust."

'"She is –" There came a pause as she hovered still only half-awake between her two worlds. She spoke very low, as if to herself, and slowly raising her hands, held them in front of her, palms outward, as if to thrust something away from her. "She was so delicate – and light. A gentle lady."

'Then – I can scarcely describe the change that came over her. It was as if understanding flooded her whole being, and with it a distress amounting to horror. It was not the distress of having betrayed herself to me. She paid no further attention to me. It was a deep, inward response, as if truth had broken in upon fantasy and she grasped the full measure of whatever it was in her conduct that she had cause to regret; as if she saw in its true and merciless light what had hitherto seemed merely the legitimate means to a necessary end. Her state was pitiable. Nevertheless, for one of my profession it was a rare moment. To have traced her obsession through all its subtle modifications, and then actually to witness the loosening of its hold! She fell to her knees, her head resting on the chair arm, and I judged it best to leave her. She did not seem to hear me go . . .

'Forgive me if I bring this letter to a close. I have notes to complete which will be of considerable interest to my old friend Wilhelm Wundt . . .'

But Mr Drigg's attitude to his fellow men is never wholly scientific. A kinder human being never lived, as his postscript reminded me:

'Since then I have called three times and found her in a faraway state. She has difficulty in understanding what I say as if she did not hear. Her health is sorely strained by neglect and inward conflict, but she is a strong woman and may continue in this state for months, even years. Rest assured that when the time for it comes, she shall have all the care we can give her. It would be best for you to keep away. The sight of you would certainly rouse painful associations and aggravate her condition. I will do all that can be done.'

I am thankful with all my heart that when the time comes, she will be in good hands. Her last sight on earth will be of the house she loves. It will be the sweet air of Gower Gill that receives her last breath and bears away her troubled spirit.

In summer whenever possible we escape from Marshall Street to ramble in one or other of our favourite country haunts. It is not unusual to come upon a solitary house in a quiet situation; to hear through the half-open door the shuffle of slippered feet; to see at the rose-framed window the wrinkled face of a woman living alone. I find the experience strangely moving and have fallen into the habit of lingering at the gate to wonder how she came there: why she stayed when everyone else went away: and whether, when the flesh fails her and her mortal days are done, she will somehow contrive to stay there still.

1 84 A 3/83

Gilbert, Anna
Miss Bede is staying. 1983 $13

T

031253471X